"Everybody out!" Caradoc gasped.

Margoth took the initiative, diving through the ragged jaws of the opening into the night beyond. Rhan and Serdor followed on her heels. Tumbling headfirst after them, Caradoc landed flat on the ground outside. As he scrambled to his knees, something dark dived at him from the top of the roof.

He rolled to get out of its way. An icy chill swept past him, borne on beating wings of darkness. Hurtling onward, the shadow banked at the far end of the field and swooped back, its pinions churning up clouds of loose dirt as it swept low over the ground.

With the winged shadow bearing down on them from above, the four fugitives hurled themselves over the wall and ploughed recklessly into the trees beyond. The shadow veered off at the last possible moment, scattering dead leaves in a sulphurous wake of roiling air.

Also by Deborah Turner Harris
published by Tor Books

# THE GAUNTLET OF MALICE

Book II
of
The Mages of
Garillon

## DEBORAH TURNER HARRIS

TOR®

A TOM DOHERTY ASSOCIATES BOOK
NEW YORK

THE GAUNTLET OF MALICE

Copyright © 1987 by Deborah Turner Harris

A TOR Book
Published by Tom Doherty Associates, Inc.
49 West 24th Street
New York, NY 10010

ISBN: 0-812-53956-7      Can. ISBN: 0-812-53957-5

First edition: January 1987
First mass market edition: September 1988

Printed in the United States of America

0  9  8  7  6  5  4  3  2  1

## DEDICATION

This book is dedicated with much love to my mother, who is a lady of redoubtable character.

## ACKNOWLEDGMENT

Special thanks are due to Elisabeth Bridges, who very kindly took time out from her own creative work to help me proofread the page proofs for this novel. "Bare is back without brother!"

# FOREWORD

THE KINGDOM OF EAST GARILLON, according to histori-
cal and legendary sources, was established nearly a millen-
nium prior to the period with which the present story is
concerned. The ancient Lay of the Morrigans tells how the
ninth king of Vesteroe, the now-lost Empire of the East,
sent his younger son Evelain over the Great Sea with five
ships to colonize the lands to the west. Evelain, so the Lay
recounts, landed his company on the east coast of the land
that was then known as Dunsinar. He made an alliance
with the indigenous race of mystics who called themselves
the Corrianon. With their help, he succeeded in carving
out for himself a new kingdom between the sea and the
mountains, which he called East Garillon (to distinguish it
from West Garillon, a savage and mysterious land to the
west of the mountains).

To ratify the bond between his own people and their
Corrianon allies, Evelain took as his wife the daughter of
the priest-king of the Corrianon. After establishing his
capital at Farrowaithe on Lake Damanvagr, he assumed
the title Lord Warden to signify that he held and ruled
East Garillon as his father's vassal. Evelain's four high-
est-ranking captains and their families in turn each received authority over a neighboring region of the country,
the head of each family taking the hereditary title of

Seneschal. These five territories, each with its principal settlement, gave rise to the Five Cities of present-day East Garillon: Farrowaithe, Ambrothen, Gand, Glyn Regis, and Tyrantir.

During the centuries that followed, East Garillon's relations with its nearest neighbors were variable. In particular, the powerful pagan kingdom of Pernatha to the south and east, across the Gulf of Mhar, represented for a long time a major threat. The southern palatinate of Minivoire on the other side of the River Tyran, likewise, had to be discouraged, as often by force of arms as by treaty, from encroaching on Garillon territory. By the time of the present story, however, diplomatic relations with both Pernatha and Minivoire had been stable for almost eighty years. Prosperous and cultured, the people of East Garillon did not suspect—yet—that in the year of the Red Boar, 1347, internal affairs in the Five Cities were about to take a turn for the worse.

The trouble started when Gwynmira Du Bors Whitfauconer, second wife of Delsidor, Lord Warden of East Garillon, decided that it would be no bad thing if the succession to the Wardenship should fall upon her son Gythe, instead of on his elder half brother Evelake. Gwynmira's brother Fyanor, the Seneschal of Ambrothen, sympathized with her ambitions, and between them they conspired to find a way to have Evelake eliminated as soon as it could be arranged.

Matters did not come to a head, however, until the spring. In the meantime, affairs in Ambrothen progressed with every appearance of normality, until the Ambrothen chapter of the Mage-Hospitallers of East Garillon convened for the purpose of examining new candidates for membership in the Order.

Founded not long after the consolidation of the kingdom of East Garillon, the Hospitallers' Order was a brotherhood of priest-physicians: men who possessed strong affinities for controlling the mysterious source of energy known as the Magia, on which the ancient mystics of Corrianon had based their power. Using disciplines handed down from ancient times, the mages communed with the Magia in mystical trance-states called Orisons, and by means of gems of power—the smaragdi, or "magestones"—they drew upon the Magia to heal injuries and cure diseases.

One of the novices scheduled for examination in the year of the Red Boar 1347 was young Caradoc Penlluathe. Despite his unusual spiritual gifts, Caradoc had failed on a previous occasion to qualify for the Order. His keen anxieties over the impending trials led indirectly to his becoming involved in a tavern brawl the night before the examinations were to take place. The incident led the Order's Council of Magisters to conclude that Caradoc was too undisciplined and unstable to be trusted to handle power as a mage. He was consequently dismissed.

Aware that his was a very special talent, Caradoc was angry and embittered over his rejection, and desperate to retain possession of his magestone at all costs. As he was seeking to drown his sorrows in a waterfront tavern, he was approached by a black-clad stranger who was, however, clearly authoritative, sympathetic, and cultured. The stranger gave his name as Borthen Berigeld. When he offered Caradoc employment and a way out of his dilemma, Caradoc accepted the offer without reservation.

Caradoc did not know that Fyanor Du Bors, through an intermediary, had sought to hire Borthen to kidnap and murder Evelake Whitfauconer. Borthen had accepted the commission, intending to betray his employer and turn the political conspiracy to his own advantage. Himself a renegade mage and a practicing necromancer, Borthen was embarking upon a campaign to destroy the Hospitallers' Order and institute his own spiritual reign of terror. Having heard rumors of Caradoc's potential talents, Borthen hoped to recruit him to help bring down the Order that had rejected him.

## FOREWORD

Borthen had been apprised of the fact that Evelake Whitfauconer was due to be returning home to Farrowaithe from Gand by way of the road that led through an old mining area known as the Grey Hill Country. Borthen and his men, accordingly, set up an ambush on the trail. At Borthen's prompting, Caradoc used the Magia to confuse and confound the outriders of Evelake's escort. As a result the boy's entourage was massacred in the ensuing attack, and Evelake himself was captured.

Already sick with disgust at the contribution he had unwittingly made to the slaughter, Caradoc was aghast when he learned the identity of Borthen's captive. His feelings turned to horror when Borthen revealed himself to be a necromancer.

Borthen proposed to use perverted mage-power to invade Evelake's mind and force the boy to forget all knowledge of his true identity so that he could be made to serve as a pawn in Borthen's deadly game. His conscience already in revolt, Caradoc sought to intervene on the boy's behalf. Borthen, however, was too strong for him. The necromancer struck Caradoc down and stole his magestone from him.

When word of Evelake's disappearance became public, a search was instituted throughout East Garillon—not only to recover the boy, but to apprehend his abductors. Caradoc was implicated in the affair by evidence uncovered by his former teacher, Forgoyle. After hearing this news from Forgoyle, Caradoc's minstrel friend Serdor set out on a quest to find the missing mage, before the law could catch up with him.

Caradoc, meanwhile, was being held captive in the secret brigand stronghold of Thyle Tarn, deprived of adequate food and sleep in order to weaken his resistance. He was still awaiting Borthen's return to Thyle Tarn when a new prisoner arrived, a man named Valoran. Upon learning the truth about Borthen and his powers, Valoran engineered his and Caradoc's escape from Thyle Tarn. He later revealed that his real name was Gudmar Ap Gorvald, and that he was acting as an agent for Evelake's father, the Lord Warden.

Gudmar attempted to persuade Caradoc to give himself up voluntarily to the authorities in order to prove his good faith. Before Caradoc could commit himself, however, the party was overtaken by a patrol of soldiers from Farrowaithe. Caradoc was arrested on the spot, and shipped south to Ambrothen to stand trial under the supervision of Delsidor Whitfauconer, who had gone there to take part in the investigations.

Unaware that Caradoc was already in custody, Serdor at last was forced to admit defeat in his search for his friend. On his way back to Ambrothen, Serdor stopped at a wayside inn and there met Rhan Hallender, a young boy indentured to the owner of the inn. Seeing Rhan lonely and mistreated, Serdor befriended him. When Rhan subsequently ran away out of fear of his master, Serdor helped him make good his escape, and took the boy with him back to Ambrothen.

Serdor arrived home just in time to learn that Caradoc was shortly to be executed for treason. Impelled by the strength of their friendship and a sense of personal commitment, Serdor devised a plan to rescue Caradoc from the castle before the sentence could be carried out. With the help of Rhan and of Caradoc's sister Margoth, he succeeded in freeing Caradoc from his cell. In the ensuing confusion, however, the boy Rhan was separated from the rest of the party. He was captured by guardsmen, one of whom recognized him as the missing Evelake Whitfauconer.

Of all the members of the boy's family, only Gwynmira Du Bors was present in the Keep at the time of his discovery. When the guards informed her of the boy's return, she took steps to poison them and the boy before the news could be made public. Unsuspecting, the guards drank the poisoned wine she gave them, but Caradoc, Serdor, and Margoth arrived in time to rescue the boy, whose true identity Caradoc was able to confirm. Leaving the bodies of the guards behind, the party set out for St. Welleran's Hospital so that Evelake could be placed under the protection of the Order. Caradoc, however, needed a place to hide.

Leaving Serdor and Margoth to deliver the boy to his beloved former teacher, Forgoyle, Caradoc hid himself in the crypt below the cathedral adjoining the hospital. Here he was apprehended by Borthen, who had come to the cathedral to meet Delsidor Whitfauconer. It was Borthen's intention to propose a trade: he would keep Caradoc Penlluathe free and clear, to control as he wanted, and in exchange he would give Delsidor the name of the man who had the Lord Warden's son kidnapped. He had earlier arranged for Fyanor to come to the cathedral as part of the entrapment. With Caradoc already back in his grasp, however, Borthen no longer needed to do business with the Lord Warden. Now perceiving how Fyanor Du Bors could continue to be useful to him, the necromancer decided to force the Seneschal of Ambrothen to murder his brother-in-law.

Serdor and Forgoyle learned of this development too late to prevent the disaster. In an attempt to salvage what they could of the situation, Serdor raced to the crypt to rescue Caradoc, while Forgoyle held Borthen at bay. In the duel of power that followed, however, Forgoyle was killed, though Caradoc escaped. Left without witnesses to speak up in their favor, Caradoc and his friends fled the city that night in an attempt to place Evelake beyond his uncle's reach until he could be restored to his right place.

This is the point at which the next stage of the chronicle begins.

*Cast of Characters*

**The Nobility**
Fyanor Du Bors: Seneschal of Ambrothen
Gwynmira Du Bors Whitfauconer: Fyanor's sister, the
    Dowager Warden of Farrowaithe
Gythe Du Bors: Gwynmira's son
Evelake Whitfauconer (Rhan Hallender): Gythe's elder
    half brother, true heir to the Wardenship
Arvech Du Penfallon: Seneschal of Gand
Kherryn Du Penfallon: Arvech's daughter
Devon Du Penfallon: Arvech's crippled son
Khevyn Ap Khorrasel: Baron of Kirkwell

**The Clergy**
Ulbrecht Rathmuir: Magister of Ambrothen
An'char Maeldrake: Grand Master of Ambrothen
Forgoyle Finlevyn: formerly a Magister of Ambrothen
Baldwyn Vladhallyn: Arch Mage of East Garillon
Earlis Ap Eadric: Inquisitor of Farrowaithe

**The Commoners**
Caradoc Penlluathe: a mage declared outlaw
Margoth Penlluathe: Caradoc's sister
Serdor Sulamith: Caradoc's best friend, a minstrel
Arn Aldarshot: an innkeeper, friend of Caradoc

## Cast of Characters

Gudmar Ap Gorvald: a merchant prince of East Garillon
Harlech Hardrada: Gudmar's associate, owner of the
    galleass the *Yusufa*
Brachen: manservant to Devon Du Penfallon
Fitch Kilrand: a master-mason of Beresfyrd
Rustiman Du Bracy: Mayor of Gand
Warryn Wingate: Justiciar of Gand
Jorvald Ekhanghar: Marshall of Gand
Tessa Ekhanghar: Jorvald's daughter
Cergil Ap Cymric: a former Farrowaithe Guard
Geston Du Maris: a friend of Cergil; also a Farrowaithe
    Guard
Duncan Drulaine: a former mercenary

**Other Dramatis Personae**
Borthen Berigeld: a renegade-mage with exceptional
    powers
Muirtagh: Borthen's lieutenant
Midrash: a Pernathan dealer in juju'bi
Feisal Al Akbar: Bey of Sul Khabir

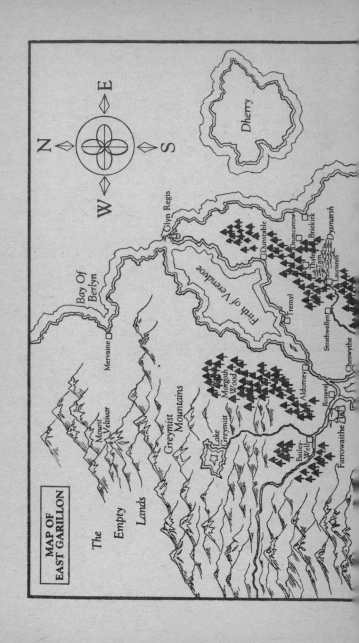

MAP OF
EAST GARILLON

The

Empty

Lands

Mount
Velivar

Greymist
Mountains

Lake
Greymist

Bailey
Well

Farrowaithe

Bay Of
Berlyn

Mervaine

Morgoth
Wood

Aldorney

Ronava

Cheswythe

Strathwellyn

Glyn Regis

Frith of Verenhue

Tremyl

Dunstable

Druncarrow
Briekirk
Thydel
Tam
Dysmarsh
Lauristen

Dherry

N
W — E
S

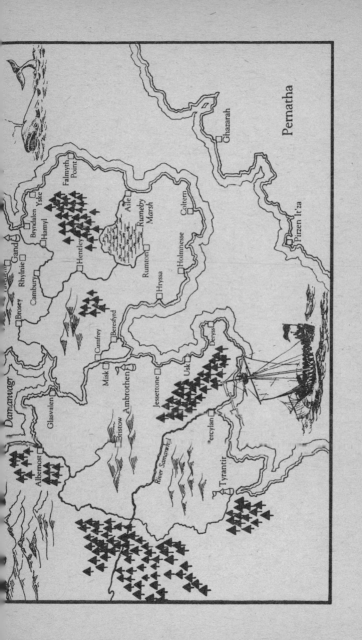

# PROLOGUE

Shortly before midnight on the fifteenth of September, Kherryn Du Penfallon, second child and only daughter of the Seneschal of Gand, was jolted out of sleep into sudden wide-eyed awareness when her bedroom windows burst apart with a crash that rocked the foundations of the floor.

Jerking herself upright, she looked wildly around her. The chamber seemed all at once full of shadows, leaping and whirling like dervishes. The casements were flapping dementedly back and forth, banging out an earsplitting tattoo against the surrounding woodwork. Clutching the edge of the coverlet, she retreated into the far corner of the big bed and cowered there as the shadows chased each other madly around the four walls.

The banging of the shutters mounted to an insane crescendo. Palms pressed to her ears, Kherryn gave a gasp of fright and threw herself flat as a wraith-trail of blackness swooped over her head and shot toward the ceiling. The casements came together again in a final tumultuous crash, and suddenly everything was still.

Her heart hammering hard against her ribs, Kherryn lay motionless for a long moment, listening to the hush. When nothing happened for the space of several breaths, she uncovered her ears and shakily raised her head.

1

She was half prepared to find furniture overturned, her belongings lying scattered in utter disarray, but to her amazement, the room seemed quite undisturbed. The casements were closed, just as she had left them before going to bed. Moonlight, streaming in through the panes, showed everything in its place.

Bewildered, she climbed out of bed and walked over to the windows. The latches were perfectly secure. She looked out across the park. The moon hung cold and white above the trees. Pale as the face of a dying man. . . .

Chilled, she was about to turn away, when a thin black line appeared at the center of the disk. Even as she stared at it in fixed horror, the line split and gaped like a gash cut into living flesh, and out of the gash boiled an effusion of dark ichor, like blood from a mortal wound.

Like blood. . . . As the analogy clicked in her mind, a pain like a bolt of frozen steel clove the bone between her breasts and pierced her to the heart.

The agony was paralyzing. Choking out an anguished cry, Kherryn stumbled against the nearest chair and folded to her knees. Her hands clawing at the upholstery, she made an effort to pull herself up, but the pain radiating from under her ribs unnerved her whole body.

Her grip slackened and she slid to the floor. Like an anlace of poisoned ice, the agony pinned her where she lay, transfixing her lungs so that she could make no further sound. There was a bubbling roar in her ears and a splitting sensation that spread in veins of searing cold from her chest, as if her body were breaking up from inside. . . .

The dagger of pain turned in her breast like a live thing. Writhing on the black brink of unconsciousness, she rolled back, her dilated gaze raking her surroundings. . . .

Darkness and firelight . . .

Vaulted stonework soaring away into shadows far overhead . . .

A dark figure kneeling over her prone body, face aflame with malice and desire . . .

2

His hand gave a sharp jerk at the blade in her chest. It left the wound burning. Blood gushed up the back of her throat into her mouth. The taste of it was the last thing she remembered. . . .

When she came to her senses, she did so sluggishly, and then only because someone close to her was calling her name, repeating it with an urgency that she could not ignore. Focusing her dazed attention in the direction of the voice, she moved her head.

Fingers passed lightly over her brow, and a voice said encouragingly, "That's better. Can you hear me? See if you can open your eyes."

Her vision was cloudy. Soft light—candlelight? —made a watery pool behind the outline of someone's head and shoulders. When she flinched and tried to pull away, the voice said, "Steady! It's only me."

Narrowing her lids, she looked more closely, and found herself gazing up into the thin, grave face of her brother Devon.

He was paler than usual, his features sharp with the kind of nervous tension to which he rarely gave way. "What happened?" he asked. "Are you hurt?"

Her clothes, her body, were miraculously unmarked. "No," said Kherryn shakily. "I don't think so."

"Thank God for that." He drew a deep breath. "Your scream woke me. I came as quickly as I could, but I was afraid I wouldn't be in time. . . ."

His voice held the raw edge of suppressed frustration, for which Kherryn well understood the cause: Devon had been born a cripple, and for him no movement came easily.

He shifted his weight, and she realized that he was kneeling, despite the pain it must have cost him to bend his twisted right leg. As he eased himself out of his uncomfortable position, another figure stepped into focus behind him.

3

"The windows are all secure, milord," said the burly officer of the guard. "I see no sign of any attempt at forced entry."

Devon assimilated this. Without taking his gaze from his sister's white face, he said, "Thank you, Captain. As long as you are satisfied, I shall not detain you any longer from your other duties."

"Very good, milord." The captain's tone was wooden. "Shall I send for Mistress Tessa?"

Meeting her brother's eyes, Kherryn wordlessly shook her head. "No. That won't be necessary," said Devon. "I'll stay with Lady Kherryn for as long as she desires company."

"As you wish, milord." The captain bowed and turned on his heel. "He thinks we're both weak-minded fools," said Kherryn flatly as the door closed behind him.

"What does that signify?" Devon dismissed the captain's opinions with a weary shrug. "I'm more interested to know what happened to make you cry out like that."

Guided by his hand, Kherryn sat up. "I had a nightmare. At least, I suppose that's what it was. But it was more vivid—more *real*—than any dream I've ever had before."

She was shivering. "You'd better get back into bed," said Devon quietly.

Moving with the careful deliberation of someone unaccustomed to thoughtless dexterity, he picked himself up, tested his balance, and bent from the waist to help her to her feet. The big four-poster on the opposite side of the room seemed suddenly very inviting. As she slipped between the sheets and drew the blankets gratefully around her, Devon hitched himself awkwardly onto the foot of the bed and tucked a stray pillow between his shoulders and the bedpost. "Now," he said. "Tell me exactly what happened."

It took a surprising amount of fortitude to summon the recollection. Kherryn recounted what had happened in as few words as possible, but even so, by the end of her recital, she was trembling again. "What do you make of

4

it?" she asked, aware of the throbbing appeal in her own voice.

Devon considered the question carefully, his dark eyes grave. "If you're asking me, do I think you were dreaming, the reply is yes. What you experienced wasn't anything *physical*. But that doesn't mean the experience itself wasn't *real*."

"What on earth would cause me to have a dream like that?" asked Kherryn.

Devon frowned slightly. "I noticed something was bothering you earlier this evening, but I knew better than to ask you about it with Father present. When people aren't allowed to talk openly about their fears, the tension sometimes breaks out in their dreams. Maybe this was a distress signal from inside yourself—"

"No! It didn't come from inside me!" protested Kherryn vehemently. "Devon, I swear to you, *it wasn't my dream*. First I was woken up. And then . . ." She started to shiver again, her voice trailing off as she began to understand a terror far worse than the implications of a horrible nightmare. "Then it all happened. *Forced* on me . . . oh, Devon, there was nothing I could do to stop it. Not even wake up!"

Devon rocked forward and wrapped both arms tightly around his sister's quivering frame. As he held her close, he privately cursed this second sight in his beloved sister—a sensitivity, unpredictable but strong, that was the bane of her young life, sometimes giving her glimpses of events she could not explain, more often plaguing her with feelings even more incomprehensible—and all anathema to their father. But she had never before been assailed by such a vivid and personally threatening "dream." Even as he struggled in his own mind to account for what had just occurred, Kherryn raised her head, her eyes hungering for answers. "Is it possible that some other person might have the power to intrude on my thoughts from outside, without my consent?"

"I doubt that very much," said Devon with firm

conviction, though he was secretly as puzzled as she was. "Only an exceptionally powerful mage—an inquisitor, for instance—would be able to do something like that. And not even an inquisitor would presume to do so except at the express request of one of the high judges, with the consent of his own Grand Master.

"No," he continued, groping for a clearer expression. "I don't think this dream was inflicted on you by some other person. I think it's more like—oh, I don't know —almost a kind of 'accident.' . . . Rather like a person with unusually acute hearing inadvertently eavesdropping on a conversation going on in another room—"

"Like a prophecy?" Kherryn was still pale and chilled.

Devon balked slightly at the question. He said with difficulty, "The ability to 'see' things and events at a distance, both in space and in time, is one of the rarer gifts of the Magia. I'm not sure I understand where far-seeing ends and prophecy begins."

He eyed her closely. "Do you think this vision of yours was significant to that degree—that it might have been foreshadowing some future event?"

"I don't know," said Kherryn. "I only know that it seemed at the time that I was sharing in the experience of death. I know now how it feels to be murdered."

She shuddered and buried her face in the hollow of her brother's shoulder. Devon stroked her hair gently, without speaking. There was nothing more he could say that could comfort her. All he could do was stay with her.

# THE PRICE OF KNOWLEDGE

THE SKY OVER PENFALLON MANOR that night was cruelly clear, but three hundred miles to the south, the city of Ambrothen lay half-suffocated under a blanket of fog. Clammy as dead men's fingers, it clogged the streets and alleyways, suffocating those unhappily abroad, and muffled the buildings in wraithlike clouds of winding-sheets. No wind stirred off the sea to the east, but with the approach of midnight the dank air carried a thin rumor of unrest.

Ulbrecht Rathmuir, Magister of Ambrothen and a healer of considerable power, sensed the growing disquiet pregnant in the dark as he followed his companion up to the fog-shrouded gatchouse guarding the entrance to Ambrothen Castle. Harlech Hardrada, squat as a capstan, made no attempt to soften his stumping footsteps as he marched across the drawbridge that spanned the dry moat. When the sentry stepped forward to challenge them, the captain of the *Yusufa* thrust out a truculent black beard and waited to be recognized.

The sentry lowered his weapon when he saw who it was. "Is that the magister with you?" he asked. And when Harlech nodded, gestured toward a dark doorway just inside the arch of the portcullis. "Up the stairs and through the doorway at the top," he said. And added, "You'd better make it quick. . . ."

A spiraling climb through draughty darkness brought them to the door the guard had indicated. At Harlech's knock, it opened and a tall man with a backswept mane of dark blond hair stepped into the gap.

"Here he is, Gudmar," said the little sea captain, jerking a thumb over his shoulder. "How's our soldier-laddie faring?"

"He's still breathing," said Gudmar Ap Gorvald, and stood back to let the other two men in. To Ulbrecht he said, "Thank you for coming so promptly."

From what Harlech had told him already, Ulbrecht knew that the case was serious. "Where is the patient?" he asked.

"In there," said Gudmar. He indicated the doorway of a small side-chamber opening off the main room.

Designed to serve as a weapons-closet, the windowless room had been hastily converted into a hospital cell with the addition of a lamp, a rough wooden table, and a makeshift pallet set up on trestles against the right-hand wall. The patient's outer clothes had been draped over one of the spear-racks. Noting the color of the livery—blue and white—Ulbrecht raised an eyebrow. "Farrowaithe Guard?"

"Aye," said Harlech, with a glance over at Gudmar. He added, "His mate was also from Farrowaithe—the one who died."

The young man stretched out on the pallet was not moving. His ashen face, sunken against its bone, showed a curious livid mottling over the cheeks and forehead. Ulbrecht wordlessly felt for the pulse at the neck, then folded back the blankets to expose his patient's bruise-marked chest. "He didn't have those blotches on him when we first found him," said Gudmar. "They only appeared later."

"Yes. That would be right," said Ulbrecht grimly, and raised his eyes. "Delayed subcutaneous bruising is uniquely symptomatic of sesquina poisoning."

8

"Sesquina—!" said Gudmar, then checked himself.

"God Almighty!" muttered Harlech. "If that's what got into the boy, it wasna by accident."

"No," agreed Ulbrecht. "Somebody appears to have had a very strong reason for wanting this young man dead."

There was a bleak pause. "Can you save him?" asked Gudmar.

"I don't know," said Ulbrecht. Seeing Gudmar's expression, he continued. "I'll do what I can, of course. But I can't begin to predict how effective the treatment will be. The next eight hours should tell us whether or not he will survive. After that, it could go either way."

"What d'ye mean by that?" asked Harlech.

"I mean," said Ulbrecht, "that he could pull out of it. Or he could remain as you see him now: to all appearances, a dead man."

His gaze returned to his patient's disfigured face. "I must ask you to leave me alone with him now."

Gudmar and Harlech traded glances. "I understand," said Gudmar. "If you need anything, we'll be waiting outside."

The patient's malady could only be eased through the deeper offices of Orison. Once the other two men had withdrawn, Ulbrecht sighed and drew out his magestone.

He cradled the gem in his hand, composing mind and will to invoke the healing power of the Magia. After a moment, a warm answering glow pulsed beneath his fingers. The warmth spread throughout his body, quickening his perceptions as the Orison of Interior Silence yielded to the disciplined ardor of Sensibility.

Before entering into affinity with his patient, he paused a moment until he could feel the strength of the Magia magnifying his own fortitude. Then, thus reinforced, he plunged into the chilly depths of the patient's illness.

It was like diving into a whirlpool. Buffeted by conflicting impressions of disorder and debility, Ulbrecht fought to create an island of stillness in the midst of chaos, and then, thus grounded, cast about him for specific information.

Neither the heart nor the lungs were functioning normally. Ulbrecht struggled to stabilize the patient's vital functions by bringing breathing and heartbeat under the governance of his own body. It took all the strength he could summon to overcome the resistance generated by the other man's unbalanced nervous system, but gradually the patient's internal organs began to respond to the regulating influence of Ulbrecht's overriding will. . . .

While the mage Ulbrecht was occupied with his patient, Gudmar Ap Gorvald, guild-master and merchant-adventurer, turned to his one-handed companion. "How much have you told him?" he asked.

"Enough tae give him a general idea what's been goin' on around here since sunset," said Harlech. He eyed his friend consideringly and added, "I told him somebody here at the castle seems tae have declared open season on the members of the Lord Warden's personal staff. And that His Lordship himself will be wantin' answers when he gets back."

Earlier that evening, Delsidor Whitfauconer, who had come to Ambrothen to investigate his son's disappearance, had ridden off to St. Welleran's Cathedral on an errand he refused to discuss even with Gudmar, who was a close friend of his. In the hours since his departure, the Keep had witnessed a series of upheavals that had begun when several prisoners had escaped from the castle gaol.

Among the escapees was a young mage by the name of Caradoc Penlluathe, who was to have been executed the next day for treason in connection with Evelake Whitfauconer's abduction. Personally acquainted with Caradoc, Gudmar and Harlech both had reason to disagree with the court's ruling concerning his guilt. Their sympathies, however, had not excused them from taking part in the castle-wide manhunt that followed the breakout.

They had been patrolling the grounds in front of the castle's guest wing, when the sight of flames in one of the upper rooms had sent them racing upstairs to the Lord Warden's personal suite. There they had found two members of the Warden's military escort sprawled out on the floor of the library next to a table which had been furnished for a meal. Gudmar had yet to come up with a satisfactory explanation for the fact that the table had been set for three people, instead of only two.

Harlech's thoughts must have been running along similar lines. He said thoughtfully, "I'd gi' a warden's ransom tae know who it was gave those lads a dose o' the de'il's homebrew."

"And I'd give twice that," said Gudmar thinly, "to find out *why*."

He scowled. "I'd like Ulbrecht to take a look at that wine-flagon we brought away with us from the library."

"Why?" asked Harlech caustically. "We already ken it's got poison in it."

"Yes," agreed Gudmar. "But a mage like Ulbrecht might be able to learn something more—"

"I might. *If* I were an inquisitor," said a light baritone voice from the doorway to the sideroom. "But perhaps," continued Ulbrecht Rathmuir, "it's just as well my greatest gifts are those of a healer."

Gudmar turned, his golden eyes kindled with sudden interest. "Then that boy in there will live?"

"He has a fair chance. I've managed to arrest the degenerative effects of the poison," said Ulbrecht. "But it's still too soon to tell for sure. He should be moved to St. Welleran's for further treatment as soon as possible."

He paused, his gaze traveling from Gudmar to Harlech and back again. "Now—what was that I overheard about a flagon?"

"I've got it here," said Harlech, and presented Ulbrecht with a graceful decanter of cut crystal which had been standing unregarded on one of the side-tables.

The decanter contained a measure of dark red wine. It washed thinly up the sides of the vessel's interior as Ulbrecht took it and turned it thoughtfully between his hands. "You may not be an inquisitor," said Gudmar, watching him, "but I understand that you are not entirely unskilled in the art of far-seeing."

Ulbrecht turned his head, his eyes as level as his voice. "I have a limited facility for recovering impressions from inanimate objects, yes. But not enough to make me eligible as an inquisitor."

He grimaced slightly. "I see you're thinking that I might be able to identify your poisoner by means of Orison. But let me remind you that only a trained inquisitor has the legal authority to pursue investigations by the means you propose. Even assuming I could find out anything at all, my testimony would not be admissable in a court of law—"

"We can sort out the legal technicalities later," said Gudmar. "Right now, what we need is information —What the hell's *that*?"

Harlech was already moving toward the shuttered window-slot on the side of the main room overlooking the drawbridge. Arriving three strides ahead of Gudmar, he hauled back the bar-bolt and wrenched the shutter open.

Excited voices crackled upward through the black water-laden air. "—He's dead, I tell you!—Yes—Yes, straight through the heart. God," said the messenger with a shudder in his tone. "There was blood splashed all the way from the altar to the foot of the chancel steps!"

Chancel?

St. Welleran's Cathedral?

His blood temperature plummeting, Gudmar wheeled in his tracks and raced for the stairs.

The clank of chains and the flicker of torches from the room at the bottom of the steps told him the sentries were raising the portcullis. Bounding past them, Gudmar shot through the doorway into the path of the messenger's white-lathered horse.

It shied wildly at the sight of him, fighting the bit as its rider bore down hard on the reins. Dodging the animal's flailing forefeet, Gudmar caught hold of the foam-flecked cheek-strap. The man in the saddle swore pungently, then took a second look. As the horse, snorting, came to earth, he gasped, "Master Gudmar! I didn't expect to find you here. Lord Delsidor—"

He broke off with a grunt as his knee scraped the left-hand wall. Retaining his grip on the bridle, Gudmar said grimly, "What about Lord Delsidor?"

The horse sidled at last to a standstill. The messenger, who wore the livery of the Farrowaithe Guard, swallowed hard. "It's bad news, sir. He—he's—"

"Dead," said Gudmar, with stark finality.

The messenger nodded and ran a gauntleted hand nervously over the lower half of his face. "His Lordship had us escort him to St. Welleran's earlier this evening. When we got there, he sent half of our detachment to patrol the adjoining streets, while the rest stood watch before the gate. He went on to the cathedral alone. While he was in there, something happened."

He paused and shivered. "Don't ask me to explain it, but all of a sudden it was as if a whirlwind had broken loose inside the church. There was a crash, and all the windows in the chancel blew outward. Our captain led the rush on the doors, but he and the men in the front rank didn't get so far as the vault inside before something—a blast of some kind—hit us and hurled us all back. At least half a dozen were killed outright. . . ."

He swallowed hard. "The cathedral's in a shambles, sir. The mages think it might have been caused by some massive discharge of power—"

"Was His Lordship killed in the explosion?" asked Gudmar.

The messenger's expression was haunted. "No, sir.

When the magisters found him, he had been stabbed. Through the heart."

"'Crueler oftimes than death itself,' wrote the poet Isembard, 'is the shape and manner of its coming. . . .'"

Gudmar felt his tongue turn to dust in his mouth. Closing his eyes—Delsidor, my friend, he thought dizzily. I wish you had seen fit to confide in me. Perhaps if you had, this night's tale of violence might have ended differently. . . .

Fingers gripped his arm. "I had hoped that the worst was over. It appears that I was premature," said Ulbrecht. "You knew His Lordship well. I'm sorry."

Gudmar nodded. Drawing himself up with an effort, he said to the messenger, "Who's directing the investigation? Your superior?"

The messenger shook his head. "No, sir. The Seneschal of Ambrothen is himself at St. Welleran's, acting in consultation with the Grand Master. I'm here by his orders to carry the news to the Lady Gwynmira."

His horse was tugging nervously at the bit. "Then I won't detain you any longer," said Gudmar, and released his grip on the bridle.

The messenger clicked his tongue, and the horse broke away at a trot. Listening to the fading hoofbeats—"It seems our night's work is only beginning," growled Gudmar. Returning to the gatehouse doorway, he leaned around the doorframe and called, "Harlech! You'd better come down here!"

Following behind him—"You're planning to go yourself to the cathedral?" asked Ulbrecht.

"Yes. I prefer to be my own witness," said Gudmar. Seeing Ulbrecht's expression, he added, "Will you stay with our young guardsman while we're gone?"

"I couldn't leave him now—even if the Order itself were in danger of dissolution," said Ulbrecht bleakly. "I daresay I'll learn the worst soon enough. In the meantime, I'd be obliged if you could let the Grand Master know where I am, and why. . . ."

# THE QUESTION OF ANSWERS

THERE WERE NO HORSES AVAILABLE for civilians. The remaining mounts in the castle stables had been reserved by order of the Marshall of Ambrothen, after dispatching half the night watch to search for—and if possible, recapture—the eight prisoners who had escaped from custody earlier in the evening. Unwilling to waste further precious time, Gudmar and Harlech, heavily cloaked and fully armed, set out on foot for St. Welleran's Cathedral. Left alone with his patient in the upstairs room of the castle gatehouse, Ulbrecht added more charcoal to the brazier standing at the foot of the bed. Then he sat down to consider Gudmar's urgent request that he call upon the Magia in an effort to unlock the stubborn mystery of the evening's disturbing events.

What Gudmar had asked him to do was simple enough in theory. In actual fact, an essay in far-seeing presented some very real difficulties for any mage not specially gifted in the art. For one thing, he could not guarantee that the impressions he received would be relevant to the inquiry at hand: it took a rare degree of talent to be selective. For another, he could not be sure that those same impressions were necessarily vehicles of actual fact: given the interpretive nature of perception, only a mage empowered with an unusual capacity for heuristic Orison could distinguish with certainty falsehood from truth.

Those rare mages who evinced a particularly well-developed gift for this kind of inquiry occupied a special place within the Order. Formally invested as inquisitors, they were granted dispensation to exercise their office in the service of the civil authorities. It had long been common practice for the Lords Chief Justice of the Five Cities to invoke the aid of an inquisitor in carrying out difficult or delicate investigations.

Examining his own conscience, Ulbrecht found himself reluctant to place over much faith in his admittedly modest gifts as an investigator. At the same time, however, he could not shake off the nagging conviction that even a little knowledge was better than none at all. The decanter holding the tainted wine was standing next to the young guardsman's bedside. Ulbrecht studied it for one long moment, then abruptly made his decision.

Leaving the patient lying quietly in his bed, Ulbrecht carried the flagon into the adjoining room and set it down on the oaken table standing against the right-hand wall. He paused a moment to collect himself, then took his magestone again between his hands.

Rarely since his investiture as ordinaire had Ulbrecht practiced the telesthetic techniques he had learned during his novitiate. It was with a strange sense of rediscovery that he now took the flagon to himself in Orison, divesting himself by degrees of all external sensation.

Magnified at first, the sights and sounds of the room around him began to subside from his field of awareness. As they faded completely away, a new range of impressions arose to take their place.

Odours first. . . . The overpowering scent of the wine itself, its sweet pungency liberally laced with the almond-like taint of sesquina. And permeating it, the earthier smells of bread and cheese, and the sap-like fragrance of apples. . . .

These, and something else.

16

The spicy, exotic tang of Pernathan spikenard.

It was perhaps what Ulbrecht expected least to encounter—this feminine savor of expensive perfume. His curiosity quickening, he probed more deeply, the elusive scent drawing him on, like a clue of silken thread, toward the heart of the mystery.

Visual images flickered like tongues of fire before him. Temples throbbing, he willed the fluctuating forms to stabilize and coalesce. Under the intensity of his concentration, the details of a scene emerged from the twilight realm of shadows . . .

A well-appointed room, its tapestried walls richly aglow with candlelight . . . a table worked in marquetry in the foreground, and beyond it three figures.

It required a painful expenditure of effort to hold the image steady. His mind's eye lanced with small needles of fire, Ulbrecht fought to catch a glimpse of the faces of the trio.

The first set of features belonged to his patient. Beside him, clad alike in the livery of the Farrowaithe Guard, stood a second man whose insignia suggested that he might be the sergeant whom Gudmar had reported dead.

The third member of the party was only a boy. Ragged, dirty, and bruised, he seemed jarringly out of place amid his luxurious surroundings. Even as Ulbrecht struggled to retain the image of the boy's angular, fine-boned face, the scene itself wavered and began to disintegrate.

Despite his efforts, the outlines of the boy and the two guardsmen softened and dulled to a grey blur. Clinging precariously to the lingering shadows, Ulbrecht became suddenly aware of a voice breaking in against the clouding backdrop of the pictured room.

A woman's voice, cool and melodic, its mellow timbre enhanced by a tantalizing huskiness. "Poor child—we can only guess at the strain of his condition," sighed the owner of the voice in satiny remorse. "Until the Grand Master can be summoned to tend him, all we can do is try to make him comfortable. . . ."

The voice faded to a murmur. His overstrained nerves on fire, Ulbrecht battled feverishly to capture the rest of what the woman was saying. The blood by this time was pounding in his ears. Surfacing briefly above the clamoring symptoms of his own fatigue, he caught a resurgent glimpse of the sumptuous room. . . .

The two Farrowaithe Guards accepted goblets of wine held out to them by a woman's slim jeweled hands. The slender fingers were perfumed with spikenard. The same inimitable female voice spoke again, in tones winningly dulcet: "I think perhaps our young friend will feel more at ease if you keep him company. There's plenty of wine. Please don't be shy of sharing it. . . ."

The almondine odor of sesquina hung like a miasma of death over the goblets. Unwary as children, the guardsmen lifted their cups and drank. . . .

Pain exploded inside Ulbrecht's skull, splintering the vision beyond all recall. Palms pressed flat against his temples, he slumped forward, biting his lips to keep from exclaiming aloud. For a long moment he remained unmoving as the tide of his anguish crashed back and forth inside his head like waves trapped among sea-rocks. Then, as the agony ebbed apace, he straightened up and opened his eyes.

The light in the room at first made him wince. Aware that he had pushed himself dangerously close to the limits of his endurance, he returned the flagon to its place on the side-table, then settled wearily back in his chair to consider the implications of the vision he had just experienced.

The anomalies were immediately striking: a street urchin in a silken prison. A lady of quality with a penchant for murder. In retrospect, the situation seemed so outlandish and unlikely that Ulbrecht wondered if his own imagination might not have been playing tricks on him.

At the same time, he realized that he could not afford

to dismiss out of hand what he had learned through Orison. At least, not until someone with greater skill and authority had the chance to put his findings to the test.

Or until the revival of one of the principal witnesses for the prosecution rendered indirect methods of questioning unnecessary. Remembering his patient's corpselike face—"Who was that woman?" asked Ulbrecht softly. "And who was that boy that she wanted him—and you —dead?"

He was still turning these questions over in his mind when he was roused from his troubled reverie by a fresh disturbance downstairs. Stiffening, he pricked up his ears to listen.

A muttered colloquy among several people yielded abruptly to a single speaking voice. The sentry's tone was markedly deferential as he delivered his report.

There was a pause. Then another voice responded in the sharp accents of impatient inquiry. Ulbrecht felt the hairs rising along the nape of his neck. The second voice belonged to a woman.

His reflexes jumping, he glanced involuntarily over at the poisoned decanter. The compulsion to put it away somewhere out of sight laid hold of him with such intensity that he rose to his feet, and only then paused to think. He was still wavering between impulse and reason when a door opened and closed two floors below and footsteps drummed smartly upward toward the landing.

A mailed fist hammered at the paneling outside. "Magister Ulbrecht Rathmuir? Open up in the name of the Warden!" called a man's voice ringingly. "Lady Gwynmira Du Bors wants a word with you."

Gwynmira Du Bors.

The Lord Warden's widow. . . .

His flesh creeping for no reason that he could put into words, Ulbrecht went to answer the summons.

When he first opened the door, all he could see was the steely glitter of plate-armor. Then the captain of the guard

19

stood aside, and Ulbrecht was left facing a slender figure mantled in fur-trimmed scarlet.

The face beneath the hood might have been sculpted from alabaster, but its consummate composure of contour and feature warred with the seething emotion pent up behind the liquid dark eyes. Bracing himself under the volcanic impact of Gwynmira Du Bors's imperious gaze, Ulbrecht bowed deeply. "Lady Gwynmira, your servant. Would it please you to enter?"

The woman on the stairs inclined her head. In response to a curt snap of her gloved hand, the captain of the guard preceded her into the room and stationed himself opposite Ulbrecht to the right of the door. Leaving the rest of her escort behind in the stairwell, Gwynmira crossed the threshold in a whisper of quilted velvet. As she passed in front of him, Ulbrecht caught the residual drift of perfume.

A haunting fragrance, spicy and exotic.

The scent of Pernathan spikenard!

Ulbrecht drew breath with an audible hiss. The Lord Warden's consort stopped and turned back to look at him. "Did you say something, Magister?" inquired Gwynmira Du Bors.

Her voice was low, with more than a hint of huskiness in it. His heart thudding erratically against the wall of his chest, Ulbrecht pulled himself up. "Forgive me, milady, if I am shamefully tardy in offering you my condolences, but I must confess that I did not expect to see you abroad. The circumstances surrounding your husband's death—"

"Demand that I find a more productive expression for my outrage than tears," said Gwynmira with cool civility. "I fully intend to bear my part in overseeing the investigations. But before I go to join my brother at St. Welleran's, there are a few mysteries here at the castle that I should like to explore."

"Mysteries, milady?"

Gwynmira was no longer looking at him. Her gaze had strayed to the flagon standing behind him on the table.

"That decanter—where did you get it?" she asked.

Watching her face—"It was found beside two stricken guardsmen in your husband's apartments," said Ulbrecht.

The brilliant eyes shifted and sharpened. "The sergeant who reported the incident to me made no mention of any such artifact."

"Perhaps he never saw it," said Ulbrecht uncomfortably. "It was delivered to me when the lieutenant was handed over into my care."

"Delivered," said Gwynmira silkily, "by whom?"

Something feline in her manner warned Ulbrecht that the question might be a trap. He said uneasily, "By Gudmar Ap Gorvald."

"Yes, of course. It was he who arrived first and discovered the bodies. It appears we owe Master Gudmar a debt of gratitude for summoning you to the Keep so promptly," said Gwynmira. Her gaze traveled speculatively toward the lighted doorway leading into the adjoining alcove. "Is Gudmar still here with you?"

"No, milady. He felt his place was at St. Welleran's," said Ulbrecht.

"Then I shall thank him when we meet," said Gwynmira. "Have you examined the flagon, Magister?"

The same perfume. . . .

The same voice. . . .

Or was it? Feeling like a man walking blindfolded through a den of scorpions, Ulbrecht this time took refuge in a lie. "No, milady."

He thought he detected a slight softening—of relief? —in the hard line of her tinted mouth. "Of course. You are not, after all, an inquisitor," said Gwynmira. She motioned to the guardsman with her. "Coryn, take that flagon and see that it is conveyed to my strongroom. It can remain there until the proper authorities arrive to deal with it."

It would be dangerous to protest. Ulbrecht stood mutely by as the captain of the guard picked up the flagon and withdrew from the room. As the door closed behind him, Gwynmira said softly, "Your patient's name, incidentally, is Cergil Ap Cymric. How is he faring?"

It occurred suddenly to Ulbrecht that the young lieutenant's life might possibly depend upon his answer. He swallowed hard. "Not well. Not well at all, I'm afraid."

"Will he live?"

Ulbrecht's eyes were drawn irresistibly to her ungloved hands. He tried to envision how they would look curled loosely around the stem of a goblet.

"I ask your opinion, Magister," said Gwynmira sharply. "What are the lieutenant's chances of recovering?"

"Your pardon, milady." Ulbrecht wrenched his gaze away. Squaring his shoulders firmly, he said, "I would not willingly deceive you with false assurances. As matters stand at the moment, I cannot foresee his recovery."

Gwynmira's dark eyes searched his face. Ulbrecht bore her regard impassively. After a moment, the Warden's consort withdrew her scrutiny. "I'm sorry the prognosis is so bleak," said Gwynmira. "May I see him?"

Fool! You should have hidden that flagon while you had the chance, thought Ulbrecht to himself. Aloud, he said, "The ravages of the poison are not sightly. As your unfortunate lieutenant is in any case unable to speak, you might well spare yourself the ordeal."

"Thank you, Magister," said Gwynmira. "But I learned long ago that duty must often outweigh sensibility."

She arched an eyebrow and waited. "As you wish, milady," said Ulbrecht. "If you would be pleased to follow me. . . ."

Somewhere at the back of his mind, the voice of doubt was shrilling, "What if you're wrong?" To which the voice of his conscience responded in a kind of desperation, "What if I'm *right*?" He stood aside to allow Gwynmira to enter the alcove ahead of him. "The facial discoloration is due to subcutaneous bleeding—" he began, then cut himself short. "Oh, my God!"

Gwynmira wheeled sharply, lips parted in unfeigned surprise. Whipping past her, Ulbrecht sprang to Cergil Ap Cymric's bedside.

He thumbed open his patient's left eye, swore under his breath, and pressed his ear to the young man's chest. "What's the matter?" demanded Gwynmira, then subsided as Ulbrecht gestured pleadingly for silence.

For a long moment he remained where he was in an attitude of listening. Then, snapping upright, he groped for his patient's left hand. Singling out Cergil's forefinger, he pinched the nail between his own index finger and thumb. He waited intently for the space of several heartbeats, then abruptly slumped in his chair.

Gwynmira's perfumed hand fell upon his shoulder. "What is it, Magister?" asked the Warden's consort.

The tension in her voice hinted at the depth of her interest. His head drooping, Ulbrecht slipped Cergil's limp hand back under the covers and reached for the hem of the top blanket. "I'm sorry, milady," he said wearily. "I'm afraid the lieutenant is dead."

And drew the blanket over his patient's clay-cold face.

# MURDER IN THE CATHEDRAL

GUDMAR AND HARLECH ARRIVED AT St. Welleran's Cathedral to find a small-scale riot in the making in St. Welleran's Square. Lights flared in the fog as Ambrothen Regulars on foot struggled to keep a jostling crowd of agitated spectators from rushing the abbey gates. The fire-shot mist rumbled with the sullen mutter of unanswered questions. Gudmar and Harlech forced their way through the forming mob, and eventually came face to face with a harried sergeant in a torn surcoat.

He waved them back with a menacing flourish of a weighted baton. "That's far enough. Who d'you think you are?"

"Friends of the Lord Warden," snapped Gudmar. He twisted the jeweled signet ring from the middle finger of his right hand and thrust it under the sentry's nose. "My name is Gudmar Ap Gorvald. If my word alone is insufficient, perhaps this will allay your suspicions."

The guardsman peered at the insignia of the Merchant-Adventurers, then threw back his head. "That won't be necessary, Guild-Master," he said stiffly. "You may pass."

The abbey grounds were seething with activity. After stopping to identify themselves to the guards at the gatehouse, Gudmar and Harlech struck out for the main entrance to the cathedral itself.

24

The grass to the right of the entryway was littered with ominous cloth-wrapped bundles. A pair of boots protruded from under the edge of the nearest tarpaulin. His expression stony, Gudmar bent and twitched a loose fold of cloth over them before mounting the three broad steps to the cathedral's west portico.

The great bronze doors beneath the tympanum were gaping wide, their hinges wrenched and twisted. As Gudmar and Harlech reached the topmost step, two stooping figures emerged from the narthex, carrying another limp, draped form between them. Standing aside as they shuffled past—"God Almighty, that makes eight," muttered Harlech under his breath. "Not including His Lordship. . . ."

His voice trailed off. Gudmar nodded grimly and stepped through the doorway into the garbled chiaroscuro of the cathedral's interior.

The chancel was an island of torchlight, remote at the far end of the nave. Even from the narthex, the evidence of destruction was visible: shattered windows, tumbled frieze-work, ruptured wood, and broken stones. Dark shapes moved to and fro in silhouette beyond the altar-rail. The murmur of subdued voices carried across the intervening gloom like the whispered echo of the sea trapped inside an empty seashell.

His footsteps ringing out hollowly over the bare flagstones, Gudmar paced the length of the aisle in grim silence. Glancing obliquely at his friend's implacable profile, Harlech grimaced to himself and kept his own counsel as they approached the sanctuary.

Two soldiers in the livery of Farrowaithe stepped forward as if to intercept them, then fell back as the flickering tapers illuminated Gudmar's set, strong-featured face. Gudmar brushed past them without speaking as his searching gaze located a broken human form stretched out on the floor ahead of him.

The Lord Warden of East Garillon lay on his back, staring vacantly up into the vaulted darkness far above the torchsmoke. At the sound of Gudmar's slow approaching footfalls, the mage kneeling over the body stood up and backed away. Gudmar saw that the stone flags were flooded with a thick spill of crimson.

The sheer volume of blood left no room for hope. Jaw muscles aching with the strain of self-control, Gudmar closed his eyes on his own blind rage. A moment later, a hand touched his shoulder. "The heart was pierced through in three places," said a voice heavy-laden with shock and weariness. "No mage in the world could have saved him."

The words clanked dully, like chains on a gibbet. Gudmar opened his eyes and found the Grand Master of Ambrothen standing at his side.

An'char's lined face was grey. "Forgive me that I have no words of comfort to offer you," he said. "What has happened here tonight transcends mere infamy. All the signs there are point to the passing presence of something *evil*."

His voice carried a quiver of revulsion. Gudmar's golden brows lifted. "Evil, Your Eminence?"

"I do not—believe me—use the word lightly," said An'char. "Look around you, Guild-Master."

Gudmar wordlessly obeyed. And caught his breath hard between his teeth.

The white marble of the high altar was no longer white. Its purity dulled to the greyness of dead skin, it was blotched with livid marks, like plague spots. On either side of the altar, the sacramental candlesticks lay like lightning-stricken trees, their forms wrenched into crippled joints of blackened metal.

"What you see is the signature of blasphemy," continued An'char. "At the time the Lord Warden was murdered, someone stood before the altar and invoked the Magia, not for healing, but for the purpose of conjuring forces that do not bear the stamp of enlightenment."

"Are you telling me," said Gudmar, "that Delsidor

Whitfauconer died by means of some supernatural agency?"

An'char's mouth took on a bitter twist. "The weapon that inflicted the wounds was concrete enough. Lord Fyanor's men are searching for it now. But whoever wielded that blade drew his strength from an act of blackest sacrilege."

He drew himself up. "Make no mistake, Gudmar: genuine evil is like a loathsome disease, and like disease, it can spread. If the plague is to be contained, its hosts must be identified and purged—without mercy or compromise."

His tone carried the hard ring of conviction. "Have you got any leads yet?" asked Gudmar.

"No—only a few theories which have yet to be tested," said An'char. "At the very least, I want to talk with Caradoc Penlluathe."

"That isna going tac be easy," said Harlech sourly. "Caradoc Penlluathe flew the coop earlier this evenin', and hasna been seen or heard from since."

An'char stiffened, and turned to Gudmar. "This is news to me. How did it happen?"

"Nobody seems to know," said Gudmar grimly. "In any event, it might not be a bad idea to find out if Borthen Berigeld has been seen in the city in the last few days."

Borthen Berigeld.

The mysterious brigand-lord who had once blackmailed Harlech into becoming a smuggler. Who had tempted Caradoc Penlluathe into forswearing his vows as a Hospitaller. Who had engineered the abduction of Evelake Whitfauconer, and God knew what else besides. . . .

"We have Caradoc's sworn statement that Borthen has a powerful and corrupt affinity for the Magia," continued Gudmar. "I remind you that even Caradoc—gifted as he is—failed significantly to stand up to Borthen in a test of power."

"There is no need to cite Caradoc Penlluathe as an

27

example," said An'char harshly. "When we entered the sanctuary tonight, we found one of our own magisters lying dead at the foot of the chancel, his body marked as though with leprosy."

There was a shocked and heavy pause. "This magister," said Gudmar. "Who was he?"

"His name was Forgoyle Finlevyn," said An'char. And added bitterly, "You will perhaps recall that he was Caradoc's teacher."

Gudmar and Harlech traded startled glances. "There is more to this than mere coincidence," said Gudmar.

"Yes," agreed An'char. "But the tale of this night's events is already so tangled that I'm afraid only Earlis Ap Eadric will be able to unravel it."

Earlis Ap Eadric. Grand Prior of Kirkwell, and Inquisitor of Farrowaithe. "I had heard he had been summoned," said Gudmar. "When do you expect him to arrive?"

"Within the next few days," said An'char.

"Well, he's going tae have his work cut out for him when he gets here," said Harlech darkly. "As if things were no' bad enough, somebody up at the castle's been goin' around poisoning."

"Ulbrecht Rathmuir is up at Ambrothen Castle at this very moment, tending one of the victims," said Gudmar. "Certainly he will want to render his report to you in person, but I should at least explain that—"

"Master Gudmar Ap Gorvald?"

The voice belonged to a gangling young servitor. "Yes," said Gudmar. "What is it?"

The servitor glanced apologetically over at An'char before replying. "I'm sorry to disturb you, sir, but your manservant is waiting outside. He begs you to allow him a word with you."

"My manservant?" A glint showed from under Gudmar's half-lowered eyelids. "Did he mention what he wanted to speak to me about?"

"No, sir," said the servitor. "He hinted that it concerned a matter of considerable urgency."

There was a slight pause. "Hmm. Then I suppose I'd better go find out what he wants," said Gudmar. "If you will excuse us, Your Eminence. . . ."

The young mage who had brought the message clearly intended to accompany them. At the corner of the south transept, Gudmar came to a halt. "I don't see any reason why we should trespass any further on your time, when you must be anxious to get back to your duties at the hospital," he said to the servitor. "Thank you for your trouble. We'll make our own way from here."

The servitor looked as if he would have liked to protest. Gudmar bestowed upon him a brief encouraging nod, and moved purposefully away from him. Jumping to catch up, Harlech waited until they were out of earshot, then gave a grunt of approval. "So much for yon sprat. Now let's go see who's had the bad sense tae volunteer for your service."

Fog was ghosting into the narthex through the gap between the broken doors. Motioning Harlech to hang back, Gudmar stepped outside.

Someone drew breath warily in the darkness off to his left. Turning in the direction of the sound, Gudmar said, "Well?" and then waited.

Three heartbeats later—"Gudmar Ap Gorvald?" inquired a voice rough with uneasy belligerence.

"That's right," said Gudmar. "Who wants to know?"

A muffled figure moved away from one of the pilasters. "A friend of Caradoc Penlluathe's."

"Indeed?" Aware of Harlech's attentive presence just inside the doorway, Gudmar folded his arms. "I didn't think Caradoc had any friends left. Have we met before?"

"No, sir," said his informant, taking two steps forward into the halo of the nearest torch. He folded back his hood, revealing a round rubicund face surmounted by an unruly thatch of brown curls. "My name's Arn Aldarshot, sir. I'm the owner of the Beldame Inn, by Candlewick Cross. Caradoc must surely have spoken of me."

"The name is certainly one I've heard before," said Gudmar. He eyed the other man up and down. "Whether or not you belong to it, however, remains to be seen."

A figure materialized at his elbow. "That's all right, Gudmar," said Harlech, his berry-black gaze taking in their summoner's ordinary appearance. "I ken well enow this mannie's face. When I found Magister Ulbrecht earlier this evening, he had twa other chiels wi' him: one of 'em a magister like himself, the other this fellow here."

"The other magister was Forgoyle Finlevyn," said the owner of the Beldame Inn. "He was Caradoc's teacher."

Gudmar's glance flickered toward Harlech. "What were the three of you doing?"

Arn Aldarshot shook himself like a bull terrier. "Caradoc's sister works—worked—for me. She'd gone missing, along with a friend of theirs. We were out looking for them. It wasn't until later that we found out what they'd been up to."

Gudmar remembered suddenly that one of the prisoners who had escaped from Ambrothen Keep had been a woman. Recalling with liberated insight the details of her description—"Don't tell me. Let me guess," said Gudmar. "They were off hatching a scheme to save Caradoc from the gallows."

"They managed it, too—God knows how," said Arn with a wondering look in the direction of the castle. "I've seen them since, and I've a message to give you from Caradoc."

He dropped his voice. "These are Caradoc's own words, sir: 'Your friend's son is alive, but in peril. If you want to see him safe, meet us at Holmnesse.'"

He paused expectantly. "That's all?" asked Harlech.

Arn nodded, and cast an appealing look at Gudmar. "He seemed certain you'd understand, sir."

"He may have overestimated my perspicacity," said

Gudmar with arid irony. He fingered his moustache, golden brows touching above the bridge of his nose. "My *friend's* son . . . Think, Harlech: of all my myriad acquaintances, which one would Caradoc know enough about to describe as a friend of mine?"

"Well, he wasna referrin' tae me—at least t'the best of my knowledge," said Harlech. He cocked a shrewd black eye at Arn. "What's the bairn's name?"

"Rhan," said Arn. "Rhan Hallender."

"Hallender? I don't know any Hallenders," said Gudmar, his frown deepening. "Can you describe the boy?"

Arn screwed up his face. "About fifteen or sixteen years old, I should say, though he's none too well grown for his age. Fair hair, straight nose, brown eyes. He has a small cleft in his chin—"

He stopped because his questioner was staring at him. "When this boy smiles," said Gudmar, "do the corners of his mouth pull down slightly, just before they turn up?"

He spoke softly, but there was an odd note of rising excitement in his voice. Arn thought a moment. "Aye. Now that you mention it, it *is* an odd trick of expression with him."

He tilted his head to get a better look at Gudmar's taut face. "Are you sure you don't know the lad?"

"On the contrary," said Gudmar. "I rather think that I might, after all." He sounded slightly breathless, like a man surfacing out of deep water. He added musingly, "All of a sudden, Caradoc's message begins to make sense."

"Not to me it doesna," said Harlech testily. He glared up into his friend's altered face. "We've obviously missed the point, so ye might as well spell it out."

Gudmar roused himself from his reverie with a small jerk. "It's a wild explanation, but it's the only one that fits. I think this Rhan Hallender—my 'friend's son'—may well be none other than Evelake Whitfauconer."

31

# PERIL IN THE CHURCHYARD

THE TWO OTHER MEN GAPED AT him. After a moment, Harlech whistled softly through his teeth. "If ye have the right of it, the cat'll soon be among the pigeons."

"Or—more properly speaking—the lamb among the wolves," said Gudmar grimly. "Master Aldarshot, I'm going to take you at your word. Harlech, are you in the mood for a change of air?"

Harlech flashed him a gold-toothed grin. "Aye. I hear Holmnesse is fairly bracing this time o' year."

"Let's go see for ourselves," said Gudmar. "How soon could the *Yusufa* be made ready to sail?"

"I wouldna mind another day for takin' on provisions," said Harlech, "but if ye've an itch to be on your way, I daresay we could lift anchor wi' the next tide."

"Excellent," said Gudmar.

"Aye. But what about yon injured soldier-laddie up at the castle—the one wi' verra vital information ye'll be wanting?"

"He won't be recovering for days and he's safe enough in the keeping of Magister Rathmuir." Turning his head, he favored Arn with a thoughtful look. "In the meantime, we'd better see what can be done to protect you."

"Me?" Arn blinked. "Why should I need protection?"

"Quite apart from the fact that you are guilty of aiding and abetting an escaped felon," said Gudmar, "there are

32

some extremely dangerous people who would like to get their hands on the information you've just given us. You may take it from me that you don't want any of them taking even a casual interest in you—Hullo, what was that?"

From the direction of St. Welleran's Square, a trumpet rang out, its harsh fanfare climbing above the uproar of the crowd outside the abbey gates. Trading swift glances with Gudmar, Harlech sprang for the nearest in a series of niches ornamenting the cathedral's west facade.

He swung himself up by means of a carven saint's outstretched arm, and peered lynx-eyed across the fog-drowned quadrangle. "More guardsmen," he reported in a throaty undervoice. "At least twa dozen."

"I don't like the look of this," said Gudmar. "What's happened here tonight smells to high heaven. They'll be clapping everyone under guard—we might be held for weeks. I think the time has come for the three of us to make ourselves scarce."

"Aye." Harlech leaped down from his vantage point, landing without a sound. "Back through the cathedral?"

"No. The Grand Master and his colleagues are still there." Gudmar was on the move, sidling toward the northern end of the porch, his gaze tracking the watchlights bobbing toward them across the lawn from the gatehouse. "We'll just show ourselves out by the back way—"

He halted abruptly. Shoulder to shoulder behind him, Arn and Harlech froze in midstep. The foggy air pulsed with stealthy activity: heavy footsteps, inadequately muffled, were converging on the cathedral porch from around the north side of the building.

Gudmar gestured his companions back. Thrusting his one hand through the crook of Arn's elbow, Harlech spun the innkeeper around and made for the shrubbery on the cloister side of the cathedral entrance. Behind them, there was a sudden drumroll of charging feet, and a voice called sharply, "Stop right there, in the name of the Seneschal!"

Instead of obeying, Gudmar lunged forward. Bypassing Arn, he caught Caradoc's messenger by his other elbow and hissed, "*Jump!*"

Darkness gaped beneath Arn as his two escorts carried him off the south end of the porch in a flying leap. They landed heavily in a loud crackle of snapped shrubbery and blundered on, leveling waterlogged bushes as they skirted the wall. The same voice, strident with outrage, bellowed after them, "Halt, I say! You're under arrest!"

Swept jarringly along between his two companions, Arn cast a breathless, walleyed glance over one shoulder. Torchlight streamed over scarlet livery as a dozen Ambrothen Regulars broke away from the anonymous darkness and hammered forward to close the gap.

The wall ended abruptly at a vine-covered archway. "Into the cloister!" ordered Gudmar, and launched Arn through the opening with a hard two-handed shove.

Bereft of volition, Arn burst through the arbor in a whirl of torn leaves and stumbled to his knees on the gravel path beyond. A second later, Harlech overtook him and hauled him upright again. "Where's Gudmar?" panted Arn, then winced as metal clashed ringingly against stone in the murk.

There was a heartbeat's baffled pause, broken by a loud rattle and a staccato series of thuds. A tall figure shot out of the shadow of the arbor amid a mounting volley of curses. "That gate won't hold them for more than half a minute," growled Gudmar, as he caught up with them. "You two make for the southeast corner of the cloister —there's a door there leading into the hospital. I'll catch up if and when I can, but don't wait for me."

He had drawn his sword. After one lightning glance at his friend's face, Harlech caught Arn by the sleeve and dragged him up the path.

Left alone, Gudmar gripped his sword in both hands. Under a vengeful battery of hobnailed boots, the wooden gate shuddered and caved in. As the foremost guardsmen swarmed over the sagging shards of split fencing, Gudmar took one step backward and laid the edge of his blade with all his strength to the base of the trellis.

Vines popped and cracked as the heavy weapon clove through everything in its path. Cut loose at ground level, the arbor abruptly collapsed, flattening two of the soldiers as it fell.

The men immediately behind them also went down in a tangle of broken slats and half-dead foliage. Turning his back on his victims' howls of surprise and confusion, Gudmar turned and bolted after his companions up the path to the hospital.

Circumventing the well in the center courtyard, he found Harlech and Arn waiting for him in the cloister. "Well?" demanded Gudmar.

"The door's lockit," growled Harlech. "And so are all the windows on this level."

Torchlight flared with sudden abandon above the barbered crowns of the patterned fruit trees. "Follow me—this way," breathed Gudmar between set teeth, and melted into the darkness.

He was making for the opposite end of the long gallery. Keeping their heads down, Harlech and Arn scuttled after him and found him waiting for them beside the last of seven winglike arches enclosing the cloister's south loggia.

"What now?" demanded Harlech.

Gudmar's grin was a mirthless flash of bared teeth. "Up," said the big merchant, and levered himself onto the saddle of masonry between the two descending arms of the last archway.

He chinned himself off the wall and vanished from view. A slight stir of movement overhead told them he had gained the roof of the passageway. Swearing, Harlech leaned out through the opening and twisted his neck around in order to look up. "What the de'il d'ye think ye're doing?" he demanded in a fierce whisper.

Gudmar's head appeared over the edge of the roof, along with his outstretched arm. "Give me your hand."

Harlech did so. Gudmar hauled him up onto the roof in a single powerful heave. Similarly aided, Arn joined them a moment later. Flattened on the tiles next to Gudmar, he pressed a hand to the stitch in his side and wheezed, "Where do we go from here?"

A sharp pinch from Harlech's wiry fingers reduced him to silence as a group of torches emerged from between the hedgerows off to their right. "Keep your head down!" hissed Gudmar. "And *don't move!*"

The soldiers marched up to the southeast entrance to the cloister and drew up around the officer in charge. Snatches of their conversation floated up to the men on the roof through the roiling mist.

"Nobody here. D'you think they might have doubled back through the cathedral?"

"If they have, Dyssart and his lads'll soon pick 'em up," said the sergeant dispassionately. "Martyn! Geordan! Tullie! You three check out the east loggia. The rest of you come with me."

The party divided and receded separately into the shadows underlying the cloister's continuing walkway. Harlech mentally counted to twelve, then raised his head a few cautious inches. "There they go," whispered Gudmar, getting to his knees. "Now then—over the rooftop."

The upper floor of the abbey's residential wing was overgrown with ivy. Edging past two darkened windows, they came at last to a point where the vines were stout enough to afford partial footholds. Measuring the distance from the tiles under his feet to the sloping edge of the dorter's steep gable—"Tricky, but not impossible," said Gudmar to Arn. "Think you can manage it?"

The innkeeper squared his shoulders. "What's the point of asking?" said Caradoc's messenger sourly. "Just give me a leg up, and I'll do the rest."

The overlapping slates yielded better purchase than

Arn had expected. Inching upward on his belly, he arrived at the roof's summit and worked a leg over the acute angle at the gable's peak.

Hugging the base of a chimneystack, he paused to recover his breath. Harlech arrived a moment later, closely followed by Gudmar. The fog swirled around them, dank and all-encompassing. Arn shivered, and had a passing thought for the Beldame Inn's comfortable fireside.

"So far, so good," he grumbled, leaning closer to the man Caradoc had instructed him to find. "Now how do we get down from here?"

"The far end of this building adjoins the kitchen," said Gudmar. "It's only a short drop from this roof to that one, and then only another nine feet or so from there to the ground. Have you got your wind back yet? We'll do it in easy stages."

"Whatever you say," said Arn, and swallowed. He muttered to Gudmar's receding back, "I'm just glad I can't see the ground for the mist."

It proved easier to get down than it had been to get up. Choosing the darkest corner of the building, the three fugitives lowered themselves stealthily into the midst of what quickly made itself evident as the kitchen midden. His lip curling at the odor of rotting potatoes, Arn knuckled the end of his snubbed nose and gave an involuntary huff. Harlech grabbed his arm and jerked him down into the shadows.

From where they knelt, it was just barely possible to make out the shape of an adjacent outbuilding. "That's the library," whispered Gudmar, pointing. "The outer wall lies just beyond it. Make for it on my signal."

A twelve-yard dash carried them to the north corner of the library. Another short sprint brought them to the base of the high stone wall. Sidestepping a neglected collection of gardening tools, Gudmar bent down and made a stirrup of his clasped hands.

A quick heave boosted Harlech to the top of the wall.

Slewing around, the owner of the *Yusufa* offered his one hand to Arn on the way up.

Puffing, Arn scrambled up beside the little sea captain and disappeared over the other side in an ungainly flutter of thrashing legs. "Stay with him!" whispered Gudmar to Harlech. "If we get separated, I'll meet you at the *Yusufa*." Harlech nodded curtly and dropped out of sight.

Left alone inside the compass of the abbey walls, Gudmar moved back to take a running leap for the copestones. Before he could start, a sudden tattoo of racing feet made him look sharply to the right as five uniformed figures shot around the north edge of the library, making straight for him.

# DANGER IN THE STREETS

THE MAN IN THE OPEN answered well enough to the description Lieutenant Dyssart had been given. The young officer was a man of courage. Seeing the big man with the golden beard at bay by the wall, the lieutenant raced forward, torch held high, brandishing the sword he clutched in his right hand and bellowing "Halt!" at the top of his lungs.

Instead of obeying, his quarry sprang for the wall. For an instant, Dyssart thought he was going to jump, but at the last second, the man whirled in his tracks and snatched up a long-handled rake from the midst of a disused pile of garden tools.

Holding it before him like a quarterstaff, he retreated until his broad shoulders met stone, then stopped. Following their leader, Dyssart's men drew up in a swift semicircle around their quarry, but kept some distance open between them. None of his subordinates, Dyssart realized, was eager to be the first to close with the big man if he chose to stand his ground.

But instead of lashing out with his makeshift weapon, the big man with the golden beard looked them over from left to right with a nonplussed air, and abruptly relaxed. Grinning disarmingly, he said, "Well, I'll be damned. I thought for a moment I was in trouble."

39

This was not quite what Dyssart expected from a man reported to have been personally responsible for more than half a dozen casualties in the space of the last twenty minutes. By no means certain how he was intended to interpret the big man's remark, Dyssart set his jaw and glared at him. "Are you Gudmar Ap Gorvald?"

The big man nodded. "That's right," he said pleasantly. Then the amber eyes turned quizzical. "Is anything wrong, Lieutenant?"

Three of Dyssart's men had been injured when someone had collapsed the arbor that formed the entrance to the cloister garden. He snapped shortly, "There is indeed, Guild-Master. I've a warrant here for your arrest."

"My arrest?" Gudmar Ap Gorvald's surprise had a genuine ring to it. "Upon what charge?"

"Withholding evidence, for purposes of conspiracy," said Dyssart, with grim relish. "Her Grace the Dowager-Consort of Farrowaithe wishes to question you concerning the deaths of two members of her husband's personal guard."

Before Gudmar could respond, he shifted his gaze. "Fentyn!"

The young man to his right saluted. "Sir!"

"Relieve this gentleman of his weapons," said Dyssart. "And then be so good as to bind his hands."

Gudmar Ap Gorvald elevated a blond eyebrow. "Really, Lieutenant. That won't be necessary."

"I'll be the judge of that," said Dyssart austerely, and motioned his subordinate forward.

Gudmar shrugged. "Please yourself," he said offhandedly. And sent the hapless Fentyn flying backward with a hard rap from the butt end of the rake.

Floundering, the boy fouled his nearest companion as the rest of his party surged forward. Trapping the lieutenant's scything broadsword among the tines of the rake, Gudmar whipped it out of his grasp, then spun away from the wall like a dust-devil.

40

The more agile of the two men in his path ducked under the rake's lateral sweep, and came up at close quarters with a poniard in his free hand. Fire scored Gudmar's left side as the blade punched through his jerkin and opened a gash along his ribs. Ramming the rake-handle against the other man's diaphragm, he thrust his opponent back. In the same instant, a heavy body landed hard upon his back and flung a gauntleted arm about his throat.

Choking, Gudmar dropped the rake and dug his fingers into the hairline crack between his windpipe and his attacker's rigid forearm. He bent over and bucked from the knees, flipping his assailant over his head into the path of the one guardsman still on his feet. They collided with a clatter.

Hand pressed hard to his bleeding side, Gudmar skipped like a ram past their tangled legs and made a breakneck dash for the library. The panes of the lower left-hand window glistened like tar before his eyes. Bunched fists extended over his head, Gudmar crashed through the glass in a headlong dive.

A carpet partially cushioned his landing. Knuckles streaming crimson, he dragged himself up out of his bed of splinters and staggered to the door in the opposite wall. It gave access to a lightless passageway. Keeping his left hand on the wall, Gudmar followed it in the dark for fifteen short paces until he came to the foot of a stairway.

Shouts of alarm and racing movement from outside drove him up the steps two at a time. His momentum cost him a fall at the top of the stairs. Wincing, he picked himself up and began groping for doors along the south wall of the corridor. The first one he came to was locked, but the second one opened easily. Clearly audible voices and a scrawling flicker of light along the wall adjoining the stairwell told him that his pursuers were only seconds behind him. Inside the room three windows were visible as dim rectangles, against which the furnishings of the room showed up as dense cutouts in black. He wedged a chair firmly against the door, and made for the window on the right.

There was more light by the window, but there was no time to look around for the latch. Snatching up a candlestick from the nearest worktable, Gudmar plucked the candle free and dashed the ribbed sconce against the center of the window's cross-frame. Wood and glass gave way with a telltale crash. Knocking out the shards with his handy sconce, Gudmar swung himself over the sill and lowered himself to the full extent of his arms' reach. He took a breath to collect himself, and then released his grip.

His bent knees and ankles absorbed most of the shock of the fall. Bouncing into a forward somersault, Gudmar let his arms take the last residual jolt. He landed sitting, with no bones broken, three feet beyond the base of the abbey's outer wall. Gulping air, he scrambled to his feet and made for the obscurity of the cobbled street ahead of him.

He left behind him a hornet's buzz of baffled voices. Dodging in and out of doorways, he took the first turn he came to that branched off in the direction of the harbor. He slackened his pace to a brisk walk. As soon as his lungs would permit it, he pursed his lips and whistled the opening bars of an obscure and scurrilous drinking-song. The verse drew no response from the surrounding darkness.

Pausing to investigate by touch, Gudmar discovered that the shallow cut across his ribs had stopped bleeding. He moved on with more confidence until he came to a second turning.

This street was no better lit than the last, its cobbles miry, its air malodorous. Gudmar watched his footing and kept his ears pricked, stopping occasionally to repeat his whistling call-signal. The darkness gave back only incidental noises: the wail of an infant, the yowl of a prowling tomcat.

He crossed over Drumlyn Burn by way of the Mercat Street viaduct. Beyond, the houses became more jumbled, the bylanes more choked with refuse and offal. Whistling, Gudmar paused for a moment on a street corner opposite an evil-smelling cul-de-sac. He was about to move on again, when something stirred in the reeking gloom of the alley, beyond a battered row of ash-cans, and somebody uttered a ripely anatomical oath with feeble but heartfelt vitriol.

The language was Pernathe, with a familiar inflection. The short hairs lifting along the nape of his neck, Gudmar clapped a hand to the hilt of his sword and bounded toward the source of the voice. Squinting in an effort to penetrate the sooty atmosphere of the alley, he whispered, "Harlech?"

There was a labored grunt at ground level. "Aye, Gudmar, it's me," wheezed the owner of the *Yusufa*.

He tried and failed to sit up unaided. Thrusting the ash-cans out of the way, Gudmar dropped on one knee beside him and offered a supporting hand. He said, "I can't see—how badly are you hurt?"

The smaller man shook himself like a wet terrier and blew air gustily through his nose. "I've taken a dint or twa, but it could ha' been worse."

There was a dark flutter of movement as he put a hand to the back of his head. "What happened?" asked Gudmar. And added with rising sharpness, "And where's the inn-keeper?"

Harlech swore again, this time in Garillan. "If he's no' here, those bully bastards must ha' taken him."

Gudmar stiffened. "Guardsmen?"

"No." Harlech's tone was grim. "Not unless Borthen Berigeld's been commissioned by the Seneschal t' patrol the city streets."

There was an appalled silence. "Oh my God," said Gudmar flatly. "Are you sure they were Borthen's men?"

"I'm sure." Harlech got his legs under him, then

43

paused. "It'd take more than this damned witch's murk tae disguise something the size of Muirtagh."

Gudmar had his own reasons for remembering Borthen's behemoth lieutenant. His face tightened. "They obviously knew what they were looking for. But *damn* it! How could that hell-kite possibly have gotten wind of our movements?"

"He couldn't have," said Harlech with black simplicity, "unless there was someone *inside* the cathedral tae pass him the word."

The servitor who had informed them of Arn Aldarshot's arrival? Or someone higher up? Gudmar leaked air through his teeth with a hiss like a dragonet.

"One thing's certain: Arn and I were followed almost from the moment we left St. Welleran's," said Harlech. "I did what I could t' shake 'em off, but they kept poppin' up again, just when I thought we were in the clear. Thinkin' back on it, they were probably just herding us along in the direction they wanted us t' go."

"Never mind that now," said Gudmar. "We've got to overtake them before they turn that wretched innkeeper over to Borthen to have his brain plucked like a guinea-fowl. Have you any idea which way they went?"

Harlech shook his head. "I didnae stay conscious that long. But I marked one of 'em wi' my dagger, and I marked him good. Unless I've completely lost my touch, he'll have left something of himself behind him t' show us where he was heading."

"Then we're going to need a light of some kind." Gudmar began raking through the rubble. "Have you got any matches on you?"

"Aye, if they've ta'en no harm from this infernal damp." Harlech probed his pockets and came up with a small box, which he passed to Gudmar. "Here. See what ye can do wi' these."

Gudmar dragged a jagged length of split planking out from under a pile of oily rags. He broke it down to size, then held a lighted match to the end of it. After the third try, the wood caught fire in a crackle of acrid smoke, and light sprang out in the fog. "Now," said Gudmar, sweeping his makeshift torch along the dirty pavement. "Let's see what we can find."

They found their first clear token not in the gutter, but on the wall of a nearby building: a partial handprint still sticky with blood. Another dark smear showed where the wounded man had rested his weight on a boarded-up shop-window before moving on.

The trail led them down several narrow lanes and through a fenced-off wilderness of derelict houses overlooking the waterfront. Breathing heavily in the gloom, Harlech stopped and gripped Gudmar by the sleeve. "Douse the light," he muttered. "I know where they went from here."

In the swirling fog the abandoned shipyard looked like a sea-bed graveyard of sunken hulls. Leading the way stealthily up to the sagging fence of strung wire, Harlech recalled with unpleasant clarity his last visit here, during the time when he had been temporarily entrapped in Borthen Berigeld's dangerous employ.

Always before there had been concealed sentries posted amid the flotsam and jetsam of general disuse. Harlech tossed a handful of loose gravel against the wall of a tarry lean-to not far from the fence, then ducked back behind a mound of broken timbers. They waited for the space of ten heartbeats, but nothing stirred across the littered expanse of the shipyard. Gnawing suspiciously on his lower lip, Harlech shrugged and crept forward again.

They slid under the fence and scuttled for the nearest available cover. Squatting next to Gudmar behind the turtle-backed bulk of an overturned keel, Harlech jabbed a blunt finger toward the dark building in the middle of the yard. "There ye see it. Are ye ready?" he growled. And when Gudmar nodded, braced his shoulders. "All right then. In by the back door."

They approached warily, with weapons drawn, but no one challenged them. The door, they discovered, was not locked. Gudmar glanced back at Harlech, then nudged it open with his foot.

It swung back on oiled hinges and bumped off the inside wall. A short dark passageway lay beyond. Without speaking, the two men stepped across the threshold and halted, listening.

The only audible sound in the hallway was that of their own muted breathing. After a moment's calculation, Gudmar pulled out the matchbox and struck a light.

The corridor ended ahead of them at a three-way intersection. There was an unlit torch standing in a bracket fixed to the right-hand wall. Gudmar lifted the torchstick down from the sconce, then paused, his eyes glinting. The charred wood above the handgrip was still warm.

"This was only recently extinguished," he whispered, as the torch flared into life again. "You know the layout of this place. Where do we go from here?"

Even as he spoke, the floor beneath their feet throbbed with a sudden vibration. From somewhere off to their left came the distant but unmistakable rumble of machinery being set in motion.

Gudmar's startled gaze flew to meet Harlech's. An instant later, he tore his eyes away and leapt for the mouth of the passageway beyond, the torch-flame streaking behind him like a banner.

With Harlech hard on his heels, he shot around the corner and made off at full speed down the left-hand branch of the corridor. After twenty strides, the passage made a sharp turn to the right. Still leading, Gudmar skidded around the inside wall of the turn and raced for the doorway at the end of the hall.

He struck the door hard with his braced shoulder. It burst open in a spray of broken hinges, spilling him into the room beyond. The room itself was empty, apart from a cumbersome array of old ship's parts. Skidding to a halt on the threshold, Harlech was about to demand an explanation for his friend's sudden impetuous behavior when his quick ears caught another sound—the dungeon-rattle of a rusty chain caught in the teeth of a moving pulley-wheel.

The noise had come from somewhere underneath the floorboards. "Quick!" snapped Gudmar. "If there's a way down, we've got to find it *now!*"

Jamming the torch in the bunghole of an upturned keg, he began shifting crates and broken furniture with whirlwind abandon. Harlech leaped forward to join in.

Their lightning assault turned the room upside down in a matter of moments, to no avail. Heaving aside a large coil of heavy cable, Harlech straightened up with a grunt and fell back panting between the staves of a derelict capstan. The wheel turned under his weight with a grinding sound, and a square section of the floor sprang up from its bedding six feet away. "That's it!" shouted Gudmar from the far side of the room. "Here, I'll help you!"

The wheel answered their fierce combined leverage with a protesting rattle of unseen chains. The trapdoor yawned like a viper's mouth. First to the opening —"There's a ladder here!" reported Harlech over his shoulder, and swung himself feet-foremost through the gap.

Retrieving the torch, Gudmar sprang after him. A steady draught of cold, stinking air streamed up his back as he descended. The ladder-shaft gave access to a narrow room, dank as a crypt. An open doorway at the far end of it led out onto a creaky wooden dock.

Water sucked hollowly at the underside of the platform. "An underground boathouse," muttered Harlech. "Of all the curst bad luck!"

The roof of the enclosure sloped acutely downward at its far end where a tunnel-mouth showed black. "The water can't possibly be more than three or four feet deep," said Gudmar. "I'll go first."

Handing the torch to Harlech, he sat down on the end of the dock and lowered himself into the water. It proved to be no deeper than his waist. Sludge drifted sluggishly up from the canal-bed as he turned to take back the torch. Muttering darkly under his breath, Harlech followed Gudmar into the stagnant pool, and together they made their way toward the tunnel-exit.

The ceiling of the passage was so low that they were obliged to stoop. Peering forward, Gudmar marked the far end of the water-course as a pale triangle outlined in black.

Something was blocking the lower part of the opening. As he drew close enough to make out what it was, Gudmar felt his stomach contract into a cold knot of sick dismay.

It was the body of a man, floating face-down in the boneless quiescence of a corpse. The back of a sodden homespun jerkin showed wet and rounded above the level of the water. Seeing that much, Gudmar knew enough to identify the body without turning it over to look at the face.

But he turned it over anyway, then stared down aghast at the dead man. Peering over his shoulder—"God!" said Harlech in shaken tones. "What did they do t' him to make him look like that?"

"I don't know." Gudmar lowered his lids to shut out the sight of Arn Aldarshot's staring eyes and insanely contorted face. "Borthen's methods of torture are unique. And devastating."

"Ye don't suppose—" Harlech swallowed and began again. "D'ye think it's possible our breaking in upstairs was their signal tae kill him?"

"If so, it was a mercy," said Gudmar grimly. "But the evidence suggests that the destruction was accomplished well before we got here."

Harlech shuddered. "I wonder how much of what he knew is now in Borthen's possession."

48

"Who can tell?" Gudmar swallowed the bile of his own nausea. "But for the sake of all concerned, we'd better assume that Borthen now knows everything. And that means we'd better get back to the *Yusufa*. If we're in for a race to Holmnesse, I want a good headstart. . . ."

# CONFLICTS OF INTEREST

ON THE SAME NIGHT THAT Gudmar and Harlech set out from Ambrothen to keep an important rendezvous at Holmnesse, Magister Ulbrecht Rathmuir, having successfully deceived the Lady Gwynmira, arranged to have a "dead" body transferred from the guardhouse of Ambrothen Castle to the precincts of St. Welleran's Hospital.

The victim's name was Cergil Ap Cymric, and he had been a lieutenant in the service of the late Lord Warden. As there were a number of questions surrounding his death, the wagon bearing his shrouded corpse through the streets was escorted by a detachment of Ambrothen Regular Militia, by order of Gwynmira Du Bors, the Lord Warden's widow.

The procession was met at the hospital's west entrance by the Grand Master's appointed secretary. A brief conversation between Ulbrecht and the gangling young servitor established that the hospital mortuary was already overburdened. The guardsmen, accordingly, were shown to a small bare room in a neighboring part of the hospital. The lieutenant's body was laid out on the table that had been prepared for it, and the Regulars, their duty dispatched, were given leave to return to the castle.

Once they were gone, Ulbrecht covered the body with blankets. He stayed long enough to make sure his patient was resting comfortably, then left the room. He locked the door behind him and went to look for his superior.

He found An'char Maeldrake in the entry hall of the library, grimly lending ear to the distracted rantings of the chief curator. Catching sight of Ulbrecht in the doorway, the Grand Master disengaged himself with a few calming words and came to meet his newly returned subordinate. "I'm relieved to see you," he said, and dropped his voice to a thin-lipped undertone. "Were you aware that your friend Gudmar Ap Gorvald was wanted by the authorities for conspiracy and treason?"

Ulbrecht's stomach tightened. "I didn't know. Have they arrested him?"

"They tried to," said An'char with arid irony. "He made good his escape from the abbey via an upstairs window in this building, and as far as I know, is still at large."

He subjected Ulbrecht to sharp scrutiny. "Have you any idea what this master-merchant may have been up to that would lend substance to these allegations?"

"No," said Ulbrecht. He added with some hesitation, "I *do*, however, have a theory that would explain why Lady Gwynmira and her brother should want Gudmar gaoled as quickly and quietly as possible."

"Indeed?" said An'char. "Tell me about this theory of yours."

Ulbrecht grimaced slightly. "I have a confession to make first: my theory is based not on ordinary physical evidence, but upon information I obtained by using techniques normally reserved exclusively for inquisitors."

An'char's brow clouded. "This is a fairly serious breach of the Rule of the Order. You do not have the Arch Mage's mandate to undertake this kind of investigation."

"I know," said Ulbrecht grimly. "But I felt that the circumstances demanded that I should make the attempt." He recounted his experiences at Ambrothen Castle in as few words as possible.

At the end of his subordinate's recital, the Grand

Master stared at Ulbrecht in dismay. "This is lunacy! Surely you can't be serious in suggesting that Lady Gwynmira Du Bors used poison—sesquina!—on two of her own men? Quite apart from considerations of her birthright and station, what on earth could motivate her to do such a thing?"

"I don't know," admitted Ulbrecht. "But given the circumstantial evidence, what explanation would *you* offer?"

"I'm afraid the most obvious explanation," said An'char, "is that your apprehension of the evidence is at fault."

"I would agree with you," said Ulbrecht, "were it not for the fact that the late Warden's consort showed what I can only describe as significant interest in the flagon that held the poisoned wine—oh, I realize that's hardly conclusive, either," he continued, before An'char could voice any objection. "But if there's even a slim chance that I *am* right about this, it seems to me that we have an imperative obligation to conceal this young man's presence here, to protect him until he recovers sufficiently to speak for himself."

An'char gave the matter a long moment's careful consideration. "Very well. I suppose it's better to be too careful than not careful enough," he said grudgingly. "I do not think it will prove too difficult to disguise your patient's true malady from the rest of our community. The secular authorities, however, could prove harder to satisfy. They have certain obligations to fulfill with respect to a man supposedly killed by poison."

"I've thought of that," said Ulbrecht. "And I believe I have the solution to the problem. . . ."

The following day the chief constable of Ambrothen paid a visit to St. Welleran's Abbey and presented a writ from the office of the city justiciar. The writ, countersigned by the Seneschal, authorized the bearer to examine the body of the late lieutenant. The magister in charge, however, having read the document over, announced gravely that such an examination would be ill-advised.

The poison which had killed the lieutenant, Magister Ulbrecht explained, possessed far-reaching toxic properties dangerous to anyone else exposed to them. His graphic description of the related symptoms significantly dampened his listener's sense of duty. Ulbrecht suggested helpfully that the constable might be content to accept a signed deposition, rather than risk jeopardizing his own health. The constable, with alacrity, agreed.

Shortly thereafter, he departed to render his official report, taking with him the proffered deposition, along with the lieutenant's personal effects. Later that evening, a coffin bearing the name "Cergil Ap Cymric" on the lid was decently and discreetly interred in holy ground beyond the city walls.

Meanwhile, in an obscure corner of the hospital, an unfortunate young man suffering from a uniquely infectious tubercular complaint was being tended in strictest isolation by Ulbrecht Rathmuir. The patient's condition having been diagnosed as highly dangerous, the rest of the hospital staff were forbidden even to set foot in the private cubicle assigned to him without prior permission from the Grand Master. The one curious young servitor who was caught prying about the patient's room was severely reprimanded. His peers, taking note from his example, prudently kept their distance.

Secluded along with the patient behind a locked door, Ulbrecht Rathmuir took turns with his superior keeping watch at the young guardsman's bedside. All through the night, and throughout the following morning, Cergil Ap Cymric remained sunken in a chill coma. His condition was stable, but his two physicians looked in vain for any sign of awakening. It wasn't until late afternoon of the second day of his confinement that his situation underwent any change.

Ulbrecht was sitting lost in thought in a chair beside the sickbed when a small rustling sound, like a bird moving through leaves, drew his instant attention to the still form beneath the heaped blankets. A moment later Cergil stirred slightly and muttered something unintelligible under his breath.

A swift examination revealed to Ulbrecht that the patient's skin was hot and dry, and that his pulse rate had risen. Brows puckered in concern, Ulbrecht plucked up a vial of cordial from the table by the bedstead. As he leaned forward to administer the medicine, Cergil made a sudden threshing motion and gripped the mage hard by the wrist.

The guardsman's wild eyes showed white all around the irises as he stared up into Ulbrecht's face. What Cergil saw, however, appeared to reassure him, for he drew a rasping breath and made a strained attempt to speak.

The young lieutenant was visibly agitated. "Take your time," said Ulbrecht quietly. "You're quite safe here, and I'm not going anywhere—"

He broke off with a grimace as his patient's grasp tightened to a viselike pinch. "Evelake!" gasped Cergil Ap Cymric. "We found Evelake!"

The sheer unexpectedness of this announcement startled Ulbrecht into losing his calm bedside manner. "Evelake?" he exclaimed. "Evelake *Whitfauconer*? Where?"

Cergil's chest rose and fell. "Outside . . . near the yew hedges," he said huskily. "Didn't know me. Ask Sergeant Runlaf . . . he'll explain. . . ."

Sergeant Runlaf. The man who had been found dead in the same room where Gudmar had found Cergil. His heart thumping against his ribs in rising excitement, Ulbrecht gently chafed the taut hand still fastened about his wrist. "The sergeant isn't here just now," he said softly. "But perhaps, if you feel able, you could tell me what happened?"

"What happened . . ." The sick man's gaze wavered, his eyes momentarily losing their focus. Ulbrecht waited with bated breath to see if he would rally, but when Cergil looked up at his attendant again, it was in helpless appeal.

"Tongue . . . burning . . ." he moaned. "Can't swallow. . . ."

It was as pointless as it would have been cruel to press him. Thrusting rampant curiosity to the back of his mind, Ulbrecht laid cool authoritative fingers over his patient's tinder-dry brow. "Rest easy," he said. "A remedy is at hand."

Even with the Magia to aid him, it cost Ulbrecht a struggle to bring Cergil's temperature under control. Grey twilight was falling beyond the window as the magister at last roused himself from Orison to find his patient sleeping deeply and naturally after his fever had left him.

It was the first clear indication that the young guardsman was firmly on the road to recovery. Profoundly relieved, Ulbrecht stood up and stretched his cramped limbs, knowing that the crisis was over.

The mysteries, however, still remained—complicated afresh by the few words that Cergil had blurted out from the threshold of delirium. Ulbrecht might have been prepared to dismiss the guardsman's utterances as the ravings of a fevered imagination, were it not for the fact that Forgoyle Finlevyn, Ulbrecht's friend and fellow magister, had had an experience the night before he died that had convinced him Evelake Whitfauconer was not only alive, but present in Ambrothen.

By his own account, Forgoyle had been examining a peculiar artifact: a curious wand of greenish stone that had possessed uncanny properties of a highly suspicious nature. The rod had been given to Forgoyle by an acquaintance of his, a minstrel who had recently returned to Ambrothen after a journey in the north. The minstrel had acquired a companion in the course of his travels: a boy who called himself Rhan Hallender. There would have been nothing especially remarkable about that, except that Rhan's brutal former master had used the rod in order to trace the boy's movements.

In trying to learn more about the rod and its maker,

Forgoyle had come up against a formidable exponent of necromancy. Having used his Orison to open up the avenues of power, Forgoyle had been driven back before a force greater than his own. The storm of hostile energies had overtaken him in his library. He had only just managed to sever the bridge between himself and his adversary before the other crossed over to destroy him.

Forgoyle had confided his experience to Ulbrecht the following day. "Why," Forgoyle had wondered, "would anyone fashion a necromancer's tool for the sole purpose of keeping track of a mere bond-servant?"

The answer had been obvious: that the boy Rhan Hallender must be far more important than his appearance would seem to indicate. Forgoyle had been killed before he could examine Rhan. But it was quite possible that another mage might successfully pursue the investigation on his behalf.

Assuming, of course, that the boy could be found. Ulbrecht had accompanied Forgoyle to the minstrel's lodgings only to discover that the rooms had already been abandoned. Now that Forgoyle was gone, Ulbrecht realized he had no idea where to take up the search. But it was just barely possible that Forgoyle's house might yield up a vital clue or two that would aid his successor.

The impulse to go see what he could find was too strong to deny. Secure in the knowledge that Cergil no longer required constant attendance, Ulbrecht turned over responsibility for his care to An'char Maeldrake. Then he himself set out alone for Maulden Court.

Ulbrecht had been a frequent guest at his friend's rambling residence, and it was with a forlorn sense of loss that he approached the front of the house to find the windows all dark and blind in the early evening gloom. Already the herb garden seemed to have taken on a look of neglect. His heart weighing heavy, despite his sense of purpose, Ulbrecht let himself in through the front gate and climbed the steps to the front door.

The air inside was close and stale. Pocketing the key Forgoyle had given him over a year before, Ulbrecht paused in the entry hall long enough to light a lamp, then moved on upstairs to Forgoyle's library, where the strange confrontation had taken place.

The scene which met his eyes when he opened the door was one of rife disorder. Tables and chairs had been overturned and scattered with wanton abandon to the four corners of the room, while pots that had contained household herbs littered the rumpled rug with spilled dirt and broken pot-shards.

Forgoyle's cherished books lay strewn about the floor, pages bent and bindings cracked. Grim-faced, Ulbrecht picked his way through the debris to the desk, and spent a moment or two gazing somberly down at the loose riot of notes and papers littering the desktop. Then with a sigh, he set down the lamp and began to gather the documents together for examination.

To his disappointment, he found nothing of import among the overwritten pages. He had just set aside the last of the papers, and was about to give his attention to the bookshelves that lined the walls, when he caught a glimpse of something glimmering pallidly on the floor beside the desk.

His brow creasing, Ulbrecht dropped down on one knee to examine the carpet, and discovered that the glimmer belonged to a small heap of greenish-white powder. He started to poke at it, then snatched his hand away as he realized what it must be.

The remains of the mysterious green rod, destroyed in the duel of power that had wrought such havoc with the room at large.

Ulbrecht drew a long breath and rose to his feet. As he did so, he noticed a foreign black binding jutting out from under a pile of other books on the right-hand side of the desktop.

The black book was old—a heavy grimoire nearly a

handbreadth thick. Searching his memory, Ulbrecht could recall no such tome among the volumes in Forgoyle's personal collection. He leaned across the desk and tilted his head to take a closer look at the lettering on the book's spine.

Though faded, the title was plainly legible: *A Studie into ye Blacke Artes, As Practysed bye Them Deluded bye ye Darke.*

"This must be where Forgoyle got his information," muttered Ulbrecht aloud to himself.

A breath of air blew through the open doorway at his back and sent the light guttering. Ulbrecht stiffened as his nostrils picked up the sudden rank odor of human perspiration.

A floorboard creaked behind him. Instinctively clutching his magestone, Ulbrecht spun around and stepped right into a driving fist the size of a small ham.

The force of the blow cracked his left cheekbone and hurled him backward against a lamp-stand. It and he went down with a clangorous crash. He caught a fleeting glimpse of a lumbering form the size of a grizzly bear before pain clouded his vision and he slumped to the floor.

He did not quite lose consciousness. Gripping his magestone more tightly, he fought dizzily to collect his scattered wits long enough to summon the Magia to his aid. His ears were full of the thud and clatter of falling objects. His unknown assailant seemed to be turning the room upside down in search of something in particular.

A document of some kind? Or perhaps some special artifact?

Artifact?

Ulbrecht's pained senses reeled. Taking a firmer grip on himself, he reached out for the stabilizing solace of Orison.

As the Magia embraced him, his foggy mind began to clear. His assailant was going systematically from one bookcase to the next, emptying the shelves from top to bottom. So it's a book he's after, thought Ulbrecht. Which one, I wonder?

Then realized that the answer was obvious.

The swelling from his broken cheek had temporarily closed his left eye. Keeping his undamaged right one on the big man who was ransacking the room, Ulbrecht gathered himself together and inched his way on his elbows to the foot of the desk.

Intent on his work, the flat-faced giant in the far corner was making enough noise to drown out any small sound the Magister might make. Reaching for the desktop, Ulbrecht pulled himself to his knees.

Heart thudding against his ribs, he edged to the right, and got his hand on the big black book. "Easy now," he told himself. "Very, very easy—"

There was someone else coming up the stairs.

The big man paused in the act of dumping a whole set of red leather volumes onto the floor. Casting all caution to the winds, Ulbrecht scrambled upright and snatched up the black book, as a tall lithe figure, swathed head to foot in a dark cloak, stepped into the open doorway.

The cowled head lifted at the sight of the dishevelled mage in grey. "Muirtagh! Get him!" ordered the newcomer in a fathomless voice, and pointed with a gauntleted hand.

The big man spun around. Growling deep in his throat like the bear he resembled, he sprang for the man clutching the book.

Ulbrecht kicked a footstool into his assailant's path and dodged behind the desk. The big man overleapt the stool and lunged across the desktop, knotted fingers spread to grip and crush.

Taking a desperate leap backward, Ulbrecht crashed against the middle window overlooking the garden. The glass shattered and gave way. He tumbled over the sill with a startled cry.

He landed hard in a bed of eyebright fifteen feet below the window ledge. The black book flew out of his grasp and bounced out of sight among the neighboring hedge-plants. Bruised and shaken in every joint, Ulbrecht tried and failed to pick himself up. Unable to run, he shouted for help.

Lights flared in the darkness as occupants in the adjoining houses flung wide their shutters to see what the matter might be. Gazing up at Forgoyle's broken window, Ulbrecht saw the lamp wink out.

He listened for footbeats. "Oi! What's going on in there?" called a voice from the street.

"Fetch the Watch!" screamed Ulbrecht. "There's a break-in in progress upstairs."

"It looks more like a break-*out* to me," said the voice. "Who are *you*, anyway?"

Ulbrecht had come to the shaky conclusion that his bones were unbroken, but the cumulative effect of his numerous bumps and lacerations was for the moment debilitating. Closing his eyes against a sickening sensation of vertigo, he lay back among the herbs. "I'm Magister Ulbrecht Rathmuir," he said indistinctly. "Once you've called for the Watch, I'd be obliged if you'd see me back to St. Welleran's. . . ."

He never knew whether or not they heard him, because at that precise moment he passed out.

# VEILS OF UNCERTAINTY

Shortly after the night bell had tolled ten, An'char Maeldrake looked in on Cergil Ap Cymric, and found the young man still sleeping as Ulbrecht had left him two hours before. Satisfied that the patient would require no further attention before the magister's return, An'char was just leaving the isolated sickroom when he heard a door open and close at the far end of the adjoining passageway amid an excited conclave of voices.

Shrill snatches of conversation accompanied the swift patter of approaching feet. ". . . Forgoyle Finlevyn's house . . . no, not common thieves—Ulbrecht Rathmuir claims they were after a book dealing with necromancy."

The footbeats fetched up short. "Necromancy!" exclaimed a different voice. "No wonder Ulbrecht wants to see the Grand Master even before he gets his injuries treated!"

It was all An'char needed to confirm his sudden fears. Jerking shut the door to Cergil's room, Ulbrecht's superior wheeled on his heel and strode off up the corridor to meet the delegation coming in search of him.

The dull, solid thump of the door closing was the first sound in three days to penetrate the dark limbo of chaotic dreams in which Cergil Ap Cymric lay submerged. Like a drowning man who suddenly feels a liferope within his grasp, he instinctively seized upon the noise he had heard. Seeking its source, he came swimmingly to his senses a few minutes later.

The small, bare room in which he found himself was totally unfamiliar—in its starkness more like a gaol cell than a bedchamber. Tilting his head, he stared in some confusion at the scrubbed, featureless walls, wondering what he might have done to earn himself a sentence of incarceration. Memory failed to explain how he had come to be shut away in this boxlike cubicle, wearing nothing but a loose woolen robe in place of his uniform.

He made an effort to sit up and discovered that his body was even less reliable than his recollection. The extent of his physical weakness was as frightening as it was unexpected. His skin prickling with cold sweat, Cergil gritted his teeth and made a second, more deliberative attempt to raise himself off the mattress. As his protesting muscles strained to comply with his demands, his disoriented mind tried to work out why he should be feeling so ill and enfeebled.

Then all at once he had it: someone had been trying to kill him!

The idea crystallized into an unbreakable conviction as he caught sight of the collection of small glass vials on the table beside the bed. Hazy memories of griping pains in his chest and bowels reinforced the suspicion that he had been poisoned. Squinting hard, he tried to read the labels on the bottles at hand, but the fineness of the printing confounded his blurred vision. Defeated, he turned his eyes toward the door.

The precise reason why anyone should want him dead eluded him, but he had a strong feeling that he must have stumbled across information that someone else wanted to conceal at all cost. Until he knew who he had to fear, he could afford to trust no one. And he could only assume that this narrow room might well be a trap.

Nudging aside the blankets, he eased his legs awkwardly over the side of the bed and tried to stand up. His first two attempts were abortive, but the third time he managed it with the aid and support of the adjacent wall. A succession of lurching steps brought him at last within reach of the door. He paused a moment to regain his poise, then tried the latch.

The door was unlocked. Surprised, but by no means reassured, Cergil peered cautiously around the doorframe. The empty passage outside was no more familiar than the room had been. Quaking with cold and exertion, he stepped across the threshold. When no one appeared to challenge him, he girded himself grimly against the impending ordeal, and set out on a halting quest for a way out of the building.

It wasn't until nearly an hour later that An'char Maeldrake returned to Cergil's room to find him gone.

An exhaustive search of the hospital and grounds failed to turn up any trace of him. None of the other mages on duty, distracted from their rounds by the news Ulbrecht Rathmuir had brought back from Maulden Court, had any clues to offer concerning his departure. A pair of wine-sodden beggars, bivouacked on the bank of the burn outside the abbey walls, might have been able to shed some light on his movements, since he had prevailed upon one of them to exchange a disreputable set of rags for a good woolen robe. But no one discovered the pair in time to ask them any questions.

And so Cergil's disappearance was added to the list of unsolved mysteries presented to the High Inquisitor of Farrowaithe when he arrived shortly before noon on the following day.

An'char Maeldrake, worn out with worry, was waiting at the entrance to the magisters' dormitory to greet the distinguished envoy from the parent house of all the Order. Having been himself a preceptor fifteen years ago in Farrowaithe, An'char recalled Earlis Ap Eadric as he had been then: a frail youth whose extraordinary gifts of perception had rendered him at times vulnerable to nervous exhaustion. Since then, however, training and commit-

ment to his vocation had transformed the temperamental
novice into a slight upright man, whose fine fair hair
framed a striking rectangular face, and whose clear-
polished skin suggested an admirably disciplined life.

The High Inquisitor, it transpired, had made the long
journey from Farrowaithe equipped with no more baggage
than a single packhorse could carry, and only a single
black-clad acolyte to attend him. Rothyl, the High Inquisitor explained, was a deaf-mute, given as an oblate to the
Order because his incurable defects had rendered him too
unsightly to be accepted in the world at large. The fact that
Rothyl made no move to loosen the hood that concealed
his features suggested that his disfigurement must be grave
indeed. An'char diplomatically refrained from comment,
and conducted his guests in person to the pair of adjoining
rooms that had been prepared for them.

He was both grateful and relieved when the High
Inquisitor proposed to embark at once upon his investigations. "With all due respect for your Magister Ulbrecht,"
said Earlis quietly, "the related matters of the Lord Warden's death and the profanation of this house must take
precedence over that of his missing patient. With your
permission, I would like to examine the cathedral without
further delay."

On the way through the hospital toward the door
leading into the cathedral's south transept, An'char described to his guest the measures already taken by the
Magisters of Ambrothen. "While the officers of the Watch
were still searching for physical evidence," he said, "my
two senior magisters and I entered into the Orison of
Seeing, hoping to learn anything we could about the
individual so godless as to compound murder with necromancy. And this much I can tell you now: the offender was
a renegade mage. The sign was plainly graven there in the
presence of his penumbra."

It was a crucial piece of evidence. Like a bright mirror
image of himself, a mage's penumbra came into being on

the first occasion that he took his magestone in hand to invoke the power of the Magia. As a man's shadow in the physical world was an extension of his corporeal body, so a mage's penumbra was an extension of his ability to project himself into the realm of the spirit. "Having perceived his penumbra," said Earlis soberly, "you were, I gather, unable to sustain your view of it?"

"It faded within the hour," said An'char somberly. "This renegade has developed his own methods of covering his tracks—physical and otherwise."

He grimaced. "All we have to go on is a hypothesis based on a name."

A starlike glint appeared in Earlis's silver-grey eyes. "What name?"

"Borthen Berigeld," said An'char, mouthing the syllables as if they tasted of wormwood. "At least, that was the name by which he made himself known to our novice Caradoc Penlluathe. But I can't help wondering . . ."

He paused, then said abruptly, "You served your novitiate at Farrowaithe. Do you recall the case of Druoch Penhallowyn?"

"The postulant who used the Magia to blind a fellow novice, and then fled the Order? Who among those of us who were there could forget?" said Earlis.

He shivered slightly, an eloquent ripple of slender shoulders. "He was a few years older than I, but I recall vividly what he looked like: a dark, handsome youth, who carried himself with the arrogance of a monarch." His light eyes sought An'char's. "Are you wondering if Druoch Penhallowyn and Borthen Berigeld might be one and the same?"

"It would explain several unsolved mysteries—not the least the fact that the Penhallowyn youth's body was never found," said An'char. "Certainly he had the potential. His teachers agreed that he possessed an exceptional affinity for the Magia, but that he was also inordinately greedy for illicit knowledge and impatient of restraint. The novice who was blinded swore that his attacker had been using the Magia to conjure and control infernal spirits—"

He fell silent abruptly. "A theory worth testing," said Earlis soberly.

Even in broad daylight, the chancel was full of shadows. Standing before the ruined altar, within mere inches of the bloodstains, the Inquisitor raised himself up to his full stature and took his magestone between his palms. Stationed off to one side, An'char became aware of a subtle change in the atmosphere around him. The air seemed all at once vibrant with energy centering on the Inquisitor's slender figure as he moved clockwise around the altar, traversing foot by foot the whole area of the sanctuary.

It was some time before the High Inquisitor roused himself from the rarified heights of Orison. Opening his eyes on the sublunary world of normal sense experience, he encountered the burning question in An'char's face. A weary sigh shook Earlis's attenuated frame. His voice when he spoke betrayed the strain that his sustained clairvoyance had placed on his vitality.

"On the night Delsidor Whitfauconer was murdered," he said heavily, "three people—besides the Warden himself, and your Magister Forgoyle—passed through this sanctuary. One of them is veiled from my sight—an image of impenetrable darkness. . . ."

He paused, his finely chiseled face hard and pale as alabaster. "The necromancer's power is such that I am prevented from seeing his face. But I have seen his adherents clearly."

"His adherents?" said An'char sharply.

"They both bear the sign of those who have trafficked with demons," said Earlis. "One is tall and young, with dark red hair. His counterpart is smaller in stature than he, with brown hair and grey eyes." He added, with a penetrating look at An'char, "They are not, I think, unknown to you?"

There was a stricken silence as An'char Maeldrake

wrestled with shock and disbelief. Then he recalled the unimpeachable authority of the High Inquisitor and forced himself to put his personal doubts aside. "Caradoc Penlluathe is tall and red-headed," he said harshly. "And he has a friend named Serdor Sulamith who answers to the description of the second man."

"Then they must be sought and found at all cost," said Earlis sternly. "The servants of darkness may lead us to the master himself."

An'char shook his head in some bewilderment. "Caradoc swore under oath that he had broken and rejected the pact he had made with Borthen Berigeld. It hardly seems possible . . ."

"That he would voluntarily return to the service of his evil mentor? You must not underestimate the powers of the shadow," said Earlis. "Evil spirits, having once taken possession of an individual, rarely abandon their own."

It remained for the Ambrothen Council of Magisters to meet as a body for the purpose of communicating a warning through Orison to all the other chapter houses of the Order within a week's journey of the city. While the meeting was in progress, Earlis Ap Eadric withdrew to his quarters. He was met at the door by a tall figure shrouded head to foot in black. As Earlis slipped past the acolyte into the room, a smoothly modulated voice spoke from within the shadow of the hood. "Well?"

Earlis paused on his way to a chair by the window. "You may well ask," he said petulantly over his shoulder. "Something's come up that could tear a sizable hole in all your well-knit schemes."

He dropped into his chosen seat and began massaging his temples with slim fingertips. His acolyte latched the door, then came to join him. Looming darkly over the Inquisitor's slight wilting form, the man in black shook back his cowl, revealing a glossy head of raven hair and a high-bred, saturnine face. "Indeed?" said Borthen Berigeld with chilly interest. "Electrify me with the details."

Earlis showed small even teeth in a smile without mirth. "Lady Gwynmira Du Bors stands in some danger of being exposed as a murderess by one of the victims, who is not so dead as the world at large has been led to believe."

There was a slight pause. "You intrigue me," said Borthen. "Who is this prodigy?"

"An officer in the Farrowaithe Guard," said Earlis.

Borthen's black gaze turned thoughtful. "Our late lamented innkeeper said that Evelake Whitfauconer had been apprehended inside Ambrothen Castle by guardsmen who recognized him and notified his stepmother. Now we know the rest of the story."

"What are you going to do about it?" demanded Earlis. "If this guardsman survives to tell what he knows, it could wreak havoc."

Borthen shrugged a negligent shoulder. "Don't let that unduly worry you. In order to make the kind of trouble you envision, this young man will have to show himself. If and when he does so, we shall be in a better position to decide what to do with him."

"What's there to decide?" asked Earlis sharply. "The sooner we find him and put him out of the way, the better."

"Not necessarily," said Borthen. "He might prove more useful to us alive."

He leaned down and caressed Earlis's upturned cheek with an elegant turn of the hand. "The Du Borses aren't significant—merely corruptible. What threatens their eminence could work to our advantage."

He straightened up. "There are other equally powerful men in East Garillon. Take Arvech Du Penfallon, for instance. Too moral to be suborned by the desire for gain, but simple enough to fall victim to guile. If he could be induced—for whatever reason—to challenge the Du Borses, it could create a useful amount of friction. With the nobility of the Five Cities busy cutting each other's throats, we would be able to destroy the Order, and go on to assume full control. . . ."

"I wondered why you were still interested enough in the Whitfauconer whelp to send Muirtagh off to Holmnesse to intercept him," said Earlis.

"As a pawn," said Borthen, "he is of inestimable value."

Earlis was silent. After a moment, he said, "What about Caradoc Penlluathe? Why is he so important to you?"

A faint flush had crept into his pearl-pale face. Borthen's winged eyebrows lifted. "Caradoc Penlluathe has a virtually incalculable potential for bending the Magia to his will," he said. "Properly conditioned, he could be molded into a formidable adjunct for our purposes."

Earlis gave a brittle laugh. There was a scintillating glint in his jewellike eyes. "I can see the prospect of breaking him to your will appeals to you."

Borthen surveyed his companion from under half-lowered lids. "I have always enjoyed a challenge," he said silkily. "Does the idea perhaps offend your sensibilities?"

Earlis bridled. "Not in the least. I only hope you'll prove equal to the task."

"Never doubt it," said Borthen. "I still have Caradoc's magestone in my possession."

"Oh yes. The key to his inner being," sneered Earlis with sudden venom. "Not that it did you much good three nights ago when you were face-to-face in the cathedral—"

The sentence ended in a gasp as Borthen made a lightning movement to seize his wrists, jerking the slighter man upward so that they stood breast to breast. "You would do well to remember who is master here," said Borthen doucely. "Unless, of course, you desire a lesson in humility?"

Earlis was breathing quickly. His face held an odd expression, half shrinking, half fascinated. After a moment, his lips began to quiver. Borthen abruptly released him so that he sprawled back in his chair.

He himself remained standing. "I—I'm sorry," said Earlis in a muted voice from which all shrewishness had fled. He added hesitantly, "What will you do if Muirtagh fails in his mission?"

Borthen gestured toward the table by the far wall. On the cloth lay a large black book, and beside it a small pouch that gaped to reveal a measure of ashy powder inside. "Articles retrieved from the house of one Forgoyle Finlevyn," he said.

Earlis gazed at the powder. "What's that? Bloodstone?"

Borthen nodded. "As the book says:

There ys a rocke wich sall be knowne as
blodestane forbye yt can be techt to drynke blode
aeftre the mannere of a leeche. Ande thys sall be
considred propre materiale for the fashionynge
of a rodde of seekynge. . . .

All I need in order to deal with the boy is something of his vital essence—in this case, the bloodstone—to help me seek him out in spirit. If we do not succeed within a reasonably short time in recovering him, I have the power to turn his own dreams against him, to destroy him."

"And Caradoc?" asked the Inquisitor of Farrowaithe.

"Caradoc?" Borthen's smile was refulgent with malice. "Caradoc Penlluathe could fly to the ends of the earth, but so long as we both live, he will never be rid of me. . . ."

# ST. AMBRYSS'S FAIR

AMBRYSS BEING THE PATRON SAINT of the river-port of Beresfyrd, the town's inhabitants had long ago been granted sanction by the Hospitallers' Order to hold an annual fair in honor of their patron on his name day, the seventeenth of September. As St. Ambryss's Fair had become an event of considerable local importance, it was not surprising that on this year's St. Ambryss's Day the road leading east into Beresfyrd was clogged with incoming fair-goers.

The countryside to the west of town was boggy, and the heavy, slow-moving carts were obliged to keep to the roadbed. The water standing high in the thickets and ditches on both sides of the causeway forced pedestrian travelers who wanted to keep their feet dry to wedge themselves in among the wagons. With the names and fees of so many visiting merchants and tradesmen to be enrolled in the ledger pages of the town's Master of Accounts, traffic progressed at a snail's pace that dawdled at last to a standstill a quarter of a mile from the Beresfyrd High Gate. The latest arrivals, unhappily situated at the far end of the long line of vehicles, were still craning their necks and grumbling bad-temperedly about the cost of delays when the sound of quick-cantering hooves coming up the road from behind them gave them something else to think about.

It was a small troupe of Ambrothen Regular Militia-men, their crimson livery catching the afternoon sunlight in bright splashes of motion. They drew rein smoothly in unison, their horses coming to a standing halt twenty yards back from the tail of the last wagon. The officer in charge raised himself up in his stirrups and surveyed the terrain ahead through narrowed eyes.

The four people huddling in the bushes a stone's throw to the north of the roadway watched the officer's movements with anxious interest. When he at last gave a twitch to his reins and led his men around the roadblock by way of the southern embankment, all four seemed to rediscover the ability to breathe.

The first of the furtive quartet to come out of hiding was a slight young man in clothes that had seen too much weathering. Shading thoughtful grey eyes with the palm of a long-fingered hand, he followed the guardsmen's move-ments until the red cloaks and horsetails dwindled to a reddish smear in the distance. "All clear," he reported.

Hands parted the branches behind him and a closely capped head appeared in the gap. "Just what we need —another patrol," observed the wearer of the cap with bitterness. "When we set out this morning, I would have said we had at least a fair chance of winning through to the Beresfyrd ferry without being stopped. Now I'd say the odds are about a thousand to one against us."

"That's what I like about you, Caradoc: always the optimist," remarked a female voice from a neighboring patch of foliage. Its owner, muffled head and shoulders in a threadbare shawl, stood up and shook out her skirts. "Forget about the odds," said Margoth Penlluathe. "We've got more important things to think about."

"Like how we're going to get inside the town walls when there are bound to be soldiers plugging every bolt-hole. Yes, I believe you're right," said her brother sourly. "Rhan, are you ready to go?"

"Any time you are." A scrawny adolescent in a torn jerkin emerged with difficulty from the embrace of a burgeoning elderberry bush. He peered up at the tall man in the close-fitting cap. "Don't worry. Serdor will think of something. He always does."

The object of this trusting reference favored his young admirer with a wry look. "If ever I'm going to prove you wrong," said Serdor Sulamith, "I hope today won't be the day."

Choosing their footing carefully, they picked their way back to the road. By the time they arrived, the stalled procession of vehicles was on the move again. They fell in among the other pedestrians, shuffling forward with a wary eye for horse-droppings. Ahead of them, across an open meadow, the walls of Beresfyrd rose grey above the particolored crowns of three score or more fair pavilions.

Glancing around her at the ruddy-faced farmers and stout, innocently self-important burghers with nothing more dangerous on their minds than the prospect of an afternoon's profitable trading, Margoth experienced a sharp pang of envy. It had been five nights and days since she and her companions had fled their home in Ambrothen, headed for Holmnesse, and every step of the journey so far had been fraught with fear of pursuit.

It was bad enough that they should be hounded by the agents of the Seneschal of Ambrothen, who had his own reasons for wanting Caradoc Penlluathe and his associates returned to custody on charges of conspiracy and murder; but there was also a chance that they were being sought by the minions of another interested party. Recalling what her brother had had to say on the subject of Borthen Berigeld, Margoth repressed an inward shudder.

Her gaze strayed sideways to the boy at her elbow. Angular, unkempt, and ill-dressed, he looked nothing like the heir apparent to the Wardenship of East Garillon. But heir apparent he was, despite the false name and the trappings of poverty which Borthen Berigeld had imposed upon him by means of necromancy. And it was up to the three of them—Caradoc, Serdor, and herself—to keep him safely out of the hands of his enemies until his spirit

73

and his memory could be made whole again. An undertaking which threatened to prove no easy task.

Rousing to the realization that they were approaching the High Gate into Beresfyrd, Margoth raised herself on tiptoe to get a better look at the gatehouse, and abruptly dropped down again at the sight of a dozen red-liveried forms clustered about the port.

The guardsmen were questioning all comers and recording the responses in writing. Coming to a halt in the middle of the road, Caradoc swore under his breath. "Well, we can forget about getting into town by *that* route," he muttered. "Now what?"

Serdor was gazing out across the bustling fairgrounds. "If we're not going to go for the gate, the most natural alternative would be to head for the fair. I think that's what we'd better do just now—before we attract unwanted attention. We can formulate more definite plans once we're safely lost in the crowd."

The broad meadow known as St. Ambryss's Common was bounded to the west and south by a deep drainage ditch. A stout bridge of heavy timbers had been laid across the ditch at the point where a wide gravel track branched off from the main road to connect with the fairgrounds. A wooden customsbooth had been erected at the southern end of the bridge for the purpose of collecting the tolls that represented Beresfyrd's share of the fair's revenue. "Too official for comfort," said Serdor. "Let's see if there's another way around."

The toll bridge, as it turned out, offered the only easy access to the fair, and in the end they were forced to get their feet wet wading across the ditch. The opposite side of the fosse was treacherously slick, and it took the combined efforts of Serdor and Caradoc to get Margoth safely up the slippery incline. Glaring over at Rhan, who was studiously not laughing—"It's all very well for you," she panted crossly. "*You've* never had to scramble uphill through mud in a petticoat."

74

"Now who's dabbling in self-pity?" inquired her brother. "Hurry up and put your shoes on before someone comes along and sees us sprawled out on the bank like so many landed trout."

St. Ambryss's Fair was laid out according to a systematic plan of aisles and squares. Passing through an open area occupied largely by caterers, Rhan drew a deep lungful of air perfumed with cookery, and wistfully eyed the steaming displays of roast meat, fresh bread, and hot pastry. "I know. I'm hungry, too," said Serdor. "We'll try to find something to eat once we've managed to get inside the town walls."

"Who are those men in the buff-colored surcoats that I keep seeing?" asked Margoth, pointing a surreptitious finger.

Serdor looked, without appearing to. "Members of the local militia, I should imagine. Probably just on hand to keep order and make sure business runs smoothly. Even so, it might not be a bad idea to open our ranks a little. If you fall back with Caradoc, Rhan and I will go on ahead."

The large number of people milling about within the precincts of St. Ambryss's Common provided ready enough concealment for anyone wishing to remain anonymous. Peripherally aware that Caradoc and Margoth were strolling along twenty yards behind Serdor and himself, Rhan did his best to conform to his friend's leisurely pace, and resisted the impulse to keep glancing back over his shoulder.

Besides, the prospect ahead of him offered plenty to catch the eye. Despite his anxiety over their immediate future, Rhan found his gaze diverted, almost against his will, to the cages full of bright-feathered songbirds; to the tooled leather bindings crowding the stalls of the booksellers; to the tents of the armorers with their dangerously glittering array of daggers and shields; to the glowing wood-and-ivory shapes suspended along both sides of an instrument-maker's pavilion.

This last drew Serdor's attention as well. Rhan saw him hesitate slightly, his glance flickering upward toward a sweetly turned lute in honey-colored fruitwood. Serdor had once possessed a lute not unlike it, which he had played with rare passion and skill. But the minstrel's lute was one of the things they had left behind in Ambrothen. And they had no time for music now.

At least, not until they reached Holmnesse, five days' journey to the southeast, where Caradoc had arranged to meet a friend of his, Gudmar Ap Gorvald, whom Caradoc had encountered while they were both prisoners of the mysterious outlaw known as "His Eminence" to his underlings. Gudmar was a guild-master of the League of Merchant-Adventurers, a man of considerable influence and power. Rhan sincerely hoped that that power and influence would suffice to extricate the four of them from the plight of the hunted, and save them from becoming the scapegoats that Fyanor Du Bors, the Seneschal of Ambrothen, intended them to be.

An honest appraisal of his own attitudes forced Rhan to admit that his concern was less for Caradoc than for Serdor, Margoth, and himself. His personal feelings toward Serdor's tall red-haired friend were mixed. Nothing Serdor had told him about the now-discredited novice mage had prepared Rhan to reckon with Caradoc Penlluathe's vital and volatile presence—a presence that Rhan, for reasons he couldn't explain, found strangely disquieting.

It was a little like living in the presence of a whirlwind: Rhan was haunted by the impression that he had wandered too close to some potent source of elemental power. The uneasiness he felt in Caradoc's company made it hard for him to place much trust or liking in the man for whom Serdor had been prepared to sacrifice his life. Conscious of the fact that there couldn't be any rational basis for his prejudice, Rhan held his tongue on the subject and hoped that in time he would succeed in overcoming his mistrust.

In the meantime, the party already had enough to worry about if they were going to win through to the Beresfyrd Ferry without being apprehended by any of the Ambrothen patrols in the area. Thrusting his private concerns to the back of his mind, Rhan squared his sharp shoulders and kept his eyes firmly fixed in front of him as they moved on through the fair.

Their peregrinations eventually brought them out onto a strip of grass between the outlying line of trade-booths and the base of the stone rampart that divided the town from the common. The party stopped to regroup at the back of a covered wooden stall. "That wall must be fifteen feet high, if it's an inch," said Margoth, measuring the barrier with her eye. "We need a ladder. Or failing that, a miracle."

"Would you be prepared to settle for a stroke of good fortune?" asked Serdor. "Look there."

The others followed the line of his pointing finger forty-five degrees to the left. "Workmen!" exclaimed Rhan. He peered at the white-clad figures clinging like limpets to the face of the curtain-wall a hundred feet from where he himself was standing. His brow wrinkled. "What are they doing?"

"Repairing the masonry," said Caradoc. He squinted. "I don't see any ladder, though."

"They're using a floating scaffold," said Serdor. And produced, apparently out of nowhere, a seraphic smile. . . .

Because the West Rampart incorporated some of the oldest stonework along the full encircling length of the Beresfyrd town wall, it was here that the masonry stood most often in need of repair. The latest signs of serious deterioration had manifested themselves the afternoon before the fair, when a sheep grazing in the shadow of the old wall had been struck dead by a falling capstone. Beresfyrd's leading citizens, after a hasty conference, had ordered the wall's immediate restoration, and work had commenced early the following day at the hands of Fitch Kilrand, master-mason, and his three assistants.

It had taken most of the morning to cut and shape the new stones that were to replace the old ones. After a trial session of measuring and fitting, Fitch dispatched his two junior journeymen to fetch water from the river for mixing the mortar.

A sheep-track led down along the town wall to a tussocky bank. Below, a greyish strip of sand flanked the water for a furlong, coming to an end at the point where the drainage canal spilled into the river. Fitch's two journeymen plodded stolidly along the path with their empty buckets clattering on their shoulder yokes. Their ears full of the noise coming from the tents on the fringes of the fairground, they didn't look back as they started down the slope toward the shore.

Because they didn't look behind them, they didn't notice that they were being followed until they reached the river-beach. And by then their two assailants were already forcefully upon them.

The struggle was brief, and largely one-sided. Donning the work-apron his unconscious victim had been wearing, Caradoc felt metal shifting against his pelvis and paused to take a look in the pockets. "It's a damned good thing we were lucky enough to take these fellows by surprise," he said feelingly, holding up a heavy chisel so that Serdor could see it. "If either of them had gotten the chance to make use of their hardware, we'd have been in real trouble!"

The minstrel peered at the chisel, then grimaced. "'Beware the tygre's silken pawe: Eche velvett padde dothe sheathe a clawe. . . .' That was the easy part. Now for the real challenge."

The trip down to the river and back was bound to take at least twenty minutes. Since there was nothing more to be done in the meantime, Fitch Kilrand sent his remaining journeyman to fetch a pottle of brown ale, while he himself sat down on the grass to take his ease, with his back to the wall and his legs spread out in front of him.

He was just getting comfortably settled when a shrill hail and an erratic patter of approaching footsteps made him start up and open his eyes. A wispy figure of a boy was floundering toward him up the path from the river. While the boy was still a few yards away, he stumbled to a halt and gulped frantically for air. "Sir!" he panted. "Sir, your two men—there's been an accident!"

"An accident?" Fitch was on his feet with more agility than his girth promised. "What happened?"

"I dunno—I was just sent to bring the message." Dancing skittishly from one foot to the other, the boy flailed a skinny arm in the direction from which he had just come. "Down at the riverbank, sir. The guardsman said you'd better hurry!"

Fitch glared at his young informant. "If this is some kind of prank, I'll see you thrashed within an inch of your life."

"It's no prank, sir!" the boy insisted. "Go and see for yourself!"

His voice held the throb of genuine urgency. Fitch brushed past him and set out at a brisk pace up the path his subordinates had taken over a quarter of an hour ago.

His peaked face intent, the boy watched the older man's receding back for a long moment. Then he turned and beckoned to someone lurking unseen among the tent-ropes fifty feet away.

"Let's go!" hissed Serdor. Linking arms, he and Margoth and Caradoc scurried across the grass to the foot of the wall.

Seizing the dangling pulley-cables, the two men swiftly lowered the floating scaffold to the ground. Caradoc glanced up at the wall-walk overhead. "I'll go first, in case there are patrols to be reckoned with."

"No, I'll go," said Serdor. "You handle the ropes."

The allure, he discovered, was unoccupied—at least for the moment. Serdor leaned out over the parapet. "It's safe," he called softly. "Rhan, you're next."

The boy jibbed. "Send Margoth. I can wait—"

"Don't argue. There isn't time," said Margoth, and pushed him toward the platform. "Caradoc and I can work the ropes in tandem. We've done it before."

To her relief, Rhan swallowed his protests and did as he was told. Margoth watched him until he disembarked safely onto the battlement. Then she and Caradoc eased the scaffold back to the ground for the third and last time.

They placed two building stones and a bucket of sand on Margoth's side of the platform to compensate for the difference in their weights. Six feet off the ground, Margoth was just beginning to breathe more easily when she became suddenly aware that there was someone watching them from the edge of the grass.

Their audience was a stocky young man in a stone-mason's work-apron. Gripping a brown earthenware ale-pot in front of him with both hands, he sputtered, "Rossyn! What the devil do you think you're doing?"

Caradoc mouthed a vehement imprecation. With a lightning glance at her brother's profile, Margoth gave a high-pitched giggle and waggled her fingers coquettishly at the man who was watching them. "I told him I didn't want to miss anything," she chirped, "and *he* offered to show me a place where I could see the whole fair all at once."

The young man in the apron changed colors. Ruffling up like a turkey-cock, he shouted, "How dare you? Come down from there this minute!"

Then he took a second look at the man on the platform.

The ale-pot he was holding slipped from his grasp and shattered on the ground. "Hey, you're not Rossyn!" he yelped, and started toward them at a lumbering run.

# THE RACE TO THE FERRY

THE JOURNEYMAN-MASON HAD TAKEN scarcely a dozen strides when a small missile, launched from above, smacked hard into the turf mere inches in front of him. Startled, he shied to the right. "That's far enough!" sang a voice from the top of the wall.

Fitch's journeyman looked up. Balanced on the edge of the parapet, the slender individual who had hailed him flung up a wiry arm, so that the man on the ground could see that he held a sling in his hand. "I'm a good shot," continued the challenger pleasantly. "Don't force me to prove it."

Torn between self-preservation and outrage, Fitch's journeyman made mouths like a haddock. The scaffold inched upward. Realizing that the three miscreants would get away unopposed unless he acted quickly, the young mason manfully girded himself up and started forward again.

There was an angry hiss and a lead plummet the size of a crab apple bounced off his left collarbone with an excruciating crack. The sky spun overhead as he cork-screwed in his tracks and went down. "I warned you," said the voice from above in tones of adult sufferance. "Now don't get up again."

Nursing what felt like a fractured clavicle, Fitch's

journeyman discovered he had no desire to get up. Bereft of the will even to hurl insults, he lay back and watched sullenly, as the sling-wielder's two companions drew even with the top of the wall and stepped off onto the parapet.

The people who had made so free with Fitch Kilrand's property vanished from view behind the merlons. A moment later, two rolled-up bundles of discarded mason's gear flopped to the ground at the base of the wall. By the time Fitch's journeyman summoned the fortitude to shout for help, his assailants were gone.

The inner face of the town's defensive wall overlooked a strip of hard-packed dirt thirty feet wide. The party lowered themselves from the wall-walk to the ground with the aid of rope salvaged from the mason's pulley, then paused briefly to reconnoiter.

The open accessway in which they found themselves ran along the foot of the wall for a hundred yards before curving away from them in the general direction of the river. A narrow alley opened up forty feet off to their left. Aware of running footsteps and inquiring voices on the opposite side of the curtain-wall, Serdor grimaced. "We'd better take ourselves off pretty smartly. Let's see where that alley leads."

The lane wound east between two rows of dilapidated houses. A short sojourn south along an adjoining thoroughfare brought them into more populous surroundings. Catching sight of a painted wooden sign suspended over the heads of the passersby thirty yards ahead of them, Caradoc gave Serdor a nudge and pointed. "The Green Parrot Inn. That looks a likely enough place to inquire about when the ferry runs."

"That sounds fine to me," said Serdor. He glanced uneasily over his shoulder. "I have a feeling the less time we spend out on the streets, the better."

Upon closer inspection, the Green Parrot proved to be a rambling two-story structure somewhat in need of fresh paint. "Good: not too fashionable," said Margoth with mordant satisfaction. She wiped a clean place in the nearest window and squinted through it into the room beyond. "It's fairly dark in there—only one lamp over the bar and a few rush candles. We shouldn't have any trouble blending in with the other patrons."

Their entrance drew only a few casual glances. Leaving Serdor to deal with the innkeeper, who was serving at the bar, Caradoc steered Margoth and Rhan to a dimly lit table on the right-hand side of the room, furthest from the fireplace. The minstrel rejoined them several minutes later, clutching two tumblers of ale in each hand. He deposited them carefully on the ring-marked tabletop, then slid onto the bench next to Margoth.

"Here's the word on the ferry," he said. "It makes three crossings daily—once in the morning, once at noon, and once at sunset. The innkeeper says the last boatload of passengers will be setting out about an hour and a half from now."

"How far is the landing from here?" asked Caradoc.

Serdor took a pull at his ale. "Our friend reckons it's about a quarter hour's walk from here through town to the riverfront," he said. "The directions are straightforward enough: right two blocks from his front door, then left onto the High Street. The High Street will take us down to the embankment. The ferry dock is located forty yards or so downstream from where the High Street comes to an end."

Margoth nodded, then quirked an eyebrow. "What do you suggest we do in the meantime?"

Serdor thought a moment. "I vote we stay put right here," said Rhan, with a glance across the table at the minstrel. "According to the placard I saw outside, we can get a hot meal for four pence apiece. I can't think of any better way to spend an hour than resting and eating."

Margoth mentally reviewed their slender resources. "Four pence each. That's four coppers short of a florin," she said thoughtfully. "We've only eight florins twelvepence left to last us the rest of the way to Holmnesse, and it's going to cost us a florin each for the ferry. . . ."

She scowled obliquely at Serdor. "I don't know. What do you think?"

Serdor was gazing at Rhan. The ale had brought a slight flush to the boy's cheeks, but his eyes were underscored with shadow and his shoulders were drooping with weariness—clear signs that the hard pace they had been obliged to set for themselves since leaving Ambrothen was weighing heavily upon him.

But in that respect, he was hardly alone: Margoth was pale beneath the golden peach-glow of suntan, and even Caradoc was slumping a little in his chair. Serdor realized that he himself was leaning forward on his elbows to ease the throbbing ache between his shoulder blades.

"I think Rhan's right," he said. "It's been a long day, and all of us would be the better for something hot to eat. Worry about the finances later. I'll go tell the proprietor we'll be taking our dinner here."

The meal—somewhat to Margoth's surprise—proved to be quite tolerable: a thick stew of mutton, potatoes, and leeks, with bread and cheese and baked apples to follow. Toward the end of the hour, chewing slowly to savor the last tart-sweet bite of his pippin, Rhan caught above the commonroom clatter of busy knives and forks the distant strokes of the town bell.

Across from him, Serdor sat up in his chair. "Six o'clock," he said. "Time to be thinking about leaving."

Margoth rolled her eyes and sighed. "I suppose it had to happen some time."

Serdor gave her a wry half smile. "I'll go settle our score with the innkeeper while you get your things together."

He stood up and slung his light pack over his shoulder. In the same instant, the door to the commonroom flew open.

Torchlight glittered on metal accoutrements. There was a collective murmur of suppressed dismay as five uniformed figures strode into the taproom and came to a halt just inside the threshold.

Two of the five men were members of the Beresfyrd militia. The other three, including a sergeant-at-arms, were wearing the crimson livery of Ambrothen. A sixth man, not in uniform, entered behind them and wormed his way to the fore, where he stopped, elbows pricked out like sparrow's knees. "You have sworn testimony from three witnesses that the miscreants came in here," said the civilian querulously to the sergeant. "What are you waiting for?"

Margoth recognized the voice and the face that went with it as belonging to the journeyman-mason of the fairgrounds. "For God's sake, don't any of you turn around!" she hissed to her companions.

But it was already too late. "That's him!" howled the victim, pointing a quivering finger at Serdor. "That's the ruffian who attacked me!"

Before the sergeant could restrain him, he lunged forward and got entangled in the outstretched legs of an innocent bystander. He went down with a crash amid an eruption of alarmed outcries and the banging of colliding chairs. As people started up from their seats, the sergeant blew three piercing blasts on his officer's whistle.

More guardsmen surged into the commonroom through the open doorway. "Let's get out of here!" rapped Caradoc.

Gripping the edge of the table with both hands, he overturned it with a single heave. "What are you doing?" shrieked Margoth above the rising din of confusion.

Instead of answering her, Caradoc stooped and rammed a shoulder under one of the uppermost tablelegs. Grey eyes ablaze with enlightenment, Serdor sprang to his aid, and together they picked it up.

Red-clad soldiers were swarming toward them up the aisle between two rows of tables. "Margoth! You and Rhan behind us!" ordered Caradoc. "Now, *charge!*"

He and Serdor sprang forward, table balanced like a

battering ram between them. The onrushing guardsmen tried to veer off and found themselves hemmed in by benches and trestles. The two parties collided headlong and ruptured into separate tumbling forms.

Caradoc landed at the foot of the bar. Scrambling to his knees, he looked wildly around for his companions. "Here we are!" called Margoth, popping up next to Rhan from behind an overturned bench.

"Where's Serdor?" demanded Caradoc. Then caught sight of his friend by the adjacent wall.

The minstrel had his back to the masonry. Dagger in hand, he was facing three men in livery.

His opponents were closing in. Peering over her brother's shoulder, Margoth spat like an angry kitten and groped for something to throw.

A pewter soup-trencher was the first thing that came to hand. Expertly launched, it struck one man below the tail of his helmet and knocked him flat. Leaving his sister to pursue her own brand of combat, Caradoc vaulted over the table and charged the nearer of Serdor's remaining assailants.

His bowed shoulder caught his victim in the back. The two of them skidded across the wine-slick floor and crashed heavily against the wainscoting. Capturing a fallen flagon, Caradoc crumped it hard against his opponent's nose-guard, and felt cartilage give way beneath. Rolling free as the other man slumped to the floorboards, he looked around again for Serdor and found him flat on his back with a burly guardsman astride his chest.

The guardsman was trying to force the point of a heavy poniard past the crossguard of Serdor's less serviceable weapon. The minstrel's arm muscles were quivering with strain as the deadlock tightened.

Caradoc gathered himself to spring to the aid of his friend. In the same instant, a slight form flashed past him and drove hip and knee against the guardsman's knotted shoulder.

The shock of the impact knocked Serdor's assailant sideways. Caradoc caught the vengeful flicker of steel as man and boy rolled over in a tangle of limbs.

Serdor called Rhan sharply by name and levered himself off the floor, but Caradoc was there ahead of him, clipping the guardsman hard on the side of the throat with the combined force of his interlocked fists. The man jerked twice, like a marionette, before all his muscles went limp. Dragging Rhan out from under the guard's unconscious body—"Are you hurt?" demanded Caradoc. When Rhan dazedly shook his head, he pointed toward the curtained doorway beside the bar. "Go! We've got to find the back door to this place before the militia throw a cordon around the building."

Shying dishes behind her, Margoth raced to join her male companions as Caradoc wrenched aside the curtain, revealing a narrow passageway. A short sprint carried them past another doorway into the Parrot's kitchen. Bringing up the rear—"Look sharp! We're about to have company!" called Serdor, and turned back in his tracks as three men in red surcoats burst across the threshold.

There was an open sack of flour on the nearest counter. Whipping it off the countertop, Serdor slung the contents in the faces of their pursuers.

Trapped unexpectedly in a blinding white cloud, the armsmen reeled back, cursing and clawing at their eyes. "This way!" urged Rhan, holding open the door to the innyard. Nodding, Serdor buried his mouth and nose in his hands and raced to catch up with the rest of his party.

First out, Caradoc plunged off the back step and pelted across the yard toward the southeast corner of the inn, where the muddy ground gave way to a gravel-strewn driveway. His three companions hard on his heels, he skirted the side of the building and shot into the lane.

There he came to a skidding halt. Directly in front of them stood a laden farm-cart.

Its axle-hubs kissing the walls of the buildings on

either side of it, the wagon filled the gap as snug as a cork. "All right, up you go!" ordered Caradoc, and swung Margoth bodily onto the tail of the cart. As Rhan and Serdor clambered after her, four running figures, floured like dumplings, careened around the corner. "Duck!" shrilled Margoth, and let fly with something the size of a baby's head.

The turnip struck the man in the lead squarely in the chest. He gave a grunt of surprise and sat down in the miry gravel. "Good shot!" crowed Rhan, then tumbled forward as the wagon gave a violent lurch beneath him.

Margoth kept her balance. One eye on Rhan, who was struggling to right himself, she stooped for ammunition, and began lobbing vegetables like stoneshot.

Behind her, the horse between the traces whinnied in panic and made a second attempt to bolt. Scrambling toward the front of the wagon, Serdor overleapt the driver's seat and snatched up the reins.

The animal reared and plunged, its heavy hooves churning up gouts of rough gravel. "Jump, Caradoc!" shouted Serdor.

At the sound of his own name, Caradoc wheeled and made a bound for the wagon-bed. He landed hard, with force enough to rock the cart on its axles. "Go!" cried Margoth sharply. Whipping the reins around one wrist, Serdor breathed a silent invocation and released the cart-brake.

The heavy vehicle lurched forward and caromed off the right-hand wall as the horse fought for control of the bit. Feet braced hard against the board in front of him, Serdor bore down with all his weight on the curb-bit and succeeded in keeping the animal on the roadbed as they fishtailed out of the driveway onto a broad thoroughfare.

Pedestrians, shrieking, scattered in all directions. His body thrown bruisingly from side to side, Serdor gritted his teeth and sawed at both reins as the wagon bucketed wildly back and forth between the gutters. A fiery head appeared at his shoulder. "Let him go!" panted Caradoc.

*"What?"* exclaimed Serdor. Then he saw what Caradoc had seen: a group of mounted Ambrothen Regulars blocking the street ahead of them.

Serdor let go of the reins and dropped to the floor of the wagon. The huge draft horse, hysterical with terror, clamped enormous teeth on the bit, lengthened his stride, and thundered down upon the mounted patrol like an equine juggernaut. Despite all their riders could do to restrain them, the light-boned cavalry mounts scattered like so much chaff as the big horse smashed blindly through their ranks in a clatter of heavy hooves and a shower of loose turnips.

Completely out of control, the wagon swept on down the street, leaving chaos and a broad trail of turnip-greens in its wake. Clinging desperately to the side of the cart —"This is insane!" screamed Margoth to Caradoc above the din of pounding hooves. "You've got to pull him up before we overturn—"

The last word turned into a shriek of dismay as she sighted water directly ahead of them. Blowing wildly, the horse sheered off at the last possible moment, plunging to the right with reins flapping wide.

As they hit the wharf, the cart slewed around to the left and banged into a pyramid of packing-cases. Above the clatter of tumbling crates, the people in the wagon heard two loud snaps and the dry crackle of splitting wood. There was a sharp ping, and suddenly the horse was free, galloping off along the wharf in a flutter of burst traces.

The wagon trundled to a rickety halt. Shaking in every limb, its four passengers clambered out. Before he had even caught his breath—"We've got to get out of here," gasped Caradoc. "Which way to the ferry?"

Tenderly fingering a bashed elbow, Serdor jerked his chin in the direction of a cluster of lights two hundred yards downriver. "Come *on!*" the tall man said impatiently. "Those guardsmen will be here any second. . . ."

Limping and shuffling, they hurried along the wharf at the best pace they could manage. They were still thirty paces away from the pier leading out to the ferryboat, when Rhan glanced behind him along the quay. He stiffened in midstep. "Regulars!" he gasped. "Back there where we left the wagon!"

"Just keep walking," said Serdor. "Don't look at them."

"But—"

"The leader's stopping to question people," said Serdor with a tight smile. "By the time he's got the information he's after, we'll be on board."

The ferry was crammed end to end with bales and boxes. The other passengers were wedged in among the cargo like so many sardines. "Can you take four more?" asked Serdor, springing down from the landing with the money ready in his hand.

The ferryman peered at the florins, then nodded dourly. He held out his palm for the fare, then pointed laconically over his shoulder as the rest of the party climbed into the boat. "Find yourselves room anywhere you can. I'm about to cast off."

# FORCED MARCH BY STARLIGHT

PICKING THEIR WAY AFT, THE fugitives from Ambrothen barricaded themselves between a large movable hencoop and a hundredweight bale of unbleached wool. The owner of the ferryboat loosed the mooring cable and moved to the tiller. Under his leisurely guidance, the flatboat drifted away from the dock and circled into the embrace of the current.

"I hope we're going to pick up speed. I could make better progress swimming backward," growled Caradoc. He peered uneasily over an intervening bulwark of stacked crates toward the receding quay. "Oh God—somebody must have sung the right tune. Here come the hounds of the law. . . ."

Their mounts coursing like harriers, the red-clad horsemen flickered in and out of the waterfront lights. Taking obstacles in full stride, they materialized as a group at the head of the pier and came to a racking standstill. Surcoats caught the light as the party dismounted. A hard voice, pitched high to carry the ring of authority, called out to them across the darkened water.

Resting his weight negligently on the tiller, the owner of the ferry looked back over his shoulder at the receding shoreline. A single crimson-clad figure broke away from the rest of the company and marched out to the end of the pier. Making a trumpet of his two hands, he shouted again.

The tone carried, but not the words. The ferryman lifted a disenchanted eyebrow and spat into the shallow wake of the boat. "You're going to have to do better than that, laddie, if you want me to make sense out of what you're doing."

There was some murmuring among the passengers. "Hadn't we better go back to see what they want?" suggested someone nervously.

"And spend the next four hours hanging about, waiting to be questioned about toll-frauds or something like that? No, thank you," said another voice tartly. "I've got a three-hour ride ahead of me once we tie up at the east bank, and I'd like to get it over with before midnight."

"But it might be something important—"

"If it's important," said the second voice, "old Hoblett here can deal with it on his return trip."

The ferryman grunted. "It'll have to keep till tomorrow morning. I won't be going back across the river again before daybreak. . . ."

This dogmatic announcement occasioned some further argument among the passengers, but clearly the ferryman regarded himself as the captain of his ship and he had no intention of turning his craft around. The four people sitting silent in the bow began guardedly to unbend again, as the cries from shore faded from earshot. "Lucky for us he's a salty fellow," murmured Margoth. Then inched closer to Serdor as an uncomfortable thought occurred to her. "You don't suppose those Ambrothen guardsmen will just simply hire another boat to come after us?"

"If they do," said Serdor, "it'll take time to make the necessary arrangements. We should be able to get at least a few hours' headstart on them once we're on the other side of the river."

"More marching? Oh goody," said Rhan with heavy irony. He shivered, and reached across Caradoc's knees for a blanket. As he did so, the yellow light of the boat-lantern showed up a discolored rent in his sleeve.

The edges of the tear were sticky with dried blood. "How did that happen?" demanded Caradoc. Then recollection dawned. "That guardsman you jumped at the inn—I thought you said he never touched you."

His tone was accusatory. Rhan peered self-consciously down at his forearm. "I didn't realize he had—until later, when it began to sting a bit."

"Why didn't you speak up?" inquired Caradoc.

The sharpness of his tone was nettling. Rhan shrugged and said defensively, "There was too much else going on."

"Well, it will have to be cleaned up, if you don't want to risk picking up an infection," said Caradoc. "Not here: we'd better not draw attention to ourselves. I'll see to it when we make camp."

His manner implied that he alone had any say in the matter. It was on the tip of Rhan's tongue to tell Serdor's overbearing friend to mind his own business, but he caught himself in time, telling himself sternly that he was being excessively sensitive. At the same time, his reluctance to let Caradoc examine him persisted. Unable to account for it, he gathered his blanket around him and tried to think of something else.

The lesser branch of the Damanrhyl was a third of a mile wide, and twenty minutes went by before the ferry drew up at the east landing, its lights dimly glimmering through a cold haze of river-mist. Disembarking with the other passengers, the party from Ambrothen made their way up the embankment and turned south along the main street of the small settlement that had grown up around the ferry dock.

After a furlong, the road left the friendly shelter of the clustered cottages and continued south, flanking the black, fog-haunted river. To the west, Beresfyrd was visible as a distant constellation of dimly twinkling lights. Overhead, true stars winked fitfully as the night air thickened.

"We'd better keep to the road for the first few miles," said Serdor. "When the moon comes up, we should have light enough to see our way inland without losing our sense of direction."

"How far do you plan on traveling tonight?" asked Margoth.

"As far as we can," said Caradoc. "Even if Fyanor's men don't make the crossing until tomorrow morning, they'll be traveling on horseback. The more miles we can put between them and us, the better."

The roadbed was pockmarked, and they had to go carefully. For a long time, there was no conversation at all. Trudging along behind Serdor, Rhan bore his fatigue like a leaden weight on his back. Before they had been on the road an hour, he felt as if his feet were growing too heavy for his leg muscles to control.

The others, however, were carrying on in stoic silence. Aware that they must be every bit as tired as he was, Rhan held his peace for another mile, until a hole opened up in the road ahead of him and tripped him up.

He landed hard, and gave an involuntary exclamation of pain as gravel bit into his palms and his knees. Before he could pick himself up, a strong pair of hands caught him under the arms and lifted him off the ground. "Steady," said Caradoc. "If you're having trouble, say so, and we'll stop and rest for a bit."

The tensile strength of Caradoc's supporting hands hinted at enviable reserves of vitality yet untapped. Rhan was mortified that the tall mage had been so quick to gain so accurate an impression of his comparative weakness. The boy felt as if he could have done without being invited to make a public confession of his lack of endurance.

Shame, added to the haunting uneasiness generated by Caradoc's potent presence, made him jerk brusquely away, his cheeks burning in the darkness. "I'm all right," he said. "I just took a false step, that's all."

Serdor's tall friend was looking at him without speaking. The sense that the mage was capable of seeing right through his defenses made Rhan feel even more unsettled.

To counteract the threat of intrusion, he snapped, "You needn't worry. I won't slow you down."

Caradoc's rangy frame stiffened. Palms pressed flat against his thighs, he studied the boy a moment longer. Then he walked away from him without a word.

"Easy, Rhan," murmured Serdor's voice at his side. "Caradoc wasn't trying to belittle you."

Feeling guilty and confused, Rhan hung his head. "I—I know. I'm sorry," he said. "I don't know what came over me."

His inflection was bitter, but Serdor could tell that the boy was genuinely distressed. "Never mind," he said comfortingly. "When you're as tired as we all are, it's all too easy to make a mountain out of a molehill."

Rhan was still gazing after Caradoc. "Do you think I ought to apologize?"

"If you think it would make you feel any better," said Serdor. "But it's not worth making an issue out of doing so. Caradoc has a tendency to be a little too high-handed, and it does him no harm to be reminded of the fact every once in a while."

With this small misunderstanding put into abeyance, they trudged on again, stopping briefly every mile or two to rest their aching legs and weary feet. By the time the waning moon rose above the hanging mists to the east, the open marshes and grass-meads to the left of the road had given way to more wooded terrain. The land itself was rising. The fugitives from Ambrothen turned off the road where it crossed over a small brook. They followed the streambed east for two or three furlongs and eventually came upon a tree-bordered clearing facing north across the water into a dense pine forest.

It was by then well after midnight. "We've come far enough," said Caradoc, surveying their surroundings. "Let's camp here for the rest of the night and press on again at daybreak."

"That's the most intelligent thing anybody's said for

the last two hours," said Margoth. She pulled her drooping shoulders back and scanned the ground. "There seems to be plenty of bracken lying about. I vote we light a fire."

"No objections from this quarter," said Serdor. "Caradoc, I believe you've got the matches. . . ."

They hollowed out a shallow firepit in the middle of the clearing and soon got a small blaze going. After arranging their meager bedding around the fire, Serdor and Margoth went beyond the clearing to gather more fuel. Left alone with Rhan, Caradoc heated water from the stream in Margoth's small cooking pan, then called the boy over to him.

Rhan came warily, seating himself with forced compliance. Outwardly composed, he was throwing off internal nerve-tremors like sparks. Keenly aware—as he had never expected to be—of the boy's interior anxiety, Caradoc was surprised and bemused. I shouldn't be able to feel this, he thought wonderingly. Not without a magestone.

More by instinct than by conscious decision, he closed his eyes to test the strength and quality of his perceptions. The impression he received was indisputable: Rhan was acutely uneasy.

But why? They had left pursuit several hours (at least) behind them. And the surrounding woods were reassuringly still— Caradoc stopped short, for it came to him suddenly that Rhan's disquiet was linked to his own presence.

Again, the tantalizing question, why? Since the boy was incapable of recalling Caradoc's former besmirching association with Borthen Berigeld, there was no obvious reason why he should distrust the man they had rescued from Ambrothen Castle. Unless there was something about Caradoc himself—some residual *power*?—that was eliciting the boy's irrational hostility.

Caradoc gnawed his lip, staggered by the thought. But the fact remained that his sensitivity to the boy was all out of proportion, amounting to something deeper and more

specific than mere comradely concern for this most vulnerable member of their party. His feelings toward Rhan
involved an intuitive and painful apprehension of the
strain dwelling within the boy's torn personality. But
perception was not the same thing as the power to heal.

His gaze dropped to Rhan's blood-soiled sleeve. Given
the boy's obvious aversion to personal contact, Caradoc
approached his task with misgivings. His reservations were
not eased by the knowledge that once he could have sealed
up such an injury painlessly, without leaving even a faint
scar. Now he was forced to resort to crude camp remedies.
In a voice roughened by a sense of self-recrimination, he
said, "All right. Let me see that cut you've got there."

Rhan wordlessly extended his arm, flinching slightly
as Caradoc touched him. His own hands deliberately
steady, Caradoc braced the limb across his knee and
carefully worked the stained cuff back to the elbow.

The exposed gash was visible as a dense red line
curving downward from the outside point of the elbow to
the inside of the wrist. Caradoc gently swabbed away the
dried blood with warm water, then examined the cut more
closely. His face darkened. "Another quarter of an inch,
and that dagger would have opened a major vein," he said.

His tone, inadvertently, implied censure. Rhan stiffened and scowled. "So?"

Frustration had already loosened Caradoc's grip on
his temper. "I'll tell you," he growled. "That was a bloody
stupid thing to do—rushing that guard the way you did.
He could have injured you seriously, and if he had, the
game would have been up for us, then and there."

The mage's hard admonitory manner made Rhan
forget all his good resolutions. "What if he'd killed
Serdor?" he flared. "Wouldn't that have meant the same
thing?" Then lost his head for the second time that night.
"Or don't you care that he's only in this trouble because of
*you*?"

Caradoc's eyes flashed emerald. For a sick instant,

Rhan thought the mage might strike him. His stomach contracted in a cold knot of anticipation, but Caradoc, after a bristling pause, merely reached for the bandage he had prepared. "It may surprise you to know that I care very much," he said softly.

There was an undercurrent of cold violence in his voice that rendered Rhan speechless. His handsome face rigid with anger, Caradoc continued speaking. "If you'd trouble to think about it, you'd realize that's why I object to your unwarranted interference. You could have done far more harm than good by getting in the way back there. Don't ever do it again."

The tone of command stung worse than a lash. Rhan jerked his arm away, his chest heaving. "Leave me alone!" he cried, and scrambled to his feet.

The discomfort connected with Caradoc's presence was becoming intolerable. "I don't take orders from *you*!" he declared hotly, and stormed off to the farthest edge of the clearing, where he halted trembling.

Serdor joined him a little while later. "It seems you and Caradoc had another argument," he said quietly.

Rhan nodded and twisted his fingers uncomfortably together. "He said I shouldn't have gone to your aid back at the inn in Beresfyrd."

"So I gather," said Serdor dryly. "Forgive me if it doesn't sound serious enough to cause a row."

"It wasn't so much what he said," muttered Rhan, "as the way he said it."

"Hmm. Yes, I can well believe that," said Serdor. He laid a light hand on the boy's taut shoulder and let it rest. "I'll grant you Caradoc's no diplomat. Still, he occasionally sees things the right way."

"Then you agree with him?" Rhan's brown eyes looked hurt. When Serdor nodded without speaking, he stamped his foot. "I couldn't just stand there! That guardsman was going to kill you!"

A grave twinkle appeared in the minstrel's grey eyes.

"Trust me to look after myself better than that," he said, and ruffled Rhan's unkempt head. "Look—it was gallantly done, and I thank you, but from here on out, you really must exercise a little more discretion in deciding when and how to act."

Rhan was looking increasingly miserable. "Caradoc accused me of getting in the way. I don't think he has a very high opinion of me."

"If it comes to that," said Serdor, "you don't like him very well, either. Do you?"

Rhan dropped his eyes. "I—I'm sorry," he said in a small voice. "I wish I did. It's just that . . ." His voice trailed off.

"Caradoc's main problem," said Serdor, "is that feelings tend to run very strong in him—so strong that sometimes they can only be expressed in violent terms. When that happens, his manner doesn't always reflect his concerns—in this instance, his regard for your welfare. Don't be too quick to take offense: there's much more to Caradoc—believe me—than arrogance and temper."

"I know," said Rhan, rather desperately. "That's precisely the trouble."

The minstrel's eyes widened a little. "I'm not sure I follow you."

Rhan chewed nervously on a fingernail. "It isn't easy to explain. But something about him makes me uneasy. He . . . he reminds me of someone. Only I can't seem to remember who."

His face downcast, he missed seeing the startled flicker of surprise in Serdor's watchful gaze. There was a pause. Then—"Come back to the fire," said the minstrel softly. "It's only six hours till dawn, and you need as much sleep as you can get. You and Caradoc can make your peace in the morning. . . ."

Rhan went gratefully enough to his bedroll. Leaving the boy curled back-to-back with Margoth on the more sheltered side of the fire, Serdor went off to consult with

Caradoc, who was standing watch down by the bank of the stream.

After listening in silence to Serdor's account of what Rhan had said, Caradoc sighed wearily. "Poor little bastard," he said. "None of this is his fault—least of all the friction that seems to be developing between him and me. I should have foreseen it, and dealt with him far more carefully than I have been doing up to now."

Serdor's expression was keenly attentive, though his eyes were heavy with fatigue. "Let's hear your theory."

Caradoc threw back his head, his gaze wandering among the scattered stars. "I was present when Evelake had his name and his memory ripped away from him. Some part of him still remembers the agony—and I'm somehow wrapped up in it."

"Some part of him . . ." Serdor frowned. "Do you think there's a chance his memory isn't *gone*, but only . . . *blocked*?"

Caradoc smiled thinly. "I think it's a theory worth testing. At some later time. And by better men than I. . . ."

# SHADOWS IN THE WOOD

DAY BROKE COLDLY THROUGH THICK clouds of ground-mist. "Of all the rotten luck!" growled Caradoc around a mouthful of stale bread. "This fog could force us back to the road, whether we like it or not."

Margoth pulled a sour face. "I suppose it's pay your money and take your choice."

She turned to Rhan. "Which would you prefer: getting lost in the woods, or getting captured on the highroad?"

"I'd prefer going back to sleep," said Rhan frankly. "But I'll do whatever Serdor thinks best."

The air, however, was steadily lightening, and by the time the party were ready to leave, the mist had begun to thin out, revealing the sun as a pale white disc in the eastern sky. Given visible points of reference, they decided to risk traveling cross-country.

At the outset, the ground was open and fairly level. For a time they made good progress, keeping the sun always in the left eye. As the morning wore on, however, the sky began to darken. Shortly after midday, the clouds closed in, and the rain began to fall.

Within minutes they were all drenched to the skin. Margoth scuffed disgustedly through sodden heaps of fallen leaves, with water dripping off the end of her nose. "If there are any guardsmen following us, I hope they're

101

every bit as miserable as we are," she said vindictively.

Serdor blinked the rain out of his eyes. "If they've got any sense at all, they'll be holed up in some comfortable hostel, in front of a blazing fire, with mugs of mulled ale in their hands."

"While we slog on through all weathers, with our shoes leaking like sieves. I wish I *were* as dangerous a necromancer as everyone seems to think I am," muttered Caradoc. "I'd soon send this poxy rain back where it came from."

They continued on their way in waterlogged silence, with the ground squelching like a wet sponge beneath their feet. Without the angle of the sun to guide them, they could only hope that they were still tending in the right general direction. Another hour passed in the unremitting downpour. They halted under a broad-beamed elm tree long enough to wolf down the last of their bread, and then moved on again.

The terrain became steadily more variable. After plodding sloppily in and out of a series of shallow folds in the ground, the party clambered laboriously to the top of a last steep incline, and there stumbled to a standstill.

By this time the rain had thinned to a fine grey drizzle. A hundred yards below them, the pattern of the trees was broken by a thin line running perpendicular to the crest of the hill. Hugging himself hard to control his shivering, Serdor shook his wet hair back from his face and took a better look.

"That seems to be a track of some kind down there," said Caradoc, pointing. "Let's see if it leads anywhere useful."

The road, when they reached it, proved to be little more than a pair of deep ruts divided by a raised hump of weed-grown dirt. "Wherever it leads, nobody's had any reason to go there for a good long time," said Margoth, surveying the unkempt roadbed with disfavor.

"What difference does that make?" asked Caradoc. "If we follow the right-hand branch, we should eventually come out of the forest within sight of the Daman Estuary."

"Assuming, of course, that we haven't gotten ourselves turned around in the wrong direction," said Margoth tartly.

Her brother shrugged. "Well, there's only one way to find out, isn't there? Come on. . . ."

He was about to step down into the middle of the road when there was a sudden loud crackle in the brush that crowned the slope at their backs.

Startled, the four people by the road whirled around as something large and dark rocketed out of the heart of a small coppice near the crown of the hill. Traveling toward them in great bounds, it planted four affrighted feet in the earth five paces from where Rhan was standing, balked, curvetted, and thundered off in the opposite direction.

Watching the bobbing retreat of the animal's white tail, Margoth gave a shaken laugh and took her hand away from her heart. "A buck deer!" she exclaimed. "Poor thing—I think we frightened him almost as much as he frightened us."

"He certainly veered off in a hurry once he caught sight of us," said Serdor. He frowned, scanning the line of the slope above them. "What puzzles me is why he started from cover in the first place."

There was a sudden jarring pause. Her heart leaping into her mouth for no discernible reason, Margoth involuntarily stopped breathing to listen.

Her three companions were standing still as waxworks. To Margoth, it seemed as if the silence underlying the steady *drip-drip-drip* of the rain had taken on a sinister quality of watchfulness that had not been present a moment before. She said in hushed tones, "I think we'd better be going."

"Yes," said her brother. "I think so, too. . . ."

They plunged off the embankment into the lane. With Caradoc in the lead, they hurried in single file along the right-hand branch of the rutted cart-track. Bringing up the rear, Serdor kept a wary eye on the high ground off to the right of the road. Though he saw nothing out of the ordinary, his nagging suspicions, once aroused, refused to be set at rest.

A double bend in the path carried them out of sight of the point at which they had come down from the hilltop. As the party pressed on, the trees closed in on either hand, their water-laden branches overshadowing the ground in some places. Serdor caught himself glancing repeatedly over his shoulder, unable to shake off an eerie conviction that all their movements were being watched. This conviction intensified as the afternoon light began to fail.

"What is it?" asked Rhan in a low voice, dropping back apace to allow the minstrel to overtake him. "What's bothering you?"

"I don't know," said Serdor with a troubled scowl. "I keep thinking I've glimpsed something moving out of the corner of my eye, but each time I turn around to take a proper look, there doesn't seem to be anything there."

Margoth overheard him. "I've noticed it too," she said, "and it's beginning to get on my nerves. I hope this road isn't just leading us deeper and deeper into the wilds. Somehow the thought of being caught out in the open after nightfall doesn't appeal to me in the least."

An exclamation from her brother prevented her from elaborating further. As his three companions gathered around him—"We're coming into habitable parts," said Caradoc. "Look there."

The three other members of the party followed the line of his pointing finger. Ahead of them the cart-track fell away into a broad wooded hollow, then climbed to the top of a low hill two furlongs away. Among the darkening trees that crowned the ridge, a pinprick of light showed yellow.

"A house . . ." Margoth stared raptly at the tame glimmer of distant lamplight. "Do you think we might beg lodgings for the night?"

"Too risky for that," said Caradoc. "But if that's a

farmstead, I certainly wouldn't turn up my nose at the thought of sharing the byre with a few sheep and cows."

"Neither would I. We could do a lot worse," agreed Serdor.

Then broke off short as Rhan gave a stifled gasp and clutched him by the sleeve. "Serdor," he breathed, "there *is* something back there!"

His three companions whipped around. "What? Back where?" demanded Margoth in a constricted undertone.

"About forty paces back up the trail," said Rhan. His eyes were wide as saucers.

"What did it look like?" asked Caradoc.

"I—I'm not sure. Just a dark shape of some kind. It vanished into the trees," said Rhan, "before I got a good look at it."

The others exchanged glances. "Let's get out of here," said Serdor. "We've only got a quarter of an hour left before the light fails altogether."

They pressed forward again with renewed urgency through the thickening dusk. Sending Margoth and Rhan on ahead, Caradoc fell back to share the rearguard with Serdor. "What do *you* think it was?" he muttered.

Serdor was keeping his eyes steadfastly in front of him. "Possibly a bear. But I rather think not."

"I agree." Caradoc set his jaw, his green eyes glinting. "Maybe we ought to go back and check it out—"

"No!" said Serdor. "Not in the dark, and certainly not so poorly armed as we are."

"All right," said Caradoc thinly. "But if there's going to be trouble, I'd rather meet it head-on than wait for it to catch up with us."

"That principle holds true only when you have some idea of what to expect," said Serdor. "We'll be out of the woods in a few more minutes. Once we're clear of the trees, we'll be in a better position to judge whether or not to take action."

The forest thinned out toward the top of the hill. The

yellow glow they had spotted from the floor of the valley was issuing from a small window at the back of a low stone croft. Hedged by trees to the east, it faced west across a downsloping meadow where sheep grazed in the darkness. The lowland edge of the meadow was bounded by a secondary line of mixed evergreens and hardwoods. Beyond and below the narrow strip of woodland, a jeweled network of lights proclaimed the presence of a fair-sized village.

Margoth sniffed the air. "I smell salt," she said. "We're not far from the coast."

"No farther away, I should guess, than that line of lights we can see from here," said Serdor. "In the morning we'll get our bearings. Just now let's see if we can find a place to camp for the night."

The pasture close at hand was encircled by a wall of freestanding stones. Giving the shepherd's cot wide berth, the party clambered over the wall and cut south across the open grass.

At the farther end of the enclosure, a thick stand of young pines separated the sheeprun from a furrowed potato field. The fugitives let themselves into the field by means of a stout wooden gate, then paused to reconnoiter.

There was a long, low building tucked back into the northeast corner of the field among the shadows of the trees. "There's your byre, if you like," said Margoth to Caradoc. "Let's go and take a closer look."

In the gloom it was hard to make out much more than the general shape of an elongated wooden barn. They felt their way to a door set into the wall opposite the fence. Serdor rummaged in the small pouch at his belt and fished out the dirty stub of a tallow candle. "Have we got any matches?" he asked.

"Yes—if this infernal damp hasn't gotten past the wrapping," said Caradoc.

He groped in the breast of his jerkin and produced a little packet bound up in a twist of oilcloth. "It looks all right to me," he said, handing it to Serdor. "Just be careful. We've only got a dozen left."

Three of the matches refused to ignite. The fourth had to be carefully coaxed into giving its flame to the candle-wick. "Are you sure it's wise to show a light?" asked Margoth anxiously.

"That cottage back there is the only other building close by, and its lights aren't visible from here, thanks to the trees," said Serdor. "If we can't see them, its occupants won't be able to see us, either."

"In that c-case, can we b-build a fire?" asked Rhan, through chattering teeth.

After a long afternoon's exposure in wet clothes, he was quaking violently where he stood, his thin body drawn in upon itself, his lips blue with cold. "We'll see to it as soon as we've taken a look inside this barn," said Caradoc. "It won't take long."

The door to the barn had been padlocked. "This looks like a job for you, Margoth," said Serdor. "After the locks in Ambrothen Castle, this one should be child's play."

Margoth's extrasensitivity to lock mechanisms had proven an invaluable gift when she had joined Serdor and Rhan in their daring bid to free Caradoc from prison in Ambrothen Keep. True to Serdor's prediction now, the lock on the barn door yielded readily to her talented manipulations. The inside of the barn was cluttered with farm tools of every description, from the heavy plough and harrow in one corner to the wide assortment of spades, reaping hooks, and other implements hung up on pegs along the other three walls. Holding the candle aloft, Caradoc ran a critical eye over the haystrewn floor. "It looks snug and dry enough in here. Margoth, if you and Rhan will lay out all of our bedrolls, Serdor and I will go gather wood for fuel. . . ."

The firwood supplied ample kindling in the form of pinecones and fallen branches. Leaving Caradoc to set up the firepit in the shelter of the trees, Serdor poked his head around the door to the barn. "I'll need the candle back," he said. "The wood's damp, but Caradoc is pretty confident he can get it to burn."

"I certainly hope so, because *we've* found supper," said Margoth. She shook out the gathered front of her skirt and spilled a dozen dark misshapen objects onto the floor.

"Potatoes!" exclaimed Serdor. "Where did those come from?"

"There's a root cellar underneath the floor of this place," said Margoth with a grin. "Rhan and I found the trapdoor in the corner next to the ploughshare."

By the time they got the fire started, the clouds overhead had parted, showing white stars in the open spaces of the night sky. They roasted the potatoes among the firecoals and devoured them with shrinking eagerness, blowing hard on their fingertips between mouthfuls. At first Rhan was not entirely at ease, haunted by the memory of a dark shape only half glimpsed among the shadows of the trees. But none of his companions seemed worried, now that they were out of the woods, and as the warmth of the fire stole over him, he began by degrees to relax.

The fire began to die, its embers glowing red under the clearing sky. Comfortably full-fed, his clothes steaming dry on his body, Rhan was nodding on the edge of sleep when a sudden thrashing in the trees a stone's throw to his right startled him into full awareness.

Caradoc was on his feet in a bound, as an animated flock of black rags erupted skyward out of the treetops. Cawing shrilly, they spiraled up on wildly flapping wings and veered eastward, traveling fast like a plume of smoke. "Crows!" muttered Serdor, gazing after them. "I wonder what set them off like that. . . ."

They were all of them thinking of the deer they had spotted earlier, but no one mentioned it aloud. "Let's get inside," said Caradoc quietly. "And barricade the door behind us. I'll take first watch. . . ."

# THE WINGED HUNTER

THEY LEFT THE FIRE TO die in its own ashes and made for the shed, taking a burning pineknot with them as a torch to light their movements. There was no bar on the inside of the door. Caradoc braced it shut with a stout length of loose board. "That's about the best we can do," he said. "The rest of you may as well lie down and try to get some sleep. I'll wake you if there's any sign of trouble."

"Wake me, in any case, in a few hours' time," said Serdor. "You need rest, too."

The inside air was chilly. Nestling into the protective curve of Serdor's limber body, Margoth was grateful for the warmth and solace of his nearness. Rhan lay down next to them and curled up in a tight knot of angular limbs.

He was shivering again. Margoth unthinkingly reached out and laid a comforting hand on his near shoulder. He flinched at her touch, like a horse with sore withers. Remembering what kind of punishment the boy's former master had been in the habit of meting out to him, Margoth jerked her hand away. "I'm sorry. I didn't mean to startle you," she said.

"You didn't," said Rhan. He sounded nervous and distracted. "It didn't take you long to get cold again, did it?" said Serdor, raising up on one elbow. "If you move in closer, we can share blankets and all sleep a lot warmer."

After a brief instant's hesitation, Rhan nodded and obeyed. Margoth twitched an extra fold of covering over him, wondering if the boy appreciated Serdor's tact as much as she did. Her acquaintance with Rhan had taught her that he was capable of going to self-punishing lengths to conceal his vulnerability to pain and fear. No one but Serdor, she was sure, could have so easily persuaded the boy to accept the comfort he would never have allowed himself to ask for.

Within minutes Rhan was asleep, his anxieties outweighed by his weariness. Lying wide-awake in the half-light, Margoth listened to Serdor's light, even breathing, and wished she could bring herself to place similar trust in Caradoc's vigilance. Though she ached with the need for sleep, a troublesome feeling of foreboding kept her fitfully on the edge of wakefulness as the long minutes ticked away toward midnight.

An oppressive stillness settled over the room. Sitting bolt-upright, Caradoc kept his eyes on the door. He could hear nothing stirring outside, but he took no reassurance from the fact. Having been schooled as a mage, he knew only too well the limitations of his own five senses.

Had he been still in possession of his magestone, he could have summoned the power of the Magia to heighten his ability to perceive what was otherwise hidden. Thus aided, he would have been able to tell, beyond the shadow of a doubt, whether or not there was anything lurking outside in the dark.

As it was, his magestone was gone—taken by Borthen Berigeld, to be used against him. And with it, he had lost the mage's gift of clairvoyance. Despoiled of the power he had worked ten years to attain, he felt like a man blinded and crippled. Having learned how bitter a trap self-pity could be when, sodden drunk, he had fallen in with Borthen Berigeld's plans, Caradoc would not unburden himself to his friends of his feelings of guilt, much less the deep sense of personal loss occasioned by the terrifying handicap under which he now labored. In the baffling silence of the night, he could feel himself straining toward heights and depths he could no longer reach.

Something quivered on the floor off to his right. Starting out of his dark reverie, Caradoc turned sharply to see what it was.

For a moment everything was still. Then, with a dry mouse-claw rustle, the straw in the corner skittered away from the wall like chaff before a winnowing breeze.

Only there wasn't any breeze.

Caradoc sprang to his feet as the straw eddied back upon itself, then settled. Glowering, he stalked over to the corner and bent down, feeling along the base of the wall for any crack or chink wide enough to admit a draft. While his back was turned, there was another faint scuffling sound behind him. He whirled about and saw that the straw-patterns on the floor had changed.

He blinked, and took a second look. "What is it?" whispered a voice he recognized as Margoth's.

Before he could answer her, the deathly quiet was riven suddenly by an eerie sibilant hiss, like wind escaping from a chasm. Faint at first, and far away, it gathered pitch and volume as it surged toward them, rising to a strident, ululating howl an instant before it swooped down upon the barn like a banshee.

There was a thunderous bang from above, as if some vast bird of prey had alighted on the roof, and the whole fabric of the barn began to shiver. Before any of the four people inside could move or cry out, the trapdoor in the far corner of the room flew up with a rending crash. There was a subterranean rumble, and the contents of the root cellar fountained upward through the opening.

Serdor, Margoth, and Rhan dived for the south wall under a punishing hail of tubers. Shielding his face with both hands, Caradoc lunged for the door and tried to knock aside the makeshift bolt.

It was locked in place as if it had been welded there.

Cursing, Caradoc threw his full weight against the door itself. The impact bruised his shoulder, but the door did not move.

"Duck!" shrieked Margoth above the rising din of breakage. He dropped to a startled crouch a split instant before an airborne hatchet flew across the room and embedded itself two inches deep into the boarding above his head.

Within seconds, the air was thick with missiles. Buckets and farm tools leapt off their pegs and converged toward the center of the room in a churning vortex that spat them out again with murderous caprice. Reeling, Caradoc got his dagger out just in time to parry a stabbing attack from a pair of wool-shears. "Hold on—we're coming!" called Margoth. "I've got an idea—"

She cried out as a flying trowel slashed open her right sleeve. Serdor snatched her by the shoulders and dragged her down as a disembodied spade whipped past them and clattered to the floor an arm's length away.

Fire from their makeshift torch was spreading along the base of the far wall. The plough was already sheathed in flame. "We've got to get to the door!" panted Margoth. "I think I can—"

"Look out!" cried Rhan, and hit the floor beside her as a stream of objects hurtled toward them. Serdor and Margoth flattened themselves to the wall as a wooden pail smashed itself to pieces overhead. "Come on then," said Serdor. "Keep together, and keep your heads down—"

He broke off with a profane gasp as a long-handled grain-flail whizzed down upon them, its free-bar whirling like a morning star. Thrusting Rhan and Margoth behind him, Serdor snatched up the fallen spade and jammed the shovel-blade into the blurred path of the swingle.

There was a splintering crack as the free-arm of the flail bit iron and flew to pieces. The stock spun into the air and lashed down like a truncheon.

The butt end of it struck the minstrel a glancing blow to the temple. As he stumbled to his knees, a two-pronged hayfork shot across the room like a bolt from a ballista, and pinned Rhan flat to the wall behind him.

For one ghastly instant Margoth thought the boy must be dead. Then she saw that by some incomprehensible miracle he was only imprisoned, his throat trapped between the two spreading tines. Rhan was struggling frenziedly, fingers locked tight into the metal collar that was threatening to choke him. "Help him!" gasped Serdor thickly, from a prone position on the floor.

The right side of his face was bloody. Margoth's temper went up in a sudden white blaze of fury. "God damn you, *stop it*!" she screamed to the room at large, and stamped her foot in sheer outrage. Behind her Rhan gave a strangled cough. She turned and flew to his side.

The tines of the fork were digging themselves in deeper. Margoth seized the handle with both hands, intending to tear the prongs loose, but to her horror, the implement turned in her grip like an adder. In her amazement and disgust, she almost let go of it, but her seething anger lent her the strength to retain her hold. "*I said stop it!*" she panted furiously, and gave the fork a vengeful twist with all her might.

To her utter astonishment, the implement came away in her hands. Freed, Rhan staggered aside, massaging his grazed throat. Margoth hurled the stave away with a shudder of revulsion. There was no time to think about the implications of what she had done. "Quick—both of you come with me!" said a voice at her elbow.

It was Serdor, pale but steady on his feet. Catching Rhan by one arm and Margoth by the other, he towed them toward the door.

They reached it amid a spattering bombardment of small missiles, and found Caradoc struggling on the floor under an imprisoning morass of smashed planking and shattered glass. "That whole bloody wall of shelves came down on me!" he wheezed. "God, my chest—"

Serdor threw himself down next to the mage and began heaving the rubble away. Rhan joined him, digging like a terrier through the lesser drift of glass shards and sawdust. Leaving them to work Caradoc loose, Margoth darted to the door and laid her hands firmly on the bolt that was holding them prisoner.

The wood quivered under her fingers as the malignant principal controlling it became aware of her presence. Instinctively Margoth tightened her grip. Hardly aware of what she was doing, she willed the bolt to move.

The bar shifted, then she met resistance. As Margoth redoubled the urgency of her unspoken directive, something lashed back at her through the fabric of the wood. She cried out and recoiled as the plank exploded into fragments.

Serdor caught her as she stumbled back. Floundering to his feet, Caradoc pushed Rhan aside and made a limping run at the door.

There was a hollow crack as he hit the portal broadside, and the center-planks burst outward. "Everybody out!" he gasped.

Margoth took the initiative, diving through the ragged jaws of the opening into the night beyond. Rhan and Serdor followed on her heels. Tumbling headfirst after them, Caradoc landed flat on the ground outside. As he scrambled to his knees, something dark dived at him from the top of the roof.

He rolled to get out of its way. An icy chill swept past him, borne on beating wings of darkness. Hurtling onward, the shadow banked at the far end of the field and swooped back, its pinions churning up clouds of loose dirt as it skimmed low over the ground.

Hands plucked at Caradoc as he lay transfixed in its path. "Get up!" cried Serdor. "We've got to run for it!"

Rhan and Margoth were already sprinting for the wood on the west side of the field. Racing flat out, Serdor and Caradoc caught up with them at the edge of the clearing.

With the winged shadow bearing down on them from

above, the four fugitives hurled themselves over the wall and ploughed recklessly into the trees beyond. The shadow veered off at the last possible moment, scattering dead leaves in a sulphurous wake of roiling air.

Lying flat next to Serdor—"God, what is that thing?" puffed Rhan.

Caradoc lifted his head. "I don't know, and I don't want to hang about long enough to find out!" he said with breathless vehemence. "Let's move before it comes back."

The belt of trees was only a furlong broad. Beyond lay more fields, bridging the quarter mile between the wood and the outlying buildings of the village. The four fugitives were halfway across the first stretch of fallows, when they heard behind them the resurgent thrum of beating wings.

The nearest available source of cover was a ditch, perhaps as much as eight feet deep, lying across their line of flight. Redoubling their pace, they gained the embankment and plunged willy-nilly over the edge as a spectral black bird-shape rose above the treetops to the east.

Spiraling upward like a column of dark smoke, it leveled off and made a soughing pass over the open ground. The four people crouching neck deep in three feet of water held their breath as the shadow coasted over the mud embankments that rose well above their heads.

The noisome wind from its wing-beats sent the ditch-water flurrying as it hovered overhead for what seemed like an eternity. Then abruptly it wheeled aside and shot away.

For a long moment no one moved. As the surrounding silence lengthened, the riled water gradually settled and was still. Raising himself cautiously, Rhan gazed fearfully up at the sky above him. "Is it gone?" he breathed.

"I don't know. I'll take a look," muttered Caradoc.

He picked himself up out of the waterweeds and began crawling up the bank. "Be careful!" hissed Margoth after him.

He nodded without looking back. A dozen heartbeats

later, he reached the top of the embankment and scanned the night from horizon to horizon. "I don't see anything," he reported.

Margoth and Serdor locked glances. "That thing didn't just disappear through a crack in the sky," muttered Caradoc's sister. "I'll bet it's off lurking in some hollow, waiting for us to show ourselves. As soon as we move, it'll attack again."

"You're probably only too right," said Serdor. "But we can't stay here. Not in these wet clothes, with more than six hours of darkness to go before sunrise. Like it or not, we're going to have to make a break for the village."

"What are you three waiting for?" Caradoc hissed above them. "Since we've nothing to gain by stalling, the sooner we move out, the better."

Rhan shook himself like a half-grown puppy and began scrambling up the bank. Serdor and Margoth clambered after him. As they reached the top, Caradoc pointed toward the faint starlit rooftops of the village. "It can't be more than a furlong and a half from here to the edge of town," he said. "We should be able to cover the distance in two or three short sprints."

He started to get to his feet. "No, wait!" said Serdor. "We're better off not running before we have to."

"Why? Stealth doesn't count for much," said Caradoc, "when your enemy doesn't have to rely on normal sensory perception."

"I wasn't thinking of the creature, I was thinking of *us*," said Serdor. "If we're all running hell-bent for leather, we won't hear anything but the sound of our own feet until it's too late."

"You may have a point there," said his friend grimly. "All right, we'll take it slowly and carefully. Let's keep together and keep our eyes and ears open."

# WHISPERS IN THE WIND

THE FIELD TO THE WEST of the ditch was ridged with rows of stubble. Hearing the squelch of wet straw under her feet, Margoth winced and tried to walk more quietly. Beside her, Serdor was treading delicately, as though on slick ice. Caradoc was working hard to minimize the muddy slosh of his own heavier footfalls.

There was a thin breeze rising. Each time the chill air stirred the sodden stalks of barley, Caradoc felt a prickling sensation at the back of his neck. His uneasiness grew stronger with every step he took. Ears pricked to catch the returning thrum of black wings, he became gradually aware of a lurking menace of another kind.

The night seemed charged with whispering too subtle to be plainly audible. Caradoc was haunted by a growing impression that there were whole conversations being carried on just beyond the threshold of his hearing.

He reached out and laid an arresting hand on Serdor's sleeve. "Stop a moment," he murmured. "Do you hear anything?"

The other three members of the party froze in their tracks. "Nothing but the wind," whispered Serdor after a moment's listening. He peered up into Caradoc's shadowed face. "What is it?"

The elusive ghost-voices had subsided. "Nothing,"

said Caradoc gruffly. "Let's keep moving."

He started forward again. But he had scarcely taken two steps before the sound of whispering rose up around him like smoke on a rising wind.

Spiteful and thin as the hissing of adders, the voices seemed to be coming from all sides at once. Their malice was no longer impersonal. Caradoc was gripped by a sudden conviction that their mockery was being directed at him.

His temper kindling almost before he was even aware of it, he strained to catch some clearer indication of what was being said against him. His restricted sensibilities confounded his efforts. Trapped yet again in the perceptual deadness left by the loss of his magestone, he was seized by a sudden bitter impulse to curse his own frail nature.

The voices in the dark took up the echo of his self-derision. Sibilant and sly, they began to taunt him as he moved forward through the low stubble of a week-old harvest. The ghostly burden of scorn mounted until it finally became intolerable. His hackles rising, Caradoc lashed out at his tormenters in a sudden silent passion of resentment.

He might as well have been a blind man swatting at wasps. The spectral voices scattered laughing before his rage, like adults fleeing in mock-alarm before a child in a tantrum, then gathered round again, jeering at his impotence.

The sense, if not the substance, of the jeers cut deep. It was as if his character were being systematically dissected, and every flaw held up to ridicule.

Caradoc groped for something to say in his own defense. But by then, the tongue of his own conscience had joined in the chorus that murmured against him. And its voice led all the others in reviling him for his abiding fecklessness and pride.

In a lacerating moment of recollection, he saw again before him a parched white valley strewn with the bodies of men dead and dying. The wraith-voices pressed in upon him from all sides, moaning and sighing in an ecstasy of condemnation.

Caradoc's sense of his own baseness was in that instant crushing. The guilty part of him welcomed the anguish as the just penalty for his crimes. For a moment he was tempted to luxuriate in the pangs of expiation.

Then it occurred to him that perhaps *that* was precisely what he was being goaded to do.

Conviction suffused his fevered imagination like a flood of cold water. Digging his nails into the palms of his hands, he embarked on a fresh struggle.

Not to open his mind to the whispers, but to shut them out.

It took a supreme effort of will to lay aside the yoke of personal guilt. To counter the dark voices wooing him to self-flagellation, he forcibly summoned other memories to his aid—memories of men and women whose pains he had eased and whose maladies he had conquered. The sudden dim awareness of Serdor's presence at his shoulder gave his efforts a fresh and powerful focus. He reached back into their shared youth, recalling how he had fought to save his friend's life.

His imagination caught itself up in reliving the struggle, and it was several minutes before he realized that the pernicious whispers of the night had dwindled to sullen mutterings. Holding them at bay like so many snarling dogs, Caradoc roused himself to take a look around him, and discovered that they had come across the full breadth of two wide fields, and were standing within a short stone's throw of the first houses in the village.

Near at hand, their way was barred by an eight-foot fence. Serdor walked up to it and peered between the stout wooden stakes. He started back at the stink of foul air, then recovered himself with a sheepish sigh of relief. "It's all right—just the village tanning yard," he said. "I wouldn't recommend going in there. It would be all too easy to

119

blunder into an acid bath in the dark."

Margoth shuddered. "No, thank you."

"If we follow the fence to the right," said Caradoc, "we should come back to the road leading down from the forest."

"Won't that be dangerous?" asked Margoth.

"The road's no more open than the fields we've just crossed," said her brother. "And it's the most direct way to the center of town."

"Do we want to go to the center of town?" asked Margoth dubiously.

"It has at least the virtue of being closely inhabited," said Serdor. "We need blankets, dry clothes if possible, and food. Can you think of a better place to start foraging?"

"No," said Margoth. "Let's go."

The moon was rising, its crescent hollowed out like a worm-eaten cheese rind. Its light glimmered palely on the pitted roadbed, showing up mirror-patches of standing rainwater in the ruts. Trudging along behind her male companions, Margoth felt uncomfortably exposed in the silvering light. She was relieved when they passed within the village boundaries.

The road curved to the left between two rows of thatched cottages. The sandy ruts gave way to cobblestones. Ignoring for the moment the unpaved lanes branching off on either hand, the four fugitives kept to the main street until it broadened out into a paved market-square.

The square was dominated at its center by a bulky monument in carven stone, set on a high plinth. On each of its four sides, a series of ascending panels displayed in low relief the trademarks of the local craft guilds. From the western entrance to the square Margoth could make out the rigged caravel of the shipwrights and the quartered malt-sheaves of the brewers pricked out by the now-bright moon. "Whatever the name of this place may be, its artisans certainly have their pride," she murmured.

Beside her, Rhan was staring up in horrified fascination at the stone gargoyle surmounting the monument. Webbed wings mantling, it gripped its pedestal with taloned feet, surveying the breadth of the square with basilisk eyes. "Charming," remarked Margoth sourly.

His gaze still riveted, Rhan made no response. Margoth was about to comment further on the questionable taste of the local tradesmen, when she realized suddenly that everything around them seemed to have gone preternaturally still.

From the tanning yard to the east, to the fishing wharf on the west, not a breath of air was stirring in the village. Margoth's mouth went dry. She tugged at Rhan's sleeve. "Come on," she said in a low voice. "It's not safe to linger here."

Caradoc and Serdor had gone on ahead. Yielding to the insistent pull on his arm, Rhan tore his eyes away from the statue. "Hurry up!" called Caradoc in a loud whisper from the south side of the square, where another street descended toward the waterfront.

Hustling Rhan along with her, Margoth hurried to join him. "Where's Serdor?" she asked.

Caradoc pointed toward the third building on the right side of the road. "He spotted an open window on the ground floor," he said shortly.

Rhan opened his mouth, then abruptly closed it again as comprehension dawned. "We'll wait for him at the bottom of the hill," said Caradoc, and started off down the steeply sloping street.

Rhan fell into step behind him. Margoth was about to follow, when she heard behind her a grainy rustle, like sand blowing over a flat rock.

She cast a nervous glance over her shoulder, but the square stood as she had left it. She turned her back firmly upon the monument and its environs, and set out after her companions.

They were still thirty yards above the entrance to the waterfront when all three of them caught the sound of light footsteps pattering down on them from the upper end of the street. A moment later, Serdor overtook them out of the shadows, clutching a bundle in front of him. "Here: two blankets, a cloak, and a sheepskin," he said. "Who wants what?"

"Give me a blanket. Rhan, you'd better have the cloak," said Margoth, thrusting it into his arms before he could demur. "What about you, Caradoc?"

"I'll take the fleece, and hope it doesn't have tenants," said her brother with a grimace.

Drawing his dagger, he made a slit down the middle of it and drew it over his head, belting it to his body like a vest. Serdor swathed himself in the remaining blanket. "That's better," he said. "Now then—"

Before he could finish his sentence, the air was fractured by an ear-splitting crack. As its echoes died away, there was a dull uneven rumbling, like the onset of a rockslide. The four people in the street wheeled round to face the noise as it thundered toward them down the narrow canyon formed by the housefronts. "Look out!" cried Caradoc, and shouldered Rhan rudely into the shelter of the nearest doorway as an avalanche of uprooted cobblestones surged down upon them from above.

Serdor and Margoth leaped into the close gap between two neighboring houses as the storm of rocks broke like a wave over the spot where they had been standing. Stone slabs thudded into the roadbed, fragmenting on impact. Shrinking back from the flying shards, Margoth glimpsed part of a malt-sheaf device on one broken piece as it landed at her feet.

"The monument!" she gasped out to Serdor above the din of colliding stonework. Then gave a cry of dismay as she caught sight of a huge mass of wrought marble plummeting out of the sky.

The stone gargoyle crash-landed in the street and exploded like a bombard. Caradoc dragged Rhan to the ground and pinned him flat as a backlash of rubble rained over them like hailstones. Eyelids clenched tight against the stinging gale of swirling grit, Caradoc heard above the dwindling spatter of rock fragments the slow beat of great wings.

He raised his head. Something dark was blocking the entrance to the square. Even as he stared at it in mesmerized horror, the shadow spread its pinions wide and lifted into the air.

Rising above the rooftops, it hovered there for a long moment. Then the shadow began its gliding descent.

Caradoc bounded to his feet, pulling Rhan up with him. "Run!" he shouted. "Run and don't look back!"

Serdor and Margoth broke from cover on the opposite side of the street. With the minstrel bringing up the rear, they pelted headlong to the foot of the hill and shot off to the right along a raised stone jetty. A foul-smelling wind beat at their backs. "Faster!" called Serdor to Margoth.

He hooked a hand through her elbow, sweeping her up into the pounding rhythm of his stride. Margoth knew a brief instant of panic as she realized that she wasn't going to be able to keep her feet at that pace. A split second later, she lost her balance and tumbled flat, taking Serdor down with her.

They skidded abrasively to a standstill at the base of a piling. Shadowy wings fanned the air above their heads in great acrid gusts. Margoth screamed and hid her face in Serdor's jerkin.

Caradoc heard her cry out. Ploughing to a halt, he spun around as the shadow gathered height and dived.

Not for Serdor and Margoth, but for Rhan.

Caradoc was there ahead of it. Leaping between the creature and its intended prey, he whipped out his poniard and hurled it with hopeless bravado into the featureless mass of darkness where the head should have been.

The blackness swallowed the blade. The creature gave an icy hiss and turned on him, midnight talons outstretched to rend his face from its bones.

Caradoc dodged under its outflung bulk and had the sheepskin torn from his shoulders. The creature hissed at him again, venomous in its contempt for his puny defenses.

The naked malice in its foul breath recalled for Caradoc the whispers that had taunted him on the edge of the wind. Incensed, he turned to defy it. As he did so, the creature lashed out at him in a wild gust of fetid air.

Barbed claws clutched at the front of his jerkin and dug in deep. Pain and a chilling sense of corruption swept over him. Transfixed, he sagged blindly toward the ground. The creature hung on, buffeting him from all sides with the surge of its black wings.

His senses were swamped with the stench of decay, as though his living flesh were decomposing around him. He tasted putrefaction on his tongue, his throat clogging with the miasma of a gangrenous wound.

His gorge rose to choke him. Retching, he writhed like a madman in the creature's ravaging grip. Despite his struggles, the reek of rotting flesh mounted until it threatened to drown him. Corruption gnawed at his bones like a canker.

For a heartbeat his life hung in delicate balance, before his healer's instincts rose in revolt against the threat of imminent dissolution. Aflame with impulses he had not known in months, he seized power from untouched reservoirs beyond the flesh to strike back at the leprous thing that was seeking to devour him.

Energy coursed through his body in a fiery stream, undamming his closed veins and quickening his deadened nerves. Throwing open the sluice-gates of ardor, he poured vitality back into his drained and desiccated flesh.

His enemy yowled at him in famished frustration, but its hold was slackening. Rising like a phoenix out of the cleansing flame newly kindled, Caradoc reached out to the shadow with the hands of a healer.

His fingers brushed the substance of darkness and

passed through it. The creature shrieked in mortal agony and writhed back, wings wildly flailing. Caradoc probed deeper, his fingertips throwing off cauterizing pulses of raw power. His enemy screamed again, on a hoarse note of disbelief, as its dark frame began to dissipate.

Thinner it blew, and thinner until he could see stars glimmering through its fading outline. Its wailing voice receded to the edge of sound, and finally was lost as its form dissolved altogether. As the creature melted from his grasp, Caradoc collapsed to the ground.

All but insensible with exhaustion, he clung for a lingering moment longer to the edge of consciousness, his mind in a turmoil of conflicting horror and wonder as he relived the struggle that had just taken place. Out of the nightmare recollections of pain and sickness, a single astonishing certainty rose to blinding prominence: the realization that he had survived the struggle not by any accident of luck or strength, but by the direct intercession of supernatural power—the power of the Magia!

The knowledge that the Magia had come to him without the instrumental agency of a magestone took his breath away. The air was full of tocsins ringing and voices shouting, but he was not aware of them. Insensible as a dead man, he lay where he had fallen without the strength to move. He did not respond when Rhan crawled to his side and called him by his name, for he had slipped beyond the reach of a human voice.

# THE FACE OF DANGER

IT WAS DARK AS A night without stars. Unable to move, Caradoc lay flat on his back, contemplating a roofless void from which all light had fled.

His straining eyes seemed unable to penetrate the surrounding blackness. Cold fear stabbed at his heart —fear that he had somehow lost the ability to see. He started to sit up, and discovered that he could not.

Something was holding him down.

In that instant, he became aware of pressure building up on his eyelids. Someone was pressing a hand against his eyesockets, fingers digging with slow malice into the vulnerable tissue of the eyeballs beneath.

Writhing wildly in sudden panic, he jerked his head away, dislodging the grip from above. Freed, he opened his eyes and looked up into the dim light of a ribbed cross vault of grey stone.

A hooded figure bent over him. Eyes like wells of black flame opened out of the shadow of the drooping cowl.

The burning gaze transfixed him. Paralyzed, he stared up into the malicious, marmoreal face of Borthen Berigeld.

Borthen smiled and lifted a hand to caress his prisoner's face. Shrinking back, Caradoc saw that the individual digits were barbed like the claws of a bird of prey.

Horror pierced his heart. He gave a strangled cry of

126

protest and recoiled as the talons curled inward to rake away his sight. . . .

"Caradoc, wake up! It's all right!" called a familiar female voice from someplace off to his right.

A small strong hand plucked at his shoulder. "It's all right!" insisted his sister. "Caradoc, look at me!"

Light was radiating from somewhere beyond Borthen's hooded form. Caradoc was torn between fear and the desire to obey his sister's command.

Margoth called his name again. His enemy's clawed fingers swept his cheek. He flinched, then realized that he was unhurt.

Borthen's black-robed figure thinned to a transparent image through which Caradoc could see another moving shape, bright and solid. A face bent close to his—a smooth oval face framed in wayward curls of auburn hair. "That's better," said Margoth encouragingly. "Can you see me now?"

Shakily he nodded his head. Margoth smiled through her concern. "You must be thirsty. Wait a moment and I'll get you something to drink."

She turned aside. Watching her, Caradoc became conscious of a gentle rocking sensation vibrating upward through the mat upon which he was lying. That, and a strongly marked smell of fish. He licked dry lips and said huskily, "The others—where are they?"

"Rhan and Serdor? They're up on deck," said Margoth.

She slipped a hand under his head and held a metal cup to his mouth. Caradoc sipped a mixture of wine and water. "On deck?"

She nodded. "The rocking isn't imaginary. We're afloat."

Caradoc looked blearily around him. He was lying well-wrapped on one side of a tiny narrow room with sloping walls and a low skylighted ceiling. The other side of the room was largely taken up by wooden lockers. "I'm afraid this is all the cabin space there is," continued Margoth. "The rest of the hold—such as it is—has long been used for transporting fish. Hence the prevailing odor of herring."

Caradoc gazed up at the skylight. It was open, and beyond it he could see a square patch of blue sky wrapped around what appeared to be the base of a ship's mast. "How did we get here?" he asked in bewilderment.

Margoth hugged her upraised knees and rested her chin on top of them, her expression seriously reminiscent. "It was after you decided to take on that *thing*, whatever it was. Before I spin you *our* yarn, I'd like to know how you managed to get rid of that creature."

It took an effort of will to call the experience to mind. "I honestly don't remember much," said Caradoc, huddling deeper into his blankets. "When it first got hold of me, it was like—oh, I don't know—like grappling with some loathsome disease. I just fought back any and every way I could. Maybe my having been a mage gave me some kind of innate resistance. Either that, or—" His voice stopped abruptly.

"Or what?" asked Margoth.

"Or else I've managed—heaven knows how—to maintain some affinity for the Magia," said Caradoc.

He spoke hurriedly, and not without reluctance. But Margoth nodded sagely. "Serdor was wondering the same thing, after you and Rhan had that row by the campfire. And after last night . . ."

She peered at her brother. "Certainly it took something more than sheer blind courage to send that demon-thing back where it came from."

Caradoc was silent, remembering the white-hot surge of energy that had stormed like wildfire throughout his whole body, to dispel the ravaging corruption bent on destroying him. Potent, purposeful, that healing power had come to his aid—but he was not prepared by any means to assert that it had come in response to his call. Quite the converse, in fact: Caradoc had taken up the sword of power in the manner of a soldier in willing service to his lord. . . .

A small movement from Margoth interrupted his reverie. "What does it feel like," she asked, "to be in contact with a force like the Magia?"

The question caught Caradoc slightly off guard. Half smiling, he said, "Why do you ask?"

"Because of something that happened to me," said Margoth, "back when we were trapped in that barn."

Seeing that she had her brother's full attention, she continued. "When I found I couldn't open the barn door, I flew into a towering rage. And the door simply *burst* open. I mean something went *through* me, so strong that it shattered the wood."

"Like lightning shooting along a wire?"

"Something like that—yes!" Margoth's eyes flew to meet her brother's. "Caradoc, do you suppose . . . ?" She left the question unfinished.

"Why not? You are, after all, my sister," said Caradoc. "And you could very well have a basic sixth sense, a talent. Certainly, real stress—fear, pain, anger—would be just the thing to bring it out into the open."

He rubbed the bridge of his nose while he continued to think out loud. "Of course, if you've been trained to use your talent in a particular way—as I've been taught to use mine for healing—maybe stress would channel along the lines of that training. Otherwise, it might just take its own natural course."

He shook his head. "I wish I could tell you more. But I'm as much in the dark about 'wild' talent as you are. I don't know how it works."

There was a small silence. "Oh well," said Margoth briskly, "the most important thing right now is that we've got away."

Caradoc nodded in agreement. "How's Rhan?"

"All right," said Margoth. "He was pretty shaken up at the time, but he pulled himself together once he realized you weren't dead. I wonder . . ."

She scowled. "It seems too much coincidence that the

two attacks—both in the barn and on the waterfront —were directed mainly at you and him."

"It wasn't coincidence," said Caradoc grimly. "It was design. And now I know *whose* design."

Margoth looked at him, blue eyes widening in comprehension. "Surely not Borthen? But how could that possibly be?"

"I don't know," said Caradoc. "Except to say that he has some frightening resources at his disposal."

Margoth shuddered. "Is there anything we can do to throw him off the scent?"

"Nothing I can think of in advance," said Caradoc. "But don't lose heart: powerful as he is, Borthen isn't omniscient, or he'd have caught us long before now. For what it's worth, I think we've got a good fighting chance."

He spoke with far more assurance than he felt, but Margoth's somber eyes lightened. "That's more like it," he said, forcing a smile. "Now tell me what happened after I passed out."

"There was quite a stir," said Margoth. "I mean, what with the pavements being torn up and that hideous monument being pulled apart, the whole place was up in arms in a matter of minutes. While the alarum bells were still going off, Serdor and I scooped you up off the ground and made for the boats tied up along the dock. This one was right at the very end."

She hugged her knees more tightly. "Once we were all on board, Serdor cut the mooring-line and we just let the boat drift out to sea on the tide. With all the confusion in the village itself, I don't suppose anyone noticed it was gone. In any case, we weren't followed. Which left us free to worry about you to the exclusion of all else."

She grimaced. "You know, you've been unconscious for nearly sixteen hours. We were beginning to think we might have to go ashore at the next town to seek out a mage to look after you. Come to think of it, you still don't look very well. Maybe it would be a good idea—"

"No!" said Caradoc emphatically. "I'm perfectly all right—apart from feeling a bit tired. A few more hours' sleep, and I'll be as fit as I've ever been."

He shifted onto his side and propped himself up on one elbow. "What's the plan from here on out?"

Margoth wrinkled her nose. "Serdor reckons we're still about sixty miles north of Holmnesse. If we hold to our present course and speed, we should arrive in about two days' time. Barring accident or mishap."

"Like running afoul of the coast-watch. Are you sure it's such a good idea to stay with this boat, when it's bound to have been reported lost, stolen, or strayed?" asked Caradoc.

His sister shrugged. "I can't see that it's any riskier than trying to complete the journey overland. And it's certainly a whole lot easier. We've got food in the lockers and enough bedding to go around, not to mention a roof—of sorts—over our heads—"

"But you don't know the first thing about how to handle a boat," protested Caradoc.

Margoth flashed him a smile. "Maybe not, but you forget how quickly Serdor and I can learn. Especially when we've got someone to teach us."

Caradoc opened his mouth and closed it again without speaking. "Rhan knows a thing or two about sailing," said Margoth in response to his unasked question. "My guess is that the Lord Warden's sons are brought up to have some knowledge of a number of practical military skills—like navigation."

She reached over and ruffled his hair. "Don't worry: we're managing to stay afloat. And anyway, we're keeping well within sight of land. Lie back and see if you can get some more sleep. We won't let you doze past dinner-time. . . ."

They anchored at nightfall in a sheltered cove where a thin rivulet of fresh water spilled down to the beach from the top of a grassy cliff-face. Serdor stripped down and waded ashore to replenish their supply of drinking water. When he returned, they ate their evening meal under a clear purple sky, then cast off again, with a light wind nudging them southward along the uneven coastline of the Garillan mainland.

Caradoc by this time had managed to shrug off the last lingering effects of his fatigue. Feeling wide-awake and well rested, he volunteered to keep Serdor company on deck while Rhan and Margoth went below to seek their bedrolls.

Margoth was grateful for the prospect of a full night's rest. Curling up in her blankets, she bade Rhan a drowsy good-night, and settled down, fully expecting to sleep uninterrupted till morning.

Instead, some time later, she was rudely startled into full awareness when the boat lurched so sharply that she bumped her head on the nearest bulkhead.

It was dark in the cabin. She sat up and put out a hand. The bedroll next to hers was empty. She got to her knees and crawled to the base of the short ladder leading up to the hatched skylight.

Even as she set her hand on the first rung, the boat beneath her gave another sudden queasy lurch. The movement threw her off balance. Shoulder pressed against the cabin's right-hand wall, she became aware of a change in the little craft's forward motion.

Instead of rocking like a cradle, their stolen vessel was wallowing like a cow, bow and stern bucking up and down in a syncopated succession of rolls and hops. The gentle lap of the waves against the hull had changed to a welter of rough slaps. Wood creaked and groaned in the darkness.

Guarding her head, she drew herself up and groped for the latch of the hatch-cover. When she released it, the hatchway snapped up on a whirl of damp wind. "Serdor!" she called up. "Caradoc! What's going on?"

A head and shoulders appeared in silhouette above her. "The weather's changing," said the minstrel. "It looks as if we may be in for a bit of a blow."

Margoth captured a whipping strand of hair and tucked it firmly behind her ear. "I'm coming up," she said. "Give me a hand."

The gusty air outside was sticky with gathering moisture. The sky to the far south of them still showed stars, but behind them to the north, the star-patterns were being devoured by a fast-moving vanguard of clouds. "What time is it?" asked Margoth.

"About two hours past midnight," said Serdor.

Caradoc was at the tiller, with Rhan beside him. Near at hand, the little boat's square sail was strained tight under the swelling force of the wind.

Peering over the side, Margoth could see that their cockleshell craft was already picking up an unnatural turn of speed. Water folded away like cream from her flanks as she plunged ahead like a wayward goat. "Hadn't we better take a reef in the sail?" asked Margoth, pitching her voice to carry above the growing whine of rope and canvas.

"Not just yet," said Serdor. "Flying along before the wind like this, we may just contrive to outrun the storm itself."

"At this rate, we'll have overshot Holmnesse by daybreak," said Margoth dubiously.

"That may be the least of our worries," said Serdor. "In case you haven't noticed, we've already been carried out of sight of land."

It was true. Scanning the western horizon, Margoth could make out no trace of the cliff-lines she remembered. Her chest tightened. To shake off the encroaching grip of fear, she gave an exaggerated shrug. "Oh well. Whatever else happened, at least we won't run aground on the seneschal's doorstep."

The wind continued to mount. Given a choice between returning to the close darkness of the cabin, and remaining on deck to confront her fate, Margoth chose the latter option. Leaving her clinging to the mainstay, Serdor went aft to confer with the other two members of the party.

Before he got there, a tall wave, overtaking them from behind, almost set the little boat on her nose. He lost his footing, but caught hold of the starboard railing. Their vessel righted itself with a shudder. "Serdor, are you all right?" called Margoth.

She herself had both arms wrapped around the foot of the mast. "I'm fine," he called back. "Just stay where you are. We'll see what we can do to stabilize her in the water."

While Caradoc fought the tiller to keep them ahead of the wind, Serdor and Rhan lowered the anchor off the bow. As the cable played out behind them, the little fishing boat settled back into the swells with comparative docility.

The sea-anchor held them steady enough in their course for the next few hours. But by dawn it was clear that they were losing the race for safe searoom.

The light, when it came, had an eerie lilac sheen to it. Keeping watch astern, Margoth followed the roiling line of clouds with her eyes as the storm converged upon them out of the north.

The darkness spread over the water like a cancer. Even as she smelled the sudden bitter tang of ozone, a thunderbolt broke over them with a deafening crack. Seconds later, the black sky above them was riven apart by a blinding shaft of white lightning.

Thunder roared again, and she cowered instinctively against the mast. A hand gripped her shoulder. "You'd better get below!" said Serdor.

Rhan was beside him. The boy's expression was mutinous, but his eyes were dilated with awe. "I want you both out of harm's way," continued the minstrel. "We're going to be running into some heavy seas in another few minutes. If you're in the cabin, you can't be swept overboard."

"What about you?" demanded Margoth.

Even as she spoke, the wind dashed a spattering of heavy raindrops across the deck. The little boat heeled over sharply, throwing her up against the mast. Looking

134

ahead, Margoth caught her breath as a deep trough opened up in the sea in front of them.

The little fishing boat ploughed into the hole like a sow bellying into a mud-bath. Water fountained all around her as she skidded down the sea-sluice to the bottom of the trough. Hauling frantically at the tiller-bar, Caradoc brought her nose up to meet the next wave. A green cascade washed the length of the deck as she butted her prow through the crest of it.

Serdor made a dive for the hatch-cover and wrenched it open. "Now!" he ordered.

With the lashing rain pinging off her shoulders like hailstones, Margoth tumbled down the steps and rolled aside as Rhan hit the cabin floor behind her. Serdor slammed the skylight after them, not quite quickly enough to shut out a second stream of cold seawater.

Scrambling sideways to avoid it, Rhan bumped into Margoth in the dark. The deck canted steeply beneath them, and they instinctively locked arms.

The little boat bounded forward with liberated violence. "I think we just lost the sea-anchor," said Margoth between set teeth. "This is where things start to get interesting. . . ."

# THE TEETH OF THE STORM

LIGHT AS A CORK, THE little fishing boat flew like a bird before the wind. Lacking ballast, she was fickle as a widgeon in the water, and it took prodigal expenditures of strength and will to keep her running straight in her courses with the rain blowing in winding-sheets through her frail rigging.

Serdor and Caradoc took it in turns to man the tiller. By midmorning, they both had open blisters on their palms from the friction of handling the bar. By midday, they were sore and bruised from repeated strains and falls. By late afternoon, they were both reeling with weariness, but the storm showed no sign of abating.

They had no way of knowing how far the gale-force winds had carried them. But as the churning sky darkened toward nightfall, they began to catch ominous glimpses of rocks among the waves, and knew from this that they had been driven into strange waters.

The presence of submarine reefs presented a host of new dangers. Leaving Caradoc at the helm, Serdor went forward to act as lookout. Eyes burning under the lash of the storm-driven brine, he clung one-handed to the railing in front of him, and directed their course with the other.

It was tricky work in the failing storm-light. Steering according to Serdor's signals, Caradoc heard above the wailing of the wind a sudden loud pop. Startled, he looked up and saw that the sail had split itself from top to bottom.

It collapsed like a burst bladder, leaving them momentarily dead in the water. Beyond the settling prow, the seas raced together and began to take shape. Climbing toward a mountainous peak, the wave gathered bulk and began to roll down on them.

Serdor saw it coming. Clutching the railing with the blistered fingers of his left hand, he gestured frantically to Caradoc with the other. "Hard a'starboard!" he shouted over the snarling of the wind.

Caradoc threw his full weight against the tiller, forcing it to the right. The boat groaned under the strain, and came sluggishly around only just in time to meet the wave head-on.

Floundering, the little vessel failed to take the curl on the upsurge. Instead, her prow obstinately diving, she struck the wave at its base and bored downward through the middle of it, courting the full weight of the crashing water as it collapsed over and around her.

Hugging the rail till his shoulders cracked, Serdor had barely time enough to snatch a last lungful of air before the murky storm-light vanished in a vibrating collision of spume. Half-choked, he heard above the gnashing of the foam a single skull-splitting crack.

For a moment they hung in limbo. The ship staggered, stern uppermost, as the comber raked her from end to end. Then, miraculously, she struggled upright through the subsiding flood.

Left breathless in a heap on the deck, Serdor painfully slackened his grip and drew himself up. In the stern, Caradoc staggered to his feet with the aid of the aft-rail. A loud popping noise flayed the air. As the boat listed to port, Serdor looked back and saw that the mast had been snapped short.

Still anchored to the stump, the tattered sail was flogging itself to ribbons in the wind, threatening to foul the foredeck. The upper portion of the mast, along with the main yard, remained anchored to the port side by a hopeless ganglion of tangled cables. Listing toward the center of a forming whirlpool, the little boat swung about like a horse on a lead line.

The deck canted dangerously to the left. Panting, Serdor turned and stumbled aft, clinging to the railing to keep his balance. Before he could get to the mast-end to cut loose the dragging weight of the fallen sail, the portside waters parted, exposing a sudden glistening fang of rock.

Caradoc shouted a warning, but it was already too late. Wallowing helpless as a lamed heifer, the little boat heeled on her side and fell with a splintering crash of wracked timbers onto the half-seen reef below.

Serdor lost his footing. Beneath him the boat writhed like a live thing, as the submerged rocks clawed their way into her womb. Caradoc let go of the broken tiller and raced for the hatch. Serdor scrambled to join him.

The tall mage flung the hatchway open. Serdor seized one of the flailing wrists offered him from the dark sieve of the cabin below. Clinging to his sleeve, Margoth came stumbling up the broken ladder. Leaving her to drag herself out of the way, Caradoc joined Serdor to snatch Rhan bodily out of the mouth of the flooding hold.

The hull was coming apart. A few yards to port, the broken masthead bobbed upright in the midst of a carnassial cauldron of rocks and spume. Water was jetting out of the hatchway to join the running tidewash sweeping the sinking deck. As the four members of the crew scrambled aft, another huge wave smashed into the little boat's starboard flank.

The force of it tore what was left of the vessel away from the handspike rocks. Planks shot skyward and scattered. Floundering toward the surface through lashings of angry foam, Caradoc caught sight of Margoth's red head as she emerged choking and sputtering from the back of the wave. "Make for the mast-end!" he shouted.

Margoth spat seawater, then nodded. As Caradoc struck out after her, another head broke the foam an arm's length away.

It was Rhan, bobbing limp with his face down. Treading water, Caradoc gripped him by the collar and hauled him over onto his back.

There was a swelling bruise above his right eyebrow. Hooking an elbow under the boy's sharp chin, Caradoc towed him through the creaming sea-froth to where Margoth was already clinging to the floating mast.

By the time they arrived, Rhan had begun to stir. Guiding his groping fingers toward handholds, Margoth flung her wet hair out of her eyes. "Where's Serdor?" she demanded.

"I don't know!" Caradoc called back. "You two hold on! I'll cast around and see if I can find him."

Giving Margoth no time to protest, he thrust himself away from the floating mast and swam back to where the wreckage was beginning to drift apart. Strung out like so many archipelagoes, they showed him the direction of the racing tide, and he followed with it, praying that if he found what he was looking for, he would be able to make his way back to the others.

A broken length of planking shot halfway out of the water at a perpendicular angle. Darting sideways with a desperate carplike twist of his lower body, Caradoc felt the brush of splintered wood against his legs as he fought his way through the treacherous undertow, the breath washing saltily past his teeth.

Foam burst into the air, flying down the wind in grey clots. Carried irresistibly to the top of a cresting wave, Caradoc rocked back in the surge, thrashing for equilibrium as he scanned the crowded waters for a single glimpse of a wet brown head among the other debris.

It was a doomed effort. Holding out grimly against the battery of wind and water, he could see nothing beyond the sheeting rain but interlacing strands of wood fragments floating half-pulped in the sea-lather of froth. Shivering with cold, his limbs leaden in the water, he flipped the tangled hair out of his face, turned, and marked the obscured drift of the mast he had abandoned. Sucking air into his sodden lungs, Caradoc made a final effort, forcing his way a few precious, futile yards further, but the storm-tides were too much for him and the current eventually bore him back upon itself, tumbling him in the direction from which he had come.

He had left it almost too late. Gasping with exertion, rib ligatures strained almost to the breaking point, he floundered back through the ship's knacker-yard, recklessly flailing the flotsam out of the way as he closed the last few feet between himself and their improvised life raft.

Margoth saw he was alone, and her throat closed up on an unuttered cry of dismay. Numbly she reached out a helping hand to her brother, but her thoughts in that moment were all for Serdor. "He'll be all right. He's a good swimmer, with a strong will to live," she told herself with desperate vehemence. But in the same instant, her searching gaze lighted upon Rhan's bruised face, and her hope was shaken at its root by the realization that even such a minor injury could well prove fatal to one castaway on his own.

Clinging to the mast with his lungs laboring like forge-bellows, Caradoc watched the dark interplay of emotions in his sister's colorless face, grateful that Rhan was still too shaken in his wits by the blow he had received to comprehend their loss. Fearing for his friend's life, he steeled himself to strike out a second time into the vicious cross-streams of the tide. Then he realized that he could not leave Margoth and Rhan alone—not now, when they were certain to have need of his strength.

It was hard to lay aside one duty in favor of another. By the time Caradoc had made his choice, the current had them firmly in its grip, driving them further and further away from the center of the wreck. The floating debris thinned out around them, dispersed on the racing waters. The three castaways clung to their improvised life raft, and let it carry them where it would.

Fighting to keep from settling into the dangerous torpor of fatigue, Caradoc kept his head up. Straining his eyes in an effort to penetrate the darkness, he glimpsed a white line of movement directly ahead of them.

Calling sharply to his two companions, he took a closer look. As he did so, the white line split and scattered, re-forming an instant later into a perilous fret of spume.

Inescapably they were being driven straight into the teeth of the disturbance. Catching above the whistle of the wind the growl of breaking waters, Caradoc stiffened, his aching body marshaling its last rags of strength to meet this new danger.

Then his trailing feet brushed something that felt, incredibly, like solid rock.

Even before the surprise had time to register in his tired brain, he touched ground again, this time more certainly. Excitement dawning, he straightened his knees, groping downward with both feet. Sand grated lightly against his bare soles, the solid, hard-packed sand of a water-covered shingle.

He had just enough fortitude left to drag himself and his two companions through the shorebreak onto the beach itself. After that, the last thing he remembered was his knees striking the rain-packed sand, and then darkness.

When he woke again, it was daylight. Lying prone in a bed of sand, he had an ant's-eye view of a crescent-shaped cove flanked by dunes. At the far end of the beach, the dunes gave rise to a narrow spit of rock jutting into the ocean. At the raised tip of this natural jetty stood a detached white tower surmounted by a quartered dome of iron and glass.

The lighthouse was not built according to Garillan conventions. Cylindrical rather than square in its construction, it ascended in tiers like a turban-shell, its rounded window-slits ornamented with tilework. Caradoc had read enough about Pernathan architecture to recognize it when he saw it. It dawned on him, hazily, that the storm must have swept them clear across the Gulf of Mhar, to leave them stranded on the ancestral shores of the Caliphs of Noor Hajid.

The realization came as something of a shock. Too far spent to think in terms of action, Caradoc winced and let his eyelids fall.

Exhaustion at once overwhelmed him. He slipped back into unconsciousness.

It was a voice that summoned him back from the fathomless depths of dreamless sleep. Ascending through the dark veils of his own extreme weariness, he rose to awareness like a diver breaking the surface of a moonlit pool. Standing alone at the pool's edge, he heard his own name spoken behind him, by a voice he had never thought to hear again.

Dread and hope together in that instant set him trembling. He spun around, and saw before him a familiar figure dressed in grey. The lined face beneath the hood was as he remembered it in life. His heart leapt for joy.

"Forgoyle!" he cried, and sprang forward, hands outstretched. "Oh God, Forgoyle, if you only knew how I have grieved for you—"

He would have clasped his old master's hands, but at the last moment Forgoyle stepped back, his expression at once whimsical and sad. "Do not touch me, Caradoc," he said gently. "That, I'm afraid, is not permitted."

Caradoc was stricken. "Why not?" he faltered.

The sadness deepened in Forgoyle's dark eyes. "Surely you remember all too well our last parting."

Our last parting . . .

Finding his answer, Caradoc lowered his head, his throat aching. "Yes, I remember. What brings you back to speak with me?"

His teacher smiled. "There are some bonds that even

death cannot break—like the love of a father for his son. Tell me what is troubling you."

Caradoc raised his eyes. "I am afraid," he said.

"For yourself?" Forgoyle's gaze was searching.

"Less for myself than for those with me," said Caradoc. "I have failed in my intent to deliver Evelake Whitfauconer to safety. And my failure has left my sister and my friend in gravest jeopardy."

"Evelake is with you?"

"Yes, and Margoth," said Caradoc. "But not Serdor. We were separated when our boat sank, and I fear he may have perished." He bit his lip, his expression pleading. "Please tell me what I should do. I have never felt in greater need of guidance."

"You must make your own decisions," said Forgoyle. "But if I may, I will give you the benefit of my counsel. What choices lie before you?"

"I don't know." Caradoc writhed inwardly. "We are so far from home—"

Forgoyle raised a hand. Light glimmered green through his fingers, and Caradoc saw that it was a magestone, twin to the one he had lost. Holding the gem delicately with his fingertips, Forgoyle reached out and touched it lightly to Caradoc's troubled forehead.

A barbed hook of fire lodged itself in his brain. He cried out as images were torn from his mind—images of the white beach, the tall dunes, and the lighthouse with its foreign design. Images of Margoth and Rhan as they lay curled in the sand beside him. His parting memory of Serdor, clinging drenched and shivering to the foot of a broken mast. . . .

He reeled back and struck Forgoyle's hand away. "What are you trying to do to me?" he cried sharply.

Forgoyle's smile deepened. The sudden feral quality in that look chilled Caradoc to the marrow. Gripped by icy premonitions of self-betrayal, he lunged forward and clutched the other man by both arms.

The flesh and bone rippled slightly under his fingers. Gazing horrified into Forgoyle's smiling features, Caradoc saw the eyes take fire and the flesh begin to melt away.

Another face emerged from the wreck of the mask that had been Forgoyle's. A smooth-planed, saturnine face with elegant bones and sharp-cut sneering lips.

The shock of recognition made Caradoc recoil as if from a deadly snake. "You're far too trusting," said Borthen Berigeld.

The barbed smile broadened in indulgent triumph. "Farewell for now," said his enemy. "I shall look for you in Pernatha."

He stepped back and turned. Beside himself with outrage, Caradoc uttered a wordless snarl and sprang after him.

A doorway lay ahead of them. Borthen stepped across the threshold and vanished. Intent on following, Caradoc hurled himself at the opening and was thrown back in a blinding concussion of light and darkness.

He landed hard on his back. Winded, but furious, he struggled to get up again, and got a sharp jab in the chest.

The pain dissolved the last vestiges of the dream-vision. Blinking in the sunlight, he peered down at his breastbone and encountered the point of a very solid and very businesslike fish-spear.

Following the line of the haft, he looked up. Three dark faces leered back at him, showing yellow teeth through oily black beards.

It was the last impression he received before the fourth Pernathan, whom he didn't see, hit him on the head from behind.

# SUMMONS TO MOURNING

THE GARDENS AT PENFALLON WERE never at their best in early autumn, in a time when rainstorms unfurled westward off the ocean, flattening the late-blooming roses under the streaming weight of the sky. Standing on a raised stone terrace overlooking the drowned checker-work of regimented flowerbeds, Kherryn turned her face to the east without flinching as the thin rain collected along her cheekbones in beads finer than spider's eggs.

To the east and at a distance, she could have made out, had she tried, the rain-blurred skyline of the city, grey in the embrace of the grey sea. Kherryn's mind, however, was elsewhere, and her wide dark eyes were fixed not upon the sea-wrack of the watery lawns, but upon the small object she held cupped in her two hands.

It was a box of crystal, and delicately fashioned, its sides worked with a frosty efflorescence of fine lines. On the lid, in low relief, was the image of a hawk, wings swept back, talons extended as if to strike.

Her small face pale and set, Kherryn studied it earnestly, deep in thought, until a rising gust of wind set her cloak swirling suddenly around her, rousing her from her reverie. Heavier raindrops made a warning spatter on the stone wall in front of her. After a single upward glance at the darkening sky, she drew her hood more closely about her face and turned back toward the shelter of the house.

Inside, the grey daylight, falling through three pairs of lancet windows, left pointed pools of dull amber on the flagged floor of the vestibule. Divesting herself of her cloak, Kherryn hung it on a peg to the right of the door, then moved into the adjoining passageway where the pattering of the rain was lost amid the precise, disciplined music of a keyboard instrument played with sustained and tutored skill.

It was only a short distance to the music room, and the door was ajar. Kherryn paused a moment, listening, then gave the door a light push so that it swung softly open.

Devon was seated at the virginals, his head and shoulders framed by the windows so that, for an instant, her impression was all one of black silhouettes against a grey background. Then her pupils adjusted to the light in the room and she could see, clearly now, the color of his doublet amid the rich sheens of inlay and mother-of-pearl: the mandolin and the guitar, the two lutes fashioned from the sweet wood of fruit trees, the psaltery with its metal strings sharp-cut in the candlelight, the harp glowing with gold leaf and quiet enamels.

Absorbed in his music, he had not heard her. Even in her present troubled state of mind, she found herself admiring, as always, the fineness of his fingers, the delicate surety of his touch. And, as always, she found herself wondering if he would ever have grown to be so superb a musician if circumstances had left him as sound in body as his more fortunate peers.

The gift of music was inadequate recompense for his solitude, forced inactivity, and the thoughtless condescension of those with sound bodies. Kherryn knew she would never reconcile herself to seeing Devon, her idolized older brother, endure the subtle humiliation of other people's pity. And the even more invidious burden of knowing that his own father, for all his forbearing consideration, despised him.

146

His deft fingers executed a rippling series of descending arpeggios, then brought the melody smoothly back into play again, theme and counterpoint moving elegantly toward their consummation. As the echoes of the final chord died away, Kherryn stepped across the threshold.

At the light rustle of her footfall on the carpet, Devon turned and smiled, a warm, wry twist of a smile that betrayed, without meaning to, his lifelong intimacy with pain. The effect, however, was one of strength, rather than of weakness, and Kherryn, placing her hands in his, felt the calm of his presence like a benison.

"Hello," he said, moving over to allow her room to sit down. "Your shoes are wet."

"I've been in the garden."

"I know. I could see you from the window." Devon's gaze was quizzical. "What were you doing out there in this weather?"

Kherryn settled her skirts with a sigh. "I was thinking. About Evelake."

"I thought that might be it," said Devon. He picked out a strand of melody with one hand, then said, "Surprising as it may seem, so was I."

It was not surprising. Of all the boys, nobly born and gently bred, who had come to serve their apprenticeship to the duties of their rank under Arvech's tutelage, only Evelake Whitfauconer alone had accepted Devon as he was, neither pitying, nor condescending.

And Devon, with a rare suspension of reserve, had admitted Evelake to his confidence. "It's been so long —nearly four months. I keep wondering," said Kherryn, watching her brother's face, "what's become of him."

Devon let his hands rest. "The only person who could tell us now would be Evelake himself."

"If they ever find him," said Kherryn. Still studying Devon, she decided to make an admission. "You're probably going to think me very silly, but sometimes, like today, I play a sort of game. I think hard about Evelake, recalling

147

every detail about his face as I remember it. And when I have his image perfectly before me, I call to him—my mind to his."

Devon glanced up abruptly from his instrument and stared at her. "I know—a curious whim for someone my age," said Kherryn. "But I have the oddest feeling that one day, if I keep trying, he just might answer me."

The expression in Devon's dark eyes warmed and deepened. Moving softly, he laid one thin hand gently against her cheek. "Who knows? If Evelake still lives—and he could answer anyone in such a way—that one would undoubtedly be you—"

He might have said more, but a respectful knock at the half-open door interrupted him. Devon, turning, saw and recognized the sturdy figure of Duroch, his father's personal valet. "Your pardon, Master Devon, Mistress Kherryn," said Duroch, bowing from the doorway, "but His Lordship has sent me to inform you that he requires your presence at once in the privacy of his solarium."

Kherryn's small-boned hands flew like startled birds from her lap, but she quieted them instantly against the dark velvet of her skirt. "Thank you for your trouble," said Devon, his tone courteously level. And made the inevitable concession. "Perhaps you would be so good as to go before us to inform my father that we are coming?"

Duroch bowed again. "It will be my pleasure, Master Devon," he said gravely, and withdrew.

Kherryn was on her feet at once, her eyes wide. "That's not like Father. Something's happened . . ."

Devon, rising jerkily from the music bench, had his eyes on the door. "I believe you're right. Something important too, or Father would have entrusted this errand to some lesser personage than Duroch. Well, we shall find out soon enough."

The solarium was separated from the music room by two flights of stairs and two long galleries. Any one of the servants could have covered the distance in a minute or two. It took Kherryn and Devon considerably longer than that because Devon, with his lame leg, could not be hurried.

Curtailing her impulse to race ahead, Kherryn cast a sidelong glance at her brother's disciplined profile as he negotiated the stairs step by careful step. It would have been infinitely easier if he had allowed himself to be carried in the chair their father had designed for him, but Kherryn knew that Devon would never permit the poisonous luxury of weakness as long as he could avoid it: he had his own brand of obstinate pride.

Duroch was waiting at the door of the solarium. By the time they drew even with the doorway, he had already announced them. As they passed shoulder to shoulder into the overglassed opulence of the solarium, he entered behind them and closed the door.

Arvech, seated upright in one of several damasked chairs, was not alone. With him already were three of his household ministers and a big ruddy man with a shrewd, good-natured face. The Mayor, Devon realized, of Gand.

And a fifth man, young and lightly made, who wore above boots damped and splashed with mud the red-and-gold quartered tabard of a herald of Ambrothen.

Arvech acknowledged the arrival of his son and daughter with a nod of his head. Devon waited until Kherryn rose from her formal curtsy before making his bow with a brevity designed to cover his lameness. Chairs were placed for them, and as soon as they were seated, Arvech cleared his throat.

"My friends, we have had laid before us this day news of grievous import. Delsidor Bran-Euan Whitfauconer is dead, struck down by the foul hand of an assassin. And we are summoned to Farrowaithe to attend his funeral. . . ."

# FUNERAL IN FARROWAITHE

DEVON, IT WAS DECIDED, WOULD not be attending the funeral offices in Farrowaithe. "At least one member of the family must remain here in Gand," said Arvech, without looking at his son's still face. "If only for the sake of appearances. You need not leave the castle, if you do not choose to do so. Commander Jorvald will be remaining here. And Bertram Du Vanderlay, should you require advice in any official matter that might arise in my absence. . . ."

It had fooled nobody, least of all Devon himself. Kherryn, informed of the proposal, had been too outraged, for once, to keep her anger to herself. "As if you were some poor, driveling idiot, needing a keeper or a nursemaid! He might at least," said Devon's sister furiously, "give you credit for possessing a mind capable of rational thought!"

"Father," said Devon quietly, "is merely desirous of preserving the state of my health." And not even Kherryn could guess whether he was being satiric or not.

The funeral party left Gand early the following morning, following an all-night flurry of preparations on the part of the household staff. They traveled west in caravan as far as Cheswythe, and from there made the barge crossing to Farrowaithe.

Arvech and his daughter, along with their retinue,

were housed, as befitted their rank, in a private manor belonging to one of the city's aldermen. Despite the comfort of their accommodations, Kherryn awoke in a strange bed on the morning of the funeral with a headache and a vague sense of foreboding.

The depression grew stronger as the day wore on. Moving solemnly in her father's wake through the somber preliminary ceremonies of the morning, Kherryn felt the weight of her gown, jet on heavy sable-trimmed silk, like a burden of guilt. At noon they dined in state at the castle, at a table presided over by Fyanor Du Bors, strikingly attired in black damask and leather. Taking her seat among the privileged, Kherryn felt her heaviness of spirit like lead in her light bones.

A dimness seemed to cling to the air of the banquet hall, brooding like a presence over tables and chairs, and tarnishing the light from the candles. Staring at the food on her plate, Kherryn could find no appetite for it. She was relieved when the meal finally came to an end and they were free to seek the open air again.

At four o'clock they made one with the formal procession escorting the Warden's bier down from the castle to the cathedral where a solemn office would be celebrated for the soul of the departed. Riding next to her father near the head of a long column of official mourners, Kherryn kept her eyes ahead on the gathered spires of the basilica, star-finials visible above the gabled roofs of houses and shops.

They turned a corner into a square lined on all sides with the citizenry of Farrowaithe. Beyond, she caught her initial glimpse of the cathedral itself, carved out of stone airy as sea-foam. The wind ruffled the furs at her throat, and she shivered.

In the cathedral yard, green-robed novices stepped forward to take charge of the horses. While the dignitaries were still dismounting, six members of the Guard of Farrowaithe lifted the black-draped corsaint from the flat bed of the caisson and bore it into the narthex, where Baldwyn Vladhallyn, the Arch Mage of East Garillon, stood waiting.

Led by black-robed acolytes holding lighted candles aloft, the procession moved into the nave. At some invisible sign, voices suddenly awoke on all sides, echoing sonorously off the archivolts in somber textures of polyphonic chant. Her ears ringing with the dark undertones racing away beneath the melody, Kherryn was assailed again by a sense of bitter cold.

This time it did not pass. As they reached their appointed place beneath the soaring vertical gulf of the vault, she was shivering almost uncontrollably. She stared at her hand, clamped fast on the thick velvet of her father's sleeve, and was quite unable to control its quivering. Wrist and forearm seemed alive with a force of their own. She swallowed, and pressed her free hand hard against her side as the mages took up their stations about the Lord Warden's coffin.

Fyanor was standing not far from the altar-rail at the side of his widowed sister, a slender shape veiled so heavily that not even the suggestion of her face was discernible to the eye. Gwynmira's gloved hand rested on the shoulder of a slim black-haired boychild of extraordinary beauty. Studying the arrogant delicacy of nose and mouth, the slight tilt to the dark, full-lidded eyes, Kherryn marveled how unlike his half brother Evelake was Gythe Du Bors, shortly to be ratified by consensus of the Great Council as the next Lord Warden of East Garillon.

The Arch Mage lifted his arms in a winged sweep of black cloth and raised up a ringing voice in the words of the invocation: "Oh God the Creator and Sustainer of all mankind, bear witness to our faith this day, preserving us in sorrow as in joy, death as in life, that the works of our hands, and the counsels of our hearts, may be acceptable before you. . . ."

Then amid the lights and shadows, the whole assembly joined with him in stately supplication, voices leaping away toward the vaulting. Wracked with cold, Kherryn surreptitiously lifted her head and cast a searching look around her. As she did so, her eyes came to rest on the lowered profile of Fyanor Du Bors, Seneschal of Ambrothen.

Sharp-featured and clever, framed in its clipped wings of raven-black hair, the seneschal's face contained a brooding capacity for violence. As he bowed his head more deeply over his formally clasped hands, Kherryn was reminded suddenly of some dark bird of prey, stooping over its meat.

The shadow of murder lurked in his downcast eyes and predatory mouth. Staring at him in horrified fascination, Kherryn felt her words of devotion falter on her lips. Her mouth dry as dust, she tried to pray, and found that she could not in the presence of this man who bore about him the secretive air of an undiscovered assassin. . . .

"Amen!"

The sonorous response from the packed congregation sprang toward the cross-beams, fracturing the icy chill of her momentary paralysis. Released, Kherryn gave a small choked sob.

Heads turned in her direction in the newly fallen silence. An admonitory hand laid itself on her arm. She started and raised her eyes to her father's stern face. His look cautioned her not to strain the studied decorum of the occasion.

Even as she acknowledged his unspoken order with her eyes, her heartbeat grew heavier and slower, as if her heart were laboring to force the congealing blood through her veins. Chilled to the marrow, Kherryn closed her eyes on the scene before her. "Death could hardly be colder than this," she thought numbly. "Am I the only one who feels it?"

The funeral liturgy continued, rolling ominously over her in dark waves. Trapped in the bitter isolation of the debilitating cold, Kherryn heard the prayers and the music as mere indiscriminate sound. Dimly aware that she had appearances to maintain at all costs, she roused herself at last from her frozen lethargy, and discovered that the funeral service was coming to a close.

The mages attending the Lord Warden's corsaint had laid aside the velvet pall covering the bier, and had lifted off the coffin-lid so that all present could view the carefully embalmed body, and pay their final respects to the spirit that it once had housed.

All around the packed congregation, men were preparing to move, twitching back cloaks of fur and brocade, shrugging rich doublets into smoother array. Kherryn saw the late Warden's widow and son step forward to the right side of the altar-rail, saw Fyanor follow suit. Her father, standing tall and inflexible at her side, offered her his arm.

Her mind beclouded still with the numbing cold, she stared at it uncomprehendingly for an instant before the significance of his gesture penetrated through the mist of her own cold fear: in token of respect for their rank, she and Arvech were to follow immediately after the Warden's family when the procession formed up to file past the bier.

Kherryn, shuddering in the shadow of shooting columns and dark, intricate carving, realized suddenly that this was the moment she had been dreading: the focal point for the mounting sense of horror that had preyed upon her since the morning.

She had a panic-stricken impulse to hang back. A gloved hand gripped her wrist and she started at the touch. Her eyes flying upward, she encountered again a stern inquiring glance from her father's dark eyes.

It spelled the inevitability of the coming ordeal. Numb with reluctance, she allowed him to tuck her nerveless hand through the crook of his arm and lead her to her place behind the Seneschal of Ambrothen.

The Grand Master of the Order stood at the head of the bier, a silver bowl containing holy water cupped between his palms. On either side of him, the two senior magisters dipped their hands in the water and sprinkled it lightly over the body, while the Master intoned: "Almighty God, whose hand once moved across the waters of the world, and called into being the life of all things—Receive into thy keeping the soul of this thy servant, that renewed in thy grace, he may dwell in thy courts forever. . . ."

It was the signal for the procession to begin. Gythe Du Bors, as heir apparent, took the lead, stepping daintily as he ascended the steps leading up to the bema. His lovely face, with its fair skin and high coloring, framed in raven-black hair, was studiously self-contained as he bent low and kissed his father on the brow in token of farewell. Gwynmira, lifting her veil, did the same. From her place at the foot of the coffin, Kherryn looked in vain for some sign of grief and saw none.

Then Fyanor approached the corpse, and for the second time that day, Kherryn felt her heart leap sickeningly into her throat.

The seneschal's face gave nothing away as he leaned over the body of his dead brother-in-law. Watching him, Kherryn stiffened, her flesh frozen to her bones.

For as Fyanor's shadow fell across the Warden's face, a spot of bright crimson broke suddenly through the snow-white lawn that covered Delsidor's shattered breast.

Too shocked even to scream, she stared aghast as the stain grew before her eyes. Unchecked, it soaked its way through linen, silk, and silverpoint, saturating the embroidered baldric lying in a jeweled line across the dead Warden's chest. The satin lining of the coffin was pulped wet with scarlet.

Kherryn bit down hard upon her lip. The taste of her own blood unlocked the frozen mechanism of voluntary movement. Wrenching herself away, she spun around, wild-eyed with horror, and found herself looking straight into a pair of black merciless eyes beneath the dark sweep of an acolyte's hood.

Pitiless as steel, they bored into her soul, exposing her terror like the white underbelly of a leveret. The impact of that cold stare was as final as a crossbow-bolt. Kherryn gave a small gasping cry and crumpled to the floor.

Her father was the first person to reach her. His face pale and set, he knelt amid the hushed murmurs of concern and inquiry and swept her up off the floor limp as a rag doll in her heavy jet-beaded gown.

A grey-robed magister rushed forward from the corner of the south transept. At the mage's whispered invitation, Arvech delivered his daughter's unconscious form into the other man's waiting arms. The magister turned and faded swiftly toward the nearest exit. Arvech drew himself up and recrossed the floor to resume his place in the broken line.

The line moved forward again as the other seneschals and their families closed ranks smoothly to heal the breach in the ceremonial procession. Raising his head after making his personal obeisance at the bier, Arvech encountered the heavy-lidded gaze of Delsidor's widow.

"I am sorry that your daughter should have been so upset by these proceedings," said the Dowager of Farrowaithe in a douce undervoice. "But then, her nerves have never been very strong. Have they?"

Arvech's hard face yielded nothing. "Not all women have your well-attested strength of purpose and character, milady," he said.

Gwynmira's long lashes flickered, then settled. "I am pleased to see that you have my measure, Lord Arvech. I hope that will make it easier for us to deal with one another in the future."

So saying, she turned away and allowed her brother to escort her back to her place beneath the carved canopy of state to the right of the nave. Following after them, Arvech was left to wonder if perhaps he had just been given a warning.

Gwynmira's enigmatic words were still at the back of

156

his mind an hour later, when he was at last free to see to his daughter's welfare. Leaving the members of his escort waiting in the outer courtyard of the basilica, he went alone to the hospital, situated across a broad swathe of lawn from the cathedral itself.

The preceptor on duty showed him upstairs to a quiet room overlooking the back garden. When the mage knocked at the door, the summons was answered by a tall blue-eyed girl whose thick fair hair framed a somewhat angular face, and whose fashionably cut gown did not quite disguise a hoydenish tendency toward lankiness.

Recognizing Tessa Ekhanghar, daughter of the Marshall of Gand, Arvech's tight mouth eased slightly. "I'm glad someone had the wit to send for you," he said.

The preceptor withdrew, closing the door behind him. Arvech glanced past Tessa toward the small figure lying wrapped in blankets on the narrow hospital bed. "How is she?"

The tone of the question was not especially tender. Tessa's blue eyes sharpened, but her expression remained otherwise neutral. "She's as comfortable as we could make her. The magister who attended her gave her something to put her to sleep. He says," continued Tessa carefully, "that she's suffering from shock."

"Shock?" Arvech's brows contracted. He glared at his daughter's plain-faced companion. "Explain."

"I'm not sure that I can," said Tessa uncomfortably. "When you and she followed the Du Bors family up to the funeral bier, she apparently . . . saw something."

"Saw what?" inquired Arvech. His face had not softened.

"We don't know yet," said Tessa. "She was so agitated that the magister here thought it best not to press her to talk about it for the time being. He hopes to get the full story later, when she's calmer."

Arvech considered this. "I hope he will succeed in bringing her to her senses," he said, after a moment's silence. "I have no wish to be unkind, but I was at her side throughout the whole of the ceremony and saw nothing —nothing whatsoever—to provoke such an extreme display of nervous sensibility."

"My lord, are you suggesting," said Tessa dubiously, "that she merely *imagined* what frightened her so?"

"It is not entirely unlikely," said Kherryn's father, with a second glance at his daughter's sleeping form. "She has always been overly fanciful."

Tessa set her jaw. "Never before, my lord, to this degree."

"That's just the point," said Kherryn's father sharply. "If my daughter cannot control her fancies, it's high time she outgrew them."

Tessa wanted to tell him that he was gravely mistaken in both his children—his son as well as his daughter. Prevented from doing so by considerations of age and rank, she stared woodenly past him and said nothing at all. After a moment, Arvech squared his shoulders. "How long will it be before she wakes again?"

"Some hours yet," said Tessa. She added, "The magister here would like to keep her overnight for observation."

"Very well. As long as he understands that she must be present tomorrow morning for the initial meeting of the Great Council," said Arvech.

"I'll tell him," said Tessa, a trifle shortly. "My lord."

If her friend's father noticed that the honorific was a bit belated, he chose to ignore it. "I would like you to stay with her," said the Seneschal of Gand.

"Yes, my lord," said Tessa. "I'll tell him that, too. . . ."

# FUEL FOR THE FIRE

WHATEVER TESSA EKHANGHAR MIGHT LACK in beauty, she more than made up for in common sense. Satisfied that he could rely on the tall girl's good judgment, Ulbrecht Rathmuir left her to keep watch by Kherryn Du Penfallon's bedside while he himself returned to the cathedral.

The fact that Ulbrecht, rather than a member of the Farrowaithe chapter, was looking after Arvech Du Penfallon's daughter was not quite accidental. Ulbrecht had first glimpsed Kherryn from the eminence of the cathedral's south gallery, where he had been sitting among his fellow delegates from St. Welleran's in Ambrothen. The numb look of suffering on the girl's small white face had roused his immediate concern, and he had kept a wary eye on her throughout the funeral service.

Already on the alert, he had seen the crisis coming, and had rushed from his seat, pushing his way to the fore among the people gathered on the ground floor. She had been running straight for him when she collapsed.

In retrospect, Ulbrecht realized that he had felt drawn to the girl from the very outset—almost as if she had been projecting an unconscious cry for help. While it was true that the Order made no provision for testing or training women in spiritual gifts, Ulbrecht saw no reason to dis-

159

count the possibility that such undiscovered talents might exist. Certainly Kherryn Du Penfallon showed signs of possessing such an untutored gift for extrasensory perception and communication.

Which was why Ulbrecht felt compelled to return to the scene of the late Warden's funeral in the hope of picking up some clue as to what might have awakened her powers of vision. Whatever that vision had been, Ulbrecht sensed that she had been its unwilling recipient—a fact which gave him cause for concern. If Kherryn were in fact "sighted," she was going to need guidance. Otherwise, there was danger that she might become the tormented victim of her own impressionability.

Dusk was gathering cloudily over the cathedral's twin bell towers as the magister from Ambrothen mounted the steps leading to the great west porch of the basilica. Turning back on the threshold, he saw there was a ground-fog rising. The sight of the mist reminded Ulbrecht forcibly of the night back in Ambrothen when he had first been summoned to attend the guardsman Cergil Ap Cymric.

Cergil's subsequent disappearance from St. Welleran's Hospital three nights later remained an unsolved mystery. When the mages of St. Welleran's failed to find him, the Grand Master—overruling Ulbrecht's protests—had called in the Ambrothen Watch to assist in the search. When their efforts likewise failed, Ulbrecht was grimly left to assume the worst.

But there was nothing he could do about that now. Pacing slowly up the deserted nave, passing from one dimly lit column to the next, Ulbrecht returned his attention to the problem of Kherryn Du Penfallon. He advanced to the head of the great aisle, then stopped. Before him lay the vault where Delsidor Whitfauconer had lain in state; behind him and on either hand lay deep caverns of shadow.

He scowled, thinking back over the chain of events that had preceded Kherryn's sudden flight. The girl's anxiety, he recalled, had only become acute at the start of the farewell processional past the dead Warden's bier. She had been following only a few paces behind the Du Bors. Prompted by a gut feeling that this fact was somehow significant, Ulbrecht started to reach for his magestone.

In the same instant, a sinewy arm whipped itself tight about his throat from behind.

Ulbrecht's startled exclamation was stifled by a second hand, armed with a muffling pad of thick cloth. Even as the mage from Ambrothen struggled against his assailant's imprisoning grip, a voice breathed harshly in his ear, "Quiet! I don't want to hurt you, I just want to ask you a question."

Ulbrecht stopped threshing and nodded. The fingers clamped across his mouth slackened cautiously. When the mage made no attempt to call out, his attacker dropped his hand altogether and said in the same husky undertone, "You're the magister who's looking after Kherryn Du Penfallon. Aren't you?"

Ulbrecht made a move to look around. "Don't look back!" hissed his assailant. "Yes or no?"

"Yes. I'm Ulbrecht Rathmuir," Ulbrecht acknowledged in a whisper. "What's this all about?"

"You don't need to know," said his assailant curtly. "I want you to arrange for me to see Lord Arvech."

ular request. Groping by infinitesimal degrees is magestone, Ulbrecht murmured, "What makes ink I wield any particular influence with His Lord-

"His daughter is in your care. He'll receive you any time of the day or night. A word from you—"

"Is out of the question," said Ulbrecht firmly, "until I know who you are and what you want."

His fingers encountered the vital smoothness of his magestone. The other man said, "My name isn't important. What matters is that I've got information that I must pass to Lord Arvech before the Great Council convenes in the morning."

The tone in the man's voice carried the throb of

genuine urgency. Ulbrecht, however, was no longer interested in vocal nuances: the impressions he was gathering with the aid of the Magia had already given him the other man's identity.

He grinned broadly into the darkness. "It's all right, Cergil," he said. "I'll be happy to do what I can to help you."

The young guardsman was betrayed into an audible gasp. The hand that still gripped Ulbrecht's shoulder tightened in suspicion. "You can't possibly know who I am," he growled. "We've never met."

"Oh, yes we have—in a manner of speaking," said Ulbrecht. "The reason you don't remember is that you were at death's door from sesquina poisoning at the time."

A stunned silence greeted this announcement. "I'm the mage who looked after you the night it happened," continued Ulbrecht. Then caught his breath as the other man seized him hard and spun him around.

"Are you the one who found me?" demanded Cergil hoarsely.

He was muffled in a tattered cloak, but Ulbrecht caught the intense gleam of his searching eyes beneath the fall of his hood. "No," said the magister from Ambrothen. "You were found by one of the late Warden's friend, man named Gudmar Ap Gorvald."

A small shiver seemed to grip the former guardsm. "Was anyone else found with me?" he asked.

"Your sergeant—dead," said Ulbrecht quietly. "There was no trace of anyone else in the room." He added carefully, "Gudmar, however, reported that he had found three wineglasses on the table, one of them apparently untouched."

"Untouched!" Cergil shook back his cowl, his gaze ranging intently over Ulbrecht's face. When the mage steadfastly withstood his scrutiny, the young guardsman drew back. "Then there's a chance he might still be alive," he breathed, as if to himself.

All Ulbrecht's unsubstantiated suspicions were clamoring for enlightenment. "Who?" he inquired sharply.

"Evelake Whitfauconer," said the former Farrowaithe Guardsman. "My sergeant and I found him wandering about in the grounds of Ambrothen Castle, the night his father was murdered. He was ragged and dirty, and out of his mind. He didn't seem to know who he was—"

Ulbrecht's friend Forgoyle had believed the bondservant Rhan Hallender to be Delsidor's lost heir. "Did he give himself any name?" asked Ulbrecht.

"He wouldn't talk to us at all," said Cergil. "That was when we sent for Lady Gwynmira Du Bors. She confirmed her stepson's identity, and insisted that he should be provided with some refreshments—" He swallowed hard and jammed the knuckles of one hand hard against his mouth.

"So," said Ulbrecht with grim finality, "she *was* the one who brought you that poisoned wine."

Cergil started. "You know? *Have known?*" His chest heaved. "For God's sake, why haven't you *done* something?"

"Because I only discovered that fact through Orison when I was trying to succor you," said Ulbrecht shortly. "And since I am not an inquisitor, I had no right to hurl accusations. For all I knew, I could have been wrong."

He shook his head. "I was waiting to see what you would have to say when you regained consciousness. But you didn't give me the chance to test my findings."

His eyes sought Cergil's. "Why *did* you flee St. Welleran's? You were safe there."

Cergil's thin mouth twisted. "I didn't know that. My impression at the time was that someone wanted me dead. The poison must have addled my wits: it wasn't until several days later that all the facts began to come coherently together."

"You had wits enough about you to give all of us the slip," said Ulbrecht dryly. "I'd dearly love to know how you managed it."

A brief rueful smile crossed the younger man's lean

face. "Luck must have had a lot to do with it. When I staggered out of my room, there wasn't anyone about. I eventually found a door, and once outside, I just made for the darkest, quietest corner of the grounds. The perimeter wall, fortunately, had recently suffered some damage: I found a place where the stones had given way enough to let me pass through without too much effort."

A small reminiscent twinkle appeared in his hollow eyes. "The banks of the stream outside the abbey walls appear to be a popular gathering place for transients. One of the beggars was only too glad to change clothes with me. A couple of others—taking me for a fellow drunk, I suppose—bore me off with them to a derelict timberyard on the south edge of town. A regular gypsy campground, if the local Watch only knew about it. I spent the next two nights lying flat on my back, being clucked over by a frowsy old beldame—God bless her!—who thought it was a great shame that a man my age should be so far gone in his vices."

He sighed. "I let on I was on the run from the law for thievery—showed off my signet ring, and said I was trying to get out of the city before the gullcatchers could apprehend me. One of the old woman's mates put me in touch with a grimy villain who runs a garbage-scow up and down the length of the Ambrothen waterfront. For the price of my ring, he ferried me a mile up the coast and turned me out on my own, with nothing but these rags on my back. Since then, I've been making my way home by the long road, trying to keep out of sight until I could seek the protection of someone powerful enough to make good use of my information—someone like Arvech Du Penfallon."

"The Order would have protected you," said Ulbrecht.

"True," agreed Cergil. "But not even the Arch Mage himself can bring criminal charges against a peer of the realm in a court of law—"

A sudden hollow rattle of a heavy door-latch, carrying

resonantly down the great length of the nave at their backs, caused both men to leap for the shadows on the dark side of the nearest pillar. "Someone's coming! They mustn't find me here in your company," hissed Cergil. "I'll meet you outside the gates in a quarter of an hour."

"Wait! How are you going to—"

"Just be there!" Cergil said through gritted teeth, and shot off into the greater darkness of the north transept a heartbeat before the great west portal swung open in a blaze of lamplight.

"Who goes there?" called a voice from the center of the light.

Incisively clear, the voice was also familiar. Ulbrecht exhaled noisily and stepped out into full view. "It's me —Ulbrecht Rathmuir, Your Grace," he called back to the High Inquisitor of Farrowaithe.

There was a slight pause. *"Ulbrecht?"* said Earlis Ap Eadric. The light began to move, bobbing up and down in time with the Inquisitor's swift stride as he started up the aisle. Ulbrecht hurried forward to meet his superior halfway. "Is anything wrong, Your Grace?" he asked anxiously, as they came together.

Gazing at him, Earlis produced a wry smile. "I begin to think not," he said. "How long have you been here, Magister?"

Ulbrecht suddenly became aware that the Inquisitor's ubiquitous acolyte was standing among the shadows several paces behind his superior. "I've been here for about half an hour, Your Grace," he said. "Why?"

The Inquisitor's ascetic face softened. "Rothyl came to me to report that he had seen someone slip inside the cathedral a short while ago. In view of what happened in your own home chapter not so long ago, I thought it advisable to investigate. I take it you've heard nothing amiss since you came in?"

"No, Your Grace. Nothing amiss."

"You relieve my mind of care," said Earlis. "Though

perhaps it wouldn't hurt to have some of the lay brethren take a look around the grounds. We can't be too careful in these dark days—don't you agree . . .?"

Ulbrecht returned to the hospital in Earlis's company, leaving Rothyl behind in the cathedral. After parting from the High Inquisitor, Ulbrecht looked in briefly on his patient. Upon receiving Tessa's assurance that Kherryn was sleeping comfortably, he departed to keep his rendezvous with Cergil.

He was of two minds whether or not to confide in An'char Maeldrake before leaving the abbey. Strictly speaking, he was bound by the Rule of the Order to seek the Grand Master's permission for what he planned to do. But time was already running short, and secrecy was of the essence. Ulbrecht breathed a short mental apology to his superior and ducked out through the abbey gate into the street outside.

Cergil was waiting for him in a dark doorway halfway along the foggy thoroughfare. "How did you get out of the cathedral without being spotted?" asked Ulbrecht breathlessly.

"I climbed out onto the roof through one of the clerestory windows, then slid down a drainpipe," said Cergil. "Come on. . . ."

Arvech Du Penfallon had accepted an invitation from the Master of Farrowaithe's League of Goldsmiths to take up residence in the guild-master's opulent townhouse for the duration of the Council meeting. Word concerning Kherryn Du Penfallon's illness had apparently been circulating discreetly among the servants, for the porter who opened the door in response to Ulbrecht's summons took in at a glance the grey robes of a magister-hospitaller and promptly ushered both Ulbrecht and Cergil inside.

The goldsmith's steward conducted them upstairs to a parlor at the back of the house which the Seneschal of Gand was using as a study. Arvech Du Penfallon was engaged in reading through a sheaf of dispatches, but he

THE GAUNTLET OF MALICE

raked them aside as Ulbrecht and Cergil entered the room. "This is an unlooked-for visit," said Arvech, disregarding Cergil for the moment. "Has there been some deterioration of my daughter's condition?"

"Forgive me—your daughter is resting quietly," said Ulbrecht. "My errand here has to do with a more . . . political matter."

Arvech's stern brow clouded. "A *political* matter? It is too early to discuss politics," he said. "It would be more seemly of you, Magister, to let such concerns wait until the Council session opens in the morning."

"Pardon me, my lord, but this concern cannot wait." Shouldering past Ulbrecht, Cergil planted himself squarely in front of the seneschal. "I have information to impart to you which cannot fail to have direct bearing on the decisions to be reached by the Council."

Arvech eyed his bristling visitor with chilly detachment. "Magister Ulbrecht, perhaps you would be so good as to introduce me to this importunate companion of yours?"

Ulbrecht clamped a restraining hand on Cergil's shoulder. "Certainly, my lord. This is Cergil Ap Cymric, formerly a lieutenant in the Farrowaithe Guards. He was a member of Delsidor Whitfauconer's escort during the late Warden's visit to Ambrothen. His account of himself and his doings since the night of Lord Delsidor's death should interest you."

He drew himself up. "As I am in a position to corroborate certain features of his story, I have taken it upon myself to act as his sponsor in these present circumstances, and to vouch for his integrity. I hope you will not deny him a fair hearing?"

Arvech Du Penfallon considered the request. "Very well, Magister," he said, then shifted his gaze back to Cergil. "Lieutenant, you may proceed."

The Seneschal of Gand listened at first with an air of sufferance as Cergil began his tale, but when the former lieutenant recounted how he had found Evelake Whitfauconer, Arvech's attitude underwent an abrupt transformation. "This is a most extraordinary claim you are making," he said sternly, leaning forward in his chair. "I hope you are prepared to defend it."

Cergil traded glances with Ulbrecht. "My lord, I was well acquainted with Evelake Whitfauconer. I served for over a year among the members of his personal escort before he was sent away to learn statesmanship and soldiering under your tutelage. This being so, I can swear with certainty that the boy my sergeant and I found in the gardens of Ambrothen Castle was none other than he —though *how* he came to be there I do not know."

"Is this sergeant available for testimony?" asked Arvech.

Cergil's jaw tightened. "No, my lord. Sergeant Runlaf is dead. He was murdered so that the world should not learn of our discovery."

*"Murdered?"* Arvech's heavy brows climbed up a quarter inch.

Cergil's gaze remained unflinching. "Yes, my lord. By Lady Gwynmira Du Bors. . . ."

At the end of a further twenty minutes, the Seneschal of Gand was in possession not only of the remainder of Cergil's story, but of all the circumstantial evidence Ulbrecht had been able to assemble in support of that story. "Gentlemen, I wish I could dismiss this tale of yours as a malicious fable," said Arvech Du Penfallon gravely. "But at the very least, the situation calls for a full investigation."

"Then you are prepared to act upon my testimony?" asked Cergil eagerly.

"I am prepared to take action of some kind," said Arvech. "The Du Bors family has always cherished extravagant ambitions. This time they have overstepped their bounds."

He sighed. "I must give some further thought to the

matter. Magister Ulbrecht, may I suggest that you return to the hospital before you are missed?"

"Of course, my lord," said Ulbrecht. "Should Cergil accompany me?"

"No," said Arvech, and turned directly to Cergil. "I think it would be best if you were to remain here, until such time as you may be called to give testimony in public. . . ."

# DISSENSION IN THE COUNCIL

On the morning following Delsidor's funeral, the delegates of the three estates of East Garillon —churchmen, burgesses, and lords, gathered on Kirkwell Common to attend the meeting of the Great Council under a clear, pale autumn sky.

It was a cool morning, with a hint of frost in the air. In the distance, to the north, beyond the fields belonging to the abbey demesne, the trees were already tipped with orichalc-gold. Near at hand, by contrast, the Common was dominated by the presence of a large amphitheater, newly built for the occasion.

Constructed of planks and roofed with bunting, the amphitheater took the form of a pentagram, with two sets of double-jointed tiers of benches flanking a raised platform. In the center of the platform, on an elevated dais backed by blue silk, sat Gwynmira Du Bors and her son Gythe.

To the right of the dais were seated the seneschals of the four sister-cities of Farrowaithe. To the left were seated the five mayors of the Five Cities in the ceremonial robes of their office. At the foot of the steps leading up to the dais two other chairs had been placed. The first of these chairs, canopied with red velvet, belonged to Baldwyn Vladhallyn, Arch Mage of East Garillon. The second was

170

occupied by the Inquisitor of Farrowaithe, Earlis Ap Eadric.

Surveying the scene from a privileged position among the higher peers of the realm, Kherryn Du Penfallon wished she could have evaded responsibility and stayed away from the Council. The general atmosphere of excitement and building contention would have been sufficiently wearing by itself, without the speculative murmurs and curious glances that seemed to follow everywhere she went. Now that she was finally in her place, she was aware of a dull headache and a dim ringing in her ears—almost as if she had been physically buffeted on her way to her seat.

Warm fingers closed gently around her cold hand. "Are you feeling all right?" asked Ulbrecht Rathmuir. "You're looking pale."

Kherryn smiled wanly over at him, grateful for his quick discernment. "I'll be all right in a minute," she said. "Large crowds of people always seem a bit overpowering to me."

It was comforting to be able to admit as much. The magister from Ambrothen nodded sympathetically. "I know what you mean. It's a little like hearing all the keys on a spinet being played simultaneously: you tire yourself out trying to make sense out of so many different sounds—"

A stir among the spectators lower down interrupted him before he could pursue his analogy any further. Sitting tall and straight-backed in the seat next to Kherryn's, Tessa Ekhanghar let fall the mangled piece of embroidery she had been worrying at for the last quarter of an hour. "No more time for philosophizing," remarked Jorvald Ekhanghar's daughter. "His Holiness is about to begin the invocation."

The cloud of depression which Ulbrecht's words had served to lighten settled in again over Kherryn's thoughts like a funeral pall. As the Arch Mage of East Garillon raised his hands in reverence, she bowed her head with those around her, but it was without conviction that she waited for the prayer to begin.

The Arch Mage's still-powerful voice carried effortlessly across the stands, endowing the formal words of the invocation with a rich grandeur of intonation.

"Guide us, oh God, in the ways of justice and of truth, that we, being mindful of the trust reposed in us, may put aside all strife and covetousness, all malice and deceit, and unfeignedly seek the common good, to the renewed peace and prosperity of this realm, and to Your greater glory. . . ."

Listening to him, Kherryn thought wearily, He sounds as if he actually believes in what he is saying. Once her father had said in her hearing, "Only fools and dotards believe in God. The only real force in the world is the human appetite for power. . . ." Studying the faces of the people seated on the platform below, Kherryn found herself more than a little inclined to agree with him.

They were all of them predators, of one kind or another. The beautiful boy, exquisitely dressed, who sat next to his mother in a chair of state that by rights should have been occupied by someone else. Gwynmira herself, splendid as a leopardess, with the subtle glitter of worldliness lending a vitreous edge to her splendor. Fyanor of Ambrothen, with the hands and eyes of an assassin. What was the phrase the Pernathan scholar Ibek Al Ribekr had used? "An arena of jackels" . . . ?

Kherryn's dark eyes moved away from Fyanor and lighted upon Earlis Ap Eadric, Inquisitor of Farrowaithe. The man was reputedly a saint, kissed (said his devout admirers) with celestial fire, but Kherryn looked in vain for outward signs of transfiguration. Rather, there was an impenetrability about his person that rendered it wholly unreadable to her probing gaze.

For some reason, that in itself was more disquieting than any naked evidence of personal rapacity. Kherryn glanced obliquely at Ulbrecht, wondering if he had any reservations concerning the High Inquisitor of Farrowaithe. Ulbrecht, however, appeared to be genuinely immersed in his devotions. Kherryn withdrew her gaze as the invocation came to a close in a sonorous responsal amen.

At a sign from Baldwyn, the members of the Council and their auxiliaries took seats in a subdued rustle of expensive fabrics. Baldwyn himself remained standing, his veined hands lightly clasped before him on the lectern from which he had delivered the opening prayer.

Then, as the capped and bonneted heads dropped into place and the rustling faded into attentive silence, he drew himself erect, his eyes roving the watchful ranks of churchmen, burgesses, and nobles as he greeted the assembly with the traditional blessing, making the sign of the six-rayed star in the air with his right hand.

"All grace and peace be unto you this day, in the name of the Lord our God."

"And unto you His favor." Joining in with the rest of the assembly, Kherryn leaned forward to get a better view of the elderly man who now addressed himself to the secular matters at hand.

"Good masters, good brethren, and good my lords, we are met here today for two purposes. To recognize by law and custom the new Lord Warden of East Garillon: in the continued absence, and, it must now be presumed, the death of Evelake Whitfauconer, we are agreed that the younger son, in the person of Gythe Du Bors Whitfauconer, shall be chosen as Lord Warden. Our second task is to choose a regent to rule in his name until he himself shall attain the age of manhood.

"You are all familiar now with the circumstances surrounding the tragic and unforeseen death of Delsidor Bran-Euan Whitfauconer, and it is perhaps better that we do not recite the details of that event again out of respect for Delsidor himself, and in charity for those who were close to him. Rather do I suggest that the time has come to look forward instead of backward, to plan for the future instead of grieving for the past.

"These are not easy tasks that we undertake. But if we seek with all our hearts to dispatch the business of this council with honesty, decency, and piety, we shall give no cause for those who come after us to reproach us for our actions. To that end, then, I present to you Gythe Du Bors Whitfauconer and pray earnestly that you will accord him the same loyalty and honor that you but lately paid to his father."

He stepped aside from the lectern, arm outstretched from the shoulder in a sweeping gesture that both singled out and summoned the boy seated on the dais behind him. As all eyes turned to him, Gythe rose unhurriedly from his chair and walked to the head of a shallow series of steps leading down from the dais to the floor.

Watching him, Kherryn marveled at his self-possession. About Gythe Du Bors there was none of the awkwardness or hesitancy natural to a boy his age. The cool, faintly arrogant air of composure was certainly out of the ordinary. How many of the voting members of the Council would be impressed by it remained to be seen.

Gythe descended the steps and approached the lectern. Dressed in velvet and vair, his blue doublet stiff with embroidery of silver and gold, he glittered like an icon in the sunlight.

Blue and gold, sable and umber and cream. For Kherryn the colors conjured up the sudden recollection of a visit paid to Whitfauconer Manor one morning in May: long grass and flowering orchards, the golden light between the branches bright with a thousand thousand butterflies. . . .

And sitting at the foot of one gnarled pear tree a small black-haired boy in blue velvet who laughed to himself as he plucked the silken wings from the living butterfly he had captured.

Searching Gythe's handsome face now, Kherryn discovered, intact beneath the glowing skin and flawless bones, the same subtle stamp of cruelty.

What was new was the disciplined grace of manner: like his mother, Gythe could exercise at will a dazzling charm. Lifting his face to the light, confident in his personal beauty, he met the impact of a thousand eyes with a practiced smile and embarked upon the brief address demanded of him by the occasion.

"My lords, my friends, I welcome you in the place of my father and express my gratitude for the services that you rendered him while he lived. As his appointed heir, I make this promise: that I will bear in mind all those who have merited my attention through their deeds, and will reward all of them according to their actions insofar as I have power to do so."

Gracefully modest, the speech was delivered with a tutored precision of phrasing and emphasis. As the solemn applause broke out all around her, Kherryn wondered if she were perhaps the only one in all the crowd to perceive the veiled threat that lurked beneath the elegant language of Gythe Du Bors's promise.

When Gythe left the lectern, it was Fyanor who took his place. His arrival was attended by a polite rustle of movement as the delegates took advantage of the breathing space to ease muscles cramped from tension.

Like his nephew, Fyanor was regally attired, with rubies large as peppercorns stippling his collar and the band of his velvet cap. The visual effect was imposing, but when he spoke, his words were more modest than his clothes.

"Good members of this meeting, I call upon you now to recall the oaths of fealty which you swore to Delsidor Whitfauconer when, at the last convening of the Council, all of us renewed the promises made at his investiture: to render to him all traditional rights, dignities, and services, and to uphold him in his office against all contenders and traitors for as long as his life lasted.

"What I ask now as the Lady Gwynmira's proxy is that the members of this Council take upon themselves as their first duty the act of pledging their individual and familial loyalty to the person of Gythe Du Bors Whitfauconer, thus formally acknowledging him as his father's successor."

"My Lord Seneschal of Ambrothen!" It was Arvech Du Penfallon who spoke, standing tall and broad beneath the green and gold regalia of his city and his family.

From his vantage point on the platform, Fyanor drew himself up to his full height and bent his gaze upon the man who had hailed him. "Yes, Lord Arvech?"

"I wish to propose an amendment," said the Seneschal of Gand.

His deep voice carried a hint of challenge. A whispered undercurrent of surprise passed through the ranks of those present. "It is now more than five months since we first grieved for the disappearance of Evelake Whitfauconer," continued Arvech. "I point out that while we do not know if he yet lives, we have no conclusive proof that he is dead. While this sad mystery remains as yet unresolved, in all decency I suggest that His Holiness administer the oath of fealty as prescribed by custom, but omit specific mention of Gythe Du Bors by name. That way we will all hold ourselves bound in loyalty to the principle embodied in the office, rather than to the individual who holds it."

The beautiful boy who was their acknowledged Warden-to-be stiffened in his chair, his face betraying an imperious flash of anger. Gwynmira's control was better, Kherryn noticed. She laid a restraining hand on her son's arm and turned her widened eyes upon her brother.

Fyanor, however, was not prepared to argue the point to the detriment of the favorable impression his family had been able to secure so far. "You will pardon me, Lord Arvech, if I find your proposition a trifle precious," said the Seneschal of Ambrothen. "Nevertheless, I will not dispute your right to make it. Let a vote be taken by show of hands."

His gaze swept the assembly. "Will all those in favor of Lord Arvech's proposal please give their endorsement?"

The majority was not overwhelming—one hundred and twenty-one to seventy-nine in favor of the proposal—but it sufficed to indicate the cautious mood of the Council. The outcome of the vote having been enrolled into the account of the day's transactions by Baldwyn's clerk, Arvech Du Penfallon was the first to take the oath in its amended form.

"I, Arvech Du Penfallon, Lord of Penfallon, Seneschal of Gand, do hereby pledge myself the loyal adherent to the Lord Warden of East Garillon, signifying by this pledge that I shall support him both in peace and in war, aid his friends and thwart his enemies, render unto him the strength of my arm and of my council, and do all such good service as he may require of me for as long as we both shall live. . . ."

The sun was halfway to the western horizon by the time all the other voting members of the Council had taken the oath. As the last of the sheriffs rose from his knees and returned to his place, Baldwyn again came forward to speak from the lectern.

"Members of the Council, we have duly recognized Gythe Du Bors Whitfauconer as the presumptive Lord Warden of East Garillon. However, since it will be three years before he attains the age of responsibility, it remains for us now to elect from among the ranking members of this assembly one man to serve as regent during that three-year interim. I call upon you now to submit the names of those men you wish to designate as candidates for this office."

The pause that followed was a mere formality: the various factions within the Council had already determined their choices days ahead of time and were merely awaiting the appropriate moment to send their spokesmen forward. Since custom dictated that members of the baronage should take precedence over members of the burgesses, no one stirred until Fyanor Du Bors rose again from his seat and came forward to address the full assembly.

The westering sun flooded the front of the dais. Standing in its warm aureole, Fyanor paused briefly and smiled before delivering the statement they were all expecting to hear.

"My lords, and members of the Council—the office of regent is no light burden to lay upon any single individual. Yet it is our privilege to do so, according to the dictates of our consciences, choosing as well as we may for the benefit of the realm."

His gaze encompassed all who listened. "Among the qualities we should be seeking in the individual of our choice are strength of mind and firmness of principle, the ability to make decisions, and the will to act upon them. But we must also bear in mind that a regent should also enjoy the trust and respect of the young ruler it will be his responsibility to guide and protect. To this end, therefore, I would like to nominate Lady Gwynmira Du Bors Whitfauconer to the office of Regent of East Garillon. If any man have cause to consider her unfit to stand for the office to which she has been designated, let that man speak now and acquaint us with the reasons grounding his objection."

Since that was a mere formality, no one really anticipated a response to Fyanor's formal challenge. And for that reason, a large majority of the members of the Great Council were taken sharply aback a moment later when the Seneschal of Gand got to his feet and announced in a voice imbued with the penetrating power of a crossbow bolt, "I, Arvech Du Penfallon, do hereby register a complaint against Gwynmira Du Bors, and do demand that she be removed as a contender for the office of regent on the grounds of criminal wrong-doing."

# DENUNCIATION AND DENIAL

THE ACCUSATION PROMPTED A GASPING outcry of surprise and bewilderment from all parts of the assembly. In the aftershock of collective incredulity, a stunned silence fell, like an undermined wall collapsing. While a number of knights, clerics, and burghers were still recovering their breath, Gwynmira rose from her chair. Her dark eyes glittering like marcasites, she turned to face her accuser.

"This comes as a surprise to all of us, Lord Arvech," she said, the temperence of her tone belied by the whiteness of her lips. "I was not aware that you, of all people, held any grievance against me."

"You misconstrue me," said Arvech coldly. "The issue here is not a matter of private grievance, but of public justice. On behalf of the citizens of East Garillon, I hereby charge you with murder, attempted murder, and treason."

If Arvech's previous announcement had silenced the assembly, this bald declaration provoked a storm of astonishment and protest. His voice stretched to the limits of oratory, Baldwyn Vladhallyn called for order. As the clamor reluctantly began to subside, Gythe Du Bors leaped from his seat. Turning on Arvech, he showed small teeth like a vixen. "How *dare* you?" he spat. "How dare you impugn my mother's honor in this vile fashion?"

"Peace, my lord." Fyanor laid a hand on his nephew's bristling shoulder. His gaze restrained Gwynmira as well.

"Let Lord Arvech speak. No doubt he is prepared to justify himself."

The words were spoken with an incisive clarity that was itself a challenge. "I, for one," continued Fyanor Du Bors, "would be very much interested to learn who it is that the Lady Gwynmira is supposed to have murdered."

Arvech, for his part, was sternly unmoved. "So you shall," he said. "Out of the mouth of one of her intended victims."

The ranks of the assembly surged and murmured like the tide at flux. "So you propose to cite a witness?" said Fyanor icily. "I hope his authority is unimpeachable."

"His birthright, no less than his record of service, is above reproach," said Arvech steadily. "He was formerly a member of the Farrowaithe Guards—until he became an obstacle in whatever game of intrigue you and the Lady Gwynmira have been playing. His name is Cergil Ap Cymric."

Gwynmira started at the name. "What cruel foolery is this?" she demanded, her voice shrill with anger. "Cergil Ap Cymric is dead. He died in Ambrothen, the same night my husband was murdered!"

"That, my lady, is what you were led to believe," said Arvech coldly. "For reasons which Cergil is prepared to disclose before this gathered assembly."

"No doubt," said Gwynmira with brittle scorn. In a swift, feline movement, she darted past her brother and halted an arm's length away from the Seneschal of Gand. "I always knew you were a man of ambition," continued the Dowager of Farrowaithe, "but I never suspected that you would stoop to employ subterfuges better suited to a rebel or a spy."

She threw back her head. "If you aspire yourself to the office of regent, do so according to the methods of honest men, and do not pollute this occasion with the substance of lies!"

On that, Baldwyn Vladhallyn moved to interpose himself between them. "This has gone far enough!" he said sternly. "I cannot and will not allow this unseemly dispute to continue at the expense of the decorum of this assembly."

He drew himself up, his deep eyes flashing, his voice carrying to the farthest edges of the crowd. "A charge has been raised, and in the right interests of justice to all concerned, cannot now be dismissed without examination. I therefore declare this assembly in recession until further notice."

He gestured to his right and to his left. "During this time, I invite the two contending parties to confer without prejudice in my hearing. Lord Arvech, you will have your witness summoned to present his testimony under the auspices of the Inquisitor of Farrowaithe. Lady Gwynmira, when you and your brother have heard the particular substance of the charges against you, you shall be given ample opportunity to offer your response."

He held the assembly a moment longer with his gaze. "If the two disputants cannot resolve the matter between them with justice, then the issue must be referred to the High Court of the realm. Until then, I call the members of this council to conduct no further business, but hold themselves in readiness."

"Your Holiness, may I speak?" Arvech's deep voice rang harsh as an iron bell. Baldwyn searched the seneschal's eyes, then gravely nodded his assent.

Arvech turned to the Council at large. "I will not keep you long," he said. "But so that you may be relieved of any uncertainty concerning my motives, I now renounce —publicly and for the record—any claim I might have had to the Regency of East Garillon. I invite my opponents to do the same."

"And thereby court a tacit assumption of guilt? No," said Gwynmira Du Bors. "You shall not have your will so easily as that. Bring on your witness, and we shall see then who has cause to be shamed!"

She stepped forward to take her brother's arm, and together they turned to leave the dais. As Gythe moved to follow them, Arvech looked stonily after him. Then, at the touch of Baldwyn's hand on his sleeve, he too made for the steps.

Holding her hands tightly clenched in her lap, Tessa glanced aside at Kherryn. The younger girl seemed deaf to the murmurs buffeting round them like storm winds rising. Bending down, she whispered into Kherryn's ear, "What does your father think he's doing?"

Kherryn made no reply. Isolated in the midst of rampant speculation, she sat upright as a bolt of brocade and watched the principal actors in the drama file past.

Gythe was plucking angrily at the hilt of his ceremonial dagger. Gwynmira retained the imperial calm of a statue in alabaster, but there was violence lurking in her chatoyant eyes. Fyanor also carried himself proudly. With his sharp profile and predatory eyes, he bore the aspect of an eagle. Or a kite.

Kherryn shuddered and wrenched her eyes away. Her refocused gaze fell abruptly on the figure of her father.

Or rather, upon the blurred outline in the center of her vision where she knew her father to be. Squinting slightly, Kherryn tried to blink away the film that seemed to be obstructing her sight, but the image before her remained indistinct and smudged, like a chalk drawing spoiled by incautious handling.

Rubbing her eyes, she glanced again at Fyanor. Details sharp-cut as crystal leapt to her perception: the studs on his collar, the smoldering unease in his dark eyes.

She returned her gaze to the dais. All there was acutely discernible: the carving on the arms of the chairs, the dark lines in the floor to show where the planks had been laid side by side. Amid all this clarity, her father's form remained peculiarly insubstantial to her eyes. He looked misty, almost like a ghost of himself.

A ghost!

The significance of her own analogy struck her like a physical blow. Her throat closed up, trapping the breath in her lungs. He's in some mortal danger! she thought wildly. And with that thought, another image sprang unbidden to mind:

The image of a man walking blindfolded toward the edge of a precipice. . . .

"He doesn't realize he's about to place his very life in peril," she thought. "I've got to warn him to take care!"

She rose shakily to her feet. As she left her seat, both Tessa and Ulbrecht started and made moves to forestall her. "Kherryn, what's the matter?" the mage called after her. "Where are you going?"

Kherryn did not answer. Pushing past Tessa, she hopped down into the stepped aisle that descended from the gallery to the ground. Tessa and Ulbrecht sprang after her. "Kherryn, wait!" cried the marshall's daughter.

Kherryn was already making her way single-mindedly toward the exit from the gallery. Even as Tessa and Ulbrecht plunged down the steps in an attempt to catch up with her, a liveried herald moved to intercept the seneschal's daughter. Kherryn came to a quivering halt, the color hectically ablaze in her cheeks. "Let me pass," she ordered imperiously. "I must have a word with my father before he leaves here for the abbey."

The herald remained where he was. "I'm sorry, my lady, but that is not permitted."

"By whose command?" demanded Kherryn.

"By order of the High Inquisitor of Farrowaithe, my lady," said the herald. Seeing Tessa and Ulbrecht approaching, he glared at them past Kherryn's shoulder. "No one," he continued, "is to be present at the Arch Mage's hearing except those who are directly involved in giving testimony."

Something of Kherryn's driving urgency had communicated itself to Ulbrecht. "Gythe Du Bors will be there," he said reasonably. "Surely this lady is entitled to the same claims and privileges?"

The herald planted his feet more firmly, his air one of

183

harassed determination. "I beg your pardon, Magister, but His Grace's orders were most specific: no one is to approach either of the disputants until after the hearing has taken place. . . ."

Jorvald Ekhanghar, Marshall of Gand and master-at-arms, would simply have removed the herald from his mistress's path. Tessa knew perfectly well what measures to take, having learned the necessary arts from her father, but the hallowed floor of the Lords' Gallery was not the place she would have chosen as a theater in which to display her martial accomplishments.

Time, however, was running short: if they didn't succeed in winning through to Lord Arvech in the next few minutes, they would lose their chance altogether. Listening in mounting agitation as Ulbrecht continued to argue in vain, Tessa abruptly hurled discretion to the four winds and apparently stumbled against the herald in their path.

Her braced forearm hooked him hard beneath the chin an instant before her bent knee took him shrewdly in the groin. The herald emitted a yowl like a strangled tomcat and folded toward the ground. Tessa let him slide, then turned to her two companions. "Come on, then!" she snapped. "We haven't got all day!"

Ulbrecht caught Kherryn by the arm and swept her past the stricken herald. With Tessa's long legs virtually sprinting along in the lead, they moved rapidly along the length of the ground-aisle and out through the egress at its end.

A thirty-yard dash brought them out into the open behind the gallery. Still going in front, Tessa skidded to a halt and uttered a well-chosen epithet. "We're too late," she announced, as Ulbrecht and Kherryn stumbled to a standstill beside her.

Her two companions looked where she pointed. A receding plume of dust marked the presence of a small troop of horsemen heading north toward Kirkwell Abbey. Kherryn gave a small, desolate cry and clutched at Ulbrecht's sleeve. He put his arm around her in mute commiseration, not daring to ask what it was she had been so anxious to tell her father before he left.

Cergil Ap Cymric was awaiting the summons at the house of the master-goldsmith of Farrowaithe. Arch Mage Baldwyn dispatched two members of his personal staff along with a captain of the Farrowaithe Guard to fetch him.

While they were waiting for him to appear, the parties concerned withdrew to the seclusion of the chapter-house at Kirkwell Abbey. The atmosphere hanging over the chapter-rooms was pregnant with pent-up hostilities. Though well schooled to say nothing, Gythe Du Bors Whitfauconer paced the meeting-chamber like a young leopard.

Before retiring to the room assigned to him, Arvech Du Penfallon took a moment to speak with the Arch Mage in private. Baldwyn gave him a penetrating look from under silvery brows, and said, "If what you are about to say to me concerns the question of Lady Gwynmira's possible guilt, I cannot in good faith hear you out without at least one member of the Du Bors family present."

"I give you my word that it does not," said Arvech.

"Very well," said Baldwyn. "What is it that you wish to discuss?"

"I have a request to make of you," said Arvech. "I would like to enlist your protection on behalf of my daughter Kherryn."

The Arch Mage's deep eyes registered surprise. "Is she in any danger?"

"Not at the moment. So far as I know," said Arvech. "But that someday might change."

"As a result of your actions today?"

"Possibly," said Arvech cryptically. He added, "Regardless of this day's outcome, there will be enmity between the Du Bors family and my own. Who is to say that there might not come a time when Kherryn might stand in need of refuge?"

For a moment Baldwyn was very still. Then he nodded. "If it should ever be so, I promise you that she will certainly find safe haven here."

"Thank you," said Arvech. "You leave me free now to follow the dictates of my own conscience."

One hour passed. Another hour went by before the disorderly clatter of hooves and the outbreak of excited voices in the forecourt of the abbey signaled the return of the delegation sent five miles downriver to Farrowaithe.

An element of feverish intensity audible in all the unmodulated activity told Arvech that there was something wrong. How wrong he did not guess until he left the abbey's chapter-house and strode down the bordered path to the abbey entrance.

There were four sweating saddle-horses standing before the gates, and four riders with them. The fourth rider, however, was not Cergil Ap Cymric. The broad face, grizzled hair, and serviceable frieze cloak belonged to the steward of the goldsmith's household.

The steward was looking flustered and dough-faced. Clambering down out of the saddle, he landed heavily on his feet and looked around him in evident consternation.

When his searching eyes lit upon Arvech's tall figure, he hurried to meet the Seneschal from Gand. Arvech cut incisively across the other man's babbling flood of apology and distress. "What has happened?" he growled. "Where is Cergil?"

The steward mopped his perspiring face. "I—I don't know, milord," he said wretchedly. "That is—"

Baldwyn Vladhallyn's soft-footed arrival caused him to break off. "Speak up, good man," said the Arch Mage with iron calm. "If some mishap has befallen the young man who was in your charge, all present need to hear the news."

The steward nodded, though his expression remained woeful. "Forgive me, milord," he said, addressing himself to Arvech. "About an hour before His Holiness's men

186

arrived, a messenger came to my master's house, claiming to be sent by you to fetch Cergil Ap Cymric to the Council. He was wearing the black robes of an acolyte of the Hospitallers' Order, and was leading a spare horse by the bridle. Master Cergil left with him straightaway—"

"Did no one think to question this man's credentials?" demanded Arvech.

The steward quailed visibly. "No, milord. After all, we . . . we were expecting just such a summons—"

A shadow fell across the ground from behind Arvech's left shoulder. "So your witness has gone missing?" said Fyanor Du Bors coolly. "What are you going to do now?"

Arvech disregarded the question. His gaze stony, he summoned the captain of the Farrowaithe Guard with a gesture. "No man simply vanishes," he said. "Have you instituted a search?"

"Yes, my lord. The city authorities have been informed, likewise the regular patrols." The officer looked warily from Arvech to Fyanor and back again.

"Let us hope they find something more telling than his corpse," said Arvech. "At least we know now that someone had good reason to fear his testimony."

"Yes, indeed," said Fyanor derisively. "How unfortunate for you if they find nothing at all."

"Yes," said Arvech, and raked the other man with an unflinching glare. "And how convenient for you."

"That hardly matters," said Fyanor. "There was never any substance in your charges from the beginning. Don't you think you had better withdraw them?"

Arvech's eyes were cold. He looked like a man contemplating violence. When he spoke, however, his voice was quite even. "I will withdraw my charges," he said. "On one condition."

"Indeed? And what condition is that?" inquired Fyanor.

"Only this," said Arvech. "That you and the Lady Gwynmira both withdraw yourselves unconditionally as candidates for the Regency of East Garillon."

There was a stunned pause. "And thus generously remove ourselves from your path? You tempt me to think," said Fyanor, "that you and this mage merely invented this tale of Cergil Ap Cymric's testimony. His absence might do you as much good—perhaps even more—than his presence."

"I am prepared to wait upon his presence, if you prefer it," said Arvech. "Or until we have some evidence to tell us what his fate may have been."

"Are you? Well, I am not," said Fyanor. "If you were to have your way, the Council might be prolonged indefinitely. I say either bring your witness, or drop your allegations *now,* and make a speedy end to what has become already too long and drawn-out an affair."

"Only if you and Gwynmira renounce the regency," said Arvech steadfastly.

"No," said Fyanor.

"Then be prepared to participate in a trial of another kind," said Arvech.

He plucked the glove from his right hand. In the eyes of all present, he walked up to Fyanor. "I challenge you, Fyanor Du Bors, on behalf of your family, to Trial by Combat," said the Seneschal of Gand. And dealt his rival a stinging blow with his glove across the cheek.

There was a horrified outcry among the spectators. Fyanor staggered back, his chest laboring, his eyes murderous with sudden rage. "Single combat: you against me," continued Arvech. "Do you accept?"

"My lords, this is barbarous!" It was Baldwyn, white-faced and noticeably shaken, who protested. "The Trial by Combat has not been invoked in East Garillon for more than three generations."

"Then the time has come to revive it," said Arvech, and returned his attention to Fyanor. "*Do you accept?*"

On Fyanor's left cheek, the mark of Arvech's blow glowed like a burn. "Yes," he said through gritted teeth. "Yes, I accept."

# LINE OF DEFENSE

ONCE THE CHALLENGE HAD BEEN hurled down and taken up again, there was little anyone else, including the Arch Mage himself, could do to quell the storm that anger and accusation had provoked. Deeply distressed by the fact that neither Fyanor nor Arvech could be prevailed upon to give ground without recourse to violence, Baldwyn Vladhallyn at last departed for Kirkwell Common, bearing the onerous news that the bitter dispute that had begun on the floor of the Assembly was destined to be resolved not by jurisdiction, but by force of arms.

Halfway back to the Council's meeting ground, the Arch Mage's small party encountered Kherryn Du Penfallon and a mounted escort that included, besides eight of her father's men-at-arms, her lady-in-waiting and the magister from Ambrothen who had been installed as her physician. Kherryn listened in tight-lipped silence as Baldwyn gravely recounted how her sire had challenged the Seneschal of Ambrothen to single combat. When the old man had finished, she fixed her dark eyes upon him in naked recrimination and said, "I will have you know, Your Holiness, that this madness might have been averted, had I not been denied the right to speak with my father before he left."

Her accusatory tone brought a furrow of concern to

Baldwyn's high brow. "Who denied you that right, my child?"

Kherryn's small jaw hardened. "Guardsmen, Your Holiness—acting upon the instructions of the High Inquisitor of Farrowaithe," she said coldly. "If there are lives to be lost tomorrow, Earlis Ap Eadric and his minions must bear some portion of the blame."

So saying, she wheeled her mare abruptly aside. Before any of the members of her party could forestall her, she gave the animal's sleek flank a sharp prick of the spur, so that it bounded past the Arch Mage's grey palfrey up the road in the direction of the abbey.

"Oh *God*!" thought Tessa half-hysterically, and sent her own mount hurtling after Kherryn's. As Arvech's livery-men closed in behind Jorvald Ekhanghar's daughter, Ulbrecht drew rein tightly to keep his sorrel gelding from following them. "Pardon, Your Holiness," he said breathlessly above the din of receding hoofbeats. "Lady Kherryn meant no offense."

"And I have taken none. She has good reason to be both angry and aggrieved," said Baldwyn soberly, gazing after the little figure on horseback. "It should have been our task—the task of the Order—to find some better resolution to this ruinous dispute. And in that aim we have failed."

Ulbrecht bit his lip. "No true resolution to any conflict can be achieved at the expense of justice, Your Holiness. The only way to prevent this murderous combat from taking place is to hand the case on to the High Court of the realm to be handled not as a political issue, but as a criminal investigation."

"On what grounds?" asked Baldwyn. "The key witness for the prosecution has disappeared."

"There is a second witness—if you choose to accept his testimony as valid," said Ulbrecht.

His diffident statement earned him a curious glance from his superior. "Indeed? Who is this witness?" inquired the Arch Mage.

190

"Me, Your Holiness," said Ulbrecht bluntly.

Baldwyn's reaction was not easy to read. His eyes were guarded. "You interest me. I had no idea you were so deeply involved in this case. Ride on ahead with me and tell me your part of the story. . . ."

With Baldwyn's attendants trailing behind them at a discreet distance, Ulbrecht furnished the Arch Mage with a terse account of all his dealings with Cergil Ap Cymric, from the night he had been called to Ambrothen Castle, till Cergil's unlooked-for reappearance in the Farrowaithe cathedral the evening before. "I realize that my testimony would not have the same weight as Cergil's," he concluded, "but I submit that the members of the Council need to hear what I have just told you, if they are going to make a knowledgeable decision when the time comes for them to decide who should be appointed as regent of the realm."

Baldwyn was silent for a difficult moment. His face was inscrutable, but his gnarled hands betrayed the tension of his inner debate in the way they clung stiffly to the reins. The party had covered nearly another furlong before the old man roused himself from his reverie. His expression as he turned to Ulbrecht was bleak.

"I'm sorry," he said quietly, "but I'm afraid I cannot allow you to present your evidence as a matter of public record."

Ulbrecht stiffened. "Why not, Your Holiness?"

The Arch Mage's manner suggested a certain dissatisfaction, as if he deprecated his own decision. "Because the information you have to offer is not firsthand. In a court of law, it would be considered inadmissable."

Seeing that Ulbrecht was about to protest, he gestured for forbearance. "I do not question your good faith. But I must point out that your credibility as a witness is open to question. You are not, after all, an inquisitor."

Ulbrecht was taken aback. "This is monstrous!" he declared. "Gwynmira Du Bors is a murderess! Surely our actions with respect to her must be dictated by considerations of justice, rather than by legalistic technicalities?"

191

Baldwyn sighed. "I understand your frustration. But those legal technicalities were instituted to safeguard individuals against false witness. Unless you are prepared to do away with the law altogether, you must accept the validity of its strictures."

Ulbrecht scowled like a thundercloud. "I see your point, my lord. But as the situation stands at the moment, Gwynmira Du Bors is the person most likely to be chosen to fill the office of regent. We can't just fold our hands and do nothing to prevent her and her brother from rising to power unopposed."

"What course of action would you suggest?" inquired Baldwyn rather sharply. "Should we go stand out on street corners, shouting accusations that we cannot prove? That would only leave us open to countercharges of calumny. Should we embark on a whispering campaign aimed at sowing suspicions where we cannot plant certainties? That *would* be a righteous way to exercise our moral responsibility. No," he finished firmly. "The matter for the moment is out of our hands. We shall have to wait until tomorrow's conflict has been resolved."

"And then what?" asked Ulbrecht.

"That will depend," said Baldwyn grimly, "on who comes off the victor."

"Isn't there *anything* we can do in the meantime?" asked Ulbrecht.

"One thing," said the Arch Mage of East Garillon. "We can consult Earlis Ap Eadric, and get his advice. . . ."

The Trial by Combat was scheduled to take place at noon, when the overhead sun would provide no particular advantage for either participant at the expense of the other. The spectators began arriving early in the morning, to find that lists had been drawn up along the center of an altered amphitheater.

It had become an arena. All through the night workmen had toiled, pulling down the two southern sections of seating so that they could be reconstructed twenty yards

192

farther down the field. Their labors had created a gap wide enough to allow the passage of a horse and armed rider from either side of the arena along a straight course marked out by a line of chalk drawn along the ground.

Three hours before the combat was to begin, Kherryn Du Penfallon, grey-faced after a sleepless night, gave up any further attempts to rest and sent for Tessa Ekhanghar. Given the ominous significance of the upcoming events of the day, Tessa did not expect to find Kherryn looking particularly well. Even so, she was not quite prepared for the ashen air of grim determination that invested the younger girl's delicately boned face with the wind-scoured angularity of a skull.

The conflicting signs of strength and of weakness made a disturbing combination. Gingerly taking the seat Kherryn pointed out to her, Tessa was conscious of a deep-seated uneasiness settling heavily into the pit of her stomach like a stone plucked from a cold riverbed. There was something fey about Kherryn's composure. Tessa had the feeling that she would have been less discomfited had she found Arvech's daughter overcome by hysterical tears.

Instead, everything about Kherryn suggested resistance. The way she occupied her chair reminded Tessa of some small animal in its lair, waiting with bared teeth for the inevitable moment when the hounds would close in to drag it out of hiding. Tessa said aloud, "I don't relish the thought of this fight any more than you do, but I don't suppose there's anything we can do to stop it now. Unless Lord Arvech's decided to listen to you, after all."

She winced inwardly as soon as the words were out. The evening before, Kherryn had accosted her father with a passionate plea that he should retract the challenge he had issued. Her vehemence had not gained his approval —in fact, quite the reverse. Recalling the curt manner with which the Seneschal of Gand had dismissed his daughter from his presence, Tessa pulled a disapproving scowl. They might at least have parted friends.

She became abruptly aware that Kherryn was watching her. The younger girl's dark eyes had an unfathomable look, as if there was no limit to their vision. Kherryn said, "How quickly could a fast courier make the journey between here and Gand?"

Tessa blinked, then thought. "That depends. A day at least to make the lake crossing from Farrowaithe to Cheswythe. After that . . . in good weather, with frequent changes of horse and no mishaps, say, three days more. Four to five days in all."

"How long would it take a large body of men—several hundred, at least—to cover the same distance?"

"Maybe twice that—"

"And how long would it take *you* to make the trip?"

"I don't know. A week, perhaps. More, if I had baggage to contend with. Less, if I were traveling light. Kherryn," said Tessa, "what's this all about?"

Arvech's daughter drew herself up. "I want you to carry a message from me to my brother Devon. The quicker he gets it, the better. How soon could you be ready to leave?"

The sinking feeling in the pit of Tessa's stomach was growing more pronounced. "If speed is of the essence, I could probably be ready in an hour," she said hardily. "But why me? Why not one of your father's messengers?"

"I want someone I *know* I can trust," said Kherryn bleakly. "Someone Devon can rely on."

Something in Kherryn's tone of voice caused a chill to race up Tessa's spine. "Is Devon in some kind of danger?" she asked.

"If our father loses this fight, he will be," said Kherryn. "That's why I would like you to be waiting outside on the green with your horse saddled, ready to ride the instant the contest of arms is decided."

"What about you?" asked Tessa.

"Ulbrecht is going to look after me," said Kherryn. "Kirkwell Abbey is near at hand. I shall seek sanctuary there, if the need should arise. . . ."

# RITE OF BATTLE

THE SKY OVERHEAD WAS CLOUDLESS, the air stainlessly clear. As his esquire finished lacing on his gorget, Arvech Du Penfallon stood motionless, watching the play of the sunlight over the soft hill to the north where the ripe uncut hay rippled like golden waves in the wind.

"There you are, my lord." Bertrant adjusted the set of breastplate and tassets and stepped back. "Now for your sword. . . ."

Lifting his arms to allow Bertrant to buckle belt and scabbard about his waist, Arvech blinked as the sunlight ran like quicksilver along the steel of his greaves. His armor, absorbing the warmth of the day, seemed to weigh more heavily than usual.

He shrugged his shoulders to ease the pressure on his clavicles. As he did so, from the far end of the lists came a flash of light reflecting off metal as two grooms in the crimson livery of Ambrothen led out a tall black stallion, the gilding on its harness clinquant in the sun.

Arvech's horse, a deep-chested bay, was tethered in the shade a dozen yards away, its high saddle hung about with the secondary weapons—morning star and miscricord—which were part of the traditional panoply of knighthood. Like Fyanor's black, it sidled restlessly back and forth, broad hooves churning up clouds of golden dust.

The white and green trappings draping its flanks were
already patched with sweat.

Bertrant, catching the direction of Arvech's attention,
left his side to quiet it. Hands resting along the upper edges
of his leaf-shaped shield, Arvech looked on as his young
subordinate ran gentling hands along the destrier's powerful neck, fending off a nervous nip with a firm shove of one
elbow. Bertrant's easy competence was enviable. If Devon
had been similarly gifted. . . .

Arvech broke the train of thought deliberately. Too
much depended upon his competence this day for him to
compromise his performance by courting reminders of a
long-standing grievance.

Behind him, a collective stir of movement from the
stands was followed by a full-throated horn-call, rising and
falling on five clear notes. As the echoes subsided, a
respectful voice at his elbow said, "My lord, Arch Mage
Baldwyn and his attendants are ready. Will it please you to
join them?"

Arvech turned slowly. The young herald, standing cap
in hand, bowed and pointed the way toward the center of
the prepared combat ground, where a knot of figures,
robed according to their clerical rank, had taken up their
station. At the opposite end of the lists, Fyanor was already
on horseback. "Thank you," said Arvech. "I will come at
once."

The bay stallion fretted under the iron control of his
hands. As he and Fyanor met in the center of the field, it
gave a sudden squeal and lunged for the black with bared
teeth. Fyanor swore and wheeled his animal aside so that it
jostled the mount of his esquire. Curbing the bay with a
twist of the bit, Arvech smiled thinly and brought the
stallion to stand several yards from where Baldwyn and
Earlis Ap Eadric, along with two black-clad acolytes, stood
poised to administer the Rite of Reconciliation.

A formal part of the ritual surrounding the Trial by
Combat, the Rite of Reconciliation was intended not to

make peace between the combatants, but to make provision for the salvation of the soul of the vanquished. Transferring his reins to Bertrant's capable grasp, Arvech dismounted and paced slowly across the grass to take up his position opposite the Arch Mage. A moment later Fyanor arrived to join him.

The sunlight glowed richly on chasuble, stole, and maniple as Baldwyn received from Earlis a small flagon of wine and a silver chalice. Holding them at chest level, the Arch Mage looked gravely from one seneschal to the other. Then in a voice pitched to carry the length and breadth of the amphitheater, he recited the opening prayer.

"Almighty God, creator of the truth, sustainer of the just, preserver of the righteous, grant that this day the truth may prevail, and that victory in battle shall be its sign."

A resounding "amen" rolled down from the heights of the amphitheater from all sides. His gaze sharpening, Baldwyn addressed himself directly to the two mailed figures before him. "It is the nature of this trial that battle shall be joined even unto the death. Are you both resolved to seek no further arbitration, but to pursue your quarrel even to this extremity?"

"This man has defamed the honor of my family," said Fyanor. "I am resolved."

"And I," said Arvech coldly. "We shall see if your honor bears defending, Fyanor."

Fyanor's jaw muscles tightened, but his eyes remained fixed upon Baldwyn. "Very well," said the Arch Mage heavily. "Since neither of you is willing to yield his claim, and both are resolved to abide the decision of divine authority, I invite you to partake of the cup which shall be poured out for you, that you may be reconciled to the judgment you have invoked. May God have mercy on your souls."

Tipping the flagon, he poured a measure of wine into the chalice he held in his left hand, then passed it to Earlis. The Grand Prior made the sign of the star over it and delivered it into the hands of one of the black-clad acolytes. The other acolyte stepped forward with a second chalice. Baldwyn filled it and blessed it in its turn before returning it to the grasp of the bearer. Then at a sign from Baldwyn, the acolytes dispersed left and right.

According to custom, Arvech dropped to one knee as the acolyte approached him. As he bowed his head, he caught a glimpse far off of a slight dark figure standing isolated in the midst of a sea of brightly clad spectators like a crow among pheasants.

Kherryn, small-boned as a cat, the pallor of her pointed face visible in stark contrast to her dark hair and black dress. The night before, she had confronted him in a strange state of agitation, begging him to withdraw from the fight. Her lack of faith in him had made him angry at the time, but now he wondered if he had perhaps mistaken care for mistrust.

A shadow fell across his line of vision and a body interposed itself between him and the sight of his daughter. Following upward the vertical lines of the acolyte's black robe, Arvech found himself gazing with sudden fixed intensity at the long hands clasped about the stem of the chalice being offered him.

The hands were beautifully modeled, the fingers fine and tapering. On the forefinger of the right hand was a golden ring set with a square green stone—a smaragdus. Its color was darker than that of any other mage-stone he had ever seen. He looked at it more closely.

Beyond, the Inquisitor of Farrowaithe lifted up his voice in prayer. "Blessed are you, Lord God of our fathers, and blessed are the works of your hands. . . ." Still gazing into the heart of the stone, Arvech lost the thread of Earlis's discourse.

Stiffening his spine, he attempted to concentrate on the litany, but despite his efforts, the sense of the words kept fading into the melody of the speaker's intonation. The smaragdus glowed before his eyes like a wheel of green fire. As he continued to stare into its depths, the wheel began to turn.

It revolved slowly at first, the square edges of the stone melting into a continuous circular rim. Then faster, gathering speed until the rim was a blur of spinning motion around a central core of piercing brightness. Enthralled, Arvech gradually became aware of another voice weaving a cunning counterpoint in and out of the gaps between the phrases of Earlis's distant prayer. Though the words were indistinguishable, the effect was like galloping across a forested landscape in a continuous flicker of light and shadow. . . .

Light . . . Dark . . . Light—Dark . . . Light.     Dark. Light—Dark . . .

"Amen!"

The word, intoned by many voices in unison, burst the momentum of the pattern like a stave hurled between the spokes of a moving cartwheel. He caught his breath sharply as the careening exchange of light and shadow shattered to a standstill.

The chalice swam suddenly before his eyes. The tall acolyte standing over him, hooded and anonymous, said, "Drink, my lord."

Accepting the chalice without demur, Arvech raised it to his lips and drank.

# TRIAL BY COMBAT

THE ECHOES OF THE THIRD call-to-arms died away. As the Master of the Lists rode out onto the field, an expectant silence worked its way through the crowd. Resplendent in cloth-of-gold and black foxfur, the Master drew rein in the center of the enclosure and raised himself high in his stirrups. His solitary voice pealed thinly across the sunlit air. "The war-horn has sounded. Let the combatants make ready!"

He flung up his arm, his baton of office quivering brightly above the ground. There was a swooping sigh from the ranks of the spectators as men and women drew breath and held it. Then, like a headsman's axe, the baton fell.

Loosed like arbalest shot, the two great horses burst through the gaps at either end of the lists and hurtled toward one another down the length of the field. Massive flanks heaving under flying draperies, they gathered speed as they swept down the center line.

Steel-barbed lances sliced down like cleavers as the riders leaned into the charge, thighs clamped hard to the saddle-skirts. A second later they came together in a crash of warring metal.

The force of the collision threw the horses back on their haunches. Meeting at cross-angles, both lances went wide, staves fracturing like so much matchwood. Arvech, righting himself with a sharp twist of the hips, was the first to recover. Bringing the bay back under control, he wheeled about and cantered back to his starting point, leaving Fyanor alone to work his left foot free of a tangled stirrup. A hoarse cheer ran along the galleries as he left the field.

They were allowed only time enough to rearm. Frothing at the bit, the bay danced nervously in place at the mark. As the master's baton swept down a second time, Arvech abruptly dropped the reins. The stallion left the ground rearing and took its stride at a bound.

From the opposite end of the lists a cloud of thunder and dust came madly careering. Out of that blur of crimson and gold bloomed a long spine of murderous steel. Flashing in the sunlight, it dipped and rose. Beyond it, Arvech caught suddenly a clear glimpse of a crested helm and damascened breastplate. . . .

At the last second Fyanor dropped his point. Barbed as a quarrel, it screamed across Arvech's raised shield and got lodged, incredibly, in the plated triangle formed by Arvech's right arm, thigh and weapon-stock.

The impact jolted Fyanor's lance from his grip. He fell forward across the bow of his saddle, gauntleted hands flung wide to break his momentum as the shaft of his lance bounced off the ground and rolled.

Bolting past one another at full gallop, the stallions separated before Arvech could press his advantage to see his opponent unhorsed. Dragging hard on the bit, he slowed the bay to a halt at the eastern end of the lists and turned back. Fyanor, he saw, had regained mastery over his mount. At a sign from the Master of the Lists, Arvech dropped the lance from his hand and set his own horse curvetting back to where Bertrant was waiting with a fresh stave.

The bay was steadier now. Velvet nostrils flaring, it complied to the bit as Arvech, inscrutable behind his visor, brought it to a standstill in the foreshortened shadow of his own banner. He accepted the lance without comment and reined the stallion around to face the arena again.

Viewed through the slits in one's visor, the panorama of the arena was spliced together from vertical slats of color. Slightly off to the left, the form of the master-at-arms was sliced through, gold and black. Gold and black. Light and dark . . .

Light . . . dark . . . The scene before him suddenly somersaulted. His vision reeling, Arvech lurched sideways in the saddle, clutching at the pommel with his reining hand.

The loss of equilibrium was sickening. He closed his eyes against the sense of being trapped at the center of a spinning wheel and swallowed hard. . . .

There was a roar from the crowd. The sound broke over him like a wave crashing against a rock. Startled, he opened his eyes. Then he saw why they had cried out.

He had missed the signal.

Fyanor's horse was in motion, flying toward him down the field like a thunderbolt. Battling his vertigo, Arvech wrenched himself upright in the stirrups. He gripped his lance hard and clapped his spurs to the bay's hard flanks.

The great horse lunged forward, bunched muscles driving it forward in powerful ground-spurning leaps, but they had already lost valuable distance. Before the bay could lengthen its stride to a full gallop, Fyanor's black pounded past the master-at-arms, carrying its rider within striking distance of his opponent.

Already targeted, Fyanor's lance-point drove a shaft of darkness through the sunlit air. Dipping under the line of Arvech's breastplate, it eluded his lance's low parrying countersweep and rose to hook itself under his gorget.

The overleafed flanges at the base of his helmet kept Fyanor's point from ripping out his throat, but the blow jarred him loose from his stirrups and lifted him out of the saddle. Fyanor's lance grated past his left ear as he fell.

Arvech's gauntleted fingers found purchase briefly in the bay's braided mane. In that instant he played the only trick remaining, using the weight of his tumbling body to

202

wrench his own lancehead around in a circular arc.

Leaping upward, it engaged with Fyanor's lance as Arvech himself lost his precarious grip. Meeting ruinously in midair, the staves crashed off one another like cymbals and fell away in a howl of twisted metal.

Arvech struck the ground inches behind the flailing threat of the bay's glancing hooves. Prone on the turf, he saw suddenly through a dense screen of dust the blurred outline of Fyanor's crested helm above a pair of striking forelegs as the black reared over him.

In a desperate jangle of mail, he recoiled, flinging himself over onto his back as the stallion's iron-shod forefeet split the dirt where his body had lain. Spurred, the black reared again. Bending low over his mount's withers, Fyanor jabbed viciously at his opponent with the pointed shard of his lance.

Sharp as a canine tooth, the broken end of the stave wedged itself between the shoulder lames of Arvech's body-armor. With Fyanor's thrusting weight behind it, it penetrated the joints, digging into the tight ligaments binding arm and shoulder together.

Blood welled greasily through the forced gap. Gritting his teeth on dust, Arvech gripped the shaft cross-handed and rolled, using his own body as a fulcrum to drag Fyanor from his seat. Intent on pinning his adversary to the ground, Fyanor found himself suddenly off balance. Poised on the brink of falling, he abruptly let go of his end of the stave and grabbed for the reins as his horse made a wheeling quarter turn to the left and broke into a canter.

Momentarily reprieved, Arvech clambered to his feet. His fallen shield lay in the dirt a few yards away. As Fyanor, snarling, unslung the morning star from his saddlebow, Arvech made a flying dive to recover the shield.

Fyanor spurred forward to overtake him. Snatching up the shield by its straps, Arvech drew his sword with his free hand. With mere yards to spare, he spun to meet Fyanor's charge.

Spiked head whirling, the morning star crashed against his shield. Genuflecting under the blow, Arvech struck out with his sword, not at Fyanor, but at the stallion's underbelly.

Squealing shrilly in pain, the destrier shot up on its hind legs, pawing wildly at the air. As Fyanor bore down hard on the reins, it overbalanced and toppled backward, spilling its rider over the crupper in a windmill of arms and legs.

Kicking and struggling, the stallion righted itself and galloped, red-eyed with panic, for the western gap in the wall. Dispassionate as a judge, Arvech hefted the sword in his hand and walked over to where his opponent lay spread-eagled on the ground.

The cacophany of cheers, groans, and catcalls from the stands died to a breathless hush. For the space of several heartbeats the point of Arvech's weapon hovered above Fyanor's chin-strap. His voice thickened with dust, Fyanor said laboredly through clenched teeth, "Strike! Damn you!"

After a brief pause, Arvech deflected his point with a flick of the wrist. His breathing uneven, he said with contempt, "And make a martyr of you? You don't deserve that honor. Get up."

He took a step backward and halted, sword-tip resting in the dirt. His eyes trained on his adversary, Fyanor slowly gathered himself into a sitting position. When the other man made no move, he shifted onto his knees and stood up, hand on his sword-hilt. "Now," said Arvech coldly, "draw your sword."

Mail chinked lightly as Fyanor stiffened. Then he said sneeringly, "Such magnanimity. Take care, Arvech. If I draw, you may regret it."

"A calculated risk." Arvech's voice conveyed a total absence of heat. He let fall his shield and lifted his blade. "Draw."

For an answer, Fyanor jerked his sword free of its

sheath and leaped. Dust-dimmed, Arvech's weapon turned the stroke and rebounded ringing. Thrown back, Fyanor sidestepped and wheeled, coming around full circle to aim a second blow at Arvech's right arm. Catching the underside of Fyanor's blade, Arvech threw it off target to the left and advanced, chopping sharply at Fyanor's right shoulder.

The edge bit into Fyanor's gorget, cleaving it partly away. It sheared on through the breastplate beneath and was stopped by Fyanor's right collarbone.

Blood burst out around the blade as Arvech yanked it free. Grunting, Fyanor stumbled back, his expression one of naked incredulity. Gripping his weapon in his remaining good hand, he fended off a second slash from Arvech with a clumsy beat to the left. His eyes glinting through the slits in his visor, Arvech swept his sword into the air with a powerful swing of the shoulders. Whining, it created an arc of wind above his head.

An arc . . .

A wheel spinning in space . . .

The vertigo smote him again, shattering vision into a maelstrom of tumbling shapes. His blade faltered in midair, then plunged under its own misdirected weight to bury itself in the earth a foot to the right of its intended target.

Reeling away from the very brink of mortality, Fyanor staggered to a complete standstill. Even as he struggled to catch his breath, a familiar voice hissed venomously in his ear, "Kill him!" Bloodless lips strained back, he looked wildly around for the speaker, then realized that the voice was speaking inside his head. "*Kill him!*" it insisted.

Fyanor jerked like a marionette. Panting like a marathon runner, he raised his sword and lunged for Arvech's unguarded flank.

Arvech parried wide and went down on one knee. Scenting the victory he had been promised, Fyanor gave a harsh sob of triumph and used the full weight of his body to ram his blade-point home between back- and breastplate into the cavity of the other man's chest.

Arvech went rigid as the steel took his breath away. Deaf to the shocked uproar from the stands, Fyanor wrenched his blade free of the wound with a brutal twist. Dark blood gushed past Arvech's lips as he crumpled to the ground. Fyanor stared down at him for a moment, then wheeled to face the gallery where his sister and her son stood beside the Arch Mage of East Garillon.

A hushed silence descended over the ranks of those present. Teeth wolfishly exposed, Fyanor flung down his weapon and raised his bloodstained hands. "Arvech Du Penfallon is dead, Your Holiness!" he called up to Baldwyn Vladhallyn. "I claim victory, and vindication—"

A breathless outcry from the gallery to his left cut him off in midsyllable. It was all the warning he had before ten inches of cold steel transfixed his windpipe.

It was like gagging on broken glass. Mouth foolishly agape, Fyanor swiveled toward his attacker and found himself gazing into the implacable eyes of Arvech Du Penfallon.

The fingers of Arvech's dagger-hand were already frozen in their death-grip, but his face in the last instant of his life was that of an avenging angel. Aghast, Fyanor looked away from the man who had just dealt him his death-wound and cast a tormented glance along the stands, searching for the black-clad figure of Earlis Ap Eadric's acolyte.

Borthen was standing by the steps leading up to the Arch Mage's gallery. It seemed to Fyanor's failing eyes that the necromancer had a faint ironic smile on his lips. . . .

# HUNTING THE HUNTER

THE AUTUMN TEMPEST THAT FOR two days had menaced shipping all up and down the Pernathan coast at last blew itself out in a series of weakening squalls. Shortly before sunset on the fourth day following the storm's passage, a dark caravel sailed into the harbor at Pirzen It'za, its black sails spread like raven's wings to catch the winds that blew out of the north from the shores of Garillon.

The black ship anchored close to the breakwaters along the quay. While the men aboard her were still hauling in her night-colored canvas, a second vessel crept into the harbor under the shadow-glow of the twilit sky.

The second ship was smaller than the first, a beak-nebbed galleass scarred by wind and wave. Sails furled tight, she nosed her way under oar-power through a floating press of cogs, galleys, and chebeq, and at last drifted to a rocking standstill within sight of the topmasts of the black caravel she had been trailing ever since leaving the Garillan port of Holmnesse.

As soon as the *Yusufa* was stationary, her crew lowered a small cockleboat into the water off her portside bow. Two men in dark cloaks subsequently descended into the cockleboat by means of a rope ladder lowered from the maindeck. The bigger of the two men took the sculls, dexterously maneuvering the little rowboat out from beneath the sheltering flank of its parent vessel. Once clear of the galleass's stern, they set out through the deepening dusk toward the string of masthead lanterns that marked the presence of the black caravel.

The sinister merchantman was only one of several large vessels moored within a stone's throw of one another. The two men in the cockleboat sculled their way through a sea-water stew of floating garbage and coasted to a standstill in the looming black shadow of a neighboring carrack.

Bracing himself against the jellylike undulations of the water beneath the cockleboat's keel, the smaller of the two men rummaged beneath his cloak and drew out a ship's glass. Setting a beady black eye to the eyepiece, he scanned the black caravel's deck from stem to stern. His companion gave him a full minute to complete his sweep, then leaned forward. "See anything interesting?"

Harlech Hardrada lowered the glass with a grimace. "It's what I *dinnae* see: there's an empty set of winches where there ought tae be a ship's boat hanging. Somebody was in a hurry tae go ashore."

"Damn." Gudmar Ap Gorvald ran a speculative eye along the light-stippled frontage of the mole. "Oh well. I suppose it was a bit too much to hope that we could get ourselves into position before our oversized friend left the ship."

He reached for the sculls. "It looks as if we're going to have to do things the hard way. . . ."

Another short stint of rowing brought them to the foot of a decaying flight of stone steps leading up from the waterline to the street that ran the length of the quay. The two men from the *Yusufa* tethered the cockleboat to a rusty ring to the right of the steps before mounting the steps. Surveying the scene, Harlech combed his beard with the point of the steel hook he had strapped on in place of his missing left hand. "All right, Gudmar," he said. "Where do we go from here?"

Gudmar carefully adjusted his cloak to conceal the

208

short sword that hung from his belt. "Muirtagh needs information as much as we do. If I were in his shoes, the first thing I'd do is go looking for a friend. Or a business associate. Do you know of anyone around here who might be involved in Borthen Berigeld's juju'bi-smuggling operations?"

"No names, I'm afraid," said Harlech. "When yon slippery blackguard had us runnin' his muck for him, it was all arranged through a go-between. But I daresay we could dig up the king mawworm in Pirzen It'za—given time and enough money."

"Just what I'm thinking myself," agreed Gudmar. "Let's go see what we can find."

Their first port of call was a squat dark taverna tucked away between two larger buildings on a stinking side-alley. Their second was a bordello three streets away. There, a modest bribe to the bordello's proprietress bought them information concerning the possible whereabouts of one D'huka Al Turoch, whom Madame Fatima described as "the eyes and ears of Pirza."

D'huka was not where the bordello-keeper had said he would be, but one of D'huka's underlings, given sufficient monetary inducement, sent them along to a cock-fighting den where, after some further negotiations, they were at last presented to D'huka himself. From D'huka—for a price—they learned the name of one particular juju'bi merchant who had grown rich through his association with a mysterious Garillan buyer with extensive connections abroad.

They also learned that Midrash Al Dakhar was not at the moment in Pirzen It'za. "Business took him south to Elhimbri three days ago," said their informant, sucking languorously at the stem of his water pipe. "His servants are not expecting him back until the day after tomorrow."

"Then we shall wait for him," said Gudmar in the man's own language. "Where does he reside?"

More money changed hands. "In a villa on the cliffs to

the south of the city," said their informant genially. "Permit me to instruct thee as to the route. . . ."

It was after midnight by the time Gudmar and Harlech took leave of "the eyes and ears of Pirza." "I'm glad ye've got *some* financial assets here in Pernatha," said Harlech, with a darkling shake of his head. "This night's work has cost us a pretty penny."

"If the search pays off, it'll be worth the price," said Gudmar. "Let's go see if we can find this villa. At this time of night, we ought to be able to take a good look around the grounds, without drawing attention to ourselves."

They followed a paved road south out of the city along the rising line of whitened sea-cliffs, where the malodorous jumble of the waterfront gave way to tended groves of orange and lemon trees. Here and there among the trees, they glimpsed the tiled rooftops of several adjacent villas. The outer walls of the house and gardens belonging to Midrash Al Dakhar were decorated in a distinctive pattern of mosaic-work. The gates, contrary to all expectation, were ablaze with lights.

Gudmar and Harlech withdrew discreetly into the shadows a safe distance away. Watching the bustle of activity surrounding the villa's entrance, Harlech swore under his breath. "What the devil's going on?"

"Midrash appears to have come home ahead of schedule," remarked Gudmar, surveying the assortment of boxes and bales with which the pack mules were laden. "Though why he should be—"

He broke off short as Harlech's wiry fingers dug into his wrist. "Look there!" hissed the little sea captain. "Do you see what I'm seeing?"

Looming large as a grizzly bear in the torchlight, the figure of Berigeld's gigantic lieutenant was difficult to miss. "Muirtagh!" breathed Gudmar, on a tight note of grim satisfaction. "We were right to play our hunch."

"Aye. He must've come straight here from that black ship o' his, tae wait for this Midrash tae show up," said

Harlech. "I'd gi' a king's fortune tae know what business they'll be hatching between 'em."

Gudmar measured the height of the garden wall with his eye. "That might be arranged more reasonably," he murmured.

As he approached the gates of his domicile, Midrash Al Dakhar was looking forward with aching nostalgia to the moment when he could transfer his bulk from the swaying unease of the horse-litter in which he traveled, to the pillowed luxury of a soft sofa. The sight of Muirtagh's massive figure planted ominously in his gateway, however, banished all thoughts of repose from his pleasure-loving mind. Round eyes agoggle, he sat up with a start that set the litter swaying, then gathered his voluminous robe about him and alighted to greet his unexpected visitor with an unctuous smile.

"Muer Tag! Effendi!" he exclaimed. "It has been many months since last these eyes beheld thee. Be welcome to this house, and thou shalt drink liquor potent as an houri's kisses, and tell me what business brings thee here. . . ."

Midrash himself conducted his visitor to an airy salon where latticed windows overlooked the gardens, fragrant with early evening. Watching with covert anxiety as Muirtagh tossed off a cup of raki, the merchant settled himself fatly into a nest of silk pillows. "Now then, honored effendi," he said. "I know thou art as the right hand of our master. What is his will of me?"

Muirtagh poured more liquor with a negligent hand. "He wants thee to find some people for him," he said in the same language. "Two men. One woman. And a boy."

Midrash blinked. "An unusual request. Who are these persons that our master wishes them found?"

"That need not concern thee," said Muirtagh roughly. "It is necessary only that thou shouldst know that they are castaways—of Garillan blood. And that His Eminence is desirous of their speedy discovery and delivery."

An errant breeze rustled through the shrubbery outside the windows. Midrash considered the problem. "Of what age and aspect are they?" he asked.

"Young—the boy only fifteen. Of the two men, one is tall with hair like unto the color of copper. The woman, being that one's sister, shall be known likewise by her hair," said Muirtagh. "The other man is poor in flesh, and of no great stature, but has the gift of a singing tongue. The boy is small too, and fair after the fashion of the north."

Midrash was silent for a moment. "It is a difficult thing that thou art asking," he said. "If they were castaways, it is likely that they would be found and sold as chattels. I respectfully remind the effendi that I am a dealer in juju'bi, not in slaves."

"And I remind thee who it is that pays thee thy wages," said Muirtagh. "Fail to dispatch this errand, and thou shalt find thyself speedily sampling the bread of poverty."

Midrash quailed visibly at the thought. "I shall do my best, Effendi Muer Tag. But I must have time to speak with those men of my acquaintance who are likely to have knowledge of such matters."

"I will allow thee the space of one week," said Muirtagh. "After that, thou shalt feel the weight of my displeasure."

"A week!" Midrash closed his loose mouth and swallowed noisily. When Muirtagh glowered at him, he bowed his head despondently. "As thou doth command. What shall I do with these thralls when they are found?"

"Have them brought here to this house," said Muirtagh. "And then send word to me at my ship. Once I am satisfied that thou hast dispatched thy duty, thou shalt receive the just reward for thy labors."

Midrash brightened slightly. "Then may heaven be gracious to thee, effendi."

Muirtagh did not acknowledge this piece of piety. His flat face impassive, he rose ponderously out of his cushions

212

and caught up his cloak. "Let me hear from thee tomorrow," he said to Midrash. "And every day thereafter, until thy task is accomplished."

Midrash bowed his head submissively. "It shall be done, effendi. Shall I accompany thee to the gate?"

As soon as Midrash and his visitor had left the room, there was a stealthy disturbance in the shrubbery just outside the windows where a shadowy figure carefully shook itself free of an ornamental boxwood and gave a sibilant hiss.

At the signal, a second figure swung lightly down out of a nearby lime tree. After a cautious glance through the latticing, he went to join the first.

Neither man spoke. Flitting from shade to shade, they retreated toward the far end of the garden where the high wall was flanked along its outer edge with crowding rows of citrus trees. The smaller of the two men mounted the top of the wall with the help of a boost from his counterpart. The bigger man chinned himself up after his companion and clambered over with powerful ease.

A moment later, both men were on the other side of the barrier, crouching in the aromatic shelter of the grove as two Pernathans in livery strolled past them on their way to complete their routine circuit of the villa and its environs. The two skulkers in black waited until the guards disappeared from view around the angle of the wall, then scuttled off like foxes through the trees, back in the direction of the sleeping city.

# THE ROAD TO PIRZEN IT'ZA

THE SWARTHY J'KHARTAN WHO HAD shared Caradoc's chains all the way from Khadesh died just before dawn.

Lying awake through the chilly star-spliced hours of the night, listening to the increasingly violent outbursts of coughing, Caradoc had helplessly witnessed the onset of the hemorrhaging, unable to do anything to ease the other man's sufferings. Once started, the bleeding did not stop, and by the time the sun had cleared the eastern horizon, it was all over.

The handlers, bundling the corpse like so much carrion into a shallow ditch at the side of the road, appeared supremely indifferent. Raging inwardly, Caradoc watched through narrowed lids as they doled out the morning's rations of bread and sour wine, and prepared to break camp as if nothing had happened.

In the past two days they had covered the better part of forty miles. It had been wearisome enough for the guards, astride their rough-coated hill ponies. For the men on foot, it had been a grueling challenge that had left its mark on every one of them.

Pitiless, the morning light singled out those whose weaknesses would cost them dearly later in the day: a spindle-shanked greybeard with the vacant face of a *khesh*-smoker; a gangling, white-faced youth only a few years

214

older than Rhan; a rabbit-plump former dandy with the rank odor of spoiled perfume clinging to the tattered remnants of a silken robe. Feeling the weight of his own weariness like lead in his veins, Caradoc wondered grimly how many more would drop in their tracks before they reached their journey's end.

Pirzen It'za. Jewel in the crown of the Prophet. Pernatha's most populous city. Caradoc understood enough Pernathe to pick the name out of the matrix of rough-tongued commands that experience had taught him to recognize in the short time since his capture. That name, and one other: Ghazarah.

Ghazarah. Where Rhan and Margoth had been taken.

The slave-dealer who had purchased them had spoken openly of their intended destination, and Rhan—white-faced and tense—had translated the instructions the Ghazarian had given their captors. That evening, the prisoners' drinking water had been drugged. When Caradoc had wakened the following morning, he had found both his companions were gone.

Picking himself stiffly off the damp ground in time to forestall a vicious blow from a horsehide quirt, he flexed his knees and surreptitiously fingered the knotted cord encircling his throat. In the course of the last few days, the rough hemp had systematically worn a raw trench in the skin above his Adam's apple. He could feel it now every time he swallowed, constricting larynx and esophagus in a maddening parody of strangulation.

The eight Pernathan handlers knew their business well. The remaining nineteen slaves who made up the straggling procession traveled in pairs chained together at the wrist, the pairs strung out in a double file and kept in order by a throttling series of nooses. Now that the J'khartan was no longer one of their number, Caradoc enjoyed a limited freedom of movement, but the handlers nearest him were watching him too closely for him to use his freedom to any advantage.

These, riding tight-reined on either hand, demanded a rigorous pace, and enforced it with the aid of their long whips. Thus driven, stoop-shouldered with fatigue, the train covered nearly eight miles by midmorning, stumbling along uneven roadbeds where the stones collected among wormhole fissures in the ground and the hollows themselves opened up to receive the unwary foot with a bone-jarring twist.

Shortly before noon, casting a dry, dispassionate eye over the array of laboring backs strung out in front of him, the foreman reined in and signaled a halt. Dropping in his tracks to nurse a growing assortment of stone bruises, Caradoc downed his meager allowance of water at a gulp and lay back on his elbows to marshal his strength for the next phase of the journey.

The overhead sun invested the wood-brown landscape with a watery glare. Closing his eyes against the sight of the empty road and the lifeless trees, he tried not to think about the others, but even fatigue could not dull anxiety, and he caught himself reliving in multiple images the events leading up to their separation.

The vision that had come to him on the beach haunted his waking hours. Caradoc was grimly certain that the magestone Borthen had taken from him had provided his enemy with the means to invade his dreams. The conviction that Borthen now knew of his whereabouts filled him with disquiet. It could be only a matter of time before Borthen, or one of Borthen's agents, came looking for him. Nor would it take them long to trace the whereabouts of his sister and the boy.

It was this thought that rendered the final bitter miles of the journey even more bitter. When the slaves all trudged into Pirzen It'za, five and a half hours later, wearing their neck ropes like ox-yokes and their chains like anchors, Caradoc alone walked erect, with a blindness in his eyes that shut out everything else—the squalid buildings, the dark faces, the foreign gibes—and left him alone

216

with the vision of Borthen's mocking smile.

Paraded like felons through the free press of bustling citizens, the slave train arrived at last at the waterfront, winding around and through a forest of crates and barrels and bales until their mounted escort brought them to an enforced halt in front of a featureless, weatherbeaten guardhouse. Here the two foremost handlers dismounted and spoke to the men stationed at the door.

From where he stood, Caradoc could hear the exchange of foreign syllables, throaty as rasps. At a sign from the foreman, the rest of the handlers dismounted and, barking orders, chivied their sodden charges toward the northern corner of the building where they were forced into an adjoining alleyway.

Hemmed in with threats, they halted again in front of a second door, waiting in resentful submission while other hands swung the door open from inside. Keeping a sharp eye on the ranks, the guards in front began to unleash their prisoners, pair by pair, thrusting them through the opening with kicks and muttered curses.

Drawing near to the head of the dwindling line, Caradoc was confronted by a smutty corridor lit at intervals by rancid oil-burning lanterns. The sickening odor of burning grease sent a mouthful of bitter fluid belching up the back of his throat and he recoiled, gagging, from the acrid air. As he stepped back, the handler behind him jabbed him viciously in the kidneys with the haft of his whip.

It was the breaking point in four days of grinding constraint. Filthy, exhausted, and shaking with fury, Caradoc wrenched himself out of their restraining hands, all his pentup tensions igniting like fire in a tinderbox.

Fingers clawed at his back and arms. Half-free still, he threw himself forward to elude a punitive lick from a darting lash, rebounded off a grimy woolen chest, and skidded to his knees with three men on top of him. Flattened by a descending weight of numbers, he twisted like a martin and got his thumb in somebody's eye, but an instant later they had him where they wanted him and exerted enough combined leverage to keep him there.

Wrenched, overtaxed, his strained muscles shot up with pure rage, he fought them all the way down the hall, his breath seething with curses as they pinned him against an inside wall long enough for two other attendants to heave open the heavy, iron-barred door at the end of a long passageway. He caught a garbled impression of firelit darkness, of steps descending into shadowy depths below, before they launched him through the doorway and he hurtled head over heels down an unyielding series of sharp-angled steps.

The floor sprang up to meet him. Rolling away from the impact in a bone-saving tumble, he lost control at the last second and crashed awkwardly, irresistibly, heavily into another human body.

The other man gave an involuntary cry of pain and rolled away into the shadows, where he dragged himself up and propped one bowed shoulder against the wall, breathing harshly through set teeth. He was cradling his right arm against his chest. Caradoc could tell that it had been broken several days before.

He raised himself shakily to his grazed knees. "I'm sorry," he muttered gruffly. "I didn't mean to hurt you—"

Then took a closer look at the drawn profile half-concealed beneath unkempt tangles of brown hair.

Caradoc's heart sprang into his mouth. Swallowing hard, he reached out a tentative hand and touched the other man's bare shoulder. *"Serdor?"* he breathed.

The disheveled head snapped up and turned. Haggard grey eyes narrowed briefly, then kindled in a sudden blaze of recognition. "Caradoc!" exclaimed the minstrel. And returned his friend's firm handclasp with all the strength of his uninjured arm.

For a long moment they could only stare at one another. "We thought you must be dead!" said Caradoc.

His green eyes were aglow with a gladness he hadn't felt in months.

"No—only a little the worse for wear," said Serdor with rueful irony. "Never mind me. What about Margoth and Rhan?"

"They're all right, too. Or at least they were, the last time I saw them," said Caradoc grimly.

He told the story baldly, while the minstrel listened in silence. "All I know for certain now is that they're bound for Ghazarah," he said at the close of his recital. "I hope they meet with better fortune there than we have so far."

"Amen." Serdor hunched his shoulders, his gaze wandering away toward the dank, cheerless walls of their prison-house. Re-collecting himself, Caradoc grimaced and pointed to his friend's injured arm. "How did that happen?"

Serdor made a wry face. "Somewhere between the wreck and the shore, I got thrown against a rock. I seem to recall there were rather a lot of them."

Which explained why his remaining clothes were in tatters. Gazing down at his friend, Caradoc noted an accompanying array of bruises and abrasions. "Yes. You do look a bit like one of Margoth's crazy quilts," he said. And added casually, "I don't suppose that fracture's been set?"

"One of the villagers who found me took a pull at my arm, and I felt something move—just before I passed out," said Serdor. "Whether or not it's set properly is another question. I'd be glad if you were to have a look at it yourself."

His voice was level enough, but his eyes betrayed his anxiety. Caradoc nodded and leaned forward.

Assuming an air of confidence he was far from feeling, he ran his fingertips lightly over the minstrel's forearm, but the flesh was so bruised and swollen that he could tell nothing about the articulation of the bone beneath. He forced a smile. "Don't worry. There's nothing the matter

219

with your arm that a mage won't be able to correct."

Serdor's expression was still worried. "Then you don't think I'll have any problems playing the lute again——"

He broke off short at a loud rattle from the door at the head of the stairs. A key turned rustily in the lock. Some of their fellow prisoners started up, muttering. Copying the angle of their upturned faces, Caradoc looked up as the door itself flew open, spilling a flood of torchlight down the steep, mired steps.

Man-shadows, inflated to monstrous proportions, overran the grey lichenous walls on three sides of the vault. Caradoc squinted upward into the heart of the light and made out against the red-gold dazzle of fresh torches a nodule of turbaned heads.

Their boots striking strident echoes off the stones underfoot, five slave-handlers swarmed down the stairs and fanned out at the bottom. Crouching next to Caradoc in the shadows, Serdor found himself suddenly confronting two handlers armed with cudgels. Before he could move of his own volition, they caught him roughly by the elbows and jerked him to his feet.

He gasped aloud as pain shot the length of his injured arm. Pinned by two more handlers, Caradoc made an abortive attempt to shake them off and got a sharp rap with a cudgel behind the legs. As he sagged toward the floor, one of his captors whipped a leash of coarse rope around his throat and slipped the knot tight. "Don't struggle. You'll only get yourself hurt," warned Serdor in a low voice.

The minstrel likewise had been collared. Their captors hustled them toward the steps and forced them to climb. "What do you suppose they want with us?" muttered Caradoc under his breath.

"We'll find out soon enough—probably too soon," said Serdor.

The handlers pushed them out into the passageway and held them there, cudgels poised at the ready, while the door-warden secured the cell door behind them. From there Caradoc and Serdor were marched along the hall to another doorway on the left.

The room inside was furnished along tawdry conceptions of luxury. Helped impolitely over the threshold, Caradoc stumbled across several feet of worn silken rug and fetched up at the foot of a low dais. Serdor arrived a few steps behind him. Shoulder to shoulder, they stood their ground and waited while a grossly fat Pernathan robed in pink brocade studied them dispassionately from the embrace of a cushioned chair.

At his side stood the master slave-dealer. After a low-voiced conversation, the fat Pernathan dipped his double chins in assent.

The slave-dealer clapped his palms twice together. Hard hands gripped Caradoc from both sides and thrust him forward. The fat Pernathan rose laboriously to his feet. Lumbering over to Caradoc, he peered intently into his face, then reached out and gave an experimental tug to Caradoc's red hair.

Outraged, Caradoc stiffened and reared back. A stick jabbed him warningly between the shoulder blades. His display of temper, however, left the fat Pernathan unmoved. Turning his head, he gave the slave-dealer another nod. At a sign from the dealer, Caradoc and Serdor were removed from the room and escorted outside under guard.

"Now why have they picked just us two?" wondered Serdor under his breath. "What good is a slave with a broken arm, for that matter?"

Caradoc made no response to his friend's speculations. He kept his own chilling suspicions to himself. At the end of ten minutes' wait, the fat Pernathan and the master-slaver emerged from the building and parted company with an exchange of bows. "Well, it seems we've just been bought and paid for," muttered Serdor.

"Yes," growled Caradoc.

He was already on the defensive, fearing Borthen's possible intervention. It was only too likely that he himself was being tracked by the brigand-leader through the power of the magestone Borthen had taken from him. That fear was uppermost in his mind as he and Serdor were transferred into the custody of their new owner's household guards.

Hustled along behind the fat Pernathan's curtained litter, Caradoc and Serdor left the slave-dealer's compound and turned left into the street beyond. Their enforced foot-journey took them along the Pirzen It'zan waterfront and up a paved road that followed the rising coastline to the south of the city. A half mile's uphill trudge brought the party to the gates of an enclosed villa, its outer walls decorated with tile work. After a barked exchange of Pernathan monosyllables, the gate was unlocked from the inside and the party passed through the entryway into an enclosed courtyard.

The ground floor of the encircling building was shadowed by a running balcony overlooking the courtyard from all sides. As the fat Pernathan alighted from his litter, Caradoc caught sight of a massive figure looming darkly within the shadow of the second-floor arcade.

His heart slammed to a standstill as he realized who it was. "What is it?" breathed Serdor.

Then went rigid as he too recognized the massive figure of Muirtagh, Borthen Berigeld's lieutenant.

# THE PRICE OF LOYALTY.

THE TWO PRISONERS FROM EAST Garillon put up a struggle as their captors dragged them indoors, but their resistance was more annoying than effective. Dourly satisfied that Midrash's men had the situation well under control, Muirtagh left the balcony and withdrew to the quiet of the villa's autumn solarium.

There he was joined several minutes later by Midrash himself. The juju'bi merchant was glowing with self-importance, his black eyes glittering in the midst of his fleshy face like raisins in a suet pudding.

Padded palms outflung in expansive bonhomie, he swooped toward Muirtagh in a downdraft of patchouli. "My esteemed friend, have I not done well by thee and our most honored master?" he asked brightly. "Behold, I have brought thee the falcon and the lark."

He eyed Borthen Berigeld's looming lieutenant with high-colored expectancy, but Muirtagh merely raised a disenchanted eyebrow. Midrash's soft face fell. "Art thou not satisfied that these men are the ones our master is seeking?"

"I am satisfied. But they are only two out of four," said Muirtagh, his guttural Pernathe grating against the ear. "Bring me the woman and the boy as well, and then we shall discuss the subject of thy continuing prosperity."

Midrash's small black eyes screwed themselves tighter. "Thou art a hard man, effendi," he said aggrievedly. "I have done my best. It is not my fault that two of thy birds have perhaps flown to the hand of another."

Muirtagh made no comment. Crestfallen, Midrash was about to protest further when a happy thought occurred to him. He insinuated himself more closely. "Effendi, might it not be that these two may know where their companions were taken?"

Muirtagh's pebble-pale eyes shifted toward the water clock on the table by the far wall. "I will ask them," he said gruffly. "Now leave me."

"Effendi?"

"Leave me," growled Muirtagh. "I will call thee if I have need of thy services."

Midrash was not disposed to argue. Once the Pernathan had departed, Muirtagh barred the door. He drew the silken drapes across the tall windows. Then he came back to the center of the room.

Standing free of the furniture, he stationed himself beneath the lamp suspended from a bracket in the middle of the ceiling. With its light eddying pallidly around him, he reached into the breast of his jerkin and drew out a small globe of greenish crystal.

Holding it cupped between his callused palms, he tilted his head downward and waited, gazing intently into its murky depths. As the balls of the water clock changed places, there was a flicker of movement in the heart of the crystal and the cloudiness boiled away like steam.

A face emerged from the midst of the dissipating fog. A dark, patrician face with high cheekbones and piercing eyes. The image wavered, then stabilized. The hard-edged mouth moved to frame an audible question. "Muirtagh. What is your report?"

Muirtagh stared impassively down into the face of his superior and spoke out loud. "Well, we've got two of 'em. Caradoc and that scrawny friend of his. Midrash's men brought them in about a quarter of an hour ago."

Borthen's full lips lifted at the corners. "Excellent. What about the brat?"

"No sign of him yet—or Caradoc's sister. They could be anywhere," said Muirtagh. "Do you still want them?"

"The boy, certainly," said Borthen. "The woman is less important, but she might still have her uses. Have you questioned Caradoc about them?"

"Not yet," said Muirtagh grimly. "But I'm going to."

"I want him undamaged—at least for the moment," said Borthen. "But you may do whatever you like with his companion."

Muirtagh grinned thinly. "I understand."

The portrait in the crystal was fading. "I shall contact you again at midnight," said his superior. "By then you should have some answers."

As his voice subsided, the mists converged again, blanketing his image from view. Straightening, Muirtagh shook his great shoulders and tucked away the crystal out of sight.

Then he unbolted the door and left the room.

The prisoners were being held in the tiled brazier-room adjoining Midrash's luxurious baths. Trussed up like a chicken, Caradoc sat with his back to the door of one of the storage cupboards and glowered over at the two men who were standing guard by the doorway leading out into the hall.

There were two more guards stationed at the louvered windows off to his right. The air was steamy with heat thrown off by the large charcoal-burning furnace that occupied most of the opposite wall. The tended embers glimmered redly through the iron gridwork of the furnace door. Feeling its hot exhalations on his face like salamander's breath, Caradoc set his teeth and steeled himself to face the worst when it came.

The worst was not long in coming. Heavy footbeats stumped to a halt outside the doorway. A moment later, the door swung inward and Muirtagh stepped across the threshold.

Caradoc recognized the look in the brigand's hard eyes, and the breath lodged in his throat. Beside him, Serdor stirred uneasily in his bonds. Muirtagh treated them both to a single contemptuous glare, then signaled to the guards. "Get 'em up," he ordered. "We've got some talking to do."

White-faced with anger and apprehension, Caradoc twitched futilely against the hands of his captors as they set him on his feet. "I've got nothing to say to you!" he spat.

Muirtagh merely grunted. "We'll see about that. Ibn! Bakhir! Truss him up to that door. I want him so he can't move."

Caradoc's guards loosened his bonds long enough to redistribute his limbs, lashing first his wrists and then his ankles to the slatted doorway of the brazier-room's drying cabinet. Pressed flat against the adjoining wall with guards on either side of him, Serdor watched with dilated eyes, but said nothing.

Once the guards had finished binding Caradoc, Muirtagh walked up to him. "Now then," said the brigand. "You're going to answer a few questions. Where is Evelake Whitfauconer?"

Caradoc glared back defiantly into Muirtagh's slablike face. "I don't know," he said. "And even if I did, there's nothing you could do to me to make me tell you!"

He waited, shrinking inwardly, for the first blow. Instead, Muirtagh turned on his heel and strolled ponderously over to where all four guards had clustered around Serdor.

At a sign from the brigand, one of the guards slashed a knife through the ropes that bound their second prisoner. As the cut cords fell away, the others caught Serdor and pinned him in an unbreakable armlock.

Muirtagh favored Caradoc with a long calculating look. Then he turned and lashed out with sudden viciousness.

The heavy backhanded blow caught Serdor full in the

face. He cried out and recoiled as far as his captors' grips would let him. While Serdor was still reeling from the stroke, Muirtagh clenched his fist and drove it hard underneath his sharply delineated ribs.

Choking, the minstrel doubled forward. "Damn you! What are you doing?" cried Caradoc. "He doesn't know anything—"

Muirtagh looked around, baring yellow teeth in a wolfish smile. "Maybe not," he said. "But I'm willing to bet you do. And if you hold out on me, he's going to pay for it."

Serdor was still retching helplessly from the force of the blow. Listening to his friend's ragged breathing, Caradoc wrenched and writhed against his bonds. "You bastard!" he shouted. "Leave him alone!"

Instead of answering, Muirtagh bent down and knotted his fingers in Serdor's disheveled hair. "It's your choice," he rumbled. And before Caradoc could forestall him, dealt the minstrel another vicious blow to the face.

Serdor raised his head shakily, blood welling from his smashed mouth. "Don't listen to him, Caradoc," he panted. "Whatever happens to me, he can't make you reveal *what you don't know*."

Racked with horror, Caradoc took the minstrel's meaning. Muirtagh, however, was unmoved. He eyed Caradoc up and down and said, "Well?"

Caradoc could only stare back at him, aghast at the choice that was being forced upon him. When he said nothing, Muirtagh reached down and took Serdor's injured arm in a swift viselike grasp.

Muscles bunched along the brigand's massive forearm as he exerted pressure on weakened bone and damaged tissue. In spite of himself, Serdor gave a broken gasp and sank toward the floor.

Muirtagh kept his grip. Seizing the minstrel by the belt, he hauled him bodily upright and plucked him out of the hands of the guards. Pivoting, he forced his prisoner irresistibly backward against the heated grill of the furnace door.

There was a venomous hiss as hot iron kissed bare flesh. Caradoc's howl of protest clashed with Serdor's wordless scream of anguish. Muirtagh held him there for a few heartbeats longer, then abruptly let him go. The minstrel sobbed and crumpled to his knees.

His exposed back was crosshatched with burns. Caradoc could bear it no longer. *"Stop it!"* he gasped, half sobbing himself with grief and rage. "Don't hurt him any more. I'll tell you what you want to know—"

*"No!"* Wild-eyed with shock, Serdor jerked himself upright. "Don't do it! For God's sake, don't—"

He broke off with a cry as Muirtagh's booted foot slammed him hard in the side. There was a brittle crackle, as of twigs snapping. Muirtagh kicked him twice more, then stood back. The minstrel rolled to a standstill, eyes closed, blood welling thinly from his mouth and nose.

Muirtagh turned to Caradoc and raised an eyebrow. "Well?" he said. "Do I have to go on?"

He drew back his foot. *"Wait!"* cried Caradoc.

Beaten, he slumped against his bonds. "Ghazarah," he mumbled. "The boy's been taken to Ghazarah."

Muirtagh shifted his weight back onto both feet. "Now we're getting somewhere," he growled. "Who's taking him there?"

"A slave-dealer. I don't know his name," said Caradoc. Then seeing the big man's muscles stiffen, cried out sharply, "I swear to God that's all I know!"

"Let's test your memory, just to make sure," said Muirtagh.

He bent over the minstrel's prone body and clapped a hand to Serdor's branded shoulder. In the same instant, there was a sudden ruinous crash, and the window behind him imploded in a geyser of glass and woodslats.

Borthen's lieutenant spun around as a blond long-boned figure vaulted through the opening and landed feetfirst on the floor, broadsword alive in his hand. "Defend yourself, you bloody meat-ox!" called Gudmar Ap Gorvald. And lunged straight for Muirtagh.

More men poured in behind him. The guards nearest the window leapt to intercept the intruders and were thrown back by a yelling influx of superior numbers. As Gudmar closed in, Muirtagh made a lightning snatch for a furnace-iron, and roared aloud as the other man's blade-edge bit into his forearm.

Metal snicked bone. Muirtagh wrenched his arm back with such force that Gudmar had the sword-hilt torn from his grasp. The weapon clattered to the floor between them. As Gudmar dived to recover it, Muirtagh lashed out with a windmilling fist.

The blow impacted on Gudmar's jaw. The guildmaster grunted and stumbled back. Left briefly unopposed, Muirtagh shot a hard-eyed glance over the melee in the room. Hearing telltale shouts from elsewhere in the building, he wheeled and made for the door, blood jetting in spurts from the wound in his arm.

Calling to his men, Gudmar picked himself up and raced after him. As the invaders surged toward the open doorway, Caradoc struggled and shouted frantically for help.

One of the men at the back turned aside long enough to slash through the rope pinning the prisoner's right wrist. "Leave me the dagger!" panted Caradoc. The man wordlessly handed him the weapon, then ran to catch up with the rest of his party.

Sobbing in his need and haste, Caradoc sawed fiercely at the cords that remained. As the last strands parted, he sprang away from the cabinet door and threw himself down beside Serdor's broken body, lying untended on the floor.

# BAPTISM OF FIRE

THE MINSTREL LAY AS MUIRTAGH had left him, battered and unconscious. Stricken, Caradoc stared down at the rampant evidence of injury. In the face of so much damage, and despite the power he had now twice called without the focus of his magestone, he realized that he hardly knew where to begin or what to do without the tool of his lost magecraft to guide him.

But Serdor's condition demanded that he act —somehow and some way—without delay. Pulling his shaken wits together, he reached out a tentative hand to touch the minstrel's blackened ribs, then snatched it back again, his fingers quaking like leaves on a windy bough.

He gulped air in an effort to steady himself, but the memory of Muirtagh's brutal assault was self-perpetuating. The sight of Serdor's seared back turned him suddenly faint and he was forced to avert his eyes to keep from being sick.

A shadow fell across the floor from the open doorway. "Caradoc?" said Gudmar's deep, familiar voice. "Are you all right?"

The question penetrated Caradoc's nausea. Starting up, he turned his head, green eyes beclouded with anger and anguish.

"*I'm* not hurt," he said bitterly. "Where's Muirtagh? Did you catch the bastard?"

Standing on the threshold, Gudmar shook his head. "Not yet: he went out through an underground passageway. By the time Harlech's men got the door panel open, he was long gone."

He came forward into the room. "Harlech's questioning some of the lackeys just now. That may give us a clue as to where our oversized friend may be heading—"

"I know where he'll be heading," said Caradoc greyly. "He'll be making for Ghazarah."

"Ghazarah?" said Gudmar. "Why there?"

Caradoc flinched. "Because I happen to know that's where Evelake's been taken."

Gudmar caught his breath, then let it out again. "You told him that?"

"Yes," said Caradoc bitterly. "I told him."

His shrinking gaze returned to the violated body of his friend. Seeing the horror creep back into the young mage's eyes, Gudmar suddenly understood.

"I'm sorry. As soon as our lookout sent word that you'd been brought here, we came as quickly as we could," he said. And added gently, "Your friend—how badly is he hurt?"

Caradoc was shivering openly, without making any attempt to control it. "I don't know," he said wretchedly. "Without a magestone, I can only guess."

His face worked. "God knows I owe Evelake my silence! I would have held my tongue, no matter what that bastard did to me—"

"Except that Muirtagh was shrewd enough to know that you couldn't sacrifice a friend as you would sacrifice yourself," said Gudmar. Watching the younger man's anguished face, he added, "You have no reason for self-condemnation—"

"Yes I do!" cried Caradoc miserably. "I should never have let it go so far—"

He hugged himself hard, gripping his upper arms with white-knuckled hands until the fingers gouged deep into the flesh. "If I was going to yield, I should have done it at once," he said in a choked voice. "At least then, Serdor would have been spared—*Oh God!*"

Blood was springing up crimson under the clawing pressure of his fingernails. Gudmar seized the younger man's taut wrists and forced his hands down. "Stop it!" he said with quiet vehemence. "If you're going to give way to shock, do it later. Right now your friend needs you!"

Caradoc's bowed head flew up as if Gudmar had struck him. "But I can't help him. I haven't got a magestone—"

"You were trained as a healer," said Gudmar in a voice incisive as a scalpel. "Even without a magestone, there must be something you can do."

He gave Caradoc's wrists a shake. "*Think*, damn it! It can't be *all* bloody mysticism."

Caradoc drew one shuddering breath, then another. His green eyes lost some of their self-destructive wildness. "No, it's not," he said, and this time his voice was steady.

His tone told Gudmar that he was beginning to think again. "Right," said the guild-master with crisp practicality. "There are some couches next door in the bathing-room. And plenty of fresh water. Let's move your friend in there and at least clean him up a bit. Then maybe you'll be able to see more clearly what you're up against."

Caradoc inhaled deeply, like a man steeling himself to dive off a cliff. "I'll take his body, if you'll take his legs," he told Gudmar. "Lift when I tell you to, and keep him level—I don't know yet which bones may be broken. . . . "

They made the transfer with gingerly care. After helping Caradoc to ease Serdor down onto one of the low divans, Gudmar departed in search of any medicinal herbs that might be found on the premises.

Left alone, Caradoc braced himself to search out and identify the graver injuries lurking below the havoc of contusions. He kept it as brief as a comprehensive survey would allow, and before long was in possession of some disquieting facts.

The break in Serdor's right arm had been displaced, and there was every likelihood that his left cheekbone had been cracked. What gave Caradoc greater cause for concern, however, was the number of ribs that had been fractured during Muirtagh's calculated assault.

There was an ugly catch in the minstrel's shallow breathing that filled him with foreboding. Lacking the means to complete his diagnosis, Caradoc was grimly aware that Serdor almost certainly was suffering from internal injuries as yet undetermined. If that were the case—if those injuries were serious—there would be nothing Caradoc could do to save his friend from bleeding to death. All he could do was treat the ills he could see, and hope.

He began by fetching clean cloths and a basin of cool water. Returning to the minstrel's side, he soaked one of the cloths and spread it, still dripping, over his friend's excoriated shoulders.

Caradoc had thought Serdor mercifully unconscious, but as the cloth touched his back, the minstrel gave a convulsive twitch and moaned aloud. He made a struggling attempt to raise his head. "Easy, Serdor," said Caradoc, and laid a gently restraining hand on his friend's outflung arm. "There's nothing to fear. Not any more."

The shocked grey eyes focused with difficulty. After a pause, the minstrel's broken lips framed a painful inquiry. "Muirtagh?"

"He's gone," said Caradoc soothingly. "It's all over now. All you have to do is lie still and rest."

Serdor's bruised eyelids drooped, and for a brief moment Caradoc thought he was going to slip back into a dead faint. Instead, the minstrel stiffened in a sudden spasm of anguish and broke out coughing.

Caradoc leaped to support him. The paroxysm lasted for more than a minute. When it finally passed, Serdor slumped against Caradoc, his mouth and chin awash with dark blood.

Horrified, Caradoc groped for a pulse. To his dismay, it was fluttering and erratic. Serdor coughed again, more blood bubbling past his lips. His face beneath the disfiguring bruises was grey as a corpse's.

In an agony of helplessness, Caradoc called the minstrel by name. Serdor's shaggy head turned, but his eyes were wildly disoriented, like those of a man poisoned by nightshade. Caradoc could only watch as the spells of coughing continued, wet and hollow. The irregular pulse beneath his taut fingers began to fail.

Caradoc's blood ran cold. "Oh no," he said flatly. "Oh my God, *no!*"

Serdor was no longer fighting. Hardly knowing what he did, Caradoc gathered the minstrel's shattered body into his arms with fierce tenderness. "Hang on, Serdor!" he pleaded. "Please hang on!"

But Serdor had already withdrawn beyond the reach of the human voice. The living warmth was pouring out of his broken flesh like water from a cracked vessel. Unable to stem the flow, Caradoc tasted the scalding anguish of his own weakness. "Help me!" he prayed despairingly. "Oh God, let my own life be forfeit, and my spirit forever in thrall, but grant me the power to save him!"

He bowed his head over Serdor's cold limbs, his vision drowned in sudden tears. In that instant, his bitter heartache converted prayer into a wordless shaft of supplication. Like an arrow vanishing into the sun, his speechless plea rose up toward heights unscalable by conscious thought or endeavor. And out of those heights there sprang a terrible answering flame.

Descending like a thunderbolt from a mountaintop, the flame clove him to the heart. Like a tree blasted by lightning, he shuddered under the fearful impact of transfiguring power. The brightness that engulfed him was too aweful to look upon. Blinded and ravished, he cried out in mingled anguish and ecstasy.

The dread fire coursed throughout his every nerve.

Storming in his veins like the risen tide, it gathered force until its influx was almost past bearing. Then, just when he thought he could contain no more of it, the tumult released him and retired with sudden supernal lightness, like a lover withdrawing from a kiss.

Caradoc opened his eyes. All around him stretched wide grey wilderlands, featureless and vast. He was standing naked in the middle of a stony roadway that divided the treeless wastes one from another. Far ahead of him, moving away from him, was a slight human figure.

Even at a distance, Caradoc recognized the averted brown head and the set of the angular shoulders. "Serdor!" he cried with a swelling voice.

The moving figure did not turn around. Caradoc knew suddenly that if he allowed his friend to pass out of his sight all would be lost. "Serdor!" he cried again. "Wait for me!" Then broke into a run.

The sharp stones of the roadway bit into his feet. Limping, he ran on, fighting to overtake the lone figure silhouetted against the grey sky.

Vast distances seemed to lie between them. Exhaustion hung chains upon his bleeding feet, weighting every step with pain. He stumbled and fell, measuring his length on the earth. Hope faltered within him. Panting, he lay where he had fallen, tasting defeat like ashes in his dry mouth.

"It's no use," he thought despairingly. "I've got too far to go. . . . " But as he lay prone in the dust of the road, Gudmar's words came back to him—"Your friend needs you!"

His resolve hardened. Gathering what little strength yet remained to him, he struggled to his feet.

And found that the gap between himself and Serdor had closed.

The road had come to an end. Beyond it, Serdor was standing at the threshold of a tall portal under an archway of stone. The door was open. Beyond it lay deep wells of roaring fire. Heat issued forth from the opening in great billowing waves, but Serdor did not appear to feel it. His face remote and intent, he stepped into the shadow of the arch.

"Serdor, *NO!*" shouted Caradoc, and lunged for the opening.

His desperate rush carried him across the threshold one step ahead of the minstrel. As the fire leapt to engulf him, Caradoc slammed the door shut behind him.

Radiance embraced him with bright agony. Bathed in glory like a refiner's fire, he felt his substance purified in undiluted ardor. The flame passed through him as light through air. Even as he cried out, he heard the pain of his purgation transfigured into song.

The song rose like a great wind. Its tide swept him across vast deserts of uncreated splendor where the moving sands had voices of fire and melody. But he himself was still fettered to a mortal body, and for him the ecstasy could not last. As the glory began to fade, he knew what was left to him to do. Reaching out into the land of the living, he found Serdor's hand and clasped it in his own.

Agony wrenched at his bones, tearing at his face, his back, his side. He opened his heart to the pain, courting a host of living wounds as a saint would invite martyrdom. Taking Serdor's injuries upon himself, he gave in return the healing virtue that had been the fire's gift.

Concentrating the force of his will, he viewed Serdor's condition with all the hallowed clarity of the magecraft he had thought lost beyond recall. With that surety of perception to guide him, he moved to seal up his friend's torn lungs and knit back his broken bones.

But Caradoc had brought to his task only as much power as his mortal flesh had been capable of receiving. And as he labored to restore the minstrel's lost vitality, he could feel that power draining away from him like water vanishing into thirsty ground.

The expenditure of energy was grueling. Fatigue

dragged heavily upon him, but he held himself sternly to his task, fighting to reinstate Serdor's breathing and pulse-beat before his strength gave out. It was slow work, heartbreakingly costly. Caradoc was seized by a sudden fear that all his efforts might still not suffice.

But by then, his own growing exhaustion was threatening to overwhelm him. A darkness swam before his eyes. He struggled desperately to keep going, but he was losing command over his own faculties.

The slow beat of his flagging heart thundered in his ears. Sensing his own collapse, he fought to hold it at bay. But even as he lost touch with Serdor, the last of the fire in his own spirit flickered and died.

# THE KEY TO LIBERTY

ALTHOUGH MARGOTH HAD NEVER BEFORE been drugged, her physical state upon waking was unmistakably the consequence of nothing else. Surfacing by degrees through a treacly darkness, she locked her teeth against the nausea and wondered how long it would take to wear off.

The furry thing in her mouth turned out to be her own tongue. After several unsuccessful attempts to spit it out, she realized as much and stopped trying. As an alternative, gulping dryly, she rolled over onto her side in an effort to come to grips with her present surroundings.

Milk-warm, the ambient air was thickly laced with the warring odors of sweat and spikenard. As unfamiliar as the glottally disruptive smell was the straw matting on which she was lying. An experimental sniff told her that the matting itself was only indifferently clean, and the discovery impelled her to try to sit up.

A hand, strong-fingered, came unexpectedly to her aid. Relying heavily perforce upon its support, Margoth dug an elbow into the floor beneath her and pushed herself up. Once precariously balanced over her crossed ankles, she summoned resolution and unlatched her eyelids.

A face swam hazily into focus a foot or two from her own. Methodically cataloguing the features one by one, Margoth realized, with an irresponsible surge of relief, that

238

it was Rhan's. And because the expression in the brown eyes was nakedly concerned, she produced from somewhere the wan simulacrum of a smile.

He did not smile back. Instead he said, "Whatever it was, they must have given you a stronger dose of it than they did me. How do you feel?"

Plexus after plexus, her nerves and muscles were beginning sluggishly to respond, but the overall effect was still that of trying to swim through lukewarm glue. Evidently Rhan recognized as much, for he said an instant later, "Never mind. Let me get you some water."

A cup materialized just below the level of her nose. Somehow she managed to free her lower jaw as he guided the rim to her lips. Cold liquid flooded the parched tunnels of mouth and throat, and swallowing, she found her voice. "Where are we?"

"I don't know," said Rhan, still watching her. "But judging from the atmosphere, we have apparently changed hands."

Yes, they were obviously somewhere other than the squalid hut that formed a backdrop for her most recent memories. Uncomfortably conscious of unwashed hands and clinging, brine-soaked hair, Margoth cast a bleary glance around her. "Where's Caradoc?"

The brown eyes dropped away from her inquiring gaze. "I don't know that, either," said Rhan. His voice was suddenly bleached white so that the anxiety showed through. "When I woke up, he was gone."

Taken, no doubt, to serve in the war-galleys of the Caliph. Or perhaps in the tin mines of Arzha. Or the stone quarries of Sul Khabir. "I see," said Margoth bleakly. There was little else to say.

Her eyesockets were throbbing fiery bits but she did not give way to tears. She pulled herself together with bitter fortitude. "I guess that means we're on our own, you and I."

"For a little while, anyway," said Rhan flatly.

239

That sounded ominous. "What do you mean?" asked Margoth suspiciously.

Rhan bit his lower lip. "While you were still asleep, I overheard the slave-dealer giving instructions to one of the handlers. I think the local Emir has been invited to come take a look at you."

It took a moment to sink in. Margoth felt the blood leave her face. She said, rather inadequately, "Oh dear."

Rhan nodded without speaking. Gazing over at him, Margoth noted for the first time how drawn he looked. Remembering how fiercely the boy had been devoted to Serdor, she wondered if her own grief had left so clear an imprint in her face.

She wrenched her thoughts away from past sorrows to present dilemmas. To cover her own fears, she said hardily, "Never mind. Perhaps the Emir will take a strong aversion to the color of my hair."

"I shouldn't think so," said Rhan. "If I understood our esteemed master correctly, the Servant of the Caliph is quite keen to acquire something a bit out of the ordinary in the way of a household peri."

"That would be just my luck," said Margoth bitterly. Her blue eyes narrowed. "Well, if nobody's told this fellow that red hair is the sign of an incorrigible temper, maybe I ought to enlighten him—"

"If you're thinking of making a scene, I wouldn't advise it," said Rhan. "Most people in authority are usually only too glad to have an excuse for hurting you."

His face had gone a shade paler. It occurred to Margoth that their impending servitude presented far more dangers for him than it did for her. Whatever indignities a Pernathan master might see fit to inflict upon her, she at least couldn't be maimed in the way he might be—as Pernathan custom dictated.

Her blood turned to ice at the thought. To counter an attack of the shivers, she hardened her jaw and said, "It seems to me that the only sure way to avoid getting hurt is to put ourselves physically out of harm's way. What would you say to the prospect of our trying to break out of here?"

Rhan grimaced. "I'd say hooray—if I hadn't already thought of that. Have you taken a good look around you yet?"

Margoth hadn't. She did so now.

The room they were in was square. Three long window slits set into one wall admitted narrow slats of aging sunlight. Furnishings were limited to three hempen mats, a water jug, and a crockery basin. The door set into the wall opposite the windows was made of heavy wood and fitted with a metal lock.

The window-openings were too small to accommodate even Rhan's underfleshed body, and the door had all too obviously been designed as a barrier. "I see what you mean," said Margoth sourly. "Not much to inspire the imagination."

"No," agreed Rhan. "Unless, of course, you happen to have a hairpin on you?"

Margoth ran her fingers through her tangled curls. "No, I'm sorry. I don't. And anyway, I think it would take more than a hairpin to trip a lock that size."

She clambered rather unsteadily to her feet and walked over to the door to take a closer look. Bending down, she put her eye to the keyhole, then ran her fingers over the lock's outer casing. "Just as I thought," she said wryly, straightening her back. "The trip mechanism is deep inside the frame. It would be hard to operate even if I had the right tools."

She frowned and ran her fingers over the lock again. Touch told her everything she needed to know about the structure of the lock and all its parts. She had a clear picture of it in her mind, along with an accompanying impression of well-oiled maintenance.

The vividness of her impressions surprised her. She could not recall ever having formed so complete a mental picture of any mechanical device she had previously dealt with. Of course, that knowledge was of no practical use to her without the proper implements necessary to the task at hand. But in spite of that, Margoth was not prepared—yet —to admit defeat.

Her brow puckered in thought, she glowered at the door, seeking fresh inspiration. Behind her, Rhan got up and walked over to the middle window.

Below the building that was also their prison-house, the seaport of Ghazarah fell away toward the ocean in a steep series of terraces. Gazing down over the stepped tiers of flat roofs, Rhan saw the zigzag line of a switchback road weaving between the terraces like a thread behind a shuttle.

Dusk was rapidly falling. "It'll be dark in another quarter of an hour," he said softly. "I wonder how much time we have left of each other's company."

Roused from her obstinate reverie, Margoth heard the forlorn note in his low voice. Her throat tightened. Oh God, hasn't he had enough yet of pain and forced partings? she thought angrily. "What more do you want of him? Or any of us, for that matter?"

Her indignation boiled up within her. In sudden sheer vindictiveness, she seized the metal fillet surrounding the lock and gave the casing a spiteful shake.

To her unbounded astonishment, her fingertips clove to the metal. Suddenly hypertactile, the nerve-ends in her fingers communicated a quivering disposition toward movement within the bowels of the lock.

The image of wheels and tumblers rose unbidden into her mind. She saw at once which adjustments needed to be made to free the spring-latch. Almost without thinking, she ordered the mechanism to turn over.

Her unspoken command translated instantly into energy. Power shot down the nerve-lanes in her arm like lightning along a wire. The surge of energy didn't stop at her fingertips. She felt the shock as the racing nerve-current discharged itself into the lock.

There was a staccato rattle of metal against metal, like a key turning in its bed. When the rattling stopped, the door swung loosely inward.

Margoth stared at the portal in dumbfounded amazement. Her whole arm felt numb, as if she had just received an electric shock. She was reminded of another door which, under extreme stress, had actually burst open when she demanded it. But this time was different. This time she had *known* each movement of the mechanism.

"Margoth! What was that noise?" demanded Rhan from across the room.

"It was the lock," said Margoth blankly. "I seem to have opened it."

*"What?"* Rhan sprang to her side. He looked from her face to the sagging door and back again in something like disbelief. "How did you do that?" he gasped.

Margoth rubbed her arm. The feeling was beginning, slowly, to come back to it. "I—I'm not exactly sure," she said dazedly. "I just *thought* about making the right parts move—and they *did*!"

Rhan blinked, then gave himself a shake. "We'll talk about it later," he said. "Right now, let's get out of here."

The passageway beyond was empty. Treading on tiptoe, they slipped across the threshold and made for the far end of the hall where the corridor bent to the left.

Hugging the inside wall of the passage, they halted at the turning. Motioning to Margoth to keep back, Rhan shot a lightning glance around the corner into the adjoining hallway.

Drawing back, he gave her hand a reassuring squeeze. "Nobody around. Come on."

The hall ended in a stairway leading down. "I'll go first," said Rhan. "Count to thirty. If you haven't heard anything out of me by then, you'll know it's safe."

He darted away from her before she could protest, and started down the steps. Crouching in the shadows, Margoth caught her lower lip between her teeth, her heart beating out the seconds. The silence held. With a quick glance over her shoulder, she straightened up and followed after her companion.

Halfway down, the stairs took a right turn at a narrow landing and continued on. Rhan was nowhere in sight. There was a door at the bottom of the steps. Margoth gulped air and kept going.

As she reached the foot of the stairway, the door opened a crack. "In here!" hissed Rhan. And pulled her across the threshold.

He closed the door behind her. The room in which Margoth found herself was long and narrow, its walls plastered white. There was a drainage conduit running along the floor from a water-pump in the right-hand corner to a tiled outlet in the left-hand one. Four bath-sized washtubs stood upside-down in front of a set of shelves along one wall. Most of the remaining floorspace was taken up by pressing boards and racks full of clothes set to dry.

Margoth knew the odor of washing soda when she smelled it. "Welcome to the laundry," said Rhan, and grinned.

Margoth plucked a linen smock off the nearest rack and held it up for inspection. "This ought to fit," she said. "I'll turn my back, if you'll turn yours. . . ."

A few minutes later, a pair of turbaned Pernathan serving-boys regarded each other with critical eyes. "There's a lock of hair sticking out from behind your right ear," said Rhan. "Yes, that's better. What about me?"

"You look fine," said Margoth, stuffing her discarded dress under a pile of dirty towels. "Now where do we g—"

Her voice plunged abruptly to a whisper as she caught the sound of footsteps approaching down the passage outside.

# BID FOR FREEDOM

MARGOTH STIFLED A GASP OF dismay behind her clenched fingers and darted for the corner on the blind side of the door. Rhan dived behind one of the washtubs. Making himself as small as possible, he wormed his way under it as the footfalls came to a halt at the door.

The latch rattled and the door swung inward. Margoth flattened herself against the wall and held her breath as a short, thick-bodied Pernathan in a food-spotted apron stumped into the room.

He went straight for the open cabinet built into the left-hand wall. Stepping between two of the washtubs, he came to a halt, arms akimbo, and peered up at the assortment of containers on the uppermost shelf.

At any moment he might turn around. Margoth's pulse pounded dizzily in her ears. Watching the intruder's back, she reached out a stealthy hand and snared a bedsheet off the top of the nearest laundry-basket.

The Pernathan stretched up to take one of the jars down from its place. When his straining fingers failed to capture it, he muttered and lowered himself onto his heels.

Still muttering, he stepped back and laid hold of the upturned base of the nearest washtub. Muscles tightening, he made a move to push it closer to the shelves.

The tub shifted a few inches, then stopped with a

bump. Scowling, the Pernathan hunkered down and raised up one side of the tub.

He caught a fleeting glimpse of a crouching figure in white before a sharp-knuckled fist smacked into his nose.

Roaring, he stumbled back and fetched up against another human body. Before he could react, this second assailant popped a sheet over his head from behind.

Blinded, he let out a bellow of rage and whirled in his tracks. His movement sent Margoth spinning into the walls. Rhan caught her before she went down. Evading the Pernathan's flailing punches, he seized a flatiron off one of the pressing boards and hurled it at one of their discoverer's sandaled feet.

The missile struck home with a thump. Leaving the Pernathan hopping and cursing, Rhan snatched up another flatiron in one hand and caught Margoth by the elbow with the other. "Run for it!" he hissed, and dragged her after him through the open door.

Behind them, the Pernathan cook was howling for help. Pounding down the length of a dimly lit corridor, Rhan and Margoth met up with two more Pernathans as the pair charged out of a side-room.

Snatching the second flatiron out of Rhan's hand, Margoth threw it at the leader's head. As he reeled back into the arms of his companion, she and Rhan shot past them into the room the Pernathans had just left.

They were in the kitchen. At the far side of the room, another doorway opened onto a darkened courtyard. Streaking between the worktables, Margoth led the way to the opening. Rhan paused to knock over a cooking brazier. As hot coals skipped across the tiled floor in the path of their pursuers, he darted outside and slammed the door.

They were in a square courtyard shadowy under a darkening sky. "The way out—over there!" gasped Margoth, pointing.

Lit by torches set into brackets on either side, a barrel-vaulted archway in the far wall yielded a tantalizing

246

glimpse of the street beyond. Without wasting breath on acknowledgment, Rhan took a fresh grip on Margoth's sleeve and broke into a run.

Before they had covered ten yards, the air came alive with shouting. Lights flared across their path from a swiftly opened door to their right and a group of shadowy figures boiled out into the yard. Behind them a man's hoarse voice called out a frantic string of directions.

Moving with unbelievable swiftness, the figures divided and scattered. In a sickening instant of panic, Margoth realized that she and Rhan could not hope to reach the gate before they were cut off.

Rhan had already seen their danger. Skidding to a halt, he wheeled sharply to the right, pulling Margoth along with him. Pelting along at his heels, panting with exertion, she could not at first see what he was making for. Then a dim opening yawned ahead of her and she discovered that he had found another door.

They had only seconds to spare before the vanguard of their pursuers caught up with them. With the thunder of following footsteps loud in their ears, they streaked across the last few yards of open ground and plunged into a lantern-lit twilight pungent with hay and horse-urine.

A figure seated to the right of the door started up as they burst across the threshold. "Close the door!" shouted Rhan and made a running dive for the other occupant in the room.

Margoth set her shoulder against the door and heaved. With her full strength behind it, the door swung shut with a boom that echoed across the rafters overhead. She slammed down the stout wooden bar across the back of the doorframe. A second later, a heavy body rebounded off the panels outside.

Hands beat and tore at the wood to the accompaniment of shouts and curses. Inside the barn, the lantern-lit air was full of snorts and the nervous clumber of hooves as the horses in the stalls took fright at the noise. The door shuddered under another ramming blow. Margoth recoiled and almost collided with Rhan as he emerged from the shadows.

There was blood on his lip. "Where's the stablehand?" asked Margoth.

"I knocked him down and he hit his head against a beam," said Rhan shortly. "Can you ride?"

"Only just," said Margoth.

"That'll have to do," said Rhan. "See if there's anything you can do to hold the door, but don't block it. I'll be back in a minute."

The din outside was mounting. The door shivered and shook under a rhythmic succession of thuds. The bar groaned under the strain. "Whatever you're doing, you'd better be quick about it!" called Margoth, then gave a stifled shriek as a large moving shape lumbered past her, almost knocking her down.

White-eyed with fright, the horse plunged to a standstill at the wall and wheeled about as two more animals bounded out of their stalls and surged toward the entryway. Margoth stumbled back and clambered onto the ladder leading up to the loft. Within seconds the central aisle of the barn was packed with tossing heads and heaving rumps.

The last horse wore a halter and lead, and carried a rider. Bearing down hard on the improvised reins, Rhan maneuvered his mount through the press to the foot of the ladder. "Quick! Climb on behind me!" he ordered.

Margoth stared down at the gelding's broad grey back in unalloyed dismay. The bar holding the door gave an ominous crack and began to splinter. "Hurry!" urged Rhan and held out his hand. Taking it, Margoth gritted her teeth and jumped.

The big horse started as she landed astride. Gripping its flanks with more strength than grace, Margoth flung an arm around Rhan's tight waist and struggled upright. No sooner was she in place than the bar-bolt gave one final

248

groan and burst apart. "Here we go!" called Rhan over his shoulder. "Hang on!"

The barn door swung inward. As the first of their pursuers stepped into the gap, Rhan gave an ear-rending war-whoop and slammed his heels hard into his mount's round sides.

The gelding lunged forward, ramming one of the other horses from behind. The collision touched off a chain reaction of startled squeals and plunging bodies. Hemmed in from behind, the riderless horses took the only escape route open to them and surged forward.

The Pernathans in the doorway leaped for their lives as the animals bolted past them. Last through the opening, the big grey gelding cleared the threshold with a controlled bound.

Men raced toward the disturbance, shouting and waving torches. The horses in the lead shied at the sight of fire and veered off to the right toward the open entryway. Still whooping like a barbarian chieftain, Rhan sent the gelding thundering after them. As they converged on the archway, he yelled, "Duck!"

Margoth did. Hoofbeats echoed hideously off the vaulted walls as the gelding slowed briefly to a trot. The sudden break in the animal's stride almost jarred her loose. But before she lost her balance completely, they were clear of the tunnel and the gelding leaped forward again into a rocking canter.

The street outside was cobbled. The gelding's shod feet struck sparks off the paving as Rhan reined him sharply to the right. Clinging to her companion like ivy, Margoth shot a brief glance over her left shoulder and gasped aloud as she found herself looking down onto the roofs of a separate level of buildings forty feet below.

The whole city was built on terraces. Her blurred gaze skipping down and down from one tier to the next, Margoth realized how high up they were. The gelding was gathering speed. She groaned and closed her eyes.

Wind rushed past her ears as the horse rumbled on in a staccato crackle of galloping hooves. The roadbed was descending at a dangerously precipitant angle. Margoth clamped her knees tighter to keep from sliding and prayed for the moment when they would reach the bottom.

Flanked to the right with walled shops and houses, the street made a shallow curve, then plunged three hundred feet toward a hairpin turn. His brown eyes widening, Rhan knotted his fingers into the ropes attached to the gelding's halter and pulled back on them with all his strength.

He might have been a fly on the big animal's back. Plunging ahead with his chin tucked tight to his breastbone, the horse held obstinately to his breakneck stride. His desperation growing, Rhan jerked twice at the halterropes with all his weight to no avail. Their mount thundered down toward the turn at top speed and only at the last second tried to slow up.

By then it was too late. Hooves smoking, the gelding sat back on his haunches. He slipped and went down on his hocks, floundering helplessly toward the slatted guardwall flanking the left side of the road. *"Jump!"* shouted Rhan, and dragged Margoth with him in a blind dive for safety as the horse crashed through the barrier and tumbled down the slope in a wild flurry of threshing legs.

Rhan hit hard and tumbled to a bruised standstill. The final impact jarred the breath from his lungs. Blackness swam before his eyes, but as his breathing caught up with him, his vision cleared. He scrambled to his knees and looked around for Margoth.

She was lying facedown several feet away. She didn't move when Rhan called her by name. Aghast, he dragged himself to her side and ran his hands along her back and limbs. When he could detect no obvious broken bones, he took her gently by one arm and shifted her over onto her back.

She had an ugly bruise on her right temple, but her breathing was easy and her heartbeat steady. Rhan heaved a sigh of relief and gave her limp hand a pat. "Nothing worse than a bump on the head," he said with a crooked smile. Then broke off short as the wind carried the sound of angry voices into his ears.

He turned around and looked back the way they had come. There was a cluster of torches descending from the crest of the hill—a large party, moving with speed and purpose. "Oh my God," muttered Rhan. He reached down and gave Margoth's shoulder a gentle shake. "Margoth!" he called with soft urgency. "Margoth, wake up!"

Her body yielded to the pressure of his hand, but she did not otherwise respond. "Margoth, please!" pleaded Rhan. "They're coming after us! Do you hear me?"

The long lashes did not so much as flicker. Rhan bit his lip and cast a worried glance around him in all directions, as the jeweled cluster of torches danced along the roadside and began to descend.

The slope above the road was all bare rock, terminating at the base of a walled villa crowning the bluff. The lower slope was gentler. Having in any case no illusions about how much strength he could bring to the task at hand, Rhan locked hands around Margoth's waist from behind and towed her over to the break in the retaining wall.

Looking down, Rhan half expected to see the dim broken outline of the grey horse, but no such sight met his eyes—evidently the animal had survived the fall with all four legs still intact. Relieved, he clambered first through the opening, then pulled Margoth after him.

Her dead weight dislodged a small avalanche of sand. Panting, Rhan took a firmer grip on his unconscious companion and began to work his way down along a shallow weed-grown fault in the hillside toward a row of walled gardens below.

The torch-bearers had reached the fatal curve in the road and were marching on toward the turn. Cradling Margoth's head against his chest, Rhan turned himself around and slid backward down the remaining twelve feet of sandy incline.

He arrived at the bottom with a cold squelch. Feeling behind him, Rhan discovered he was sitting in the middle of a thin spill of water a few inches deep.

From somewhere off to his right, he caught the sound of liquid trickling. Squinting in the darkness, he made out the dim cylindrical opening of a drainage conduit.

The spill was free of the taint of raw sewage: apparently the pipeline had been designed to transport water from a reservoir on the hilltop to nourish the gardens on this level of the town. Overhead, the pursuers were approaching the point where the horse had broken through the wall. Looking from the conduit to Margoth and back again, Rhan made a swift irrevocable decision.

The mouth of the conduit was only twenty inches across, but that was wide enough to accommodate one human body at least. Rhan wrestled Margoth's limp body feetfirst into the gap and nudged her further back up the pipe until her head was concealed from view.

He was breathless and sweating by the time he finished. "God knows I hate to leave you here like this," he told her softly, "but it's the best I can do for you just now. If I keep my freedom, I'll come back for you. If not, you'll at least still have a chance."

The voices of their pursuers were clearly audible now. He bent and kissed her lightly on the brow. "I've got to go," he whispered. "Good-bye, and good luck."

And so saying, he turned and slipped away into the dark.

# THE LEPER OF GHAZARAH

SEEN FROM THE SEA, THE port of Ghazarah was a dazzling confection of white walls and red-tiled roofs, rising out of the zircon waters of the Bay of Ghaza in seven concentric terraces. After a five-day voyage up the coast from Pirzen It'za in the teeth of a contrary wind, Harlech Hardrada's galleass the *Yusufa* dropped anchor at last within easy rowing distance of the mole.

After a brief delay, two longboats put out from the *Yusufa*. The first carried Duote, Harlech's black-skinned J'khartan first mate, to the northern end of the quay to report their arrival to the local harbor-master and pay the necessary anchorage dues. The second carried Harlech himself and Gudmar Ap Gorvald to another docking area at the opposite end of the long wharf, where the shops and warehouses gave way to a jumbled collection of other establishments, more varied and less reputable.

Leaving Hassan the pilot with two boat-hands to watch the launch, Gudmar and Harlech spent the greater part of the afternoon visiting a selection of tavernas, juju'bi dens, and brothels. They asked questions of all and sundry, but by the time the sun was westering, they had little enough for their pains, and none of that encouraging.

No one on the waterfront had seen any trace either of a red-haired Garillan woman, or of a fair-haired Garillan

253

boy. And just about everyone on the waterfront had seen the looming Garillan giant with a flat face and a bandaged arm, who had made his presence known in that quarter the day before, and who was also interested in Garillan slaves.

The last taverna Gudmar and Harlech entered was near the top of a stepped sidestreet. After a brief conversation with the owner—in which they learned nothing new—they decided to return to the *Yusufa.*

Harlech was glowering like a gargoyle. "That bastard Muirtagh!" he growled. "It gripes the soul of me wonderin' how he managed to get a whole day's headstart on us, when I could swear we left that poxy black ship of his stalled in its moorings like a dead goose."

"It wouldn't surprise me to learn that he traveled overland," said Gudmar. "With a fresh series of relay-horses, he might well have covered the distance between here and Pirzen It'za in a third less time than it took us to bring the *Yusufa* up the coast."

"I wish *we'd* thought o' that," grumbled Harlech. "An' let's hope it wilnae cost us. I wonder if that whoreson sack of guts is still in town."

Gudmar was prevented from commenting by a sudden yammering outburst of anger and dismay from up the street at their backs. Voices—male and female—muttered fearful imprecations. There was a flurry of feet running and doors banging shut.

Gudmar and Harlech turned and looked back. A twisted figure swathed head to foot in dirty rags was wending its limping way along the curbing, ringing a small bell as it advanced.

A veiled woman gave a shrill cry and snatched her child out of the path of the hunched apparition in grey. She paused on her own doorstep to make a sign of warding, then vanished inside with a swish of black skirts.

"A leper," muttered Harlech, watching the figure's slow progress. "Poor devil. Come on, Gudmar, we'd best leave him to his misery—"

"In a moment," said Gudmar. His eyes had narrowed.

254

Delving into the pouch at his belt, he took out a coin and flipped it into the dust at the leper's rag-wrapped feet. "May God's mercy be upon thee," he said in Pernathe.

The leper knelt in the dirt to recover the coin. "Charity's the same in any language. Thank you very much," said a light voice in clear unaccented Garillan.

The eyes that went with the voice were a vivid cornflower blue. "We *have* met before," continued the leper in the same matter-of-fact tone. "I knew you at once—though I wouldn't expect you to recognize me. At least, not in these clothes."

The leper raised a hand to the veil swathing the lower half of his face, and Gudmar saw that although the hand was dirty, the fingers themselves were sound and shapely. The veil dropped away, and he found himself gazing into an unflawed oval face with a firm mouth and a decided chin.

The family resemblance was as strong as he remembered it. "Good God!" said Gudmar. "The *other* Penlluathe."

The girl grinned thinly. "You have a good memory. At any rate, for faces."

"I'm not so bad at names, either," said Gudmar. "Yours is Margoth."

She nodded in acknowledgment. Harlech made an explosive sound in his chest. "Well, I'll be damned!" he exclaimed. "D'ye ken, we've been trailin' our boots up and down the length o' this bloody wharf for nigh on four hours, tryin' t' wring some word out o' somebody as to where you might ha' got to—"

"Easy, Harlech," said Gudmar dryly. To Margoth he said, "We got your brother's message."

He did not mention the fact that the messenger was dead; Caradoc would know how to break that news more gently. "We were supposed to rendezvous at Holmnesse," said Margoth. "How did you know to look for us here?"

"If you mean here in Ghazarah, we got that," said Gudmar, "from Caradoc."

The cornflower eyes flew wide. "Caràdoc!"

"We managed to pick him up in Pirzen It'za," said Gudmar. "Along with that silver-tongued friend of his—"

*"Serdor!"*

"Yes, that's his name," said Gudmar. "They're both aboard Harlech's ship." His golden eyes deepened. "We were given to understand that you and the boy were brought here together. Can you tell us where Evelake is?"

All the light went out of the girl's bright face, leaving it looking grey and exhausted with worry. "I—I'm afraid I don't know," said Margoth.

And surprised herself by bursting into tears.

Oblivious to the shocked and curious spectators peering down at them from behind shuttered windows, Gudmar took her gently by the hand and gathered her into the bracing shelter of his arm. "This is no place to stand and talk—especially since we have reason to believe that there may be enemies around. We'll send you back to the ship, where you can rest and re-collect yourself, and get news of your friends."

After the *Yusufa* docked at Ghazarah, two men who were not members of the crew spent part of the afternoon on deck, playing chess on an improvised game-board. The slighter of the two was about to declare checkmate when the man on port watch sang out the word that one of the longboats was returning.

Caradoc stood up and peered out across the water toward the shore. "That's Hassan," he said. "But no sign of either Gudmar or Harlech. There's someone else with him."

Serdor clambered stiffly to his feet. "Who?" he asked.

"I don't know," said Caradoc. "Whoever he is, he's all muffled up—"

Even as he spoke, the anonymous figure in the bow of the boat turned and shook back a concealing hood. Sunlight shone with sudden coppery brightness off blown tresses of red hair. Serdor caught Caradoc by the sleeve. "It's *Margoth*!" he gasped, and tightened his grip in a reflex of excitement. "They've found Margoth!"

He snatched up the loose linen shirt he had discarded earlier and dragged it awkwardly over his head. Caradoc moved to help him. "Careful—you'll disturb those burn-dressings if you don't watch out," he said warningly. Then grinned. "Won't she be surprised to see us!"

"She's already seen us," said Serdor. And waved his unbandaged arm. "Come on," he said to Caradoc. "Let's go meet her at the gangway."

Margoth came on board with the assistance of Harlech's Pernathan pilot, who had a familiar face. Hassan helped her up the rope ladder from the longboat and deposited her into her brother's waiting arms.

Her vision misty with painful relief, Margoth hugged Caradoc close with all the strength she could muster. "I thought I'd never see you again!" she said, her wet cheek pressed hard against his chest. "Or Serdor, either. Where is he?"

"I'm right here," said a warm, ironic voice from behind Caradoc's right shoulder.

Margoth caught her breath. Caradoc released her, and she flew like a bird to nestle in the minstrel's arms.

He wore bandages under his clothes. Disquieted in the midst of her gladness, Margoth withdrew her mouth from his and tilted back her head to look at him.

He looked thin and drawn, as though he had recently suffered a serious illness. His features showed fading bruises. "You're hurt!" she exclaimed. Then fell silent at the feathery touch of his finger against her lips.

"Never mind me for the moment," said Serdor. "What about Rhan?"

"Yes," said Caradoc. "Were you and he brought here to Ghazarah together?"

Margoth nodded. "We shared the same cell—until we broke out and made a run for it."

She told her tale briefly. When she described how she had come to unlock the door to their cell, Caradoc and Serdor stared at her in amazement.

"Do you mean to tell me," said Caradoc, "that you just laid hands on that lock and it *opened*?"

Margoth blushed. "There was a little more to it than that," she said. "I was in a temper, and—well, it surprised me as much as anyone. The thing is, I *knew* the shape of the lock just from touching it. Then I got mad—and power went from my hand into the lock like a current." She shrugged impatiently. "It's hard to describe. It's almost as if I was *at one* with the mechanism."

Listening to her, Caradoc drew a deep, wondering breath. A mage might well have described the Orison of Affinity in similar terms. He recalled the long hours —years—he had spent learning to identify himself with his patients, physically and spiritually, in order to heal their ills through the agency of the Magia.

He nodded slowly. "Quite an impressive feat—even for someone as talented at lock-picking as you are sister mine." He added thoughtfully, "I wonder if you could do it again if you had to."

"Maybe. If I got angry enough," said Margoth. But her eyes were serious. "I don't really know what came over me—except that at the time there was something I desperately needed to do—and not just for my own sake. . . . "

She dropped her eyes. "I'm not sure how much good it did in the long run. Rhan and I stole a horse and made our break for it, but the road was steep and we had an accident. I hit my head. When I woke up, I was lying flat on my back in a drainpipe, and Rhan was nowhere to be seen."

She grimaced. "I suppose Rhan must have hidden me there. The pursuit wasn't far behind us, and undoubtedly he was forced to flee. When I came to, I tried to find him, but since I don't speak Pernathe, I wasn't able to learn anything much. I even sneaked back to the hostel where the slaver had been keeping us, but that turned out to be a waste of time—at least as far as I was concerned."

258

"That was risky. I'm surprised you weren't picked up," said Caradoc.

Margoth gave a wry smile and displayed her discolored rags. "Nobody wants to get that close to a leper," she said.

Serdor's grey eyes warmed to a smile. "Well done!" he exclaimed. "Now tell us how you found Gudmar."

"More by luck than by judgment," confessed Margoth. "I'd just about decided that the only thing left for me to do was hang about the harbor and hope some decent Garillan merchant or trader might come along who would help me."

"Luck *and* judgment," said Serdor. "Where are Gudmar and Harlech now?"

"They've gone to question the keeper of the hostel," said Margoth. "Here's hoping they come back with news."

Serdor looked over at Caradoc. "All right. Suppose Rhan is still at liberty. He speaks Pernathe like a native, and he's no fool. If he's in hiding, he's likely to stay there unless he has good reason to risk showing himself—"

"What are you getting at?" asked Caradoc.

"I think you and I should go ashore and take a look around," said Serdor. "You're conspicuous enough with that hair of yours to attract notice, even at a distance. Rhan would recognize you even from far off, and come to us—"

"It might also draw attention from another quarter," said Caradoc. "We know Muirtagh is here somewhere. I'm not sure it's such a good idea to advertise the fact that we're right behind him. If *he* were to spot me, he could turn the tables on us."

"Very well," said Serdor. "Then I'll go alone."

"You can't be serious!" protested Margoth. "I don't have to be a mage to see you're in no fit state to be tramping the streets—"

"I'm well enough," said Serdor firmly. "My arm's sound enough for me to do a bit of juggling. And I still have the use of my voice. Rhan would know me by that, just as

259

surely as he would know Caradoc by his hair."

"That's not good enough. Muirtagh would recognize you if he got a good look," said Caradoc. "The bastard's almost killed you twice now. The third time he just might succeed."

"But Rhan is in trouble—wherever he is. And it's up to us to help him any way we can," said Serdor. "Caradoc, I wasn't given back my life just to hoard it like a miser!"

"No. But neither should you squander it like a prodigal," said Caradoc. "We both know how much it is worth."

His voice held a note that Margoth had never heard before. "Caradoc," she said softly. "What happened to you—to both of you—in Pirzen It'za?"

Serdor and Caradoc traded glances. "We ran afoul of Muirtagh," said Serdor. "He seemed to think we knew where you and Rhan had been taken, and he was prepared to use force to make us tell him."

His bald statement laid bare the story behind the bruises, and the general air of recent injury. Margoth flinched as she understood, and drew closer to him. "It's all right," said Serdor. "There was no lasting harm done —thanks to Caradoc."

"But—" Margoth turned to look at her brother.

He seemed at a loss for words. "Caradoc summoned the Magia to heal me," said Serdor quietly. "And he did it without a magestone."

A long moment of stunned silence followed this disclosure. Margoth eyed her brother in dawning wonder. "Is it true?" she asked breathlessly. "Are you sure it's the Magia?"

Caradoc nodded. "I don't pretend to understand how, much less why. Certainly not for any intrinsic merits I may possess," he said. "But it seems I have been elected to wield a singular gift. I can only hope that time and events will reveal to me the purpose for which I am intended to use it."

Another silence fell. "If ever I need proof of my own fallibility," said Caradoc. "I have only to review my own past actions. My judgment may not be equal to my gifts. Until I learn better, I will have to weigh my every action carefully—beginning here and now."

He sounded almost frightened. "You are not alone, you know," said Serdor. "Any burden is lighter if it's shared among friends."

A crooked smile plucked at the corners of Caradoc's handsome mouth. "I'll remember that," he said.

He might have said more, but before he could put his thoughts into words, a loud hail from the masthead attracted their attention. As one, the three companions turned to the port railing. A moment later they saw what the lookout had seen: the captain's launch returning, with Harlech and Gudmar on board.

Standing by the railing as the two men came on board the *Yusufa*, the three fugitives from East Garillon could see from the expression on Gudmar's face that the news wasn't good. Gudmar was brief to the point of being brusque. "The boy, it seems, was caught trespassing in the grounds adjoining the mosque. Apparently he cut through the gardens in an attempt to evade the men who were chasing him, and got picked up by the janissaries guarding the premises."

"What did they do with him?" asked Margoth fearfully. "Did they hand him back to the slave-dealer?"

"Nothing sae straightforward as that," said Harlech, with a glance over at his friend's stony face. "The jannies haled the boy up before the Imam, who ordered him shippit off to the quarries of Sul Khabir."

"What?" Caradoc was stiff with dismay. "How could they do that?"

"It's a capital offense for an infidel to invade a sanctuary of the Prophet," said Gudmar. "The chief Imam has full discretion to pass sentence in such a case."

He drew a breath. "The quarries are maintained by conscript labor—often foreigners arrested for infractions against the Code of the Prophet. Very few people who get sent there ever come out again."

There was a bleak pause. "How long ago did the slave train leave Ghazarah?" asked Serdor.

"Two days ago," said Gudmar. "We'll make up a party and leave tonight, following the same road. But it's a hard journey through desert wasteland. Our chances of overtaking the train before it reaches Sul Khabir are going to be slim."

"What happens if we fail?" asked Margoth.

"Then we'll really ha' trouble on our hands," said Harlech Hardrada.

# THE FACE IN THE MIRROR

Shortly before sunset on a mid-October evening, while most of the citizenry of Gand were engaged in having their dinners, Devon Du Penfallon stood alone in his bed-chamber in Gand Castle, and critically regarded his own reflection in a full-length mirror.

It was not an exercise he enjoyed. Despite his firmest resolutions, it was difficult not to dwell drearily on the physical shortcomings the mirror so dispassionately recorded: dark eyes too large for their setting; a thin, awkward body; the all-too-obvious aberration in the bones of the right leg. When he had asked that the mirror be installed six months ago, even Kherryn had been surprised, though with painful tact she had refrained from questioning him about it. Only Evelake Whitfauconer might have guessed the intent behind the request.

For it was Evelake who had given him the sword he now held in his hand.

It was a gift that he had longed for, and one that he treasured. Surrounded by his father's servants and appointees—people who unquestioningly accepted his father's crippling assessment of him—it was good to have something of his own. The sword had come to represent a means by which he could test and affirm his own strength. In teaching himself to use it, he was learning new ways to repudiate his father's view that he was an impotent weakling.

Not all the limitations were physical. His knowledge of the fencer's art was confined to what he had been able to glean from reading and from observation, rather than from actual experience. With no fencing partner other than his own reflection in the glass, he was uncertain about the quality of his progress. Nevertheless, he had persevered doggedly, painstakingly setting himself to achieve a degree of manual dexterity with the blade that would compensate for his comparative immobility.

Standing now before the mirror, he gravely saluted his own image and struck up an attitude en garde. From this position he embarked upon the series of drills he had devised for himself.

Counting slowly at first in whispers, he presented each attack and parry combination to the figure in the mirror, minutely adjusting the set of point, wrist, and elbow so that the individual movements led with formal precision into one another. The initial drill completed, he repeated the sequence of movements, more quickly and in a different order, disciplining hand and eye to produce time and again the desired exactitude of style. Then again, with more changes, at an increased tempo. Then faster . . . and faster . . . and faster still, until the point of his blade created a silver blur in the mirrored air.

So intent was he on his task that the interruption of a knock at the door betrayed him into a nervous start. Backing hurriedly away from the mirror to the bed, he flung up one corner of the counterpane and thrust his sword under the mattress. As he patted the coverlet back into place and straightened up, a hand rattled the latch and a voice from the corridor called anxiously, "My lord? Master Devon, are you all right?"

The voice belonged to his elderly valet. "Yes, quite all right, thank you, Brachen," said Devon. "Give me a moment and I'll be right there."

Limping quickly, he recrossed the room and turned

back the key in the lock. As he opened the door, Brachen gave him a searching look and said accusingly, "You're looking feverish, Master Devon. If you've taken a chill—"

"I haven't," said Devon patiently. "What's amiss?"

Brachen gave himself a shake. "I beg your pardon, my lord. Master Jorvald's daughter is downstairs . . ."

He paused, clucked his tongue, then said with labored neutrality, "She arrived a few minutes ago with a letter for you from Mistress Kherryn. Shall I show her up?"

"Tessa!" Devon's level brows came sharply together. "Yes, by all means—no, wait, I'll call her up myself."

Tessa moved at the sound of her own name. Making the most of her long legs, she bounded up the stairs two at a time. At the far end of the corridor, Devon's door stood ajar. Her boots ringing off the floor, she covered the distance in a dozen swift strides and rapped smartly on the lintel.

"Yes, Tessa. Please come in," said Devon's lightly resonant voice from the room beyond.

He was seated, she discovered, behind the inlaid writing table at the far side of the room, but his empty hands told her he had designedly removed himself there in order to receive her. As she stepped forward onto the carpet, he smiled and rose to his feet. It was so smoothly accomplished that had Tessa not known him well, she would never have suspected that in rising he had made strategic use of his arms, rather than his legs.

There was an amused glint in his dark eyes as he studied her. "Now I understand Brachen's peculiar manner," he said. "Never mind. You show off a tunic and breeches to decided advantage."

Tessa peered self-consciously down at her unimpressive chest. "If you're in a hurry, petticoats can be a serious hindrance," she said ruefully. "And there was the possibility that I might be followed on the way back here—"

"Followed?" Devon's gaze narrowed. "Tessa, what's been happening at Kirkwell?"

He looked suddenly very frail and vulnerable. Abruptly confronted with the painful difficulty of her task, Tessa squared her shoulders and said, rather unsteadily, "I'm afraid I've been elected to play the storm-crow. Devon, my news isn't good. There was a major upheaval in the proceedings of the Council. Your father—"

Her throat closed up before she could bring herself to complete the sentence. Watching her face change—"What about my father?" inquired Devon carefully.

There had been little enough affection between Arvech and this crippled son of his, whose worth the father had consistently misunderstood. That fact alone, however, hardly made matters any easier. "Your father is dead," said Tessa grimly. "And it is the official consensus of the Council that he died a traitor."

Devon's sharp chin jerked up. For a long moment he sat very still. Tessa could sense what she was not permitted to see: the stern, almost brutal enforcement of self-control. When the boy moved at last, it was with studied iron calm. "Tell me how it happened," said Devon Du Penfallon.

Tessa nodded. Summoning a hard-won fortitude, she recounted the series of events that had begun in denunciation and ended in tragedy. "I don't doubt there was some kind of conspiracy afoot," she said darkly at the end of her recital. "Given time, and the will to undertake a proper investigation, we might have been able to get to the bottom of it. Kherryn did her best to try and persuade your father to follow a more cautious plan of action. But he had already chosen his course."

Her shoulders drooped. "As it is, with both your father and Fyanor dead, nothing is settled—except that Gwynmira has been allowed to assume the regency. I don't doubt she and Gythe will want revenge. We'd better be on our guard."

"Give me Kherryn's letter," said Devon. "My sister has always had a peculiar gift for perception."

Tessa had the feeling he had been about to say more, but then had thought better of it. Wordlessly delving into the pouch at her belt, she drew out the sealed parchment

266

Kherryn had entrusted to her, and handed it over to Devon. He paused to look at the seal before he broke it. Then he opened the letter and bent his head to read.

Concentration did not come easily. His mind was churning with fears and speculations, with a growing sense of desolate loss and the knowledge that he would never now be able to measure up in his father's eyes—abruptly he concentrated on the letter. Kherryn's handwriting was feverish and shaky. Her opening sentence seemed to waver before his eyes like a guttering flame:

"By the time this message reaches you, our father will be dead, our family disgraced, and our city declared forfeit—"

Our city declared forfeit?

Devon's thin fingers tightened on the page he held before him. The stone floor beneath his feet seemed unstable, as if it might dissolve at any moment. "The Du Bors family now hold sway over Farrowaithe as well as Ambrothen," his sister had written. "They plan next to annex Gand. You must not allow them to take it, as you value your immortal soul. . . ."

"I understand now the dream I had. . . ."

The writing before Devon's eyes seemed to blur. He saw again in a flash of recollection his sister's white upturned face as she lay writhing on the floor of her room in terrible empathy with the victim of some distant act of violence. "What would cause me to have a dream like that?" Kherryn had asked at the time. At Kirkwell, apparently, she had found the answer.

He forced his attention back to the page to learn what it was she had discovered. The starkness of her words commanded his belief. "I now know Fyanor Du Bors to have been the Lord Warden's murderer. By the fact that the proofs of this go beyond what can be known from nature alone, be sure that he—and the Lady Gwynmira as well—have entered into some unholy alliance with what is totally evil. . . ."

A chill seemed to pass through the room. "Be warned.

The Du Bors family will shortly be sending an army against our city," Kherryn had written. "I am in sanctuary at Kirkwell Abbey and may not leave its precincts. It must be your task to convince the people of Gand that they must fight. And even if they will not listen to you, you must fight alone. Never yield while a single stone of Gand Castle yet stands in your defense. . . ."

Devon's lame body was trembling by the time he reached the end. He willed the trembling to cease before he turned to Tessa. His pale cheeks had no color left to lose, but the bone structure of his face had hardened. "My first act as my father's successor seems to be to convene a council of war," he said. "Will you go now, Tessa, and ask your father to join me here at his earliest convenience?"

The qualities were there: the strength and courage to command. Tessa inclined her head. "At once, my lord," she said. And went to do as he had asked.

Two hours after Tessa Ekhanghar's arrival in Gand, seven men of varying ages and aspects assembled in a room in the west wing of Gand Castle to meet with the new seneschal of the city: Devon Du Penfallon, the twelfth of his line. With them, present in the capacity of material witness, was Tessa herself.

There had been no time between fetching her father and returning to the Keep to change her clothes. Standing now at her father's side in her boots and breeches, Tessa felt the weight of disapproving eyes. She could only hope that her appearance would not count against her in helping Devon to present his case to the Mayor of Gand and the five aldermen who shared with him the responsibility for the governance of the city.

It was evident from the outset that Devon recognized what he was up against. Straight-backed and outwardly collected, he greeted each member of the group with courteous reserve. Having invited them all to be seated, he remained on his feet to break the news to them: that

rvech was dead, and that their daily lives were shortly to
c disrupted.

He left it to Tessa to supply a firsthand account of the
etails. Of the seven men present, only Jorvald had been
orewarned. He gave his daughter a nod of encouragement
s she stood up to speak. Then, as she reported, brisk
nd terse, all that had transpired at Kirkwell, he ad-
isted his position to compensate for his blind left eye,
nd took a long hard look with his right at his new over-
ord.

It wasn't the first time he had done so, though he
uspected that he was unique in that regard. Devon Du
enfallon, frail-seeming and aloof, had aroused his curiosi-
y some time ago when it had become apparent that the
oy was interested in swordplay. Remembering a wraith-
ke adolescent sitting hour by hour on a bench overlooking
ie Keep's training green, Jorvald wondered what possible
ttraction martial exercises could hold for a boy brought
p by his father to think of himself as a cripple.

Unless the young man had enough strength of charac-
er to draw for himself the distinction between a cripple
nd a weakling.

Absorbed in his own thoughts, Jorvald became aware,
uddenly, that his daughter had stopped speaking. All
round him the atmosphere of the room was charged with
ension as the ministers of Gand shifted their attention to
ie gaunt young figure standing at the center of the
emicircle formed by their assembled chairs.

Sustaining the impact of their wary expectation,
Devon said quietly, "From what you have just heard,
entlemen, it must be as clear to each of you as it is to me
hat the manner of my father's death has left us facing a
risis. It is a situation rendered all the more difficult by the
act that it calls for us to trust one another before we have
ven become acquainted. Nevertheless, I hope it will be
ossible for us to devise a course of action that will allow
s to weather the storm."

What he gave them next was his own version of th
warnings contained in Kherryn's letter. At liberty to stud
her father and his colleagues, Tessa watched them closely
trying to gauge the effect of Devon's presentation.

It was obvious that his calm strength had taken then
all, to some extent, by surprise. Whether or not they woul
suspend their preconceptions about him long enough t
give serious consideration to the logic of his argument
remained to be seen.

At least they were listening. The fact that they allowe
him to proceed without interruption counted for a grea
deal. The end of his speech was followed by a silenc
pregnant with speculation. Scanning his audience from lef
to right, Devon let the silence prolong itself for a momen
longer, then said gravely, "Gentlemen, you have the facts
Now I would welcome your comments."

It was hard to tell what to expect from these men, wh
were not soldiers like her father, but merchants an
guild-masters—solid, hard-headed, and prosperous. Wh
knew trade, and business, and the administration of good
and property, but knew perhaps too little of fervor and no
enough of faith to let their hearts be kindled in defense of a
cause in which the issues were those of conscience rathe
than of material welfare.

Not that they were exactly to blame. Dealing daily i
the realm of the physical, the tangible, the concrete, the
had never experienced the need to develop the depth o
vision necessary to recognize moral evil as a real an
terrible danger. Dedicated to the maintenance of the law
and the enforcement of public order, they would mistrus
any call to action that would seem to place law and order in
jeopardy. It would take more—much more—than rhetori
to convince them that they stood to lose more by yieldin
than they would by fighting.

Devon knew this, too. And so his speech was moder
ate. "I am not asking you to rend your garments and take
to the streets crying havoc throughout the city," he said
"But I *am* asking you to recognize the fact that this city is

danger, and to take steps to prepare against the threat. You have heard Lady Tessa's testimony. By her account, it may be only a matter of days before we find ourselves with a hostile army encamped before our gates. I urge you to use that time to firm up our defenses, so that they will not catch us off our guard."

At this, the Mayor of Gand stood up. "If I understand the matter correctly," said Rustiman Du Bracy, "this is a private dispute between your family, and the family Du Bors. We the citizens of Gand have long-standing obligations to the Seneschals of Gand Castle. But I am not certain that those obligations include espousing a personal quarrel as if it were a public issue."

Devon inclined his head, his dark eyes sober. "I understand your objection, Master Du Bracy. Certainly, I would be a poor seneschal indeed if I were to drag this city after me into a family feud. Tessa, however, has already attested to the fact that the Du Bors family has been mustering not only the Farrowaithe Guards, but also several mercenary companies from the Brotherhood of the Red Gauntlet. Since the realm of East Garillon is otherwise at peace, we can only infer that these forces are to be sent to counter the threat we represent to Du Bors supremacy. And if we grant that much, then it seems to me that the young Warden and his family have already raised this dispute above the level of family hostilities."

"I agree," said Jorvald Ekhanghar. He looked to Devon and when the boy nodded, he continued. "Speaking as a soldier, I point out—not without a certain amount of shame—that soldiers who are called into a fight do not always stop to make distinctions among persons. If we are destined to fall under danger of attack—as I believe we are—then I would not count on your being excluded from the consequences of an invasion just because you declare yourselves impartial. The least we can do is take steps to fortify the walls and muster up the militia, so as to offer our families as much safeguard as we may."

"I disagree." That came from Warryn Wingate, the

city justiciar. "Suppose Gythe Du Bors does send an army against this city? If its commander finds the walls already held against him, he must assume that *all* within are enemies."

"Possibly." Devon's tone yielded nothing. "But he will also think twice about proceeding any further without stopping to parley."

A stir of relief ran around the table. "Then you *are* prepared to parley?" asked the justiciar with some eagerness.

"Certainly," said Devon. "But only up to a point."

This time his voice had an edge. As the members of the group turned to him in fresh consternation, he hardened his jaw. "Conflict—warfare—is a great evil. But it is not the greatest. A supreme injustice has been committed —brutally and deliberately—against my family. And because it is precisely that—an injustice—its effects will surely extend to the people of this city."

He drew himself up. "Will I parley? Yes. But I will *not* compromise with evil. It remains for you to decide whether you will accept me as your arbiter. Or whether you will strike a separate bargain with the enemy for yourselves, and hope you will not be cheated."

Though shadowed with fatigue, his eyes were steadfast. But from the uncomfortable silence that settled over the room, Tessa knew that he had failed to sway them to their own defense.

Through no fault of his own: the rulers of the city were too afraid of what they might lose to perceive what was really at stake. Clearly they would take no formal steps that might compromise what they saw as their neutral position.

Her heart ached for Devon, whose gallantry had gone untried until this moment, and yet who had shown his fighting spirit. It was through a mist of tears that she saw the mayor rise from his seat to speak denial on behalf of the city council.

It was a final verdict. Having failed to move them, the

new seneschal gave the town dignitaries leave to depart. Once the mayor and his associates had gone, Devon sank down in his chair and said nothing for a long time.

His face was grey with strain and the despondency of defeat. He's wondering if they would have listened to him if he had been whole and sound—a hero to lead them into battle, thought Tessa. And added to herself in bitterness, "It wouldn't have mattered, one way or the other. They would still have left him to do this alone."

Then she caught her father's eye. "Not quite alone," she thought. "Not alone, after all."

Jorvald Ekhanghar released his daughter's gaze and stepped forward. Halting next to the table, he addressed himself to the slight bowed figure who sat there so quietly. "If we are to prepare this castle to withstand siege, we had better start at once," said the Marshall of Gand. "What are your orders, my lord?"

Startled, Devon looked up into the scarred face of Tessa's father. For a moment man and boy gazed at each other in appraising silence. Then Devon smiled, and offered Jorvald his hand.

# DEFENDERS OF THE KEEP

OF THE THIRTY MEN-AT-ARMS who made up the permanent garrison at Gand Castle, twenty-four remained in residence at the Keep to complete preparations against the impending assault. Six others—men whose skills extended to hunting and tracking—laid aside their uniforms and rode out of the city in pairs to take up scout duty in the woods and on the roads between Gand and the lake-crossing at Cheswythe.

Some of the household staff also elected to stay. Devon Du Penfallon was both surprised and touched when Brachen, his venerable valet, refused unconditionally to leave. He was profoundly grateful for such loyalty. Like the sword he now wore openly at his side, it was a treasured gift.

For three days the garrison labored from sunup to sundown under the speculative eyes of the townsfolk, building up the defenses on the castle walls, laying in stores of arms, provisions, and combustibles. Not officially numbered among the defenders of the Keep, Tessa Ekhanghar rode out to Dorley, her family's manor several miles south of the city, to see to the ordering of the household there.

She was able to muster fifteen men from among her father's tenants. Under Tessa's direction, they spent the better part of two days doing what they could to fortify the manorhouse—digging trenches and setting up traps.

The following day, they moved most of the Ekhanghar livestock, along with the families of the Ekhanghar dependents, up into a deep vale among the wooded hills six miles to the southwest of the manse. The movement of people and provisions took all morning and most of the afternoon to complete. The sun was sinking when Tessa and her escort turned their backs on the small village of tents and started back in the direction of Dorley.

There was no real path to follow until they reached the edge of the forest, a stone's throw from the shore of a small pond. A broad cattle-track ran north from the pond to one of the outlying farmsteads a few furlongs away. Tessa and the three men with her had not gone more than a hundred yards toward the farmhouse when a sudden outburst of frantic movement among the darkening trees to their left made them look sharply around.

Tessa and her party reined in to listen. The noise drew closer in fits and starts, as if some wounded animal were dragging itself from covert to covert, desperately trying to keep ahead of the hounds that pursued it. Upon Tessa's signal, her three men-at-arms dismounted and faded into the shrubbery at the side of the road. Tessa herself reached for the yewbow hanging from her saddle and drew an arrow from the quiver at her back.

A voice, thick with exertion, shouted out a command to halt. There was a wild thrashing among the shadowy leaves in a small coppice a rod's length from the pathway, and a man clad in green staggered out onto the open grass beyond.

His jerkin was soaked through with blood over his right side. He ran unsteadily, with his hand pressed over the wound. Even as he stumbled to his knees in the tussocks, his three pursuers burst through the underbrush, swords brandished high.

Their livery proclaimed them mercenaries—Brothers of the Red Gauntlet. The foremost of them rushed up on the wounded man and flung back his sword-arm as if to drive the blade through the other man's back.

Tessa shot him cleanly through the shoulder. The arrow penetrated his chainmail and hurled him back as if he had been struck by a thunderbolt. The two other mercenaries with him checked abruptly and dove toward the edges of the clearing. Their injured prey dropped flat and dragged himself forward in the direction from which the arrow had come.

Tessa vaulted out of the saddle. Slinging her bow over her shoulder, she ran to meet the injured man.

Leaving her companions to deal with his pursuers, she knelt at his side. The blanched face he turned to her was one that she recognized as belonging to one of the scouts her father had sent out from Gand Castle.

He recognized her as well, and clutched at her arm with bloodstained fingers. "Lady Tessa," he panted. "The Du Bors forces are on the march. They'll be within sight of the city by nightfall."

Tessa's blood ran cold. "How many men?" she asked.

"Four hundred horse. A thousand foot, about a hundred of them archers," said her informant.

He tightened his grip on her sleeve, his face twisted with pain. "Jastock was brought down by an arrow as we rode to warn the garrison," he said. "My horse . . . was killed under me—"

"Rest easy," said Tessa grimly. "We'll see to it that the warning gets through."

A clumping of footsteps behind her made her look swiftly around, but it was only her own men. "They made off like stoats," said Owain, her squire. "It'll take some tracking to run them to earth. Do you want us to make the effort?"

Easing the wounded man to the ground, Tessa stood up. "No," she said. "The danger is too close. Go warn our people to get ready. Take this man with you and see that his wounds are tended."

Owain jerked a thumb over his shoulder. "What about that mercenary?"

"Is he still alive? Then take him with you too

276

—blindfolded," said Tessa. "I'll talk with him when I get back."

"Where are you going, milady?" asked Owain.

"To Gand. For all the good it may do," said Tessa, with grim fatalism. And turning, stalked back to where she had left her horse standing.

The big black—her father's prize stallion—was strong and swift, and needed no spurring. Thundering up the road toward the Bridge of Ambre, Tessa took the last hill at a smoking gallop and only drew rein at the top where the trees opened up on the left side of the road to show her, half a mile distant yet, the wide sweep of the river Amberhyl, and beyond it, the fertile downs of Gandia.

From the crown of that hill, on a clear day, a traveler could see the line of the West Road for several miles inland, until it vanished among the trees. In the early dusk of an autumn evening, Tessa marked the course of the road as a broad band of moving fires, all converging purposefully on the city from out of the west.

The deadly pageantry of numbers confirmed what the scout had already told her concerning the size of the boy Warden's mercenary army. Massing down in the hollows, they would have the benefit of cover until they were within a quarter mile of the city walls.

Given the cautious attitude of the city's aldermen, it was questionable whether or not the guards at the West Gate would recognize the threat for what it was, and send a warning to the castle. Her face pale and set, Tessa wheeled the stallion sharply to the right and sent him ploughing into the midst of the trees to the east of the roadway.

After casting about in the failing light for a heartwrenching minute or two, she found what she was looking for—a narrow hunter's track that branched off northeast from the causeway toward the seacoast. Bending low over the saddle, she urged the stallion forward from a trot to a canter.

Low branches caught at her clothes and her hair. Bending, she ducked lower and after innumerable twists and turns, saw ahead of her the dim shimmer of water under the evening sky.

At the lip of the cliffs, the brush yielded to grass. Rising out of her stirrups, Tessa looked out across the dark expanse of Amberhyl Bay and saw the watchlights of Gand Castle shining down into the water on the far side of the estuary.

It was much too far for the human voice to carry a shout of warning, but there were other ways to let the garrison know that the enemy was coming. Tessa vaulted out of the saddle and groped in her pack for matches. Then at the cliff's edge, she gathered dead gorsewood and set herself to kindle a fire.

Jorvald Ekhanghar was standing on the southeast rampart of Gand Castle, staring moodily out over the water, when a yellow aster of firelight blossomed out of the dark brush that crowned the clifftop on the far side of the river. He straightened up and peered at it, his eagle's gaze keenly intent. A moment later, a golden pinprick of flame separated itself from the ground-fire. It danced briefly in the dusk like a firefly, then suddenly soared skyward in a tailed arc, like a comet.

Its flight drew a warning cry from the sentry in the adjoining tower. "Look, sir—a fire-arrow!"

"I see it," said Jorvald grimly. A moment later, the mysterious archer across the water shot another flaming missile into the air.

The sentry left his post and hurried along the wall-walk to where Jorvald was marking the rise and fall of a third pinprick of light. "Who is that?" asked the sentry. "And what does it mean?"

Jorvald knew who was doing the shooting. "If you can't win through to me in person," he had told his daughter, "send up a warning flare. And then get back to our people up the vale." When he turned to the sentry, the lines in his face had deepened. "Unless I miss my guess," he said evenly, "it means that Gythe Du Bors's commander-in-the-field is shortly going to be knocking at our front gate."

He drew his cloak more tightly about him with a dour flourish. "Go inform Lord Devon that the Du Bors forces have been sighted," he said to the sentry. "You may add that he may, if he pleases, join me at the west barbican to give them a suitably warm welcome. . . ."

The handful of soldiers on duty at the West Port of the city were few and had no orders to offer any opposition when Khevyn Ap Khorrasel, with a combined force of fourteen hundred men at his back, rode up to the gatehouse and demanded their immediate surrender.

In addition to three hundred mercenary cavalrymen recruited from among the Brotherhood of the Red Gauntlet, Khevyn had at his disposal a hundred mounted Farrowaithe Guards, dispatched by a direct order from Gwynmira Du Bors to take part in the assault. Leaving them to the task of securing the chain of secondary guardposts running the length of the city walls, the expeditionary commander led the rest of his forces into the city itself.

He made certain they moved quickly, pressing on toward the Keep which represented their chief objective. Because his men knew their business, the sporadic outbursts of protest on the part of belligerent civilians were quelled with a swift efficiency calculated to discourage anyone who might be cherishing similar intentions. Nevertheless, by the time the greater part of the regent's expeditionary force had reached the castle, the sky over the city was lit from beneath by several burning rooftops, testimony to the outrage of private householders.

The pillar of hard rock on which Gand Castle stood had once been part of the mainland, but centuries of erosion had worn away all the softer sediments, leaving a chasm forty yards wide between the castle rock and the bluff that represented the eastern boundary of the city itself. Normally traffic came and went between the castle and the town over a stout bridge that had been constructed across the gap from the city side. Supported on wooden pilings from beneath, it could sustain the weight of the heaviest wagon and withstand the bitterest winter storm.

Built to hold out against considerable strain, the bridge could reasonably be expected to resist a hasty attempt at demolition. Khevyn Ap Khorrasel, therefore, was considerably surprised and not at all amused, upon emerging from the shelter of the town's outbuildings, to discover the whole structure in flames.

A wind off the ocean carried the hot smoke chokingly into the faces of the men lining up along the cliffside. From the acrid tang underlying the stench of charred wood and burning creosote, it was clear that the timbers of the bridge had been supersaturated with oil before being put to the torch.

Hissing and crackling balefully, the fire had had time to build to hungry maturity. Directed by officers on horseback, the men under Khevyn's command formed up into hastily organized brigades. Transporting water by hand in upturned helmets from horsetroughs and wells, they damped their cloaks and rushed out onto the bridge, beating back the climbing flames as they came.

In the midst of their efforts to contain the blaze, a volley of well-aimed arrows fountained over the castle battlements, plunging with deadly effect among the men in the vanguard of the fire-fighters. Figures toppled and dropped from the bridgehead as those behind turned and bolted for the safety of the buildings at the west end of the castle causeway. A thin chorus of jeers followed them from the castle walls.

They made two more abortive attempts to save the bridge, and both times were repulsed by a rain of arrows from the defenders of the Keep. By that time, it was doubtful that anything further could be done to bring the damage under control. Summoning his lieutenant with a curt snap of one gauntleted hand—"Do you recall the orders I gave prior to our assault on the West Port?" inquired Khevyn with perilous sweetness.

Warned, the lieutenant drew himself up. "Yes, my lord. 'The gates are to be secured as quickly as possible. All members of the city guard are to be taken and detained, pending interrogation. . . .'"

"*All* members of the city guard. . . . Your memory," said Khevyn, "seems accurate enough. Why was the order not carried out?"

The lieutenant opened his mouth, then prudently shut it again.

"It should be apparent even to you," said the regent's deputy cuttingly, "that one of the guards at the port managed, somehow, to slip through your fingers and ran to warn the garrison. Had we taken the castle unawares, we would very probably have been able to shatter whatever rudimentary defenses they might have mustered. As it is, your negligence, lieutenant, may render the taking of the Keep a costly and a time-consuming enterprise."

With a roar and a blinding explosion of sparks, a sizable section of the bridge dropped away, sending a blast of heat rippling across the cliff face. Shielding his eyes from the glare with one hand—"We have lost our chance at taking the castle by force," said Khevyn. "Let's see if there is anything to be achieved by parley."

Fierce as the breath from a forge, the billowing heat from the blaze had already driven most of the company back from the cliff's edge. The voracious roar of the flames drowned out, for the moment, the clamor of confused voices and the sounds of scattered fighting from the streets adjoining the castle.

"We'll have to wait until the fire dies down," said Khevyn after a moment's consideration. "Lieutenant, leave fifty of your men here with me. The rest may be better employed in securing the outlying areas of the city. They are to take prisoner any person who does not immediately comply with the order to lay down arms. . . ."

At the end of two hours, little remained of the bridge but a collection of smoldering wreckage through which the smoking remnants of the pilings protruded like so many stumps of charred bone. By that time, the wind had shifted round to the north. Glimpsing through the drifting smoke sporadic flickers of movement along the Keep's crenellated battlements, Khevyn gestured to the trumpeter who had ridden with the company out of Farrowaithe on the eve of Fyanor's triumph.

Rough as a raven's cry on the parched air, the horn crowed its challenge to the silent watchers on the walls. As the echoes of it died away, Khevyn drew off his helmet and rode forward bareheaded to the foot of the causeway.

"I am Khevyn Ap Khorrasel, Deputy-Commander of the Field Companies of Farrowaithe. On behalf of Gythe Du Bors Whitfauconer, Warden of East Garillon, and on the authority of Gwynmira Du Bors, Regent of the Realm, I order you to abandon your weapons and surrender this fortress, or be arraigned on charges of highest treason against your rightful overlord!"

The sea-wind, sweeping across the intervening gap, carried his words upward in a floating swirl of incandescent debris. For a moment there was no response from the castle's anonymous defenders. Then suddenly on the roof of the barbican to the right of the portcullis, a torch flared into life and a single dark figure stepped into the gap between two merlons.

Slight to the point of attenuation, the figure occupied the center of the light in stark silhouette. As Khevyn, squinting, tried to penetrate the glare, a voice spanned the scorched ravine between them.

"We do not recognize the authority of the Du Bors family. Still less do we recognize yours. In entering this city by force as an enemy, you have displayed the rank lawlessness of a common brigand. To surrender to you would be an act of betrayal against the very laws you have invoked."

The voice carried a degree of authority oddly at

variance with the youth suggested by its thin clarity. Without rising from his stirrups, Khevyn addressed himself to the shadowy speaker on the wall. "If we are raising questions of authority, boy, may I ask by what right *you* speak on behalf of this garrison?"

His tone was deliberately insulting, but the figure on the battlements showed no sign of retreating. The clear voice out of the aura of torchlight called back, "The right of inheritance, my lord. I am Devon Du Penfallon, after my father acting Seneschal of Gand. The command of this castle is a sacred trust committed to me by my father at his departure. While I and those with me yet live, no breakers of a lawful peace shall enter here!"

This declaration provoked an undercurrent of muttering among the men ranged along the cliff. Quelling the murmurs with a slicing movement of his hand, Khevyn said sharply, "Do you claim, Devon Du Penfallon, to have succeeded to your father's eminence? Do not expect that claim to carry much weight with me. Even your father found it difficult to accept the legitimacy of a cripple."

Watching from the right of the crenel in which Devon stood balanced, Jorvald Ekhanghar saw the boy flinch. His jaw jutting angrily, he closed the distance between them, but even as he reached out to touch Devon's angular shoulder, Arvech's son threw back his head.

Raising his voice again, he called out to the emissary on horseback below, "My legitimacy, nevertheless, is unimpeachable. And I stand by the decision I have made."

There was a pause. "Then you must be prepared to see the people of Gand suffer for it." The voice of the emissary was tight with suppressed temper.

"That," said Devon, "is your decision, not mine. The men who stand behind me now are here by their own choice. I lay no commands upon the rest of the inhabitants of the city: they are free either to submit to you or to resist you according to their individual consciences. But this castle shall stand. And its defenders with it!"

# STRIKE AND PARRY

WHILE KHEVYN AP KHORRASEL WAS exchanging verbal ripostes with the defenders of Gand Castle across the smoldering gap left by the destruction of the castle causeway, the mercenary army of Gythe Du Bors Whitfauconer was spreading like wildfire through the city streets. Their progress was attended by sporadic outbursts of fighting, as some of the hardier citizens turned out to defend their homes and their families. Resistance, however, was doomed to failure. The professional soldiery dispatched by Gwynmira Du Bors in the name of her son smashed through the ranks of the dissidents, stopping only to take prisoners before moving inexorably onward to secure the city, neighborhood by neighborhood.

Not even the hallowed precincts of St. Berengar's Abbey and Hospital escaped the night's turmoil. Despite the rigorous objections of the Grand Master and his senior magisters, those agitators who applied for sanctuary under the auspices of the Hospitallers' Order were dragged summarily forth from the protection of the cathedral porch and marched off at sword-point to the city guildhall, which had been converted into a temporary prison. The cripples and beggars who enjoyed the time-honored privilege of sheltering within the abbey's forecourt were driven forth with blows and ribald threats of violence. Those who resisted were arrested on the spot, and one peg-legged beggar who assaulted a guardsman with his crutch was beaten unconscious before being hauled off to join the other prisoners taken in the fighting.

By morning all the streets were empty, and all shops boarded up tight. Those citizens who had played no direct role in standing off the invaders huddled fearfully behind locked doors, waiting to be told what price they would have to pay for the night's toll of violence. Those partisans still at liberty fled and hid before the advance of the roving patrols whose task it was to crush the final embers of resistance.

Only the Keep remained inviolate, a stark stubborn monument to the fighting spirit of Arvech Du Penfallon. Above the topmost tower of the central donjon, the green and white pennon of the seneschal floated defiantly against the rising sun. Across the gap, beyond the cinders of the causeway, the Du Bors troops were already setting up guardposts and barricades.

The siege of Gand was set to begin.

Lacking the heavy artillery necessary to force matters, Khevyn Ap Khorrasel, commander-in-chief, had no other choice for the moment but to play a waiting game. Unable to occupy the castle, he was obliged to look elsewhere for accommodation, and in the end selected as his personal headquarters the handsomely appointed townhouse belonging to the Mayor of Gand.

Rustiman Du Bracy, haggard from sleeplessness, received in tight-lipped silence the news that he and his household had been singled out to play unwilling host to the man who had so forcibly trampled underfoot the pride of the burghers of Gand. Seating himself without preamble in the armchair in Rustiman's personal study, the Baron of Kirkwell stripped off his gloves and cast them on the desk in front of him. "I do not pretend to be an easy man to deal with," said Khevyn Ap Khorrasel curtly. "Do as you are told, and you will suffer only a minimum of unpleasantness. Do otherwise, and you will speedily find out how dispensable you are."

Rustiman cast an uneasy backward glance at the sergeant-at-arms standing within an arm's length of him. Elsewhere in the house soldiers were coming and going with casual insolence. His mind dwelling apprehensively on the present condition of his wife and three children, the Mayor of Gand said stiffly, "What is it that you require of me?"

"I require you," said Khevyn, "to act as liaison between me and the other worthies of this city. From this day forth, you will be responsible for communicating my orders to your fellow administrators. It will be up to all of you to see that these orders are carried out."

Implicit in the baron's tone were a host of unspoken threats. His expression wooden, Rustiman said, "What are your orders?" And grunted aloud as the sergeant jabbed him rudely in the lower back with the butt-end of a baton.

"You will begin by addressing me as 'my lord,'" said Khevyn coldly, "recalling that I am now territorial governor of this city and its environs, and the military representative of His Highness Gythe Du Bors."

His senses still swimming painfully from the blow, Rustiman was startled into blurting out the two words that penetrated the haze. "His *Highness*—?"

"That is correct," said Khevyn. "As heir by birth to the lordship of Ambrothen and Farrowaithe, and overlord of Gand by default of fealty, Gythe Du Bors has taken to himself the title of King of East Garillon."

Such a move, in brazen defiance of an ancient and jealously maintained tradition, spoke volumes of the extent of the Du Bors ambitions. Unable to contain his dismay, Rustiman said, "How have the Seneschals of Glyn Regis and Tyrantir responded to this development—my lord?"

"That is none of your concern," said the territorial governor of Gand. "The inhabitants of this city—believe me—already have trouble enough on their hands without borrowing more."

Which was, as it turned out, something of an understatement: Khevyn's list of new regulations was both comprehensive and onerous.

The edicts included the imposition of a sunset curfew, and a strict prohibition against both public and private assembly except at the instigation of the governor himself. The penalties for various kinds of seditious activity were graphically outlined, and other activities, such as travel, were to be restricted.

The governor's demands, however, did not end there. Rustiman was informed that the citizens of Gand would be required to bear the cost of housing and maintaining the troops stationed within the city's boundaries. The families of the leading burghers, furthermore, would be constrained to deliver up hostages to ensure their cooperation. These evils were crowned by a final penance, as outlined in the language of the Warden's chancery:

> Inasmuch as His Highness's esteemed uncle, Fyanor Du Bors, was beguiled to his death by one Arvech Du Penfallon, lately Seneschal of Gand, but now proclaimed recreant traitor, restitution for this grievous loss shall be made by the people of Gand on behalf of their former overlord to the value of a tithe of the income of each household within the city walls. . . .

Khevyn Ap Khorrasel took vindictive satisfaction in watching the mayor's face blanch under the staggering impact of the reckoning yet to be paid. Having thus revenged himself on the burghers of Gand, the new governor was given further opportunity to vent his spleen later in the morning, when his adjutant reminded him that he had yet to decide the fate of the individuals arrested in the street-fighting of the night before.

It meant paying an unscheduled visit to the guild-hall. Short on sleep, and even shorter on patience, Khevyn ran a bad-tempered glance down the list of names tendered him by the officer in charge. "There are about five score of them in all," said the lieutenant. "What do you want us to do with them?"

Khevyn tossed the paper away from him with a disdainful flick of the wrist before raising his eyes. "Did we lose any men to these bumpkins?"

"About a dozen," said the lieutenant.

"Find out which prisoners were responsible for the deaths and set them aside to be executed," said Khevyn. "As for the rest . . ."

He thought a moment. "We'll give them a choice. They can either pay a fine of thirty gold nobles each, or join their companions on the gallows."

Khevyn left his subordinates to implement his decision, while he himself returned to his chosen lodging to draft his report to Lady Gwynmira Du Bors. By the time the men on guard duty had established which prisoners could raise the fine money, it was approaching sunset. While the lucky ones were still yielding up their gold, those prisoners who lacked the resources necessary to buy back their lives were herded down into the cellar of the guild-hall and left there to await execution at dawn.

The proclamation of their impending doom was cried through the streets at dusk. As darkness settled sullenly over the city, the city gates were locked, and the great guard-chain was drawn across the harbor-mouth, sealing off all shipping within the bay. As a further measure to discourage any nocturnal demonstrations of discontent, the commander of the occupation forces ordered that a full third of his men should be out on patrol at any given time during the watches of the night.

While these strong measures were being taken to convince the captive population of Gand that Khevyn Ap Khorrasel intended to rule with an iron hand, these same

288

measures did not prevent one agile, black-clad figure from slipping over the city wall shortly after midnight. After eluding three separate patrols, this figure—which the defenders of the castle would have recognized as one of their own scouts—made off south through the woods on the other side of the river, toward the Ekhanghar manor of Dorley.

Inside the city walls, the night passed uneasily, but without major incident. At daybreak the forty-three prisoners who had been unable to arrange ransom were driven out into the cold grey dawn and roped together into three straggling lines. Escorted by fifteen Red Gauntlet mercenaries, the doomed men were marched down Mercat Street to the city's West Port. From the port, it was another half a mile west along the Gand High Road to a dreary plot of cleared ground known as Felon's Green.

Carved out of the dense woods at the left side of the road, the green was dominated by the grim black timbers of a high gallows. As the prisoners rounded the last sharp bend in the road, the ones in front fetched up short at the sight of a second, newly wrought gibbet on the right side of the road, opposite the green itself. Its extended framework supported a whole series of iron cages that dangled free from lengths of strong chain. The light moving airs of early morning picked up the funereal jangle of metal on metal —a ghoulish reminder that Garillan law called for the bodies of traitors to be displayed unburied for the benefit of all who passed them by.

The other prisoners straggled numbly to a halt behind those in front. There was a shocked and sheeplike moment of uncertainty, but before the prisoners' guards could goad them on to cover the last few yards, a voice from the back of the line gave a sudden unexpected crack of scornful laughter. "God, lads, I think we must have given these buggers a scare the other night. They're so afraid of us, they're even going so far as to lock up our corpses!"

Somebody else, taken off guard in the midst of his

tension, sniggered out loud. A subtle stir of movement passed along the prisoners' ranks, like the first breath of a wakening wind. "His Highness the Governor must be in quite a flap," continued the first voice. And soared into cackling falsetto mimicry. "Good God, Griswold—take every precaution! We don't want to risk getting caught with our knickers down—"

Out of the ashes of cold fear burst a spontaneous round of ribald chuckles. The sergeant in charge whipped around in his saddle, looked about for the instigator, and singled out a tattered grey figure at the very end of the procession. "You there! Watch your tongue," he growled.

The prisoner, who had a peg leg, planted the stump of it firmly in the ground and leaned insolently on his crutch. "What are you going to do if I don't, dung-breath?" he asked derisively. "Execute me?"

The gibe provoked a supportive burst of jeers from his fellow prisoners. The men on the ground began shifting apart, fingering their hempen leashes. Sensing a potentially dangerous situation developing, the sergeant signaled his men to close ranks. As they kneed their horses forward to hem in the prisoners, he turned back to the peg-legged beggar and took a hard grip on his riding-whip. "You stinking bag of lice, you'll be wishing you'd been first to greet the hangman by the time I've done with you," he snarled, and lashed out at the other man's seamed face.

The beggar turned the blow with an unexpectedly dexterous sweep of his crutch. "Have at 'em, lads—we've got nothing to lose!" he shouted. And caught his assailant by the wrist of his gauntlet.

The triple line of prisoners erupted into sudden chaos. Shouting orders furiously, the sergeant wrenched his arm back and groped for his sword.

The blade flashed blue as it cleared the sheath. Grinning mirthlessly, the sergeant flung back his arm to strike.

In the same instant, a green-clad figure leaped upright among the bushes at the southern edge of the green. A singing arrow slit the sunlight. It struck the descending sword-blade with a hard clang, and both weapons flew apart in a clash of sparks.

The sergeant started back with an oath. The green-clad archer gave a piercing whistle, and suddenly the clearing was alive with racing green-clothed shapes.

The two parties came together in a dissonant clatter of mixed weaponry. While their erstwhile guards struggled for fighting room, the prisoners began wrestling free of their neck-ropes. Left with only a dagger to defend himself, the sergeant wheeled his horse around and gave it an impatient jab with the spurs. As the gelding shouldered the one-legged beggar to the ground, another figure darted forward in swift pursuit.

Using every ounce of momentum her long legs could give her, Tessa vaulted onto the gelding's crupper. She landed cleanly, and threw a grappling arm around the sergeant's waist.

The rings of his hauberk grazed her cheek as he flailed with both elbows in an effort to dislodge her. Clinging headdown like a limpet, Tessa worked the point of her poniard into the chink at the back of his shoulder, and when he swung his own dagger downward to hack at her knee, she rammed it home.

Men on the ground surged forward as he slumped. Before Tessa could intervene, hands plucked him roughly from the stirrups, and he vanished under a storm of pummeling fists. Thighs clamped hard to the horse's heaving barrel, Tessa rode its frantic plunge sideways, changed grips, and leapfrogged into the saddle. Leaning forward, she groped for the trailing reins, and when she had them, flung a swift glance over the melee.

Overwhelmed by the first rush of numbers, several other Red Gauntlets had fallen. The rest were holding their attackers at bay with broadswords and hand-axes as they retreated toward the causeway. Pitching her voice to carry above the din of fighting, Tessa shouted, "Owain! Bowmen to the ready!"

Her five archers at once broke away from the struggle

and began nocking arrows. Tessa was about to dismount to join them, when a voice from the ground called sharply, "Look out, girl!"

Warned, Tessa whipped around to see another horseman spurring straight for her, whirling a morning star with deadly proficiency. Dragging hard on the reins, Tessa forced her horse back on its haunches.

The animal reared and lashed out with iron-shod forefeet. One hoof grazed her adversary's helmet. He threw himself flat against his own mount's withers, then flicked the ball-end of his weapon toward Tessa's exposed thigh.

The spikes opened four short gashes in her breech-hose as she recoiled. Before her adversary could recover his balance for a second blow, a gaunt grey figure darted around under his horse's neck and dealt him a ringing blow on the back of the helm with a stout wooden crutch.

The stroke jarred the rider out of the saddle. As the horse shied sideways, the beggar in grey gave a grim mutter of satisfaction and hit his opponent a second and final time.

Her would-be assailant settled into a limp heap on the ground and Tessa brought her own mount back under control. Her grizzled ally gave her a dour nod. Tessa acknowledged it with a wave, then spun away to join her men in cutting off the mercenaries' retreat.

The small force of Red Gauntlets did credit to their training, but in the end, the fact of superior numbers told against them. One by one they were picked off—some by arrows, others by sticks and hurled stones—until at last there were none left standing. Leaving Owain to deal with prisoners, casualties, and loose horses, Tessa went looking among the ranks of the men they had rescued from the gallows to see if she could find the man in grey who had lent her his aid.

She found him sitting alone on the steps leading up to the gallows. He was examining the shaft of his crutch, but he looked up as she approached. "I just thought I'd come

292

say thank you for your timely intervention back there," said Tessa.

He gave her an inscrutable look from under bushy grizzled eyebrows. "I figured I owed you a favor. That was some very pretty shooting."

"And that was very pretty staff-work," said Tessa. She added, "That kind of skill takes training. Who taught you to fight?"

He grinned thinly. "Allard Ap Alwyn."

Tessa blinked. Twenty years after his death, Allard Ap Alwyn was still revered as one of the greatest arms-masters the Brotherhood of the Red Gauntlet had ever known. Aloud, she said, "Indeed? That accounts for your performance."

"It also accounts, in a roundabout way, for *this*," said the former mercenary with arid humor, tapping his wooden leg with the haft of his crutch. He gave her another glinting look from under his heavy brows. "Fighting's a thankless profession, girl. Why involve yourself in it?"

"Because at the moment there doesn't seem to be anyone else," said Tessa frankly. "With the seneschal and my father holding Gand Castle, and the city itself under martial law, *somebody's* got to put up a show of resistance on the outside and pull together some support for Gand."

She surveyed her companion for a moment longer, then said with point-blank directness, "Would you be interested in helping us?"

Dour amusement flickered deep in the former mercenary's grey eyes. "Two days ago, I would have said no. But now I've got a few scores to settle. Yes, you can count me in."

"In that case, welcome to the Free Company of Gand," said Tessa. "May I know your name?"

"You may," said her new ally. "It's Duncan. Duncan Drulaine."

His gaze shifted away from her face to the littered grass of the Green. "If you'll take my advice now, we'd better all be going as soon as possible. Have you ever had to live like a fugitive before?"

"No," said Tessa. "But I daresay I'll be learning how soon enough."

"Learn well, then," said Duncan. "Because from here on out there won't be any turning back." He regarded his tall, blond fighting partner with distinct approval. "We'll need to go underground for a while, to build up strength. And after that, it's going to be a long war."

Neither he nor Tessa seemed to be in the least dismayed by this prospect.

# THE QUARRIES OF SUL KHABIR

THE CHAIN OF SLAVES FROM Ghazarah approached the stone quarries of Sul Khabir from the west along a baked clay road that ran a weary zigzag course through a series of yellow-grey foothills. The first objects that the new conscripts saw of their destination were the frowning box-turrets of the stockade guarding the entrance to—and exit from—the quarry-pits themselves.

The next thing they saw was a spiked iron portcullis leading into a ten-foot-long tunnel. The tunnel in turn led into a parched courtyard dominated by a square keep that was both a guard-tower and a residence for the overseers and soldiers who supervised the working of the quarry. Here the newcomers were presented to the commander of the garrison for inspection before being herded off under guard through a second tunnel at the rear of the stockade, and downhill into the dustbowl of the quarry-pits themselves.

Rhan was one of the last in the long line of slaves who had made the five-day journey on foot across the arid empty wasteland of bare rock and shifting sands that the native Pernathans called Khazar Mu'jakr—"the anvil of the sun." Even a month past the autumn solstice, it had been a grueling trip. Rhan shuddered to think what it would be like to attempt the crossing in the baking heat of high summer.

As it was, his shoulders were blistered with sunburn and his lips cracked with thirst. Like all the other slaves in his train, he limped when he walked, his bare feet leaving crimson blots in the dry sand. He was so tired that he could hardly keep himself upright. But despite thirst and exhaustion, his weary mind kept turning over and over the events of his last night in Ghazarah.

His first thought upon leaving Margoth behind had been to put as much distance as he could between himself and her, in order to draw off their pursuers. The Pernathans had come down the slope more quickly than he had expected, however, and he had been forced to show himself sooner than he had planned.

Once they spotted him, they gave chase, ploughing over walls and through hedges in their efforts to overtake him. Intent on keeping ahead of them, Rhan had cut across a series of orchard-gardens, where the lush shrubbery offered a welcome promise of cover. He had not realized —until it was too late—that the grounds he had invaded belonged to the Great Mosque of Ghazarah.

The grim, bare-chested janissaries who had captured him took him at once before the Imam, where he was summarily tried and sentenced. The following morning he had been led off in chains to join a whole convoy of other prisoners bound for the quarries of Sul Khabir.

He had trouble recalling the five days of the journey as distinct from one another: they represented a monotonous blur of heat and thirst and dust and weariness. The nights, however, were another matter. Ever since leaving Ghazarah, Rhan's sleep had been broken by a series of strange and terrifying dreams, that left their mark on his waking thoughts like a shadow in the light of day.

It was not the first time he had been tormented by horrors generated by the coming of night. During his days as a servant at the Manticore Inn, he had suffered from recurrent nightmares of a vivid and disturbing nature. Serdor Sulamith had obtained his release from that servitude, and during the weeks that followed, the dreams had ceased to plague him. Now, however, the black visions had returned with new and terrifying virulence. In the four nights since he had left Ghazarah, he had come to dread the quiet of the dark more than the heat of the day.

There was a covered well at the far end of the first circle of cliffs, not far from the point where a narrow ravine gave access to the inner pits of the quarry. The new conscripts were given a sparing allowance of drinking water before being marched off to their quarters: rude caverns hollowed out of the feet of the overhanging rocks.

Rhan was taken, along with three others from his train, to a cave in the northeastern wall of the enclosure. When the guards hustled them through the rough-hewn doorway, other dust-whitened bodies stirred on the floor as the slaves already in residence turned to stare at the newcomers.

There was a guttural spatter of comment from somewhere toward the back of the cave. Glancing up at the tall black-skinned men on either side of him, Rhan wished that he could have spoken Nhuboran as well as he spoke Pernathe. It would have been some comfort to have had at least an acquaintance among all the strange chalk-powdered faces that ringed him round.

He felt in that moment desperately alone and vulnerable. Making himself as small and insignificant as possible, he sidled to the wall and huddled in a noisome corner with his back against the stone. But the men and boys whose quarters he was sharing had already lost what little interest they had shown in the newcomers. Worn out by day-long toil under the scorching sun, they lay back amid the rubble on the floor and subsided again into the beaten somnolence of leaden fatigue.

Outside, the twilight deepened into inky blackness. Looking toward the torchlit mouth of the cave, Rhan could see their armed guards crouched over a game of dice. In his present state of mind, the *click-click* of the bones conjured up the ghostly rattle of dead men's fingers. He shivered and hugged his knees tighter to ward off a sudden chill.

Hunger gnawed at his midsection, but a greater sense of emptiness that was not of the body struck Rhan to the heart. He was filled with a desolate yearning for the friends he had lost. In his mind's eye, he saw again the moments of parting: Serdor vanishing under a collapsing wall of water; Caradoc raising a narcotic-laced cup to his lips; Margoth lying unconscious in the culvert where he had been forced to leave her. Wherever they were now—dead, enslaved, lost—he could not help them.

And none of them could help him.

Shifting his position to ease his aching limbs, he pressed his forehead wearily against the wall to his right. In an effort to keep awake, he forced himself to recall verses of poetry, fragments of prayer, snatches of song. A stanza plucked from nowhere in particular reiterated itself with peculiar insistency:

> What is a name, then?
> What is it for?
> Is it a talisman?
> Is it a door?
> Something of fortune?
> Something of fame?
> Something of sorrow?
> What is a name? . . .

What is a name? he thought tiredly. "Something to remember your friends by, when you don't have anything else left. . . ."

"Rhan . . ."

The sound of his own name, spoken in a whisper, startled him into sudden full awareness. He jerked his head upright and looked around him.

Everything was as it had been before he had turned his back and allowed his eyelids to droop. The dim flicker of the torches at the cave's mouth showed him a shadowy array of sleeping bodies, with here and there a face upturned in illuminated relief. Something in the sprawled, loose-limbed attitudes of his fellow slaves made him think, suddenly and for no good reason, of corpses littering a battlefield. He shrank back against the wall and turned his face away.

"Rhan . . ."

The whispered call came from beyond the entrance. His brown eyes wide in the darkness, Rhan shifted gingerly onto his hands and knees and crawled to the cave's jagged mouth.

The guards were nowhere in sight. His heart thudding erratically against his ribs, Rhan clambered to his feet. A light gust of wind caught the torchfires, sweeping them into serpentine curls like the snake-locks of a lamia. In the same instant, a shadow moved among the rocks off to his left.

Rhan turned sharply to face it. A tall cloaked figure stepped forward and gestured swiftly for silence. Strong, shapely hands plucked back the concealing hood. Auburn hair drew the torchlight with sudden splendor above a familiar face with proud bones and winged brows.

Rhan caught his breath. "Caradoc!" he exclaimed in muted amazement.

The red-haired mage laid a warning forefinger against his lips and beckoned with his other hand. His pulse pounding, Rhan cast an instinctive look around him. Nothing was moving under the dense starlit sky. There were no guards anywhere to be seen. Caradoc beckoned again, then turned. Rhan sprang forward after the tall man's receding form.

Caradoc kept to the shadows, moving smoothly from shade to shade without a sound. Buoyed up between apprehension and excitement, Rhan flitted along behind him, his bare soles raising not so much as a patter from the rocks underfoot.

His guide led him along the western hem of the cliffs to a point where the rock face was broken by a V-shaped ravine. Racing to keep up with the tall man who had called him out of sleep, Rhan panted, "Where are you leading me?"

Instead of speaking, Caradoc pointed toward the far end of the ravine. Another cloaked figure stood waiting in dim silhouette at the foot of the overhanging wall. "Who's that?" demanded Rhan. Then closed his mouth at a flashing look from his summoner's piercing eyes.

The second muffled figure uncovered a shuttered lantern. A narrow cone of light stabbed upward through the dark. Its peripheral radiance gave shape and identity to the face beneath the cowl.

A lean face, with lightly hollowed cheeks and a warmly ironic mouth. . . .

Rhan froze in midstep, transfixed between astonishment and delight. *"Serdor!"* he gasped.

The corners of the minstrel's mouth lifted. He set down the lantern and wordlessly held out both hands.

Rhan hesitated a moment longer, struggling to contain a riot of emotions ranging from bewilderment to joy. Then abruptly he stopped trying to explain his friend's presence, and darted like a mudlark for Serdor's welcoming embrace.

The minstrel's mantled arms folded around him like the wings of a bat. His forehead resting briefly against Serdor's spare shoulder, Rhan drew a deep sigh.

Then choked as his nostrils picked up the sudden unmistakable odor of corruption.

The minstrel's clothes were charged with the stench. His gorge rising, Rhan gasped and tried instinctively to pull away. Serdor's arms tightened like a snare around his body. Rhan pushed against his friend's chest and felt the flesh give way under his fingers like rancid fruit-pulp.

He recoiled as if he had been stung by a scorpion, and found himself gazing up into Serdor's livid face. In that instant horror closed his throat.

The minstrel's eyes had liquified into a blind sump of

300

decay. The eyesockets showed white beneath dissolving layers of tissue. Rhan stared without voice at the decomposing face that had belonged to his friend. As he did so, the dead man's head fell forward as if to press a loose kiss on the boy's blanched brow.

Serdor's breath was rotten. As his shriveled lips parted, Rhan could see that his friend's tongue was a blackened stump of putrefying flesh. The boy screamed and struck out with all his strength against the dead matrix of bones enclosing him.

The dead arms broke apart. One skeletal hand clattered to the ground. Rhan reeled back, retching as if he would vomit up his own heart. The corpse that had been Serdor lurched forward in a rattle of unpicked bones.

Rhan's reason broke. He turned tail and fled screaming into the black void of the night. . . .

It was after midnight when the guards on duty on the northeast side of the quarry were roused from their gaming by a terrified shriek from the inside of the nearest cave.

Earsplitting in its shrillness, the cry tore across the compound and echoed off the walls. The guards abandoned their dice and dashed to see what the trouble was.

A few yards from the mouth of the cavern, two burly Nhuboran were bending over a scrawny slip of a boy who struggled like a madman against their efforts to restrain him. The boy's lips were bloodless, his eyes blind and staring. The two men were having trouble holding him down.

The other conscripts were pressing forward, trying to see what was happening. Driving them back with whip-cracks and curses, the two Pernathan guards went back to the boy writhing wildly on the ground.

He was still raving, his thin voice raw with horror. The bigger of the two guardsmen knelt down and dealt the boy a backhanded slap across the face.

The young Garillan hardly seemed to feel the blow.

Nor did he respond to the sharper promptings of the whip. The Pernathan guards exchanged fatalistic glances. The bigger of the pair turned to the Nhuboran and gestured with his quirt.

The black men wrestled the boy to his feet. Under the watchful direction of the overseer, they dragged him outside and set off across the compound to a covered pit in the southwest corner of the enclosure.

By the time they arrived, the boy was sobbing with exhaustion, but his dilated eyes were still deranged with terror. The overseer jerked aside the grid covering the mouth of the pit. At his signal, the J'khartans nudged the boy to the edge and sent him tumbling into the blackness below.

# ACROSS THE KHAZAR

THE PLAIN OF KHAZAR MU'JAKR was a cracked brown plate a hundred miles broad from the inland foothills east of Ghazarah to the dyed red peaks of the D'Jinnar Mountains. The land that lay between was baked hard as a brick by the harsh sun, its geography crazily mapped out in jagged canyons and jutting table-bluffs, standing yellow and grey in the waterless glare.

The only settlement between Ghazarah and Sul Khabir was the Well of Tushir, a dusty handful of misshapen freestone houses clustered around an ancient deep-shafted watering-hole. The water-hole lay at the bottom of a shallow ravine where the road to Sul Khabir dipped down between low ranks of flat-topped cliffs. The only building in the settlement bearing any semblance of prosperity was the hostel located on the north side of the well—a long low building of dressed stone blocks, with a horse-paddock at the back of the house where the bluff sloped down to meet the floor of the hollow.

Four days out from Ghazarah, Gudmar's party, numbering fifteen in all, approached the well from the west. While they were yet a healthy distance away, they turned off to the left of the road and rode around the back of the rocky incline flanking the roadway, carefully making their way up the gully that paralleled the road. Here the ten volunteers from the crew of the *Yusufa* got down from their horses and waited, while their leaders, plus the three newcomers from Ambrothen, crept to the cliff's edge where they could overlook the settlement from above.

There were eight horses standing in the paddock. Two of them were pack-ponies. The other six, under saddle, showed better breeding despite the fact that their coats were patchy with sweat. Harlech peered around an outcropping of rock, then jogged Gudmar's bent elbow. "Look at that harness, will ye?" he said. "Those'll be regular troops from the Agha's fortress at Ghazarah."

"Possibly on the way back from escorting prisoners to the quarries," said Gudmar thoughtfully. "I believe I should like a word with them."

The sight of a liveried figure lounging in the shadows told them that the party had posted a guard over their mounts. "Best get *him* out of the way. Then—" said Harlech.

"Right. If you can manage it without making too much of a fuss," said Gudmar.

"Och, it'll be child's play," said Harlech contemptuously. "Yon laddie's mind's no' on his work."

He twitched the end of a two-foot length of waxed cord from the cuff of his left sleeve, and Margoth saw that it was anchored with a knot about the base of the hook he wore in place of his hand. Securing the cord with a second twist, Harlech began sidling away cautiously toward the eastern face of the bluff where a descending fault in the rock offered promise of both footholds and cover.

Nimble as a goat, the little sea captain scuttled down from the top of the cliff like a spider running down a wall-cranny. At the bottom he vanished briefly from view behind a sagging storage shed.

From there a short crawl brought him to earth behind an empty stone watering-trough. He got his legs back under him, tensed, and sprang for his victim's averted back.

The Pernathan's helmeted head gave a sharp jerk as a

waxed cord whipped itself tight around his windpipe.
There was a short, fierce tussle that ended abruptly and
quietly when the Pernathan ran out of air. Harlech let him
down gently and waved to the people on the cliff-top.

Gudmar summoned the rest of the *Yusufa*'s men with
a sweep of his arm. They came quickly, with no unnecessary noise, swarming down the slope with the ease and
economy of men accustomed to moving through ship's
rigging in all weathers. Four of them followed Gudmar in
through the hostel's back door. The others remained
outside to guard the exits.

The fight never really had a chance to get started.
Making the most of the advantage of surprise, the attackers
swarmed into the hostel's front room. They bowled over
their opponents in a single rush and sealed the issue with
shrewd raps of their cudgels. The one Pernathan quick
enough to get a sword out had his blade promptly muffled
in a dirty tablecloth. The rest were relieved of their
weapons in short order and bundled ignominiously into a
corner.

The officer was a lean tough man with obstinacy
deeply graven into his hard eyes and thin mouth. His men,
however, proved less impervious to threats, and in the end,
after only a minimal use of force, Gudmar had all the
information he wanted concerning the layout of the stockade and the quarries, along with an account of the garrison
and its ordering. Plus separate confirmation from each of
the men he had questioned that among the prisoners
delivered to Sul Khabir two days ago had been a young
Garillan boy with fair hair and dark eyes.

The following day, not long before sunset, Feisal Al
Akbar, Bey of Sul Khabir, received word from the sentries
on duty at the front gate of the fort that a new band of
conscripts had just arrived from Ghazarah, under escort
from the alcazar. The officer in charge—so the messenger
reported—was requesting permission to enter the stockade with his foot-sore prisoners and his two mounted

subordinates. The messenger added, his face somewhat flushed with excitement, that the party included another less orthodox member—a veiled and lissome figure that could only be female.

This announcement kindled a startled glea... of keen interest in the Bey's dense black eyes. Throwing on his second-best outer robe, he left his quarters and followed the messenger out of the keep-tower down to the gatehouse where the party from Ghazarah was waiting.

Here he discovered that the messenger had told the truth: behind the half-naked huddle of new labor-conscripts and between the two subordinate Aq'yahs sat a veiled figure on the back of a bay palfrey, hands folded, head bowed, yet not so muffled in drapery that Feisal could not make out the suggestion of ripe breasts and a slim waist.

If the Prophet himself had appeared to shower largesse upon Sul Khabir, Feisal would have been scarcely less mystified. He transferred his gaze to the officer in charge, a squat, ill-favored individual who sported a patch over one eye and a hook where his left hand should be.

Comprehension entered the other man's remaining berry-black eye. He stepped forward and saluted. "S'ihar-Feisal, I am Koori Al Banr. Apart from these seven miscreants which it has pleased the justice of the Prophet to send thee for their wickedness, I bring these two things: first, the greetings of His Excellency the Agha of Ghazarah; and secondly, this female slave, which His Excellency sends thee in token of his favor for thy unremitting service here."

Feisal's eyes widened. He ran his tongue over his lips. "May Heaven prosper His Excellency and reward his generosity," he said with rare and fervent piety. "Bring thy prisoners inside that they may the more speedily be delivered into the hands of my overseers."

The new conscripts were a mixed lot. The pair of J'khartans looked stolid and inscrutable. Their two

306

Pernathan counterparts seemed equally fatalistic. Of the three Garillans, the first was negligible—a skinny specimen with a pale hollow-cheeked face and a scarred back. The big deep-chested man with the blond hair, however, still had the eyes of a fighter, and the tall redhead behind him was lean and nervy as a young racehorse, with the same drive to run written into his every movement.

Feisal beckoned his lieutenant forward and pointed out the likely troublemakers. Then he returned his gaze to the woman as Koori led her horse into the compound. The girl lifted her veiled face to look at him, and he saw that her eyes were blue.

Koori—in the more proper person of Harlech Hardrada—assisted Margoth to dismount. "Are ye all right, lassie?" he whispered out of the corner of his black beard.

Margoth gave an almost imperceptible nod. "Thank God, that's one obstacle overcome. When Gudmar swore you could speak Pernathe like a native I only half-believed him, but I see now he wasn't exaggerating."

Her glance flickered worriedly after the receding forms of her brother and his companions as the overseers of Sul Khabir herded them down the pathway that led down into the quarry pits. "Dinnae fret yourself," said Harlech in a bracing undertone. "They'll no' be in there long enough tae get into any real trouble."

He took her elbow with a show of authority and led her around by the horse's head. "I just wish Serdor would have consented to stay back with Hassan," muttered Margoth. "He still hasn't recovered his strength."

"Aye, well, there's no arguin' wi' a man when he kens he's in the right," said Harlech philosophically. "Be sure Gudmar and your brother will see to it he comes t' no harm. Or the boy either, when they find him."

He lowered his voice and darkened his brow. "Look sprightly now, for here comes yon black ram. Ye ken what t' do. Make sure he takes yon potion. Ye'll not have t'play him along for verra long once it's down his black gullet. I'll join ye as soon as I may."

As Feisal approached to take charge of his prize, Koori turned and unloosed a small ornamental flagon from the palfrey's saddlebow. This he presented to Feisal with a ceremonial gesture.

"What is this?" asked Feisal.

Koori's black eye took on a sly glint. "A potion," he said, "to enhance and prolong thy pleasure. Partake of it before thou liest with the maid, and thou shalt have such a night of pleasure as the blessed taste in Paradise."

Feisal accepted the flagon with something akin to reverence. "His Excellency's munificence is without bounds," he murmured.

As the Bey took Margoth's hand to lead her away —"Aye," muttered Harlech under his breath. He added with malice, "Enjoy yourself, ye gormless rascal."

The stone box tower at the center of the stockade at Sul Khabir was divided inside into three levels. With Harlech following behind, Margoth padded beside her new master across a stone-floored undercroft where several wizened scullions, too old for work in the quarries, were laying out bowls and plates for the soldiers' evening meal.

A switch-backed stairway at the back of the building took them up through the wooden floor of the second level. Margoth glimpsed through a narrow doorway the sight of men donning helmets and chainmail, and realized that she and her companions must be passing the living quarters of the lower-ranking members of the garrison.

The Bey's apartments were at the top of the tower to the left of the stair. There were two guards standing at the door. Feisal waved them aside with a dismissive hand. "Do thou see that Captain Koori here is properly housed, and his men likewise. I and this peri shall take food in my quarters. Let no one disturb us during the night that is to come."

# ASSAULT FROM WITHIN

AT SUNSET THE MEMBERS OF the day-watch relinquished their posts to the men of the night-watch. The new conscripts were left standing by the well for nearly a quarter of an hour before the exchange was completed. By the time the head overseer arrived to look over the new men, the sky was wholly dark, apart from a thin red line along the western horizon. The surrounding cliffs showed deep pockets of shadow where the watchlights did not penetrate.

The overseer had been warned concerning the two potential troublemakers. They were easy enough to single out, and he did so at once, giving orders that the pair were to be relegated to the cave in the northwest corner of the first quarry-pit, where conditions were most secure.

Since it was taken for granted that the new prisoners had nothing left to hide, nobody bothered to search them. The tall redhead and his big blond-bearded counterpart were led away under guard, but no one suspected that they might have weapons concealed among the rags of their clothes.

The entrance to the cavern was a narrow one, a wormhole tunnel only wide enough to allow its inmates to come and go in single file. The two guards on duty at the cave's mouth manhandled the new conscripts into the passage and drove them back toward the cave with a few well-placed cracks of two long whips. Then they settled down to while away the dark hours of their vigil over a game of panca vimsati.

The night deepened and the stars flamed out in a white bloom of lights. Hunched over their game, the guards were aware of the distorted mutter of voices from inside the cave but paid them no heed. After a time, the conversation from the slaves quartered there gradually died away.

A silence settled over the compound, broken only by the occasional whisper of desert wind and once or twice, the slight scurrying sound of a lizard scrabbling from rock to rock. The broader of the two guards won three games in succession. His companion was cursing his luck when there was a rustle behind them at the cave's mouth, and a tall bronzed figure lunged at them out of the blackness of the tunnel.

The game pieces went flying. The first guard grabbed for his spear and got kicked in the chin. The other guard fumbled for his sword. Before he could get it free from its scabbard, a second prisoner leaped through the cave opening and rushed at him.

Both prisoners had daggers. Flat on his back with his blond-bearded opponent sitting on his chest, the first guard fought to keep the other man's blade-point away from his throat. More convicts were pouring out through the tunnel. The second guard managed to howl out a brief syllable of warning before he was overborne by angry numbers and dashed to the ground under a vengeful torrent of blows.

The cry of alarm drew echoes from elsewhere around the compound. Within seconds, the whole quarry-pit was boiling with shouts and grappling figures. Crouching shoulder to shoulder with Harlech in a pool of deep shadow at the quarry's entrance, Margoth started up at the sudden outburst of combat. "That's the signal," said Harlech. "Let's go!"

Raschid and Saladek fell in behind them as they

sprinted down the track. Like Harlech, they had discarded their uniforms and were running bare-chested as any conscripts might be.

There was a dead soldier lying on the ground at the foot of the north wall. The feathered shank of a barbed arrow protruded from under his left breast.

Margoth recognized the feathering in the hectic light from the torches around the quarry's entrance. Hassan and his three archers had taken up their part in the assault.

The air was riotous with hoarse shouts in several different languages. The ground throbbed with the thud of bare feet over dusty earth. Harlech led the way swiftly down the path and out into the open bowl of the pit. As they cut to the left along the rock-wall, Margoth overlooked a scene of rife disorder.

The floor of the quarry was alive with moving forms, leaping and capering. The torchlight picked up here and there a wild-eyed face drunk with the sudden prospect of freedom. From the box tower in the stockade an alarum bell clanged out. Lights flared from beyond the ravine with sudden fierce brilliance.

The knowledge that the rest of the garrison was on the move seemed to galvanize the men down in the pit. Hooting and howling, brandishing stolen weapons and makeshift clubs, the half-naked yelling crowd surged up the path toward the stockade.

The noise was deafening. Stumbling after Harlech, Margoth caught sight suddenly of a familiar red head surging toward her across the pouring tide of released prisoners. She clutched at Harlech's arm and pulled him to a halt. Caradoc joined them a moment later.

"Where's Gudmar?" demanded Harlech.

"I don't know—we got separated," Caradoc called back above the din. "I haven't seen Serdor, either."

Caradoc was bruised along one side of his face and there was a bleeding cut across his left thigh. "What about Rhan?" cried Margoth.

He shook his head. "No one in our part of the compound remembered seeing the boy. Maybe Serdor will have had better luck—"

Above them within the compass of the stockade the torchlight rang with the clash of weaponry. Scurrying in single file along the perimeter of the quarry, they collected three more of Harlech's men and learned that a fourth had been wounded in the initial assault on the guards.

There was still no sign of Gudmar or Serdor. "If you want to go pick up Sassam, I'll cut across to the opposite side of the quarry to see what I can find," said Caradoc to Harlech.

"I'll go with you," said Margoth, and caught her brother by the arm. "Come on!"

The floor of the pit was patched with lights and shadows. The moving sweep of the conflict had left behind it a groaning flotsam of injured bodies. Caradoc closed his ears grimly to the sounds of anguish in the darkness and strode on with Margoth flitting dimly at his side.

They came across two more dead guards, rolled like so much bunting against the base of the overhanging cliff. Then suddenly Margoth gave a cry and pointed. "Look!" she said. "Isn't that Gudmar over there?"

It was. There was no mistaking the leonine set of the head and the broad shoulders. The guild-master was not alone. "That's Serdor with him!" exclaimed Caradoc.

Gudmar and Serdor were standing at the brink of a hole in the ground. The mouth of the hole had been stopped with a heavy iron grid. Both men turned at the sound of running footsteps approaching. "Oh, there you are, Caradoc," said Gudmar crisply. "Come here and give me a hand."

Serdor stepped back as Caradoc leaped to comply. Looking from the iron grid to Serdor's pale face, Margoth clutched at his arm. "What's going on?" she asked. Then gulped as a dread thought occurred to her. "I-is Rhan in there?"

"I think so," said Serdor. "At least that's what I gather

312

from the other slaves in my part of the compound. He apparently had some kind of seizure, and the guards ordered him removed. The man I spoke to says that this is where they always put the ones who run mad—"

He shut his mouth abruptly. Margoth shivered and clung to him more tightly. "I called to Rhan through the grid, but I didn't get any answer," continued Serdor. "The grid itself was too heavy for me to move by myself."

His normally level voice was ragged with anxiety. Seeing the stark expression on his face, Margoth laid her cheek against his shoulder. "It'll be all right," she whispered through dry lips. "He'll be all right. . . . "

The metal grid came up with a rusty groan. Muscles bulging, Caradoc and Gudmar heaved it to one side. There were torches still burning around the mouth of the nearest cave, some thirty yards away. "I'll fetch a light," said Margoth.

Caradoc knelt down and peered into the blackness below. "Rhan!" he shouted down. "Rhan, are you there?"

No voice replied, but his straining ears caught something—the ghost-rustle that might have been movement. Gudmar's face was set like granite. "Rhan, it's me!" Caradoc called. "Can you hear me?"

Still there was no vocal response—just another whisper of motion, as of someone huddling more tightly into a corner. "I'm going down," said Gudmar shortly.

He hunkered down and swung his legs into the opening. "No, wait!" called Serdor's voice behind them.

The sharpness of his tone was arresting. Gudmar and Caradoc looked around as he joined them. "You'd better let me go," said the minstrel. "If the boy's hurt or suffering from shock, one of you might frighten him out of what wits he's got left."

"What do you mean?" snapped Gudmar. "I've known Evelake ever since he was a baby—"

"The last time he was confronted with someone from his past," said Serdor, "the strain almost unhinged his mind. He was stronger then than he is now."

"Serdor's right," said Caradoc. "We can't predict what might happen if you and he were to meet without warning while he is still under Borthen's foul influence. I can't go to him, either. For the same reason."

Gudmar drew a short sharp breath. "You're right," he said. "Go ahead. But if those Pernathan bastards have injured him, don't expect me to stand by and do nothing."

Margoth materialized with the torch and passed it wordlessly to Serdor. He sat down at the edge of the pit and Gudmar and Caradoc lowered him down through the opening.

It was a short drop to the floor of the pit. At the bottom, a dark cul-de-sac angled away to the left, like the toe of an old boot. Torchlight leapt crazily up the sloping walls of the cavern. Its flickering tongue washed over a pale huddled shape in the farthest corner of the cave.

The boy was drawn up into a tight ball of emaciated limbs, his face bowed between his upraised knees. His averted back showed taut ribs under scarred skin. Serdor felt the last remaining color leave his face. Stepping very softly, he came forward until he stood only a few feet away. "Rhan," he said quietly. "Rhan, turn around. It's me —Serdor. I've come to fetch you away from here."

A small moan broke from the boy's unseen lips. He shuddered and hunched himself tighter. Deeply disturbed, Serdor dropped down on his knees beside him. "Rhan, what's the matter?" he said. "Don't be afraid. There's no one here but me. I give you my word."

The boy's angular shoulders twisted. "Go away!" he whispered. Then gave a sob. "Oh God, I can't bear it!"

The tortured note in his voice hinted at unspeakable anguish. Serdor's throat felt suddenly as dry as the sands of the Khazar desert. "Can't bear what?" he asked. "Please tell me."

Rhan began to rock back and forth. From the ragged sound of his breathing, he was almost choking in his distress. "If I tell you, will you go away and not make me look at you?" he whimpered.

314

The strangeness of the demand left Serdor more bewildered and disturbed than ever. "Why don't you want to look at me?" he asked.

The boy's wretchedness seemed to wrack him from head to foot. "Because you're *dead*!" he sobbed with broken vehemence. And gave a wordless moan of pain.

He was groping along the floor for something. Serdor couldn't see what it was. He leaned forward to look and caught his breath as he saw that there was blood under the boy's downpressed hand.

Jamming the torch into a crevice in the wall, Serdor made a dive for Rhan's bony wrist. Rhan cried out as he felt the minstrel's hand on his. Too distraught himself to heed the boy's protests, Serdor forced the frail fingers to open. A sharp-pointed rock tumbled to the floor, its tip engrailed with crimson.

Aghast, Serdor stared down at Rhan's open hand. The flesh at the center of his palm had been gouged out with relentless cruelty. The boy had his eyes screwed tight. He was sobbing in near hysteria, "I must wake up. . . . I *must* wake up. . . ."

Serdor caught Rhan by the shoulders and held him hard. "Listen to me!" he said. "I don't know who told you I was dead, but you've got to believe me when I tell you it was a lie!"

He took the boy's wounded hand in his and wrapped the fingers around his own. "Feel that!" he urged. "My flesh is as warm as yours. Isn't it?"

The boy gave a gasp and bit his lip. "Isn't it?" insisted Serdor. He seized the boy's other hand and held it against his face. "Touch me!" he challenged. "I'm here—alive and well!"

Rhan's icy fingers trembled, then traced, shrinkingly, the lines of his lips, his nose, his eyes. "I don't pretend to know what vile deception has been practiced upon you," continued Serdor. "But a deception it most certainly was. Believe what your hands tell you, and don't be afraid to look at me."

Rhan was quaking where he sat. His stark ribs rose and fell. With sudden courageous abandon, he threw back his head and opened his eyes.

His pupils were wildly dilated. Serdor remained very still, his hands steady against the boy's trembling arms. A long moment passed, hammered out in heartbeats between them. Then Rhan blinked and drew a long shuddering breath. "It really *is* you," he said. "Isn't it?"

Serdor nodded. "No deceptions this time."

Rhan's reddened eyes were suddenly full of tears. "Serdor." He whispered the name as though it were a talisman. "Serdor," again and again. And let his head fall exhaustedly against Serdor's supporting shoulder.

There was a scuffling noise behind them, followed by a thud. "What's happening down here?" demanded Gudmar from the ruddy pool of torchlight directly beneath the mouth of the pit. "Where's Evelake? Is he here?"

His tone was rough with anxiety. Rhan flinched at the intrusion of a new voice and huddled closer to the minstrel. Serdor laid a reassuring hand on the boy's bent head. "Yes, he's here," he said over his shoulder.

Gudmar's gaze dropped to the slight crumpled figure on the floor. "Oh God!" he said flatly, and leapt forward.

"No, wait!" cried Serdor, but Gudmar was already kneeling over the boy, his horrified gaze encompassing all the physical evidence of hunger and hard usage. The guild-master's golden eyes were full of grief and outrage. Before Serdor could forestall him, he reached out to trace with shrinking fingers the scars that marred the boy's thin shoulders.

Rhan jerked away from the big man's touch and looked sharply around. His haggard eyes found Gudmar's face with its strongly marked features and rich leonine coloring. For a moment he stared at the guild-master in shrinking incomprehension. The next instant, he gave a piercing cry of pain and collapsed senseless to the floor.

316

# ONSET OF CRISIS

THE PARTY FROM THE *Yusufa* camped that night in a rocky ravine a mile to the north of the quarries of Sul Khabir. Though they had achieved their aim without suffering any losses, the air prevailing over the company was one of gloom rather than of triumph.

The boy they had come so far to find lay in a cold, trancelike swoon, beyond the reach of all their anxious solicitude. His friends sat by him, watching and waiting. They had done all they could to make him comfortable, but all their attempts to rouse him had failed.

Their failure filled Caradoc with deepest foreboding. He alone of all of them had firsthand knowledge of Borthen Berigeld's capacity for cruelty, and he alone could guess the kind of punishment the necromancer could bring to bear to enforce his control over the boy's mind and memory.

How much damage had already been done Caradoc could not say. But growing ever stronger in his own mind was the certainty that Borthen had not finished with his victim. A chill sense of impending crisis laid hold of him. Unable to shake it off, he at last relinquished his vigil to Serdor and Margoth and sought the solitude of his own thoughts in the darkness beyond the reach of the party's watch-fires.

A narrow goat-path led out of the ravine, winding upward to the crest of a low flat-topped hill where three desiccated cedar trees struggled for life among the rocks. Caradoc sat down in the midst of them. Drawing his cloak tightly around himself, he gazed out east across the barren wind-scoured plateau and wrestled in silence with the turmoil in his heart.

The night air was gravid with rumors of dark events yet to come. He could hear whispers of malice on the edges of the desert wind. The evil-to-be was encroaching like the rising of the tide. Alive to its building presence, Caradoc steeled himself to consider both sides of a difficult and dangerous dilemma: whether to leave Rhan alone, and hope that this deadly malady would ease of its own accord. Or to confront the evil that was threatening to destroy the boy, and risk both their lives in trying to cast it out.

It was no easy choice. If Caradoc did nothing—if he allowed himself to be ruled by caution—there might be nothing to stop Borthen from taking full possession of the boy Evelake to warp and twist as he chose. But the other alternative—that of challenging Borthen on his own terms —seemed foolhardy beyond belief. Caradoc bit his lip in an agony of indecision. "What chance could I possibly have?" he muttered aloud to himself. And shrank from the thought of what such an ordeal would mean to him.

An hour went by. He was still no closer to making a decision when a shrill hail with a piercing note of urgency from halfway down the slope roused him sharply from his reverie.

It was Margoth, white-faced and panting hard. "You've got to come back at once to camp!" she gasped. "It's Rhan—he's been taken in some kind of fit!"

As they reached the foot of the ravine, the sound of moaning, hoarse and sustained, flared into sudden audibility. Ahead of him, Margoth checked involuntarily, then forced herself to proceed. The voice rose and fell, then swooped upward to a shrill pitch of anguish. Listening, Caradoc felt his hackles rise.

Gudmar was with Serdor inside the makeshift tent, watching aghast as the boy writhed in the minstrel's protective grip. Rhan's eyes were open, but his terrified gaze was focused upon something they could not see. Shouldering past Gudmar, Caradoc asked, "How long has he been like this?"

"Not long—just these last few minutes." Serdor's lean face was blanched under its transparent layer of weathering. "It came on all of a sudden—"

Caradoc bent down, peering hard into the boy's whitened eyes. As he straightened up, Rhan screamed, a thin tearing sound as if his lungs were about to rupture.

Twisting among the disordered blankets as if they were winding-sheets of fire, he tore frantically at the minstrel's restraining hands. Unable to hold him, Serdor gave a stifled exclamation and fell back, blood springing from the marks of the boy's nails.

Free, Rhan lunged for the side of the tent. Fending off the boy's frenzied attempts to claw him, Caradoc got an elbow braced across his chest and thrust him back. "Get his feet!" he called over his shoulder to Gudmar.

Even as the guild-master sprang to his aid, Rhan went limp—so abruptly that Caradoc landed prone on top of him. Scrambling to recover himself, he pressed an ear to the boy's chest. To his horror, he heard nothing.

His face communicated starkly his dismay. "What is it?" demanded Gudmar. "Why has he stopped breathing?"

"I don't know!" Caradoc pressed anxious fingers against the side of the boy's throat, where there should have been a pulse. The taut skin beneath his fingertips yielded no sign of life.

Margoth read the truth in Caradoc's stricken gaze. Her own heart gave an agonizing lurch of fear. "Help him!" she pleaded. "You've got to do something!"

Her brother's face was almost a death mask. "You don't know what you're asking," he whispered.

Margoth was about to protest when she caught a warning look from Serdor. "You're right. We don't," said the minstrel. "Only you can decide," he said to Caradoc.

It was the moment Caradoc had been dreading in all the shrinking terror of his mortal flesh. But now the time had come, he knew—as he had known from the outset —that there was only one choice, shaped by the holy pledge he had given in exchange for Serdor's life. Drawing breath as though for the last time in the land of the living, he laid his hands upon the brow and breast of the boy who had served so long as hostage in the camp of the enemy. "Help me!" he beseeched of the keeper of the pledge. And entered into communion with the boy he hoped against hope to save.

Evelake's mind was dark—a temple bereft of light. But it was not empty: an intruder had taken up residence in the chambers of the mind, a black usurper who had seized control of the altar and ruled as an enemy. Standing on the threshold of darkness, Caradoc wrapped himself in the thin protection of the Orison. The world fell away from him. Standing tall despite his fear, he called the despot by name.

"Borthen!" he shouted. "Borthen Berigeld!"

The name echoed along unseen corridors steeped in shadow. Out of that lightless gloom, came back the mocking answer. "I am here!" hissed the voice of his enemy. "Come to me—if you dare."

A dark doorway opened up before Caradoc. The blackness beyond seemed utter and eternal. "Come, Caradoc," invited the evil, beautiful voice of the adversary who had once seduced him. "I await you."

Caradoc was shivering as though with ague. He took a firm grip on himself and stepped into the passageway, feeling his way along the walls like a blind man.

The tunnel worked its way down and down, in convolutions twisted as lies. After a time, he saw far ahead of him a glimmer of infernal light, red as the mouth of a forge, and knew that he stood upon the edge of conflict.

The passage opened up into a great vault, vast as the

subterranean hall of a mountain king. Dark firelight crawled up and down the walls in crimson trails like flayed serpents. At the far end of the great chamber stood a dais crowned by a dark throne.

As Caradoc stared at the throne, he saw that there was a shadowy figure seated there. The figure rose in a flowing ripple of dark robes. "Greetings, Caradoc," said the familiar sibilant voice the failed mage had grown to hate. "Have you come to plead with me?"

Borthen Berigeld was clothed in black. He held a black staff in his hand, its head crowned with two green stones that gave off a sullen interior glow. One of the stones Caradoc immediately resonated to—his own smaragdus that Borthen had stolen from him long months before. "No, I have not come to plead," he said harshly. "I have come to challenge you." His voice grated in his throat.

"To challenge *me*?" said Borthen Berigeld. "You know better than that, surely? But then you always were a fool."

He threw back his head and laughed. The sound of his laughter leapt around the chamber in quivering echoes of intransigent merriment. "You have the boy Evelake in your power," said Caradoc. "I want you to release him."

Borthen stopped laughing. His smile was chillingly indulgent. "Is that so? I'm afraid you're too late, my sweet impetuous child. Evelake is dead."

The necromancer's eyes were glittering like jewels in the head of an asp. "You're lying!" said Caradoc.

Borthen lifted an eyebrow like a feather of darkness. "Am I?"

"He was to be your passport to power," said Caradoc evenly. "Why would you want to kill him?"

"Out of my hands he is no use to me," Borthen replied with a shrug. "Why should I let him live to become a problem?"

The cold logic of it chilled Caradoc to the bone, but some part of him refused to grant Borthen any vestige of faith. "I don't believe you!" he shouted defiantly, and hurled himself at the dark figure standing before the throne.

Borthen stepped back and gestured with the jeweled head of his staff. A raw surge of power slammed Caradoc in the face as the necromancer vanished before his eyes. "Then see for yourself," called Borthen's mocking voice from somewhere overhead. "And share the same fate!" An instant later, his ghostly presence withdrew, leaving his victims for lost.

The floor of the vault heaved underfoot, throwing Caradoc to his knees. As he struggled blindly to rise, a black rift opened in the rock beneath him, sucking him down into a sudden roaring abyss.

He dropped with a cry, clawing wildly at the rushing darkness that shrieked past his ears. The air currents buffeted his plummeting body as he fell, tumbling head over heels through unfathomed gulfs of shadow. He gathered momentum as he plunged, dragged helplessly down by his own weight. He left his wailing voice behind him as the void claimed him for its own.

The noise and darkness confounded his senses. Spinning deaf and blind in the midst of a cyclone, he closed his eyes, and did not see the grey light gathering like a cloud beneath him until his falling body ripped through it and he found himself hurtling down upon a barren wilderness of jutting ice and eternal snow.

He closed his eyes and braced himself for the terrible impact that would shatter his bones like glass. Instead, the ice broke around him, crumpling like hoarfrost. Layer after glassy layer gave way beneath him until suddenly, without warning, he struck something that did not yield and shot sideways in a searing glide across a broad lake of black ice.

More numbingly frigid than any winter he had ever known, the air flayed his lungs with a biting frost that made every breath an agony. A searing gust sent him eddying into a snowbank. He struggled up and found himself at the foot of a gaunt peak of snow-blasted rock.

There was a stone sarcophagus lying at the base of the rock, its sides half-buried in drifting snow. Caradoc staggered to his feet and went forward to look at it.

The tomb was lidded with a sheet of ice like a pane of thick glass. Bending over it, Caradoc could see a slight male form imprisoned under the ice. The face of the corpse was that of Evelake Whitfauconer.

Caradoc's blood ran cold in his veins. Seizing the edge of the coffin-lid, he wrested it aside and sent it tumbling into the snow.

Evelake lay naked in the tomb, feet together, hands crossed over his breast. Reduced to its slight bones, his body might have been an effigy on a gravestone. Caradoc stared down at him in dread dismay. Then grief kindled to defiance. "Damn you, Borthen!" he shouted. "It's *not* too late!"

Stooping, he gathered Evelake out of his cold bed and wrapped the folds of his own cloak about the boy's chilled body. He laid Evelake flat on the ground before him and gently parted the cold lips with one hand. Masking the rest of the boy's face with the other, he began breathing his own breath into his patient's mouth.

Nothing happened. After ten breaths, Caradoc folded his hands over Evelake's hollow diaphragm, alternately pressing and releasing in an effort to stimulate the impulse to breathe independently. When this had no effect, he repeated the procedure from the beginning.

And again.

And again.

A deadly chill settled round them as Caradoc labored on, his knees aching, his lungs dry as parched leaves. At last, dizzy and gasping with fatigue, he slumped across the body of the boy. When he had recovered his breath, he slowly pushed himself up and looked down at Evelake's still face, his heart breaking. Pity and anger flared up anew in him. As long as I have strength to draw breath, he thought, you shall have at least the chance to try. And he steeled himself to make a final effort, willing to breathe out his very life.

Evelake's blue lips quivered. A moment later, his chest rose and fell of its own accord. As he took his first breath, there was a deafening crack from somewhere up the mountainside.

Caradoc started up as a deep rumbling tremor shook the frozen earth. He flung out a hand to steady himself and touched water.

*Water.* Not ice!

Clear as crystal, the rivulet flowed like spring rain over the ice-locked earth. Raising his eyes from his wet fingers, Caradoc followed the freshet upward to where it spilled from a freshly riven cleft in the rock.

His heart in that instant soared. Returning his rapt gaze to the sleeping face of his patient, he took the boy's thin hands in his own. "Evelake Whitfauconer!" he called. "Evelake, wake up!"

The shadowed eyelids fluttered. A heartbeat later, the boy opened his eyes.

His expression was at once vacant and bewildered. "Your name is Evelake Whitfauconer," said Caradoc. "Do you remember?"

Before he could urge the boy further, there was a sudden malevolent hiss and a chill gust of wind swooped down upon them. Evelake shuddered and seemed to shrink among the folds of Caradoc's cloak. Turning, the mage looked behind him and gasped aloud as he realized that a night-black shadow, like a gathering storm, was bearing down on them.

The shadow-storm was shot through with flickering tongues of dark fire. It was sweeping toward them with predatory speed. Hearing the howl of a legion of voices, Caradoc leaped to his feet. Seizing the boy's near wrist, he hoisted Evelake's slight unresisting weight across his shoulder and ran for the cleft in the rock.

# SHADOW AND FLAME

THE MANY-MOUTHED DARKNESS WAS almost upon Caradoc by the time he reached the opening. Its corrosive breath seared his back as he plunged through the gap. To the right of the stream lay a stairway, cut into the living rock. As Caradoc leapt panting up the steps, the water in the bottom of the cleft boiled up in sudden fury.

Frothing like a whirlpool, the cataract surged toward the opening, its white rage sealing off the cleft even as the blackness stooped to enter and follow them. After one glance down Caradoc dared not look back. Burdened with Evelake's passive weight, he climbed like a mad thing, climbed and stumbled and climbed again, foot by foot, bent forward to balance the burden on his back, feet and hands moving up step by step.

Ribs burning with the strain, he at last reached a point where he felt he could go no further. His hands could feel no steps, around him was pitch-darkness, nor could he go back. Half fainting with exhaustion, he faltered to a halt and sank down blindly, turning to cradle Evelake in his arms. Wearily he sagged, his mind a blank pleading, he knew not for what, and eventually sank with vast relief into unconsciousness.

At length a glimmering of light forced its way past his eyelids. Opening his eyes, he saw near at hand a pedestal of crystal. On top of the pedestal, a beacon in the dark, a lamp glowed with soft light.

The light was white and clear, like the radiance of a full moon in summer. Life and movement dwelt within it, as within a clean flame. Evelake stood beside the lamp, gazing into its depths. Its light shone upward into his face with transfiguring luminescence.

Caradoc rose shakily to his feet and stepped forward to the boy's side to share in his wonderment. As he too looked into the heart of the white flame, he knew suddenly what he must do on Evelake's behalf.

A taper burned at the core of the flame, sheathed in brightness, but not consumed by it. Its radiance was one with the perilous fiery heat of the Magia, but its substance was separable. Caradoc reached out to the light and felt it sear the palms of his hands like a foretaste of immolation. Ruling himself with an iron rod of resolution, he caught his breath and plunged his hands into the heart of the fire.

Agony washed up his arms. Blinded with tears of pain, he gathered the taper into his burning fingers and drew it out through shimmering waves of flame. The fire released him at the last, and he saw that despite his pain, his flesh was still intact.

The taper glowed with silvery brightness, as though the evening star had come to rest at its tip. As Caradoc turned to the boy at his side, Evelake stretched out a tentative hand. "Take it," said Caradoc softly, though the tears stood out in his eyes. "It is yours. Take it."

He guided the boy's fingers to receive it. Holding it, Evelake raised his eyes and smiled dreamily. Like a somnambulist, he turned away and raised the taper aloft.

Light flowed toward a stone archway, dimly penetrating the chamber beyond. Evelake walked slowly toward the opening. Caradoc followed after him.

The room they entered was a dark vault. A dead lamp stood on a pedestal at the center of the floor. Evelake approached the lamp and halted. "You must light it from the taper," said Caradoc.

The boy obeyed. As the flame in his hand kissed the lamp, the room's four walls came suddenly to life in a breathtaking surge of colors.

Evelake's pale lips parted. He looked around him in dawning wonder. Gazing with him, Caradoc watched the interplay of color and shape. Though the images shifted too quickly for him to see them, he sensed that the boy at his side was drinking deep of all that passed before him.

For a time the colors and images ebbed and flowed in great tides. When at last the flowing patterns subsided, the boy at Caradoc's side turned to look at him with eyes that were no longer vacant. "Hello," he said. "I'm Evelake."

Caradoc's feelings in that moment threatened almost to overwhelm him. His pulses pounding with an exultation that was almost as painful as grief, he had to swallow twice before he could speak. "I'm Caradoc," he said. Then found he could say nothing more.

It was the beginning of a long journey upward. Stairway by stairway, room by room, lamp by rekindled lamp, it was a triumphal progress, but it was not without its price.

Time and again Caradoc saw Evelake falter in the midst of his visions, his face wrung with pain whenever some double-edged stab of memory cut him deep. Unable to help, Caradoc watched anxiously for some sign of rejection, but Evelake bore the invisible wounds of recollection without complaint.

Until they reached the top of the last flight of steps.

The room beyond was like all the many others that had gone before. But as Evelake stepped forward to light the final lamp, he hesitated at the last instant and shrank back as though in fear.

His face betrayed a sudden revulsion. "What is it?" asked Caradoc.

Evelake turned to him, brown eyes hollowed out with dread. "I don't know," he whispered. "I'm afraid."

"You were afraid before, but you lit the lamps of memory anyway," said Caradoc.

"Yes," agreed Evelake. "But this is different."

He cast a darting glance around him, scanning the four walls with the mistrust of a small animal who feels itself trapped. For a moment Caradoc thought he would succumb to his fear. But then Evelake raised his head, his gaunt young face hard with desperate and bitter resolve.

He reached out with a shaking hand and touched the star-taper to the lamp. A glow sprang up in the dim air, and a tall arched portal materialized in the center of the opposite wall.

Evelake remained where he was for the space of several heartbeats. Then he walked up to the door. Caradoc heard the sharp intake of breath before the boy forced his hand down upon the latch.

His fingers took hold. In the same instant, there was a sudden malevolent hiss, and the door itself burst inward.

The force of its implosion hurled Evelake back. A wild influx of shadows snapped at him like a pack of mad dogs. He cried out and made a floundering retreat. Before Caradoc could spring to his aid, a cowled black shape stepped into the open doorway.

Looming inhumanly tall, the figure filled the opening. Yellow eyes shone fierce beneath the sweep of the hood, horizontal pupils smoldering with dense heat, arms mantling like great wings.

Evelake cringed and cried out as the creature flicked its wrist. Darkness crackled from its gnarled fingers like whip-thongs. The ribbons of shadow wrapped Evelake's slight body in a vampirous embrace. As the boy writhed screaming on the floor, Caradoc launched himself with desperate precision at the thing's unseen throat.

His clutching fingers scraped off hide like horn. While he was still groping for a handhold, his adversary spat at him with vicious malice and slashed its claws the length of his right arm.

Venom boiled into the wounds. Transfixed in sudden agony, Caradoc reeled back. The creature swept after him, its long arms mowing the air like scythes. As Caradoc made a frantic lunge to get out of its path, he took another poisonous gash along his spine.

The poison burned like acid as it took to his veins. Borne along his bloodstream, the pain coursed throughout his body like a disease run rampant, disrupting nerves and rupturing muscles. His tissues were breaking down, his flesh dissolving. He knew in an instant of torment that he was being devoured from within.

He could neither hear nor see. The raging necrosis beat at the doors of his mind, seeking to infect his spirit itself. Under its battering assault, the barriers were crumbling. He gave a voiceless scream of terror and protest as the devouring presence brutally rammed its way through his defenses to rape the inner chambers of his soul.

Its force penetrated deeper than a sword-thrust. The presence itself was obscene, a will wholly devoted to absorption. His soul writhing in revulsion under that unutterable lust, Caradoc lashed out in desperate resistance, suddenly savage with fury that all his risk and effort, and all Evelake's courage and response, should end in the foul corruption of this invader.

His screamed defiance provoked his assailant to fresh voracity. But even as the dark hunger pressed in to engulf him, he felt the surge of burning glory as the Magia blazed to his defense.

A stream of white fire, the power sprang from the disciplined recesses of his own will, coursing through his body, driving back the ravening dark with tongues of coruscating flame. Arrested in the last instant before consummation, the black invader howled in rage and frustration, then turned and fled yammering before the searing brilliance of that divine restoration.

Light enfolded Caradoc. Its touch was inconceivably tender, and he surrendered gladly to its ministering grace. Health and vigor flowed back into his withered flesh and violated spirit. When at last the light parted from him, it was an achingly gentle benison.

The exquisite pain of that parting left him weak with yearning, but there was one thing yet that he knew he must do. He opened his eyes, wearily pushed himself up and looked about him.

He was still in the vaulted chamber. Beyond him lay the tumbled form of the boy Evelake. Caradoc stood up and walked over to him. The taper Evelake had borne out of the depths lay flickering dimly a few inches beyond the reach of his hand. Caradoc bent down and carefully picked it up.

A deep pulse in his own body was throbbing with residual power. Holding the star-taper in his hands, Caradoc released that power into the service of the lesser light.

In response to the mage's gift, the dim flicker quickened to a glow. As Caradoc poured more power into it, the glow blazed up with new splendor. The boy at his feet stirred softly, like a sleeper awakening. Caradoc knelt and returned the taper to his hand.

"Come," he said softly. "You and I are free to go."

Serdor and Margoth watched Caradoc battle for the mind of Evelake Whitfauconer. They could only dimly sense the equally hard-fought battle for his body. But when, at last, the boy opened sane eyes on the world, the total exhaustion of both mage and patient was self-evident.

Margoth took charge of her brother, assisted by Gudmar. Wordlessly the friends agreed that Serdor had best stay with Evelake. All were aware that days of possibly difficult recovery lay ahead and there was much that would need to be carefully handled, for none knew yet exactly how much memory Evelake had recovered.

With Caradoc safely asleep, Margoth sought the fire, or rather the reassurance of company. She had never seen her brother look so gaunt. Coming directly to the point —"How much d'you think Rhan'll remember?" she asked of Gudmar.

He shook his head. "Not Rahn," he said. "Evelake.

It's sure he knows who he is—but beyond that, who knows? The death of his father, for instance, and all the hell that must be breaking loose back there. . . ." He looked grim.

"No point to fretting about it," Harlech offered. "He's got his mind back and that's the best news we've had in quite a while. We've got a couple of other things to worry about, y'ken. D'ye realize, laddie, we're all wanted fugitives back in Ambrothen? Course it's nothing new t'me, but we're going to have to do some mighty carefu' stepping in getting things sorted out. Come to that, we don't ourselves know what the devil's been going on. Now, do we?"

"You're right. There's no telling what we'll find when we get back." Gudmar smiled at Margoth. "But Serdor's well on the mend, Evelake's a courageous lad with a lot of his father's strength, and Caradoc"—he paused—"well, that young man is surprising us all, himself included." He put a bearlike arm around Margoth. "Best get some rest, girl. We're all going to need your help. I must say I feel as though I've done a day's work myself."

Margoth laughed, hugged the two men, and departed for grateful rest. Quiet settled over the camp as the fire died to embers.

# EPILOGUE

EVELAKE WHITFAUCONER AWOKE SHORTLY BEFORE sunrise. Through the open flap of the tent he saw the golden brightening of the eastern sky. Silhouetted against the light was a familiar figure, thin and supple, wearing obviously borrowed clothes. Evelake drew a quiet wondering breath. "Serdor?" he called softly.

The figure turned its head. "Yes, my lord?" said the minstrel from Ambrothen.

Evelake had grown so accustomed to Serdor's easy, unfailing companionship that he was taken slightly aback by the formal note of deference in his friend's response. Then he realized that with characteristic delicacy, the minstrel was offering him the freedom to redefine their relationship if he chose. His brown eyes warmly affectionate, he smiled crookedly up into Serdor's lean quicksilver face. "I think honorifics are silly between friends," he said softly. And added, "Or am I wrong in assuming that you and I are friends?"

It was a question that they had bandied between them on more than one significant occasion. An answering warmth dispelled the minstrel's carefully cultivated restraint. "You are *not* wrong," he said, and this time his voice held its familiar note of wry irony. "But I wasn't entirely sure you'd remember."

"After all you've been through on my account, how uld I forget?" asked Evelake. And stretched out his hand.

Leaning forward, Serdor took it in a firm, light clasp. he did so, there was a small scuffle at the door of the nt, and another face appeared behind the minstrel's bent oulder. "I thought I heard the two of you talking," said a cided female voice. "Since you were both obviously vake, there didn't seem to be any reason why I shouldn't me and wish the Lord Warden of East Garillon good orning."

"Be my guest," said Serdor. Releasing Evelake's hand, edged back to allow Caradoc's sister room to enter.

Evelake was staring at her in mingled joy and aston- hment. "Margoth!" he cried. "I thought . . . that is, . . How did *you* get here?"

"On muleback, just like everybody else," said argoth literal-mindedly. And gave a small pleased chor- e as Evelake rocketed upright and flung both arms around er neck. Returning the hug he gave her, she said in quite nother tone, "Welcome back."

Evelake's embrace tightened briefly before he took his ms away and settled back, the color blazing high in his in eager face as he looked from Margoth to Serdor. Thank you both—for everything," he said simply.

Margoth and Serdor traded smiles. "I'm glad to hear ou say that—even after all the scolds I've given you," said e minstrel wryly. "From here on out, I shall have to ard my tongue."

It drew a chuckle from Margoth. Their evident high pirits reassured Evelake on another account. "I'd like very uch to see Caradoc," he said. "That is," he amended, "if e's not too exhausted to see me."

"Far from it," said Margoth. "He's waiting just out- ide."

She wriggled backward to the tent entrance and called er brother by name. "Wait! This tent isn't big enough for ll of us," protested Serdor. To Evelake he said, "With

your permission, Margoth and I will go see if anyon‹
given any thought to breakfast yet."

Puzzled, but agreeable, Evelake nodded his asse›
Margoth, after a backward glance, disappeared from vie‹
Left briefly alone with Evelake, Serdor said softly, "I thi›
Caradoc was hoping for a word with you alone." Then
turned and followed Caradoc's sister outside.

Evelake lay back and waited, his newly awaken‹
memory supplying a kaleidoscope of images—Serdor sic›
ening and putrescent in his hands, and then Serdor mira
ulously whole and real again; a great terrifyi›
golden-bearded man who, remembered, was transform‹
into the beloved hero-figure of his childhood and lifetin
friend of his father; and Caradoc—Caradoc curt a›
dictatorial, Caradoc with hands as gentle as a woman's
heal his hurts, Caradoc fighting savagely to save his ra
aged mind. Recalling how selflessly the young mage ha
spent himself in his efforts to undo all the evils Borth‹
Berigeld had wrought, Evelake felt a passionate surge ‹
gratitude. He was still wondering how he had managed ·
find such friends as Serdor and Caradoc when a shado‹
fell across the tent's opening, and a tall rangy figu›
dropped to one knee on the threshold, blocking for
moment the ascendant light of the morning sun.

"May I come in, my lord?" inquired Carad‹
Penlluathe.

Like Serdor, he sounded hesitantly formal. U›
daunted, Evelake held out his hands. "Please—" he bega›
then stopped short as he caught his first clear glimpse ‹
the man who had saved him. "Caradoc!" he gaspe‹
"What's happened to your hair?"

Somewhat self-consciously Caradoc fingered the tw‹
broad streaks of silvery white waving back from h
temples. "A legacy from our encounter last night," he saì‹
"Margoth assures me it looks quite distinguished, but stil
it's going to take a little getting used to."

He seemed utterly exhausted, his green eyes heavil›

adowed, his normal air of golden vitality—the vitality
at Rhan Hallender had both envied and resented
-painfully subdued.

"Last night?" Evelake echoed. "Was it only last
ght?" He felt as though he had lived through several
'etimes since Gudmar and his friends had rescued him
om the pit. He looked again at the mage. Caradoc was
aring at his patient, his manner diffident and searching.
e said anxiously, "How do you feel, my lord? Are you
ite all right?"

His speech was slurred with fatigue. Brown eyes
emused, Evelake said, "I feel very much myself again.
hanks to you."

A difficult smile plucked at the corners of Caradoc's
andsome mouth. "It was the least I could do," he said
altingly. "I had so much to atone for. . . ."

It was hardly the word that Evelake, in his weary
xuberance, would have chosen. "To *atone* for?" he asked,
uzzled by Caradoc's off turn of speech.

The mage's face hardened, as if in self-recrimination.
I was at least partly to blame for all you've been through,"
e said. "I'm sorry."

This misplaced guilt prompted Evelake to reach out
nd clasp his rescuer's strong wrist. "You've suffered as
much—if not more—than anyone because of Borthen
erigeld," he said gently. And then suddenly a little
hy—"We have come through so much together, Caradoc.
nd I only because you were there to help; I only hope you
von't leave me now to my own devices. I have a strong
eeling that I'm going to need you if we're to put matters to
ights back home."

Caradoc's troubled brow cleared. All at once he
miled, taking the boy's hand between his own. "Margoth
lways says I can be an obstinate fool. My sister has an
nfuriating habit of being right, and I must learn to trust
er judgment more often—beginning with now."

Then all at once he laughed, like a man joyfully

shedding a heavy burden once and for all. "You know, y
and Serdor are—" he hesitated in surprised recognitio
"my first *real* patients. Through you two I've learned mo
about myself than the whole college of mages taught me
ten years! Believe me, if you want my help, I give it with
my heart. And my friendship with it."

Evelake gripped the hands that held his. "There is o
other from whom we two have learned," he said wi
unexpected maturity, and looking into the questionin
depths of the mage's green eyes, he murmured, "Borthe
Berigeld." Very earnestly they regarded one another. "Tl
measure of his power is the measure of your strengt
Caradoc."

"I will remember," the mage said.

Evelake grinned in sudden boyish delight. "No. V
*both* will remember!"

From that moment the commitment between ther
was sealed. Victims together, they needed no words now
share their determination to be victors together.